Bitter Blood

THE MORGANVILLE VAMPIRES NOVELS

THE
MORGANVILLE
VAMPIRES

Bitter Blood

Rachel Caine

NEW AMERICAN LIBRARY

NEW AMERICAN LIBRARY
Published by New American Library,
a division of Penguin Group (USA) Inc.,
375 Hudson Street, New York, New York 10014, USA
Penguin Group (Canada), 90 Eglinton Avenue East, Suite 700, Toronto,
Ontario M4P 2Y3, Canada (a division of Pearson Penguin Canada Inc.)
Penguin Books Ltd., 80 Strand, London WC2R 0RL, England
Penguin Ireland, 25 St. Stephen's Green, Dublin 2,
Ireland (a division of Penguin Books Ltd.)
Penguin Group (Australia), 250 Camberwell Road, Camberwell,
Victoria 3124, Australia (a division of Pearson Australia Group Pty. Ltd.)
Penguin Books India Pvt. Ltd., 11 Community Centre,
Panchsheel Park, New Delhi - 110 017, India
Penguin Group (NZ), 67 Apollo Drive, Rosedale, Auckland 0632,
New Zealand (a division of Pearson New Zealand Ltd.)
Penguin Books (South Africa) (Pty.) Ltd., 24 Sturdee Avenue,
Rosebank, Johannesburg 2196, South Africa

Penguin Books Ltd., Registered Offices:
80 Strand, London WC2R 0RL, England

First published by New American Library,
a division of Penguin Group (USA) Inc.

First Printing, November 2012
10 9 8 7 6 5 4 3 2 1

 REGISTERED TRADEMARK—MARCA REGISTRADA

LIBRARY OF CONGRESS CATALOGING-IN-PUBLICATION DATA:

Caine, Rachel.
   Bitter blood: the Morganville vampires/Rachel Caine.
      p. cm.
   ISBN 978-0-451-23811-5
   I. Vampires—Fiction   I. Title.
   PS3603.O557B58 2012
   813'.6—dc23   2012032958

Set in Centaur MT

Printed in the United States of America

ALWAYS LEARNING   PEARSON

FEB 19 2013

To Heidi Berthiaume, an exceptional woman
of grace, vision, strength, and passion . . . I only wish Claire
could be half the hero you are, every day.

To Sarah Brooke, also a hero. *Literally.* In this book.

ACKNOWLEDGMENTS

To Sarah Weiss, for keeping me as sane and organized as it's possible for me to get . . . You seriously rock.

To the lovely crew of the *Azamara Journey*. There will never be a nicer place to be panicking over a deadline. Thanks for the support, the love, and the cheers.

To *you*, dear reader, for making Morganville a living place that continues to be (for me!) a joy to visit.

AUTHOR'S NOTE

You'll be seeing several points of view in this book. Claire's is our basic story, with Amelie, Oliver, Shane, Michael, and Myrnin adding their own points of view to what's happening. So be sure to note the chapter headings.

INTRODUCTION

Morganville, Texas, isn't like other towns. Oh, it's small, dusty, and ordinary, in most ways, but the thing is, there are these—well, let's not be shy about it. *Vampires.* They own the town. They run it. And until recently they were the unquestioned ruling class.

But the vampires' reputation for invulnerability has taken some hits lately. The troublesome underground human revolt, led by Captain Obvious, never seems to die; even though the Founder of Morganville and her vampire friends defeated their most dire enemies, the water-monster draug, they needed human help to do it.

Now Morganville is rebuilding, and it's a new day. . . . But without the threat of the much-feared draug to hold them back, what's to keep Morganville's vampires from regaining their iron hold on the town?

One thing's for sure: there's going to be trouble.

And where there's trouble, there's Claire Danvers.

PROLOGUE

AMELIE

"I have a surprise for you," Oliver said.

I—not without reason—expected him to perhaps present a velvet box cradling rare jewels, or even a new pet ... but instead he held out a piece of expensive, heavy paper marked with the Morganville seal in the corner in thick, still-warm wax.

"Read it."

He collapsed into one of my brocaded armchairs across from my desk, crossed one leg over the other, and gave me a long, slow smile that made me shiver. Not in dread—oh, no. In something far more complex, and far more terrifying. We had been enemies a long time, uncomfortable allies for the past few years, and now ... now, I hesitated to put a name on what we were.

In more-ancient days, the word would have been *intimates*, which meant everything or nothing, as the situation required.

I lowered my gaze from that knowing expression and read the words inscribed in gorgeous, flowing script—the hand of a trained clerk, obviously, who'd been given proper education in a time when that truly mattered.

WHEREAS the Elders' Council of Morganville, concerned for the safety and security of all within its borders of influence, has resolved to enact a law requiring the identification of all persons, whether mortal or immortal. Such identification shall further be carried upon the persons of residents at all times. Whereas such proof of identity is vital to the health of our community, we also are resolved that the violation of such requirements shall be considered a direct offense to the council, and as such may be punishable with the First, Second, and Final Actions as written within the codes formulated by the Founder from the earliest foundation of this great community.

In approval of these requirements, and of these punishments, the Founder of Morganville sets her signature hereupon.

I froze, pen at the ready, and frowned. "What's this?"

"As we discussed," he said. "The requirement for citizens of Morganville to carry appropriate identification. For the vampires, of course, the requirements are somewhat different, but they'll still carry a card. It wouldn't do to appear to be discriminatory."

"Indeed not," I said, a ripple of irritation gliding through my tone. "I thought we discussed waiting a year to implement such identification measures, until they could be properly explained."

"I would have believed it was possible to wait that long had I not heard a rumor that Captain Obvious was once again among us, and agitating against us." Oliver's voice carried a bitterly dark undertone now, and his distaste for the nom de guerre of our most bothersome human adversary showed in the expression on his sharp, angular face. Age is of no consequence to vampires, of course, save in what power it brings with it, but Oliver was a rarity—a vampire who had been turned in his later years, and retained that appearance in his immortality, with gray threading his brown hair and lines pinching his skin at the eyes and mouth. He could appear warm and friendly when he chose, but I had long ago learned that Oliver was first, last, and always a warrior.

And this . . . Captain Obvious, as the humans of Morganville now named him, was cut from the same cloth. A fighter, determined to bring us harm. We had killed him a dozen times in the past hundred years, and, mortal lives being what they are, we'd never expected at first for the problem to resurrect itself again, and again, and again; yet as soon as a Captain Obvious fell, another stepped forward, masked and hidden, to take his place.

And now, it seemed, we were forced to endure yet another would-be avenger.

I felt Oliver's gaze on me, warm and yet challenging; for all the barriers that had fallen between us, his ambition wasn't one of them. He demanded more of himself, and thus more of me. It was a dangerous dance, and that was part—if not most—of the attraction.

"Yes," I said. "If they feel confident enough in their own power to openly follow yet another rabble-rouser, then I suppose we must have our own answer." And I penned my elaborate signature, all loops and swirls and slashes, to the bottom of the formal document. In true modern-age fashion, this would be photographed, digitized, transferred to bland and simple words on a screen . . . but the effects were the same. The word of a ruler was law.

And I was now the uncontested ruler of Morganville. All my enemies had fallen; the sickness that had crippled vampires for so very long had been conquered at last, thanks to the intervention of humans, most notably that troublesome young Claire, apprentice to my oldest friend, Myrnin. We had likewise dispatched at last my father, Bishop, that blood-maddened beast. And just in the past few months, the cool, cruel draug, who had hunted us to the edge of extinction, had been destroyed and were no more.

Now, nothing stood between my people—the last of the vampires—and the power and status that were rightly due us.

Nothing, that was, but the too-confident pride of the humans in this town—humans I had chosen, brought together, allowed to grow and flourish and prosper in cooperation and under strict conditions; humans who had repaid me, in large part, with fear, spite, and resistance that grew stronger each year.

No more.

"No more," Oliver said aloud, and rose to take the decree from my hand. "No more will these vassals think they can slip away in secrecy from their crimes. It's our time, my queen. Our time to ensure our final survival." And he captured my hand in his, bent, and touched his cool lips to my equally cool skin.

I shivered.

"Yes," I said. "Yes, I believe it is."

His lips traveled up my arm, in slow and gentle kisses, and found my neck; he unpinned my hair from its heavy crown and let it fall loose. His strong hands went around me and pulled me to him. He was as irresistible as Newton's gravity, and I gave up politics and pride and status for the sheer, novel joy of being wanted.

And if there was a part of me, a small and hidden part, that questioned all this and understood that the more power I took for the vampires, the more the humans would rebel . . . well, I buried it with ruthless efficiency. I was tired of being alone, and what Oliver drew from me was pleasant, and in some measure necessary.

The old ways of Morganville . . . They were my past.

Oliver was my future.

ONE

CLAIRE

🌙

Claire Danvers was in a rare bad mood, and nearly getting arrested didn't improve it.

First, her university classes hadn't gone well at all, and then she'd had a humiliating argument with her "adviser" (she usually thought of him that way, in quotes, because he didn't "advise" her to do anything but take boring core subjects and not challenge herself), and then she'd gotten a completely unfair B on a physics paper she knew had been letter perfect. She would have grudgingly accepted a B on something unimportant, like history, but no, it had to be in her major. And of course Professor Carlyle wasn't in his office to talk about it.

So she wasn't fully paying attention when she stepped off the curb. Traffic in Morganville, Texas, wasn't exactly fast and furious, and here by Texas Prairie University, people were fully used to stopping for oblivious students.

Still, the screech of brakes surprised her and sent her stumbling back to the safety of the sidewalk, and it was only after a couple of fast breaths that she realized she'd nearly been run over by a police cruiser.

And a policeman was getting out of the car, looking grim.

As he stalked over to her she realized he was probably a vampire—he was too pale to be a human, and he had on sunglasses even here in the shade of the building. Glancing at the cruiser to confirm, she saw the extreme tinting job on the windows. Definitely vampire police. The official slogan of the police was *to protect and serve*, but her boyfriend called the vampire patrol the *to protect and serve up for dinner patrol.*

It was unusual to see one so close to the university, though. Normally, vampire cops worked at night, and closer to the center of town, where Founder's Square was located, along with the central vamp population. Only the regular residents would see them there, and not the transient—though pretty oblivious—students.

"I'm sorry," she said, and swallowed a rusty taste in her mouth that seemed composed of shock and entirely useless anger. "I wasn't looking where I was going."

"Obviously," he said. Like most vamps, he had an accent, but she'd long ago given up trying to identify it; if they lived long enough, vampires tended to pick up dozens of accents, and many of them were antique anyway. His facial features seemed . . . maybe Chinese? "Identification."

"For walking?"

"Identification."

Claire swallowed her protest and reached in her backpack for her wallet. She pulled out her student ID card and Texas driver's license and handed them over. He glanced at them and shoved the cards back.

"Not those," he said. "Your town identification."

"My . . . what?"

"You should have received it in the mail."

"Well, I haven't!"

He took off his sunglasses. Behind them, his eyes were very dark, but there were hints of red. He stared at her for a moment, then nodded.

"All right. When you get your card, carry it at all times. And next time, watch your step. You get yourself hit by a car, I'll consider you roadkill."

With that, he put the sunglasses back on, turned, and got back in his car. Before Claire could think about any way to respond, he'd put the cruiser in gear and whipped around the corner.

It did not improve her mood.

Before she could even think about going home, Claire had a mandatory stop to make, at her part-time job. She dreaded it today, because she knew she was in no shape to deal with the incredibly inconsistent moods of Myrnin, her vampire mad-scientist boss. He might be laser focused and super-rational; he might be talking to crockery and quoting *Alice in Wonderland* (that had been the scene during her last visit). But whatever he was doing, he'd have work for her, and probably too much of it.

But at least he was never, ever boring.

She'd made the walk so often that she did it on autopilot, hardly even noticing the streets and houses and the alley down which she had to pass; she checked her phone and read texts as she jogged down the long marble steps that led into the darkness of his lab, or lair, whichever mood he was in today. The lights were on, which was nice. As she put her phone away, she saw that

Myrnin was bent over a microscope—an ancient thing that she'd tried to put away a dozen times in favor of a newer electronic model, but he kept unearthing the thing. He stepped away from the eyepiece to scribble numbers frantically on a chalkboard. The board was *covered* in numbers, and to Claire's eyes they looked completely random—not just in terms of their numerical values, but in the way they'd been written, at all angles and in all areas of the available space. Some were even upside down. It wasn't a formula or an analysis. It was complete gibberish.

So. It was going to be one of those days. Lovely.

"Hey," Claire said with fatalistic resignation as she dumped her backpack on the floor and opened up a drawer to retrieve her lab coat. It was a good thing she looked first; Myrnin had dumped an assortment of scalpels in on top of the fabric. Any one of them could have sliced her to the bone. "What are you doing?"

"Did you know that certain types of coral qualify as immortal? The definition of scientific immortality is that if the mortality rate of a species doesn't increase after it reaches maturity, there is no such thing as aging . . . black coral, for instance. Or the Great Basin bristlecone pine. I'm trying to determine if there is any resemblance between the development of those cellular colonies with the replacement of human cells that takes place in a conversion to vampirism. . . ." He was talking a mile a minute, with a fever pitch that Claire always dreaded. It meant he was in need of medication, which he wouldn't take; she'd need to be stealthy about adding it to his blood supply, again, to bring him down a little into the rational zone. "Did you bring me a hamburger?"

"Did I— No, Myrnin, I didn't bring you a hamburger." Bizarre. He'd never asked for that before.

"Coffee?"

"It's late."

"Doughnuts?"

"No."

"What good are you, then?" He finally looked up from the microscope, made another note or two on the board, and stepped back to consider the chaos of chalk marks. "Oh dear. That's not very—is this where I started? Claire?" He pointed at a number somewhere near the top right corner.

"I wasn't here," Claire said, and buttoned up her lab coat. "Do you want me to keep working on the machine?"

"The what? Oh, yes, that thing. Do, please." He crossed his arms and stared at the board, frowning now. It was not a personal-grooming highlight day for him, either. His long, dark hair was in tangles and needed a wash; she was sure the oversized somewhat-white shirt he was wearing had been used as a rag to wipe up chemical spills at sometime in its long life. He'd had the presence of mind to put on some kind of pants, though she wasn't sure the baggy walking shorts were what she'd have chosen. At least the flip-flops kind of matched. "How was school?"

"Bad," she said.

"Good," he said absently, "very good . . . Ah, I think this is where I started. . . . Fibonacci sequence—I see what I did. . . ." He began drawing a spiral through the numbers, starting somewhere at the center. Of course, he'd be noting down results in a spiral. Why not?

Claire felt a headache coming on. The place was dirty again, grit on the floor that was a combination of sand blown in from the desert winds, and whatever Myrnin had been working with that he'd spilled liberally all over the place. She only hoped it wasn't too toxic. She'd have to schedule a day to get him out of here so she could get reorganized, sweep up the debris, stack the books back in some kind of order, shelve the lab equipment. . . . No, that wouldn't be a day. More like a week.

She gave up thinking about it, then went to the lab table on the right side of the room, which was covered by a dusty sheet. She pulled the cover off, coughed at the billows of grit that flew up, and looked at the machine she was building. It was definitely her own creation, this thing: it lacked most of the eccentric design elements that Myrnin would have put into it, though he'd sneaked in a few flywheels and glowing liquids along the way. It was oblong, practical, bell-shaped, and had oscillation controls along the sides. She thought it looked a bit like an old-fashioned science fiction ray gun, but it had a very different use . . . if it had ever worked.

Claire hooked up the device to the plug-in analyzing programs, and began to run simulations. It was a project Myrnin had proposed months ago, and it had taken her this long to get even close to a solution. . . . The vampires had an ability, so far mysterious and decidedly unscientific, to influence the minds and emotions of others—humans, mostly, but sometimes other vampires. Every vampire had a different set of strengths and weaknesses, but most shared some kind of emotional-control mechanism; it helped them calm their prey, or convince them to surrender their blood voluntarily.

What she was working on was a way to *cancel* that ability. To give humans—and even other vampires—a way to defend themselves against the manipulation.

Claire had gone from building a machine that could pinpoint and map emotions to one that could build feedback loops, heightening what was already there. It was a necessary step to get to the *control* stage—you had to be able to replicate the ability to negate it. If you thought of emotion as a wavelength, you could either amplify or cancel it with the flick of a switch.

"Myrnin?" She didn't look up from the analysis running on the laptop computer screen. "Did you mess with my project?"

"A little," he said. "Isn't it better?"

It was. She had no idea what he'd done to it, but adjusting the controls showed precise calibrations that she couldn't have done herself. "Did you maybe write down how you did it?"

"Probably," Myrnin said cheerfully. "But I don't think it will help. It's just hearing the cycles and tuning to them. I don't think you're capable, with your limited human senses. If you'd become a vampire, you'd have so much more potential, you know."

She didn't answer that. She'd found it was really best not to engage in that particular debate with him, and besides, in the next second he'd forgotten all about it, focused on his enthusiasm for black coral.

On paper, the device they'd developed—well, she'd developed, and Myrnin had tweaked—seemed to work. Now she'd have to figure out how to test it, make sure it exactly replicated the way the vampire ability worked . . . and then make sure she could cancel that ability, reliably.

It might even have other applications. If you could make an attacking vampire afraid, make him back off, you could end a fight without violence. That alone made the work worthwhile.

And what happens when someone uses it the other way? she wondered. *What happens if an attacker gets hold of it, then uses it to make you more afraid, as a victim?* She didn't have an answer for that. It was one of the things that made her feel, sometimes, that this was a bad idea— and that she ought to simply destroy the thing before it caused more trouble.

But maybe not quite yet.

Claire unhooked the machine—she didn't have any kind of cool name for it yet, or even a project designation—and tested the weight of it. Heavy. She'd built it from solid components, and it generated considerable waste heat, but it was a prototype; it'd improve, if it was worthwhile.

She tried aiming it at the wall. It was a little awkward, but if she added a grip up front, that would help stabilize it—

"Claire?"

Myrnin's voice came from *right behind her*, way too close. She whirled, and her finger accidentally hit the switch on top as she fumbled her hold on the machine, and suddenly there was a live trial in action . . . on him.

She saw it work.

Myrnin's eyes widened, turned very dark, and then began to shimmer with liquid hints of red. He took a step back from her. A large one. "Oh," he said. "Don't do that. Please don't do that."

She shut it off, fast, because she wasn't sure what exactly had just happened. *Something*, for sure, but as live trials went, it was . . . inconclusive. "Sorry, sorry," she said, and put the device down with a *clunk* on the marble top of the lab table. "I didn't mean to do that. Um . . . what did you feel?"

"More of what I already felt," he said, which was uninformative. He took another step backward, and the red didn't seem to be fading from his eyes. "I was going to ask you if you'd send over some type AB from the blood bank; I seem to be running low. And also, I wanted to ask if you'd seen my bag of gummi worms."

"You're hungry," Claire guessed. He nodded cautiously. "And it . . . made it *stronger*?"

"In a way," he said. Not helpful. "Never mind the delivery from the blood bank. I believe I shall . . . take a walk. Good night, Claire."

He was being awfully polite, she thought; with him, that was usually a cover for severe internal issues. Before she could try to figure out exactly what was going on in his head, though, he'd headed at vampire-speed for the stairs and was gone.

She shook her head and looked at the switched-off device in irritation. "Well, that was helpful," she told it, and then rolled her eyes. "And now I'm talking to equipment, like him. Great."

Claire threw a sheet over the machine, made notes in the logbook, turned off the lab's lights, and headed home.

Arriving home—on Lot Street—didn't do much for her mood, either, because as she stomped past the rusty, leaning mailbox on the outside of the picket fence, she saw that the door was open and mail was sticking out. It threatened to blow away in the ever-present desert wind. Perfect. She had three housemates, and all of them had somehow failed to pick up the mail. And that was not her job. At least today.

She glared up at the big, faded Victorian house, and wondered when Shane was going to get around to painting it as he'd promised he would. Never, most likely. Just like the mail.

Claire readjusted her heavy backpack on one shoulder, an automatic, thoughtless shift of weight, snatched the wadded-up paper out of the box, and flipped through the thick handfuls. Water bill (apparently, saving the town from water-dwelling draug monsters hadn't given them any utility credits), electric bill (high, again), flyers from the new pizza delivery place (whose pizza tasted like dog food on tomato sauce), and . . . four envelopes, embossed with the Founder's official seal.

She headed for the house. And then the day took one step further to the dark side, because pinned to the front door with a cheap pot-metal dagger was a hand-drawn note with four tombstones on it. Each headstone had one of their names. And below, it said, *Vampire lovers get what they deserve.*

Charming. It would have scared her except that it wasn't the first she'd seen over the past few weeks; there had been four other notes, one slipped under the door, two pinned on it (like this one), and one slipped into the mailbox. That, and a steady and growing number of rude storekeepers, deliberate insults from people on the street, and doors slammed in her face.

It was no longer popular being the friend of the only mixed-marriage vampire/human couple in Morganville.

Claire ripped the note off, shook her head over the cheap dagger, which would snap in a fight, and unlocked the front door. She hip-bumped it open, closed it, and locked it again—automatic caution, in Morganville. "Hey!" she yelled without looking up. "Who was supposed to get the mail?"

"Eve!" Shane yelled from down the hall, in the direction of the living room, at the same time that Eve shouted, "Michael!" from upstairs. Michael said nothing, probably because he wasn't home yet.

"We *really* need to talk about schedules! Again!" Claire called back. She briefly considered showing them the flyer, but then she balled it up and threw it, and the dagger, in the trash, along with the assorted junk mail offering discount crap and high-interest credit cards.

It's just talk, she told herself. It wasn't, but she thought that eventually, everyone—human and vampire—would just get their collective panties unbunched about Michael and Eve's getting married. It was nobody's business but their own, after all.

She focused instead on the four identical envelopes.

They were made of fancy, heavy paper that smelled musty and old, as if it had been stored somewhere for a hundred years and someone was just getting around to opening the box. The seal on the back of each was wax, deep crimson, and embossed with the Founder's symbol. Each of their names was written on the outside in flowing, elegant script, so even and perfect, it looked like computer printing until she looked closely and found the human imperfections.

Her instincts were tingling danger, but she tried to think positively. *C'mon, this could be a good thing,* she told herself. *Maybe it's just a thank-you card from Amelie for saving Morganville. Again. We deserve that.*

Sounded good, but Amelie, the Founder of Morganville, was a very old vampire, and vamps weren't in the business of thanking people. Amelie had grown up royalty, and having people do crazy, dangerous (and possibly fatal) things on her slightest whim was just . . . normal. It probably didn't even call for a smile, much less a note of gratitude. And, to be honest, Claire's once almost-friendly status with the Founder had gotten a bit . . . strained.

Morganville, Texas, was just about the last gathering place for vampires in the world; it was the spot that they'd chosen to make their last stand, to forget their old grudges, to band tightly together against common threats and enemies. When Claire had first arrived, the vampires had been battling illness; then they'd been after one another. And four months ago, they'd been fighting the draug, water creatures that preyed on vampires like delicious, tasty snacks . . . and the vampires had finally won.

That left them the undisputed champions of the world's food chain. In saving Morganville, Claire hadn't really stopped to consider what might happen when the vamps no longer had something to fear. Now she knew.

They didn't exactly feel grateful.

Oh, on the surface, Morganville was all good, or at least getting better. . . . The vamps had been fast on the trigger to start repairing the town, cleaning up after the demise of the draug, and getting all of their human population settled again in their homes, businesses, and schools. The official PR line had been that a dangerous chemical spill had forced evacuations, and that seemed to have satisfied everybody (along with generous cash payments, and automatic good grades to all of the students at Texas Prairie University who'd had their semesters cut short). Claire also suspected that the vampires had applied some psychic persuasion, where necessary—there were a few of them capable of doing that. On the surface, it looked like Morganville was not only recovering, but thriving.

But it didn't feel right. On the few occasions that she'd seen Amelie, the Founder hadn't seemed right, either. Her body language, her smile, the way she looked at people . . . all were different. And darker.

"Hey," her housemate Eve Rosser—*no*, it was Eve *Glass* now, after the wedding—said. "You going to open those or what?" She walked up beside Claire, set a glass down on the kitchen counter, and poured herself a tall glass of milk. Her ruby wedding ring winked at Claire as if inviting her to share a secret joke. "Because the last time I saw something looking that official, it was inviting me to a party. And you know how much I love those."

"You almost got killed at that party," Claire said absently. She passed over Eve's envelope and picked up her own.

"I almost get killed at most parties. Hence, you can tell that's how much I love them," Eve said, and ripped open the paper in a wide, tearing swath. Claire—who was by nature more of a neat gently-slice-the-thing-open kind of person—winced. "Huh. Another envelope inside the envelope. They do love to waste paper. Haven't they ever heard of tree-hugging?"

As Eve extracted the second layer, Claire had a chance to do the usual wardrobe scan of her best friend . . . and wasn't disappointed. Eve had suddenly taken a liking to aqua blue, and she'd added streaks of it in her black hair, which was worn today in cute, shiny ponytails on the sides of her head. Her Goth white face was brightened by aqua eye shadow and—where did she find this stuff?—matching lipstick, and she had on a tight black shirt with embossed crosses. The short, poufy skirt continued the blue theme. Then black tights with blue hearts. Then, combat boots.

So, a typical Wednesday, really.

Eve pulled the inner envelope free, opened the flap, and extracted a folded sheet of thick paper. Something fell out to bounce on the counter, and Claire caught it.

It was a card. A plastic card, like a credit card, but this one had the Founder's symbol screened on the back, and it had Eve's picture in the upper right corner—taken when she'd been without the full Goth war paint, which Eve would despise. It had Eve's name, address, phone number ... and a box at the bottom that read *Blood Type: O Neg.* Across from it was a box saying *Protector: Glass, Michael.*

"What the ... ?" *Oh,* Claire thought, even before she'd finished the question. This must have been what the vampire cop was asking her for. The identification card.

Eve plucked the card from her fingers, stared at it with a completely blank expression, and then turned her attention to the letter that had come with it. " 'Dear Mrs. Michael Glass,' " she read. "*Seriously?* Mrs. Michael? Like I don't even have a name of my own? And what the hell is this about his being my Protector? I never agreed to that!"

"And?" Claire reached for the letter, but Eve hip-checked her and continued reading.

" 'I have enclosed your new Morganville Resident Identification Card, which all human residents are now required to carry at all times so that, in the unlikely case of any emergency, we may

quickly contact your loved ones and Protector, and provide necessary medical information.'" Eve looked up and met Claire's eyes
squarely. "I call bullshit. *Human* residents. With blood type listed?
It's like a shopping list for vamps."

Claire nodded. "What else?"

Eve turned her attention back to the paper. "'Failure to carry
and provide this card upon request will result in fines of—' Oh,
screw this!" Eve wadded up the paper, dropped it on the floor, and
stomped on it with her boots, which were certainly made for
stomping. "I am *not* carrying around a Drink Me card, and they
can't ask for my papers. What is this, Naziland?" She picked up the
card and tried to bend it in half, but it was too flexible. "Where
did you put the scissors . . . ?"

Claire rescued the card and looked at it again. She turned it
over, held it under the strongest light available—the window—
and frowned. "Better not," she said. "I think this is chipped."

"Chipped? Can I eat it?"

"Microchipped. It's got some kind of tech in it, anyway. I'd
have to take a look to see what kind, but it's pretty safe to say
they'd know if you went all paper dolls with it."

"Oh great, so it's not just a Drink Me card; it's a tracking device, like those ear things they put on lions on Animal Planet?
Yeah, there's no way that can go wrong—like, say, vampires being
issued receivers so they can just shop online for who they want to
target tonight."

Eve was right about that, Claire thought. She *really* didn't feel
good about this. On the surface, it was just an ID card, perfectly
normal—she already carried a student ID and a driver's license—
but it *felt* like something else. Something more sinister.

Eve stopped rummaging in drawers and just stared at her.
"Hey. We *each* got one. Four envelopes."

"I thought they were only for human residents," Claire said. "So what's in Michael's?" Because Michael Glass was definitely *not* human these days. He'd been bitten well before Claire had met him, but the full-on vampire thing had been slow-building; she saw it more and more now, but deep down she thought he was still the same strong, sweet, no-nonsense guy she'd met when she'd first arrived on the Glass House doorstep. He was definitely still strong. It was the sweetness that was in some danger of fading away, over time.

Before Claire could warn Eve that maybe it wasn't the greatest idea, Eve shredded open Michael's envelope, too, yanked out the inner one, and pulled out his letter. Another card fell out. This one was gold. Shiny, shiny gold. It didn't have any info on it at all. Just a gold card, with the Founder's symbol embossed on it.

Eve went for the letter. "'Dear Michael,'" she said. "Oh, sure, he gets *Michael*, not *Mr. Glass*.... 'Dear Michael, I have enclosed your card of privilege, as has been discussed in our community meetings.'" She stopped again, reread that silently, and looked down at the card she was holding in her fingers. "*Card of privilege?* He doesn't get the same treatment we do."

"Community meetings," Claire said. "Which we weren't invited to, right? And what kind of privileges, exactly?"

"You'd better believe it's a whole lot better than a free mocha at Common Grounds," Eve said grimly. She kept reading, silently, then handed the paper stiff-armed to Claire, not saying another word.

Claire took it, feeling a bit ill now. It read:

Dear Michael,

    I have enclosed your card of privilege, as has been discussed in our community meetings. Please keep this card close, and you are welcome

*to use it at any time at the blood bank, Bloodmobile, or Common
Grounds for up to ten pints monthly.*

Wow, it really was good for free drinks. But that wasn't all.

*This card also entitles you to one legal hunt per year without
advance declaration of intent. Additional hunts must be preapproved
through the Elders' Council. Failure to seek preapproval will result in
fines of up to five thousand dollars per occurrence, payable to the
family's Protector, if applicable, or to the City of Morganville, if there
is no Protector on file.*
    Best wishes from the Founder,
    Amelie

For a moment, Claire couldn't quite understand what she was
reading. Her eyes kept going over it, and over it, and finally it all
snapped into clear, razor-sharp focus, and she pulled in a deep,
shaking breath. The paper creased as her grip tensed up.

"Yeah," Eve said. Claire met her gaze wordlessly. "It's telling
him he gets a free pass to kill one person a year, just on a whim. Or
more if he plans it out. You know, like a special treat. *Privilege.*"
There was nothing in her tone, or her face, or her eyes. Just . . .
blank. Locked down.

Eve took the paper from Claire's unresisting hand, folded it,
and put it back in the envelope with the gold card.

"What—what are you going to say to him?" Claire couldn't
quite get her head adjusted. This was wrong, just . . . wrong.

"Nothing good," Eve said.

And that was the precise moment when the kitchen door
opened, and Michael stepped inside. He was wearing a thick black
canvas cowboy-style duster coat, broad-brimmed hat, and black

gloves. Eve had teased him earlier that he looked like an animé superhero, but it was all practical vampire sun-resistant gear. Michael was relatively still newborn as a vampire, which meant he was especially vulnerable to the sun, and to burning up.

Now, he whipped off his hat and gave the two of them an elaborate bow he'd probably copied from a movie (or, Claire thought, learned from one of the older vamps), and rose from that with a broad, sweet smile. "Hey, Claire. And *hello*, Mrs. Glass." There was a special gentleness when he said *Mrs. Glass*—a private kind of thing, and it was both breathtaking and heartbreaking.

Heartbreaking, because in the next second, he knew something was wrong. The smile faltered, and Michael glanced from Eve to Claire, then back to Eve. "What?" He dumped the hat and his gloves on the table, and shed the coat without looking away from Eve's face. "Baby? What's wrong?" He walked to her and put his hands on her shoulders. His wedding ring matched hers, even down to the ruby inset, and it caught the light the way Eve's had earlier.

Bloodred.

It was terrible, Claire thought, that he was still so much *Michael*—still exactly as he'd been when she first met him—eighteen, though they were all catching up to him now in age. It wasn't fair to call him pretty, but he was gorgeous—tumbles of blond curls that somehow always looked perfect; clear, direct blue eyes the color of a morning sky. His pallor gave him the perfect look of ivory, and when he stood still, as he was now, he looked like some fabulous lost statue direct from Greece or Rome.

It wasn't fair.

Eve held the gaze between herself and her husband, and said, "This is for you." She held up the inner envelope with his name written on it in flowing script.

For a second, Michael clearly didn't know what it was . . . and then Claire saw him realize. His eyes widened, and something like horror passed over his expression and was quickly hidden underneath a blank, carefully composed mask. He didn't say anything, but just took his hands from her shoulders and accepted the envelope. He stuck it in his pocket.

"You're not even pretending to be curious?" Eve said. Her voice had gone deep in her throat and had taken on a dangerous edge. "Great."

"You read it?" he asked, and took it out again to open it up. The card fell out, again, but he deftly snatched it out of the air without any effort. "Huh. It's shinier than I thought it'd be."

"That's all you have to say?"

He unfolded the letter. Claire was no good at reading those micro-expressions people on TV were always talking about on crime shows, but she thought he looked guilty as he read it. Guilty as hell.

"It's not what you think," he said, which was exactly the wrong thing to say, because it made Claire (and almost certainly Eve) think about every guy ever caught cheating. Luckily, he didn't stop there. "Eve, all vampires get the hunting privilege; it's just part of living in Morganville—it's always been the rule, even when nobody in the human community knew. Look, I don't want it. I opposed the whole idea at the meetings—"

"Which you didn't tell us about at all, jerk," Eve broke in. "We're *community!*"

Michael took a deep breath and continued. "I told Amelie and Oliver I wouldn't ever use it, but they didn't care."

"Doesn't matter. You have a free pass for murder."

"No," he said, and took her hands in his, a gesture so quick she couldn't avoid it, but gentle enough that she could have pulled away if she'd wanted. "No, Eve. You know me better than that. I'm trying to change it."

Her eyes filled with tears, suddenly, and she collapsed against his chest. Michael put his arms around her and held her tightly, his head resting against hers. He was whispering. Claire couldn't hear what he was saying, but it really wasn't any of her business.

She took the glass of milk Eve had poured for herself, seeing as how it was sitting there unwanted, and drank it. *He still should have told us,* she thought, and slit her envelope open with a steak knife to take out her own letter and ID card. It felt weird, seeing her information on there. Even though the vampires had always known what her blood type was, where she lived . . . it felt different, somehow.

Official.

As if she were some kind of commodity. Worse: with the chip in it, it meant she couldn't hide, couldn't run. She now, as Eve had said, *had papers,* just as they demanded in those old black-and-white war movies; she had to carry the card or get arrested (today's encounter had proven that), and it meant that they could round her up whenever they wanted . . . for questioning. Or for sticking her in some kind of prison camp.

Or worse.

One thing was certain: Shane Collins was not going to like this at all . . . and just as she thought about that, Shane banged in the swinging door of the kitchen, headed straight for the refrigerator, and snagged himself a cold soft drink, which he popped open and chugged three swallows of before he stopped, looked at Eve and Michael, and said, "Oh, come on. Don't tell me you guys are fighting again. Seriously, isn't there supposed to be a honeymoon period or something?"

"We're not fighting," Michael said. There was something in

his voice that warned this was a bad time for Shane to get snarky. "We're making up. We'll be upstairs."

Shane actually opened his mouth to say something else, but he suddenly shivered and took a step back. "Hey!" he said, and looked up at the ceiling. "Stop it, Miranda! Brat."

Miranda was . . . well, the Glass House teen ghost. A real, official one. She'd died here, in the house—sacrificed herself, in the battle with the draug—and now she was part of it, but invisible during the day.

She could still make herself felt, when she wanted to; the cold spot she'd just formed around Shane was proof of how she felt about his impulse to harass Michael and Eve just now. Miranda couldn't be heard or seen during the daytime, but she could sure make her displeasure known.

And they'd probably hear about it tonight, in detail, when she materialized.

Claire sighed as Michael led Eve out of the room with an arm around her shoulders. "Here," she said, and passed Shane the envelope with his name on it. "You should sit down. You're really not going to like this."

Sitting Shane down to discuss things didn't help, because all it accomplished was an overturned chair, and Shane stalking the kitchen in dangerously black silence. He tried to throw his ID card in the trash, but Claire quietly retrieved it and put it back on the table, along with hers. Eve's still sat abandoned on the counter.

"You're going along with this?" he finally asked. She'd been watching him as he paced; there was a lot to learn about her boyfriend when he wasn't saying anything, just from the tenseness of his muscles, and the way he held himself. How he looked right now was telling her that he was on the verge of punching something—preferably something with a set of fangs. Shane had gotten better about controlling his impulses to fight, but they never really went away. They couldn't, she supposed. Now he stopped, put his back to the wall, and used both hands to push his shaggy, longish hair back from his face. His eyes were wide and dark and full of challenge as he looked at her.

"No," she said. She felt steady, almost calm, really. "I'm not going along with it. None of us is—we *can't*. Are you coming with me to talk to Amelie about it?"

"Hell yes, I'm coming with you. Did you think I'd let you go alone?"

"Do you promise to keep your cool?"

"I promise I won't go starting any fights. But I'm taking a little insurance, and you're carrying, too. No arguments. I know you don't think Amelie's exactly on our side anymore, so trusting her's off the table." He pushed off the wall and opened the cabinets under the sink; under there were several black canvas bags of equipment, all of it damaging to vampires in some way.

Claire wanted to be brave and say that she didn't need any kind of defenses, but she was no longer sure of that. Morganville, since the defeat of the draug, was . . . different. Different in small, indefinable ways, but definitely not the same, and she wasn't sure that the rules she'd learned about interacting with Amelie, the vampire Founder, were the same, either. The old Amelie, the one she'd gotten almost comfortable knowing . . . that woman would not have hurt her just for disagreeing.

But this new, more powerful Amelie seemed different. More remote. More dangerous.

So Claire looked at the contents of the bag he'd opened, and took out two vials of liquid silver nitrate, which she put in the pockets of her blue jeans. She wasn't exactly dressed for vampire fighting—not that there was a real dress code for that—but she was prepared to sacrifice the cute sky blue top she had on, in an emergency. Pity she hadn't picked the black one this morning.

Ah, Morganville. Where dressing to hide bloodstains was just good daily planning.

"We should talk to Hannah first," she said as Shane picked out a thin-bladed knife that had been coated with silver. He checked the edge on it, nodded, and jammed it back in the leather sheath before he stuck it in the inside pocket of his leather jacket.

"If you think that'll help," he said. Hannah Moses was the newly minted mayor of Morganville—she'd been the police chief, but with the death of Richard Morrell, she'd ended up being appointed the First Human of the town. It wasn't a job Hannah wanted, but it was one she'd accepted like the soldier she'd once been. "Though I figure if Hannah could have done anything about this, it would have already been done. She doesn't need us to bring her the news."

That was true enough, but still, Claire couldn't shake the feeling that they needed allies at their side before dropping in on Amelie. Strength in numbers, and all that; she couldn't ask Michael, not without asking Eve, and Eve was a hot button for the vampires right now. Michael and Eve were married, really, legally married, and that had cheesed off a good portion of the plasma-challenged in their screwed-up community. Apparently, prejudices didn't die, even when people did.

Not that the humans seemed all that happy about it, either.

"Still," she said aloud, "let's go talk to her and see what she can do. Even if she just comes with us . . ."

"Yeah, I know—she'd be harder to make disappear." Shane stepped in and bent his head and kissed her, a sudden and warm and sweet thing that made her pull her attention away from her worries and focus utterly on him for a moment. "Mmmm," he murmured, not moving back farther than strictly required for the words to form between their lips. "Been missing that."

"Me, too," she whispered, and leaned into the kiss. It had been a busy few months, rebuilding Morganville, finding their lives and place in things again. Then she'd been focusing on getting caught up at school again—once Texas Prairie University had reopened, she'd been determined not to have to repeat any credit hours she'd missed during the general emergency. Her boyfriend had been through some rough times—more than rough, really—but they'd come out of it okay, she thought. They understood each other. Best of all, they actually liked each other. It wasn't just hormones (though right now, hers were fizzing like a shaken soda; Shane just had that effect on her); it was something else. Something deeper.

Something special that she thought was actually going to last. Maybe even forever.

Shane pulled back and kissed the tip of her nose, which made her laugh just a little. "Gear up, Warrior Princess. We've got some adventuring to do."

She was still smiling when they left the house, hand in hand, walking through the blazing hot midafternoon. Lot Street, their street, was mostly intact from all the troubles Morganville had seen; it even had most of its former residents back in place. As they passed, Mrs. Morgan waved at them as she watered her flowers. She was wearing a bathing suit that was—in Claire's opinion— way too small, especially at her age, which had to be at least thirty. "Hello, Shane!" Mrs. Morgan said. Shane waved back, and gave her a dazzling grin.

Claire elbowed him. "Don't bait the cougars."

"You just don't want me to have any fun, do you?"

"Not that kind of fun."

"Oh, come on—she's not serious. She just likes to flirt. Gives her a thrill."

"*I'm* not thrilled."

Shane's smile this time was positively predatory. "Jealous?"

She was, surprisingly, and hid it under a glare. "Disgusted, more like."

"C'mon, you think that actor guy is hot, and he's probably as old as Mrs. Morgan."

"He's on TV. She's modeling a bikini for you two doors down from us."

"Oh, so it's about access. In other words, if he lived two doors down and was walking around in his Joe Boxers . . ."

She elbowed him again, because this was not turning out to be an easy win of a conversation. He grunted a little, as if she'd hurt him (which she hadn't, at all), and he put his arm around her shoulders. "Okay, I surrender," he said. "No more cougar baiting. I won't even go outside without a shirt on when I mow the lawn. But you have to make the same promise."

"Not to go outside without a shirt? Sure."

"No," he said, and suddenly he was completely serious. "No flirting with older guys. Especially the really old ones."

He meant Myrnin, her vampire boss, friend, mentor, and sometimes the bane of her existence. Crazy, wildly sentimental Myrnin, who seemed to like her more than was good for either of them.

And she sometimes hadn't done a very good job of handling that, she had to admit.

"I promise," she said. "No flirting."

He sent her a sidelong look that was a little doubtful, but he nodded. "Thanks."

Other than Mrs. Morgan's bright orange bikini, it was an uneventful walk. Morganville wasn't a huge place, and from Lot Street to the mayor's office was about ten minutes at a stroll—in the current late-spring temperatures, just about enough time to really start to feel the burn of the sun beating down. Claire was a little grateful when Shane opened the door and she stepped into the cooler, darker space of the Morganville City Hall lobby. It had been rebuilt, mostly, but one thing about the vampires: they demanded high standards on their civic buildings. The place looked great, with new marble floors and columns and fancy-looking light fixtures overhead. Old-world elegance in the middle of Nowhere, Texas.

A round wooden information desk was situated in the center of the lobby, staffed by a good-looking lady probably only a few years out of college. The nameplate in front of her said she was Annabelle Lange. Looking up as Claire and Shane stopped in front of her, she gave them a warm, welcoming smile. She had chestnut brown hair worn long and glossy, and big blue eyes . . . entirely too pretty, and all her attention focused on Shane immediately.

This was worse than Mrs. Morgan by a whole lot. Annabelle wasn't old. And she didn't have to wear a Day-Glo bikini to get attention.

"We're here to see the mayor," Claire said before Annabelle could speak or ask Shane for his phone number. "Claire Danvers and—"

"Shane Collins," Annabelle interrupted her, still smiling. "Yes, I know. Just a moment; I'll see if Mayor Moses is available."

She turned away and got on a telephone. While she was busy, Claire sent Shane a look—a significant one. He raised his eyebrows, clearly amused. "I didn't do anything," he said. "Totally not my fault."

"Stop being so . . ."

"Charming? Attractive? Irresistible?"

"I'm going with arrogant."

"Ow." Before he could defend himself, the receptionist was back, all smiles and dimples.

"Mayor Moses is in a meeting, but she says she can work you in immediately after. If you'd like to go upstairs and wait in her office . . ."

"Thanks," Shane said. And the girl actually did that lip-biting shorthand for *I'm available* and gave him the under-the-lashes look. Textbook. Claire couldn't help but roll her eyes, not that she actually existed on Annabelle Lange's planet at all.

Shane noticed, though. Definitely. He hustled Claire on, fast, to the elevators. "C'mon, that wasn't worth all that effort at a reaction. She's just . . . friendly."

"If she were any friendlier, she'd be giving you a lap dance right now."

"Wow. Who turned you into the Green-Eyed Monster? And don't tell me you got bitten by a radioactive spider. There's no superhero of jealousy." When she didn't reply before they reached the elevators, he punched the button, then turned toward her. It wasn't just a casual kind of look; it was a level stare, very direct, and it caught Claire a little off guard. "Seriously. Are you really thinking I'm into Mrs. Morgan? Or what's-her-name back there?"

"Annabelle," Claire said, and wished she hadn't remembered the girl's name quite that fast. "No. But—"

"But what?" It wasn't like Shane to be so serious. "You know I was just kidding about Mrs. Morgan, right? I wouldn't go there. Or anywhere. I mean, I look at girls, because c'mon, that's biology. But I love you." He said it so matter-of-factly that it sent a shiver through her, deep down to her toes. When Shane was serious, when he got that steady, calm look in his eyes, it made her hot and cold all over. She felt as if she were floating someplace very high, where the air was terribly thin but intoxicating.

"I know," she whispered, and stepped closer to him. "That's why I'm jealous."

"You know that doesn't make sense, right?"

"It does. Because now I have so much more to lose, and more every time you kiss me. I think about losing you, and it hurts."

He smiled. It occurred to her that Shane didn't smile much with other people, only with her, and certainly not *that* way. It was so . . . hot, having that all to herself. "You're not losing me," he said. "I straight-out promise that."

Whatever else he was going to say—she would have managed to think about it in the ringing, happy silence of the afterglow— was interrupted by the soft bell of the elevator. Shane offered his arm, and she took it, feeling stupid and a little bit giggly, and let him escort her into the elevator.

As soon as the doors slid shut, Shane pushed the button for the third floor (it had a boldly lettered MAYOR'S OFFICE sign on it) and then backed her up against the wall, bent his head, and kissed her for real. A lot. Deeply. His lips felt soft and damp and sweet and more than a little too hot for being in public, and she made a protesting little sound that was half a warning that the door was going to open *any second*. The other half of her was begging him to completely disregard the warning and just keep going . . . but then he pulled back, took in a deep breath, and stepped away as the doors opened.

He was still smiling, and she couldn't stop staring at him. In profile, those lips were just . . . yeah. Delicious.

"Claire," he said, and gave her an after-you gesture.

"Oh," she said brilliantly, and pulled her head together with an effort. "Right. Thanks."

The warm spell of the elevator was broken, because as she and Shane stepped out into the hallway, a door slammed hard down the hall, and a tall girl in a short skirt and designer heels came striding around the corner. The season's color was hot pink, and she was practically glowing in the dark with it . . . the skirt, the shoes, the nail polish, the lipstick.

The lips took a particularly bitter curl when Monica Morrell spotted the two of them. Her steps slowed for a second, and then she tossed her glossy hair over her shoulders and kept coming. "Somebody call security—vagrants are getting in again," she said. "Oh, never mind. It's just *you*. Here visiting your parole officer, Shane?"

It sounded classically Monica, Mean Girl, Deluxe Edition, but there was something different about her, Claire thought. Monica's heart didn't seem quite in it anymore. She looked a little pale under her must-have spray tan, and despite the up-to-the-minute makeup and clothes, she seemed a little lost. The world had finally and decisively knocked the props out from under Monica Morrell, and Claire wished she could have more satisfaction in that. She still felt the pulse of dull anger and resentment, sure; that was pretty much hardwired inside, after the years of abuse Monica had heaped on her since she'd arrived.

But, knowing what she knew, there was not nearly enough delicious revenge to be had in seeing Monica off-balance.

"Monica," Shane said. Nothing else. He watched her the way you'd watch a potentially hostile pit bull, ready for anything, but he wasn't reacting to her jibe. Monica didn't return the greeting.

"Nice dress," Claire said. She meant that. The hot pink looked particularly good on Monica, and she'd obviously taken a lot of time with the whole look.

Monica punched the elevator button, since the doors had already shut, and said, "That's it? *Nice dress?* You're not even going to ask me if I mugged a dead hooker for it or something? Lame, Danvers. You need to step up your efforts if you want to make an impression."

"How are you?" Claire asked. Shane made a sound of protest in the back of his throat, a low warning she disregarded; maybe this was useless, trying to be empathetic with Monica, but it wasn't really in Claire's nature not to try.

"How am I?" Monica sounded puzzled, and for a moment, she looked directly at Claire. Her eyes were expertly made up, but under the covering layers they looked tired and a little puffy. "My brother's dead, and you jackasses just stood there and let it happen. That's how I am."

"Monica—" Shane's voice was gentler than Claire expected. "You know that's not what happened."

"Do I?" Monica smiled slightly, her eyes never leaving Claire's. "I know what people *tell* me happened."

"You were talking to Hannah," Claire guessed. "Didn't she tell you . . ."

"None of your business what we talked about," Monica interrupted. The elevator dinged for her, and she stepped inside as it opened. "I don't believe *any* of you. Why should I? You've all hated me since forever. As far as I'm concerned, you all thought this was payback. Guess what? Payback's a bitch. And so am I."

Monica looked . . . alone, Claire thought, as the doors slid closed on her. Alone and a little scared. She'd always been insulated from the real world—first by her father, the former mayor of Morganville, and by her faithful mean-girl companions. Her brother, Richard, hadn't coddled her, but he'd protected her, too, when he thought it was necessary. Now that Richard was gone, killed by the savage draug, she had . . . well, nothing. Her power was pretty much gone, and with it, her friends. She was just another pretty girl now, and one thing Monica wasn't used to being . . . was ordinary.

"I thought she'd be less . . ."

"Bitchy?" Shane supplied. "Yeah, good luck. She's not the reforming type."

Claire elbowed him. "Like you? Because as I remember it, you were all bad-boy slacker bad attitude when I met you. So you've what, forgiven her? That's not like you, Shane."

Shane shrugged, a slow roll of his shoulders seeming to be more about getting rid of tension than expressing an emotion. "Could have been wrong about some things she did before," he said. "Doesn't mean she isn't a waste of general air space, though."

Well, he was right about that, and since Monica was gone, there was no point in spending time discussing her, anyway. They had an appointment, and when they rounded the corner toward the mayor's office, they found the door open, with the receptionist at her desk.

"Yes?" The receptionist here, unlike the one downstairs, was all business . . . matronly, chilly, with X-ray blue eyes that scanned the two of them up and down and rendered a verdict of *not very important.* "Can I help you?"

"We're here to see Mayor Moses," Claire said. "Uh—Claire Danvers and Shane Collins. We called up."

"Have a seat." The receptionist went back to her computer screen, completely uninterested in them even before they moved to the waiting area. It was comfortable enough, but the magazines were ages old, and within a few seconds Claire found herself itching to do something, so she pulled out her phone and began scrolling through texts and e-mails. There weren't very many, but then her circle of tech-savvy friends wasn't very large. Most of the vampire residents of Morganville hadn't mastered the knack and didn't want to ever try. Most of the humans were too wary of network monitoring to commit much to pixels.

However, Eve had linked her to a funny cat video, which was a nice break from the usual vampire-related mayhem. Claire watched it twice while Shane flipped through a decade-old *Sports Illustrated* before the receptionist finally said, "The mayor will—" She was probably going to frostily pronounce that the mayor would see them now, but she was interrupted by the door opening to the mayor's inner office, and Hannah Moses herself stepping out.

"Claire, Shane, come in," she said, and cut a glance at her assistant. "We're not that formal here."

The receptionist's mouth tightened into a lemon-sucking pucker, and she stabbed at the keys on her computer as if she intended to sink her fingerprints into them.

Mayor Moses—that sounded so strange, honestly—closed the door behind the two of them and said, "Sorry about Olive. She's inherited from two previous administrations. So. What was so urgent?" She indicated the two chairs sitting across from her desk as she took her own seat and leaned forward, elbows on the smooth wood surface. There was something elegant and composed about her, and something intimidating, too. . . . Hannah was a tall woman, angular, with skin the color of very dark chocolate. She was attractive, and somehow the scar (a souvenir of Afghanistan and her military career) just worked to make her more interesting. She'd changed her hair; the neat cornrows were gone now, and she'd shaved it close to her head in a way that made her look like a beautiful, scary piece of sculpture.

She'd exchanged her police uniform for sharply tailored jackets and pants, but the look was still somehow official . . . even to the Morganville pin in her lapel. She might not have a gun anymore, but she still looked completely competent and dangerous.

"Here," Shane said, and handed over his ID card. "What the hell is up with these things?"

He certainly wasn't wasting any time.

Hannah glanced at it and handed it back without a smile. "Don't like your picture?"

"C'mon, Hannah."

"There are certain . . . compromises I've had to make," she said. "And no, I'm not happy about them. But carrying ID cards isn't going to kill you."

"Hunting licenses might," Claire said. "Michael's letter said they were back in force. Each vampire can kill one human a year, free and clear. Did you know that?"

That got her a sharp, unreadable look from the mayor, and after a moment, Hannah said, "I'm aware of it. And working on it. We have a special session this afternoon to discuss it."

"Discuss it?" Shane said. "We're talking about licenses to murder, Hannah. How can you sign up for this?"

"I *didn't* sign up for it. I was outvoted," she said. "Oliver's got . . . influence over Amelie now. In defeating the draug—which we had to do, for the safety of the human population—we also removed the only thing that vampires really feared. They certainly aren't afraid of humans anymore."

"They'd better be," Shane said grimly. "We've never taken any of this lying down. That's not going to change."

"But—Amelie promised that things would change," Claire said. "After we defeated her father, Bishop. She said humans would have an equal place in Morganville, that all this hunting would stop! You heard her."

"I did. And now she's changed her mind," Hannah said. "Believe me, I tried to stop the whole thing, but Oliver's in charge of the day-to-day business. He's put two more vampires on the Elders' Council, which makes it three to one if we vote along vampire versus human lines. In short, they can just ignore my votes." She looked calm, mostly, but Claire noticed the tight muscles in her jaw, and the way she glanced away as if reliving a bad memory.

Claire followed her gaze and saw a lone cardboard moving box in the corner. Hannah hadn't had the job very long, so it could have just been unpacking left to do . . . but from what she knew of her, Mayor Moses wasn't one to just let things sit around undone.

"Hannah?"

The mayor focused on her, and for a second Claire thought she might talk about what was bothering her, but then she shook her head. "Never mind," she said. "Claire, please take my advice. Drop this. There's nothing you can do or say that will change her mind, and Amelie's not the person you knew before. She's not reasonable. And she's not safe. If I could have put a stop to this, I would have; seven generations of my family come from Morganville, and I don't want to see things go south any more than you do."

"But—if we don't talk to Amelie, what are we supposed to do to stop it?"

"I don't know," Hannah said. She seemed angry, and deeply troubled. "I just don't know."

At times like these, Claire was sharply reminded that Hannah wasn't just some small-town sheriff upgraded to mayor. She had been a soldier, and she'd fought for her country. Hannah had taken up arms in Morganville before, and in a fight there wasn't anybody Claire wanted at her back more (except Shane).

"That's not an answer," Shane said. He tapped the identification card again. "You're not serious about really carrying these things."

"That's the new law of the land, Shane. Carry it or get fined the first time. Second time, it's jail. I can't advise you to do anything else but comply."

"What do we get the third time, stocks and public mockery?"

"There wouldn't be a third time," she said. "I'm sorry. I really am."

He looked at her for a long moment, then silently put it back in his pocket. Claire knew that look, and she saw the muscle jumping uneasily along his jawline. He was counting to ten, silently, letting go of the impulse to say something crazy and suicidal.

When he let his breath out, slowly, she knew it was okay, and she felt tension she didn't even know she had start to unbraid along her spine.

"Thanks for seeing us," Claire said, and Hannah stood to offer her hand. Claire accepted, though she still felt awkward shaking hands. Trying to be professional always made her seem like a fraud, like a kid playing dress-up. But she tried to hold Hannah's gaze as she returned the firm, dry grip. "Are you sure you won't come with us?"

"You're intent on going to see Amelie?"

"We have to try," Claire said. "Don't we? As you said, she used to listen to me, a little. Maybe she still will."

Hannah shook her head. "Kid, you've got guts, but I'm telling you, it's not going to work."

"Will you make an appointment for me, though? That way there's a record."

"I will." Hannah looked to Shane. "You're going to let her do this?"

"Not alone."

"Good."

Ten seconds later, they were out in the waiting area, under the judging gaze of the assistant, and then in the hallway. Claire took in a deep breath. "Did we actually accomplish anything?"

"Yeah," Shane said. "We figured out that Hannah wasn't going to help us much. Go figure, a Morganville mayor whose hands are tied? Who saw that coming?" He stopped Claire and put his hand on her shoulder. "I'll go with you to see Amelie."

"That's sweet, but having you with me is kind of a walking invitation to trouble."

"Just because they know I prefer my vampires extra-crispy..."

"Exactly." Claire covered the hand on her shoulder with her own. "I'll be careful."

"I meant what I said. You're not going in there alone," he said. "Take Michael. Or—and I can't believe I'm actually saying this—take Myrnin. Just have somebody at your back, okay?"

It was really something if Shane suggested she go anywhere at all with Myrnin, and for pretty good reasons.... Myrnin had feelings for her, and he had feelings for Shane, too, but in the opposite way entirely. As in, Myrnin probably thought about the death of her boyfriend, and Shane had the same fantasies. It was a mutual, weirdly cheerful loathing, even if it didn't come to outright conflict.

"Okay," Claire said. She didn't mean it, but it touched her that he was so genuinely concerned about her safety. She'd survived a lot in Morganville—not as much as Shane, granted—and she thought of herself as pretty tough these days. Not indestructible, but... sturdy.

One of these days, she'd have to sit him down and explain that she wasn't the fragile little sixteen-year-old he'd met; she was an adult now (she *so* didn't feel that status yet, despite the birthdays) and she'd proven she could meet the challenges of survival around here. And while it was sweet and lovely that he wanted to protect her, at a certain point he really needed to understand it wasn't his job to do it, twenty-four/seven.

He linked his arm with hers and walked her to the elevator. There was no repeat of the kissing, which was a little disappointing, but he outright ignored his would-be stalker Annabelle down in the outer lobby. That was better.

After the chill of the lobby, walking into the sun was like hitting a furnace face-first, and Claire blinked and grabbed her sunglasses. They were cheap and fun, blinged all to heaven—a gift from Eve, of course. As she adjusted them, she saw something odd.

Monica Morrell was still here. Standing at the bottom of the steps, leaning against a forbidding granite pillar (the courthouse was built in a style Claire liked to call Early American Mausoleum) and shading her eyes to peer out at the street. The hot wind stirred her long, glossy, dark hair like a sheet of silk, and that dress—as ever—was dangerously close to violating decency laws when the breeze inched the hem up.

Shane saw her, too, and slowed down, shooting Claire a sideways glance. She silently agreed. It was odd. Monica didn't just *stand* places, at least not unless she was making a statement of some kind. She was always on the move, like a shark.

"Huh," Monica said. "That's weird. Don't you think that's weird?" She addressed the remark to the air, but Claire supposed she intended it for her and Shane. Kind of.

"What?" she asked.

"The van," Monica said, and tilted her head toward the street. "Parked on the corner."

"Sweet," Shane said. "Somebody got new wheels."

"*This* year's model," Monica said. "I know for a fact that our lame-ass car lot doesn't even have *last* year's model. I had to go all the way to Odessa to buy my convertible. Morganville doesn't exactly keep up with the cutting edge."

"Okay." Shane shrugged. "Somebody went to Odessa and bought a new van. Why's that weird?"

"Because I'd know about it if they did, stupid. Nobody in Morganville's bought a new van in years." She sounded confident. Monica was the queen of town gossip, and Claire had to admit, she had a point. She *would* know. She'd probably know the serial numbers of each purchase, and how many times it had driven through town, and what the driver had been wearing on each occasion. "Besides, that shine? That's so *town*, not country. And check out the tinting."

"So?" Claire asked. Most glossy cars in Morganville had superdark windows, because they were owned by people who were— to put it mildly—allergic to the sun.

"That's not vampire shades," Shane said. "Dark, but not *that* dark. Custom stuff. Huh. And there's a logo on the side. Can't really see it, though, and . . ." His voice trailed off as the doors opened on the van. Three people got out.

"Oh," Monica said. "Oh. My. God. *Look* at him."

There were two men who'd exited the van, but Claire knew exactly what she meant. . . . There was only one *him*, even at a distance. Tall, dark, Latin, *hot*.

"That," Monica continued, in a voice that sounded very much like awe, "is some serious man candy." Shane made a throwing-up sound in the back of his throat, which brought out a leisurely smile on Monica's lips. "I'll bet if I licked him, he'd even taste like fruit. Passion fruit."

There was a woman, too—tall, leggy, with blond hair pulled

back in a bouncy, glossy ponytail. She seemed pretty, too, but Claire had to admit, her attention was on Mr. Man Candy. Even at a distance, Monica had nailed the description.

Monica pushed away from the pillar and set off in a runway stride, high heels clicking on the hot concrete sidewalk.

"Come on," Shane said, and tugged Claire after her. "This, I've got to see. And maybe get on the Internet."

TWO

CLAIRE

As they got closer to the van, Claire realized it was big—Texas-style big, with a high roof. It looked more like something to haul equipment than people. The logo on the side of the van was on a magnet backing, and it was red on black. There was some kind of skull with a microphone and hard-to-read letters, not that she was paying a lot of attention.

Monica's target was clearly Mr. Man Candy, who, Claire had to admit, did not suffer from closer inspection. He was tall (as tall as Shane), and broad-shouldered (like Shane) . . . but with an expensive-looking style to his thick dark hair, and perfect golden brown skin. Whether it was airbrushed or natural, it looked good on him. He had on a tight knit shirt that showed off his washboard abs, and his face was just . . . perfect.

"Hi," Monica said, and held out her hand to him as she came

to a stop about a foot away from him. "Welcome to Morganville."

He smiled at her with dazzlingly white teeth. "Well," he said,
and even his voice was perfect, with just a little hint of a Spanish
accent to give it spice. "Morganville gets points for having the
loveliest welcoming committee yet. What's your name, lovely?"

Monica was not used to being one-upped in the flattery game,
Claire guessed, because she blinked and actually looked a little
taken aback. But it lasted only an instant, and then she smiled her
biggest, brightest smile and said, "Monica. Monica Morrell. And
what's *your* name?"

His smile lost a little of its luster, and those sparkling dark
eyes dimmed a bit. "Ah, I thought you knew."

Monica froze. Shane muttered, "Thank you, God," and took
out his cell phone to start recording. "It's like arrogant matter
meets arrogant antimatter."

Monica unfroze long enough to snap, "Put that away, Shane.
God, are you six?" before focusing back on Mr. Man Candy. "Don't
mind him—he's the village idiot. And she's the village Einstein,
which is nearly as bad."

He accepted that as an apology, Claire guessed, because he
took the girl's hand and bent over it to plant his lips on her knuckles. Monica looked dazzled. And a little scared. Her lips parted,
her eyes widened, and for a moment she looked like a normal, regular girl of nineteen who'd been knocked off her feet by an older,
slicker man. "My name is Angel Salvador," he said. "I am the host
of the show *After Death*. Perhaps you know it?"

It sounded vaguely familiar—one of those ghost-hunting shows
Claire never watched.

Shane pivoted and focused on the girl. "And you are . . ."

"His cohost," the woman standing a few feet away said. She

was just as pretty as Angel, but she was frosty. . . . Even her hair was a pale, watery blond, and her eyes were very light blue. Unlike Angel, she looked uncomfortable in the harsh sunlight. "Jenna Clark."

The other guy snorted and said, "Since nobody's going to ask my name, it's Tyler, thanks. I'm just the one who does all the work and hauls all the equipment and—"

Jenna and Angel said, in perfect, bored synchronicity, "Shut up, Tyler." Then they threw each other poisonous looks. Clearly, there was no love lost there. Or maybe some gone bad.

"*After Death*?" Shane asked. "Don't you guys do some kind of spirit-hunting thing?"

"Yes, exactly," Jenna said, and seemed to focus on Shane as an actual human being for the first time. She smiled, but to Claire's relief it was more of a professional kind of attention, not a *Wow, you're hot* kind of thing. "We're looking for the permits office."

"Permits?" Monica had recovered her composure, at least a little. Angel had stopped kissing her fingers, but he hadn't let her hand go, and Claire thought her voice sounded a little higher than usual. She was also a little more blushy than normal. "Permits for what? Are you moving your business here?"

Angel laughed, low in his throat—a sexy laugh, of course. "Alas, no, my lovely. Our studio is out of Atlanta. But we are interested in filming some local sights here. Perhaps conducting a nighttime investigation of your graveyard, for instance. We always pay a visit to the local offices for our filming permits. It avoids so many problems."

Claire could not even count how many ways this was a bad idea. . . . Television people. In Morganville. Filming at night. She was mesmerized by the flood of horrible possibilities that ran through her brain.

Luckily, Monica wasn't one for deep thought. "Oh," she said, and smiled so warmly that Claire was almost fooled. "I see. Well, I wouldn't waste my time. Morganville doesn't have anything special for you. Not even a decent ghost to hunt. We're just really . . . boring."

"But it's so scenic!" Angel protested. "Look at this courthouse. Pure Texas Gothic Renaissance. We passed a cemetery that was perfect—elaborate tombstones, wrought iron, and that big dead white tree—such a striking color, very photogenic. I'm sure we'll find something."

Shane muttered to Claire, "If they hang around there at night, they definitely will, but I don't think it's what they're hoping for."

"Sssssshhh!"

He cleared his throat and raised his voice. "Monica's right—it's very boring." He sounded like he was still struggling not to laugh. "Unless you want the world's least interesting reality show. The weirdest thing that happens around here is old Mr. Evans running around naked at midnight and howling, and he only does that on special occasions."

"That's unfortunate," Jenna said. "It does seem perfect."

"Well, it won't hurt to get the permits. At least we'll contribute to your local economy, yes?" Angel said, and flashed them all an impartial movie-star smile. "*Adios.* I'm sure we'll meet again." He gave Monica's hand another brief kiss, and then he and Jenna were striding up the walk toward City Hall, with Tyler scrambling in their wake while carrying a small camcorder—though what kind of filmable drama there'd be in applying for a permit, Claire couldn't imagine.

"Crap," Shane said. He still sounded *way* too amused. "So. Any bets on how long they last before the vamps make them go away?"

"No bet," Monica said. "They won't last long." Looking dreamy-eyed, she sighed and cradled her hand. "Too bad. *So* pretty. And totally manscaped under that shirt, I'll bet."

Shane sent her a revolted look, then put his arm around Claire. "And on that note, we're out."

"Really?" Claire said, and couldn't help but smile. "That's what creeps you out. Waxing. You can take on vampires and draug and killers, but you're afraid of a little chest-hair pulling?"

"Yes," he said, "because I am sane."

They walked on a bit, and it took a few minutes for Claire to realize that although they'd left behind the ghost hunters, they still had an unwanted visitor: Monica. She was keeping pace with them. Uninvited. "Yes?" Claire asked her, pointedly. "Something we can help you with?"

"Maybe," Monica said. "Look, I know I've been historically kind of a bitch to you, but I was wondering . . ."

"Spit it out, Monica," Shane said.

"Teach me how to do that stuff you do."

"What, be awesome? Can't do it."

"Shut up, Collins. I mean . . ." She hesitated, then lowered her voice as she brushed her hair back from her face. She slowed down and stopped on the sidewalk, and Claire stopped, facing her. Shane tried to keep going, but eventually he looped back, defeated. "I mean that I want to learn how to fight. In case I need to do that. I always sort of thought—my father always said we didn't need to worry about the vampires, because we worked for them. But Richard never trusted that. And now I know I shouldn't, either. So I want to learn how to make weapons. Fight. That kind of thing."

"Oh *hell* no," Shane said. "And we're walking."

He started to, but Claire stayed put. She was studying Monica with a frown, feeling conflicted but oddly compelled, too. Monica looked serious. Not defiant, or arrogant, or any of her usual poses. Her brother had told Claire before he'd died that he thought Monica could change—and had to change.

Maybe she was starting to understand that.

"How do we know you won't sell us out at the first possible opportunity?" she asked.

Monica smiled. "Shortcake, I probably *would* if it got me anywhere, but these days, it wouldn't do squat. The vampires aren't looking at us like collaborators and enemies anymore. We're all just . . . snack foods. So. I understand what a stake is for, but you guys seem to have all the killer toys. What do you say we work out a sharing arrangement?"

"We'll take it under advisement," Shane said, and grabbed Claire's elbow. "We're going. Now."

They left her, and when Claire looked back, she thought Monica had really never looked lonelier. The other girl finally walked to her red convertible, got in, and drove away.

"We are *not* getting cozy with her," Shane said. "She's got vamp problems? Boo hoo. She spent her whole life siccing them on anybody who pissed her off. Smells like justice to me."

"Shane."

"C'mon, this is a girl who tormented me most of my life. Who beat you up and tormented *you*. She's a bully. Screw her."

Claire gave him a long look. "You're the one who was nice to her when Richard died. And she saved your life."

"Yeah, don't remind me," he said, but after a moment or two, he sighed. "Fine. She'll always be an ass, but I guess it doesn't hurt to teach her to use a stake or something. Basic self-defense."

"That's my guy." She squeezed his arm. "Besides, if you teach her self-defense, you get to smash her into the floor when you tackle her."

"Suddenly, I am all about this plan."

They got about half a block before Shane stopped in front of the used-parts store to talk to the guy who ran it—something about needing a new hose for Eve's always-being-rebuilt hearse. Claire lost interest after the conversation began sounding like a foreign language, and she ended up staring into a store two windows down. It was a junk store, really, full of discarded stuff (some of it actually good), and she got on the creepy track of wondering if people had actually brought it here to resell, or if it had been scavenged from abandoned houses after the owners' disappearances. Maybe both.

The storefront was blessedly in dark shade, and so was the narrow brick alley next to it . . . which was why she didn't see the attack coming. It happened so fast, she saw nothing but a blur out of the corner of her eye, and then felt the sensation of hands crushing her shoulders, and then a rush of dizzy motion. When she caught her breath to scream, she was slammed up against the brick wall, and a cold hand pressed over her mouth to seal in the sound.

"Hush!" Myrnin said urgently. "Hush, now. Promise me."

Claire didn't want to promise anything, because there was a manic gleam in her vampire boss's dark eyes, and he looked . . . especially disheveled today. Myrnin was prone to eccentric dressing, but this outfit looked as if he'd picked it out in pitch-darkness by feel—some kind of moth-eaten velvet trousers that would have been deemed too out-there for the 1970s, a loose-fitting lemon yellow shirt that was buttoned up wrong, and a vest with cartoon characters. He'd matched it up with a hat that a Pilgrim might have worn and, just to top it all off, neon Mardi Gras beads—three strands.

He was also—she cringed to see it—totally barefoot. In an alley. That was disturbing.

She nodded, which wasn't so much a promise really, but he accepted it as one and took his hand away. She finished drawing in the breath, but held off on the scream, just in case he wasn't crazy at the moment, bare feet aside.

"I heard that you spoke with Mayor Moses?" he asked.

"You forgot your shoes."

"Bother my feet! Moses?"

"Yes, we talked to her."

"Did she tell you that Amelie has just announced an election?"

Claire blinked. "For what?"

"For *mayor*, of course. She has removed Hannah from office, effective tomorrow, since Hannah has refused to agree to sign some of her more-aggressive new decrees. The election will be held next week to appoint someone more ... friendly to the new agenda." Myrnin seemed not just agitated, but really worried. "You see why I object."

"Uh ..." *Not really.* "You do remember you're a vampire, right?"

He gave her an utterly sane and baffled look. "The fangs and the fact I crave blood do give me a general clue, yes. And being a vampire, I am naturally interested in the survival of my species. Therefore I feel I ought to stop Amelie and that damn Roundhead from ruining everything we've accomplished of value here."

"Myrnin, you're not making any sense."

"Oh, aren't I?" He let go and stepped back from her, and she had to admit, despite the haphazard wardrobe, he looked a whole lot more together than he often did. His eyes were steady, dark, and focused; he held himself still, with no more than a minimum of fidgeting. "I came to Morganville to create something unique in the history of the world ... a place where humans and vampires could coexist in relative safety, if not always peace. I will not allow Oliver to pervert that achievement into nothing more than his own personal . . . hunting preserve! It's a perversion of what Amelie intended here. And if she won't recognize it, I must do it for her."

Shane must have just noticed she'd gone missing, because she heard him call her name, a sharp and urgent note of alarm in his voice. He knew how easily people could vanish here, even in broad daylight. It didn't take him more than a few seconds to identify the alley as the most likely peril, and she saw his broad shoulders block out about half the murky light.

"Bother, it's your overprotective young man." Myrnin sighed. "Remember this: we must have a plan of how to counter Oliver's influence. Perhaps another human on the council. If not Hannah Moses, then someone in opposition to Amelie's agenda. Preferably someone sane, of course. Work on that. I'll be in touch soon." He sent a blistering look down the alley as Shane approached, then briefly bared thin, razor-sharp eyeteeth before just . . . vanishing. He didn't actually disappear in a mist, Claire knew; he just moved faster than her eye could track, so the human brain filled in something similar for reference.

And then Shane was there, staring first at her, then around at the shadows. "What the hell, Claire?"

She pulled in a deep breath, and wished she hadn't. Alleys. Disgusting. She thought of Myrnin's bare feet, and shuddered. "Let's get out of here."

A phone call to Michael sorted out her vampire escort problem for her upcoming audience with Morganville's Founder; he was willing—in fact, eager—to talk to Amelie along with her. Claire was especially grateful, since if she hadn't been able to land his support, Shane would have insisted on going with her, and she could foresee how *that* would turn out. She didn't need to be a psychic to know Shane's mouth would get them both in trouble, especially with Amelie's own attitude these days.

Michael brought his car and picked Claire up on the street in front of the Glass House. It was a standard-issue vampire sedan; having fangs in Morganville came with wheels, for free, as well as a membership on the withdrawal side of the town's blood bank. The downside of riding in Michael's car was that Claire couldn't see anything out the windows, since it was vampire custom-tinted.

"So," she said after they'd driven a couple of blocks in silence, "are you guys okay? Eve seemed . . ."

"She's okay," he said in a tone that meant he wasn't going to go over the details with her. "She's not happy with me for not telling you guys about the cards, but having a heads-up wouldn't have done anything but given you room to complain more. I was trying to keep the peace as long as I could." He shot her a look, eyebrows up. "Was I wrong?"

She shrugged. "I don't know, honestly. Everything's so weird these days, maybe you were right. At least we got to have some nice argument-free evenings out of it."

"Yeah," he agreed. "But those days are over."

Claire thought he was probably right.

Hannah might have called ahead, but that didn't mean word had gotten down to the level of the guards on duty near Founder's Square—two vampires, both wearing police uniforms, only this time they were female . . . a tall one and a short one. The taller one wore her white-blond hair in a thick braid down her back. The shorter one wore hers cropped close to the skull.

ID cards were the first thing they asked to see. Michael silently produced his gold card, but the two cops hardly even glanced at it. They wanted Claire's.

The taller one smiled as she looked it over. "Good blood type," she said, and handed it to her partner, who admired it in turn. "You take care of yourself. Wouldn't want to see it wasted."

Claire felt particularly weird about that. It was like being exposed, as if she'd had some kind of privacy taken away. Michael must have felt it, too, because he said, in a dangerously soft voice, "You've checked her out. Knock it off."

"You're no fun," the shorter one said, and winked at him. "Just like your grandfather. And look where that got him."

"Dead," the taller cop agreed. "All for trying to treat humans like equals. Seems like the Glass family members just never learn their lessons."

Michael's eyes flickered a sudden, bright crimson, and he said, "I'll take any comparison to my grandfather as a compliment. And you really need to stop screwing with us now."

"Or?"

"Viv, dial it down," the other cop said, and handed Claire's ID back to her. "We're done. They're cleared for the Founder's office."

"I'm sure we'll see you again," Viv said, and grinned, showing fangs. "Both of you. Hunting season starts soon."

Michael rolled up the window and put the car in gear. Claire let out a breath she hadn't realized she was holding, and finally said, "That was completely creepy."

"Yeah," Michael agreed. "I'm sorry. It was." He seemed to be almost apologizing for the two women, or maybe for vampires in general. "This might not have been such a great idea, coming out here. It's not like it was before."

"I have to try."

"Keep this short, then. I don't want you out here once the sun sets. Not even if I'm with you."

That was very unusual to hear from him, and unsettling, too. Claire looked straight ahead—at nothing, because the view was pretty much pitch-darkness. Michael's pale face and golden hair were tinged a little with blue from the dashboard light, and he glowed like a ghost in the corner of her eye. "What's happening to us?" she asked. She didn't mean to; it just came out, and it revealed way too much of the growing dread she was feeling. "They looked at me like meat in a supermarket. I know there have always been a few vampires like that, but . . . they were *police.* That means they're supposed to be the best at holding back their instincts."

Michael didn't answer her. Maybe he didn't know how. The dig they'd thrown about Sam Glass, his grandfather, had hit home, and she knew it. Michael's grandfather had physically looked about like Michael did now, only with more reddish hair. He'd been a sweet man, probably the most human of all of the vamps Claire had ever met. Sam had been a force for good in Morganville, and he'd paid for it with his life. Michael hadn't forgotten that. Claire wondered whether he thought about what might happen to his own life, if he kept trying to stay in the middle, squarely between humans and vampires, and whether he thought about being killed.

Of course he did. Especially now that he'd married Eve, against the wishes of both sides. They both had everything to lose.

Michael eased the car down, following the curve of the ramp as it led below Founder's Square. The vampires had excellent parking, all covered. When he'd pulled to a stop and turned off the engine, he finally said, "It's going to get bad, Claire. I know it. I feel it. We've got to do everything we can to stop it."

"I know," she said, and held out her hand. He took it and held it lightly—a good thing, because he could have easily shattered bones. "Glass House gang forever."

"Forever," he said. "If we're going to be a gang, we need a good sign to flash. Something intimidating."

They tried a few silly, strange attempts at flashing signs, but the efforts looked awkward. "We," Claire said, "are the worst gang *ever.*"

"Bad idea," Michael agreed, straight-faced. "Shane's the only one of us with real street cred anyway."

They got out of the car, and Claire was watchful of the shadows; so was Michael, but he must not have spotted anything out of the ordinary, because he nodded and escorted her to the elevator. While they waited for it to descend, Claire kept looking behind them, just to ensure that nobody had decided to stalk them.

Nobody did.

Someone had decided the elevator music had needed a change, so this time up, Claire was treated to an orchestral version of "Thriller," an oddly appropriate choice. Even vampires had a sense of humor, though it was mostly atrophied. Either Michael didn't think it was funny, or he was too focused to notice— probably the latter, because he seemed very self-contained just now. He must have been gearing up for whatever would be waiting for them.

The doors opened on a dead-white vampire, bald as a cue ball and dressed in formal black. Claire didn't know if he was security or just a very intimidating greeter, but she took a step back, and Michael tensed beside her.

The man looked them both over in silence, then abruptly turned his back on them and walked away. As he did, one hand snapped up to give them a follow-me gesture.

"Do you know him?" Claire asked as they trailed their black-suited guide into the paneled hallways. Vampires seemed to deliberately design all their buildings to confuse people, but the two of them didn't really need a personal escort; they'd spent a lot of time here, over the past couple of years. "And is he always this friendly?"

"Yes, and yes." Michael put his finger to his lips, asking her for silence, and she complied. They were passing closed, unmarked doors and watchful portraits of people she recognized as still walking the streets of Morganville, even though they'd been painted in ancient styles of clothes. Their escort moved fast, and Claire realized that even though it was tough for her to keep up, it was probably just standard vampire walking speed. It was oddly telling that the vamps no longer felt they needed to slow down to accommodate mere mortals.

She saved her breath and hurried, while Michael strode along beside her, matching her speed but not pushing her. He was watching the doorways, she realized. She'd never seen him quite this alert before, at least not here, in what should have been a safe place for them both.

It all became clear when a vampire slid out of the shadows ahead, lowered his chin, and bared his teeth. Claire knew him slightly, but he'd never looked quite so . . . inhuman. He was bone white, and his eyes were flaring crimson, and he gave off waves of menace that made her slow down and look at Michael in alarm.

Because that menace wasn't (for a change) aimed at her.

It was directed purely at her friend.

"You're not welcome here," the vampire said in a low, silky voice that was somehow worse than a growl. "Those who consort with humans use the servants' entrance."

"Ignore him," Michael said to her, and kept going. "Henrik's not going to hurt you."

"What's this one? Another little wife-pet you're planning to marry when you tire of the one you have?" Henrik's grin was full of cruel amusement. "Or won't you bother with the church's blessing next time? It's perfectly fine to eat them, you know. You don't need to sanctify them first. They still taste delicious."

Michael's eyes fixed on the other vampire, and his own eyes started turning red. Claire saw his hands flexing, trying to knot into fists. "Shut up," he said. "Claire, keep walking. He'll move."

This time there was something like a growl, or a rattling hiss, and Henrik's eyes turned even darker red. "Will I? Not for you, boy. Certainly not for your pet."

Claire kept walking, but she also reached into her pocket and pulled out a small glass vial. It had an easy-open pop-top, and she flicked it with her thumbnail, never taking her eyes off Henrik. "I'm not a pet," she said. "And I bite." She held up the vial. "Silver nitrate. Unless you want to spend a couple of hours nursing your burns, back off. We're here to see Amelie, not you."

His eyes fixed on her for the first time, and she felt a shock of fear; there was something really violent inside him, something she could only barely understand. It was a blind, unreasoning instinct to hurt—to kill.

But his teeth folded up into his mouth, like a snake's, and his smile took on more human proportions . . . though it remained intimidating. Serial-killer intimidating. "By all means," he said. "Pass. I'm sure we'll meet again, flower."

He made an elaborate bow and retreated into the shadows. Claire kept her eyes on him as she edged through, but he didn't move at all.

When Michael followed, though, there was a sudden burst of movement, a blur punctuated by a soft outcry from Michael . . . and then the other vamp was walking calmly away in the other direction.

"Michael?" Claire turned toward him, crying out when she saw the damage to his face. The blood was bad, but it was flowing from claw marks down the side of his face from temple to jawline. They were deep gouges—nothing that wouldn't heal, but still . . .

Michael stumbled and caught himself against the wall, shut his eyes, and said, "Maybe you'd better go on without me. I'm going to need a minute." His voice was shaking, both from pain and—she assumed—from shock. "It's okay. I'll be fine."

"I know." Claire put away the silver nitrate and rummaged in her pockets, coming up with a pack of tissues, which she handed over. "Here."

He looked at her, gave her a weak flash of a smile, and took the packet from her. One after another, the tissues soaked red, but each successive one did so more slowly. By the time he'd used most of them, the wounds were sealed over—gruesome still, but steadily better.

"This isn't the first time, is it?" she asked. "You were expecting this. I could see how tense you were. It's about your marrying Eve. They're bullying you because of it."

Michael shrugged and scrubbed the last of the damp stains off his skin. "We all knew how they felt about it. Pretty much like Captain Obvious and his crew of humans-only believers feel, too. Everybody sees us as traitors to whatever their cause is."

"That's stupid. You two—you've been together for years!"

"Not *married* together. They're funny about that. In vampire circles, marrying someone is a huge deal . . . vampires being immortal and all. It hardly ever happens, and when it does, there's— power involved. The lesser partner gets elevated up to the status of the greater. So now Eve's technically got all the rights and powers and privileges that I do. And being Amelie's direct bloodline, that's kind of a big deal." He stuffed all the bloody tissues in his pocket and nodded to her. "Let's keep going. I don't like being a sitting duck around here."

Their escort hadn't waited for them, but he was standing in front of Amelie's office when they arrived, and he opened the door to shoo them inside. He didn't follow, and Claire heard the latch click shut with a finality that made her wonder if they were, in fact, locked in.

If they were, the receptionist inside gave no sign of it. Her name was Bizzie, and she'd been with Amelie a long time. She gave Claire a cool, impartial nod, and ignored Michael almost completely, though her gaze flicked quickly to the wounds on his face. She didn't ask what had happened. In fact, she didn't speak at all, which in Claire's experience was a little unusual; Bizzie had always been cordial in the past.

Things had changed.

Claire and Michael waited silently in the armchairs lining the small wood-paneled room, and Claire spent her time studying the portraits hanging high on the walls. Amelie was in one of them, looking just as she did now but with a more elaborate hairstyle that reminded Claire of movies she'd seen in high school about the French Revolution. Elegant in white satin, Amelie was shown lit by candles, and in her right hand was a mirror dangling negligently by her side. The fingers of her left hand rested on top of a skull.

Creepy and beautiful.

"The Founder will see you," Bizzie said, though Claire hadn't heard any phone or intercom. As Claire rose to her feet, the inner door swung open without a sound.

Deep breaths, Claire told herself. She didn't know why she was so nervous; she'd met with Amelie dozens of times, probably nearly a hundred by now. But somehow, this felt strongly like walking into a trap. She glanced back at Michael, and their eyes met and held.

He felt it, too.

Deep breaths, Claire thought again, and took the plunge.

*   *   *

The office looked eerily the same: high bookcases, big picture windows treated with anti-UV tinting to reduce damage from the sunlight, candles burning here and there. Amelie's desk was massive and orderly, and behind it, the Founder of Morganville sat with her hands folded on the leather blotter.

Behind her stood Oliver.

The two vampires couldn't have been more different. Amelie was polished, silky, pale haired, every inch a born ruler. Oliver, on the other hand, had the angular toughness of a warrior, and with his graying hair and ruthless smile, he might as well have been wearing armor as a turtleneck and jacket. Amelie's pantsuit was a pristine white silk, and it contrasted completely with his all-black—deliberately; Claire was certain of it.

Amelie was also wearing her hair down in flowing, gorgeous waves. Very *not* the old Founder.

Oliver had his hand on Amelie's shoulder, a gesture of easy familiarity that would have been odd in the time before the arrival, battle, and defeat of the draug. He and Amelie had been enemies, then unwilling allies, and then, finally—something else.

Something more dangerous, obviously.

Claire looked around, but the chairs that had once been in front of Amelie's desk, the ones for visitors, were gone. She and Michael would be expected to stand.

But first, apparently, they were expected to do something else, because Oliver watched the two of them for a moment, then frowned and said, "Pay proper respect, if you wish to speak with the Founder."

Amelie said nothing. She'd always been a bit of an ice queen, but now she was unreadable, all pale, perfect skin and cool, assessing eyes. There was no telling what she felt, if she felt anything at all.

Michael inclined his head. "Founder."

"I see you've been recently injured," she said. "How?"

"It's nothing."

"That doesn't answer my question."

"It's my problem. I'll handle it."

Amelie sat back in her chair and cast a glance upward at Oliver. "See to it that Henrik understands I do not condone this kind of behavior within these walls. Michael, you'd do well to answer my questions when I ask them next time."

"Since you already knew the answer, I don't see the point." He was almost as good at hiding emotions as Amelie. "If you really cared about stopping him and the others like him, you'd publicly acknowledge our marriage and put a stop to it."

"You didn't obtain permission from me, and it's my right as your blood sire to give or withhold it," she said. "I don't have to acknowledge anything you do without my blessing. And we've traveled this road before, to no good purpose. What brings you here, then?"

Claire cleared her throat and took a step forward. "I—"

Oliver interrupted her. "Greet the Founder properly, or you'll not utter another word."

Amelie could have quelled that; she could have just waved it away as she normally would have . . . but she didn't. She waited, her gaze on Claire's face, until Claire swallowed hard and bent her head forward just a little. "Founder," she said.

"You may speak, Claire."

Gee, thanks, Claire wanted to say with a liberal dose of sarcasm, but she managed to choke it back. Shane would have said it, which was why she hadn't let him come along on this little venture. "Thank you," she said, and tried to make herself sound truly grateful. "I came to talk to you about the identification cards."

Amelie's face did show emotion after all—anger. "I have heard all of the arguments that I am prepared to endure," she said. "The measure ensures that all Morganville residents have proper care in case of emergency, that their Protectors are properly identified, that they can be found in case they go missing. Whatever resentments you have come from a false sense that you are free to do as you will. You are not, Claire. No one is in this world."

"I thought you took Sam's goals seriously. You told me you'd make humans equal partners in Morganville, that we had rights just like vampires. You *told* me that!"

"I did," Amelie said. "And yet I find that where humans are allowed a little freedom, they will take more, until their very freedom destroys our way of life. If it comes to a choice, I must choose the survival of my own. Yours are certainly far too numerous as it stands. What is the count now, seven billion? You'll excuse me if I believe we might be at a slight numerical disadvantage."

"Is that why you're allowing hunting again?"

Oliver laughed. "A tempting side benefit, but no. Hunting is buried as deep in the vampire nature as the need to reproduce is in humans. It is not simply a thing we can turn off. For some, hunting allows them to control a dark and violent side that would be much more damaging. Think of a dammed-up river, with a flaw in the structure. Sooner or later, that torrent of water will break free, and the damage it does will be considerably worse than a slow and controlled release."

"You're talking about water! I'm talking about people's lives!"

"Enough," Amelie said flatly. "This is not a human concern. You and your friends need have no fear; the law does not touch you. The things you've done in Morganville have ensured my personal patronage for you, as you can see on your cards. And any vampire is free to refuse to hunt. Michael has done it. No doubt many will do so."

Somehow, relying on the goodwill of individual vampires wasn't what Claire could see as a positive solution, but it was pretty clear that Amelie wasn't interested in her opinions. "Then the humans need to know," Claire said. "They need to understand that going without a Protector means they're being hunted again. Let them at least have a chance to defend themselves!"

"Tell them if you wish," Oliver said, and smiled. "If it makes you feel safer to be prepared, tell them to go armed. Tell them to stay in groups. Tell them whatever you wish. It will not make any difference but to make the hunt more challenging."

"This is your doing, isn't it?" He just watched her without replying. Claire turned her attention back to Amelie. "You're going to let him destroy everything," Claire said, and locked her gaze on the Founder's. That was dangerous; Amelie had power, a lot of it, and even when she wasn't trying to project it, there was something truly frightening about looking deep into her eyes. "You're really going to let him turn this town into his own personal hunting preserve."

"You're always free to leave town, Claire," Amelie said. "I've said so before, and I've given you more than generous terms. I urge you to take the opportunity before you make me regret having given you so much... consideration. Remember, I can always withdraw Protection."

"Maybe I will leave! And what are you going to do then? Because I don't think Myrnin really likes any of your new ideas, and you can't control him, can you? But anyway, they're not really *your* ideas." Claire transferred her stare to Oliver. "Are they?"

Oliver went from standing still as a statue—if statues could smirk—to rushing at her full speed, a blur she instinctively flinched away from.

Michael got in the way, and shoved Oliver violently off course, into a side table, destroying a probably priceless antique vase. Oliver rolled to his feet, hardly slowed at all by the fall, and came at him.

"Enough," Amelie said, and Oliver just . . . froze. So did Michael. Claire felt a crushing sense of pressure in the room and realized that Amelie had just *made* them stop. It must have hurt, because even Oliver's face contorted in pain for a second. "I've had quite enough peasant-style brawling in my presence. Michael, your loyalty is misguided, and I've had enough of your thinking that your personal choices outweigh your duty to me. You owe me your *life*. If a choice is to be made, be very careful how you make it. A vampire alone is vulnerable to many things."

"I know," Michael said. "You can quit trying to threaten me. I'm not giving up the people I love, no matter what you do. And in the words of my best friend, bite me. Come on, Claire. We're not getting any favors from her."

She reached out to him, but in the next instant, his blue eyes went wide and desperately blank, and he went straight to his knees—driven there by the force of Amelie's fury. It felt like a storm, lashing over Claire as an afterthought, and she found herself on her knees next to him, reaching for his hand and holding it with shaking strength. He was trying not to crush hers, but it still hurt.

Amelie rose from behind her desk, took an elegant silver-coated letter opener from her desk, and walked to look down on Michael. As she turned the knife in her hand, thin wisps of smoke escaped; she wasn't invulnerable to the silver, just stronger than most.

"Don't test me," she whispered. "I have survived my father. Survived the draug. I will survive *you*. Learn your place, or die where you kneel, right now."

Michael somehow managed to laugh and turn his face up toward her. For the first time, Claire thought, he really looked like one of them.

Like a vampire.

"I know who I am, and I'm not one of *you*," he said. "Screw you."

She drove the letter opener down, and Claire had time to gasp in horror; she had a terrible, vivid flashback to the time she'd seen someone else stab Michael—in the earliest days of their friendship. He'd survived that. Not this. Not with silver. *No, I can't tell Eve this. No, please . . .*

Amelie drove the silver knife into the floor, to the hilt, an inch from Michael's knee. She rose gracefully, turned her back, and walked away, dismissing them both with a flip of her hand.

Oliver, after a long look at her that Claire couldn't read, said, "Count yourself lucky. Both of you, get out. Now."

Claire stumbled to her feet, still holding Michael's hand, and managed to get him up. He leaned heavily on her. He looked dazed, but his eyes were as crimson as the blood dripping from his nose and ears. He was, Claire thought, ready to go for Oliver's throat, so it was lucky he was too weak to try it. "Come on," she whispered to him. "*Michael!* Come on! You're supposed to be the calm one, remember?"

He closed his eyes, which was about all she sensed she was going to get from him in terms of agreement, so she half carried him to the door.

Which remained closed.

Behind her, Oliver said, "If you come here, you come as supplicants. Anything else, and next time, the knife won't miss."

Claire was smart enough to keep her *Screw you* to herself.

THREE

CLAIRE

G etting out of Founder's Square wasn't quite as bad as getting in, but with Michael staggering and only really able
to stand halfway through, Claire was worried that Henrik, or someone else with similar feelings, would step out to finish
the job Amelie and Oliver had started. He was hurt . . . maybe not
in terms of the obvious wounds, but she was convinced that the
blood that still stained his face near his nose and ears was a sign of
some kind of internal hemorrhage. She had no idea what to do for
him, but vampires could heal from most things without help.

Still, he probably was going to need blood, and she didn't want
to be the only source standing nearby if a sudden craving came
down hard. She'd seen that happen, and the aftermath. It might
not ruin their friendship, unless he actually killed her, but it would
make things very awkward around the dinner table.

"Can you drive?" she asked him anxiously as they arrived at the garage level. She kept a hand on his arm, though he was moving under his own power now; he hadn't said much at all, but now he nodded. "Are you okay?"

"No," he said. His voice sounded hoarse, as if he'd been screaming. "Not yet. Will be."

"You probably need a drink." She said it the matter-of-fact way she'd heard Eve phrase it, and he seemed relieved that he didn't have to bring it up. "I don't mind waiting in the car if you want to stop at the blood bank. Michael . . . I'm sorry. I didn't think it would go so . . ." *Wrong. Violent. Crazy.* But Shane somehow had intuited that, or he wouldn't have insisted on someone else going with her. Someone strong enough to fight off Oliver and Amelie . . . or who'd be willing to try.

If I'd had the machine finished, I could have used it. Canceled out her power. Maybe it would have worked. Maybe it would have even canceled out Oliver's influence on Amelie, made her go back to the old Founder, the one Claire sorely missed.

And maybe it would have only made things worse.

It humbled her to think how much danger Michael had put himself in, for her. And it showed just how much danger there was for all of them. Hannah had been right after all. There wasn't any point in trying.

In the car, finally, Claire felt safe enough to broach the subject she'd been frantically turning over in her mind during the long walk. "What's happened to Amelie? She wasn't like this. Could the draug have, I don't know, infected her? Done something to her?"

"Maybe," Michael said. He coughed, and it was a wet sound. Claire cringed. "Maybe it's got something to do with Oliver; he has the ability to influence people. She always kept him at a distance before. Now it's as though they're channeling Sid and Nancy."

"Who?"

Michael groaned. "It's sad how much you don't know about music, Claire. Sid Vicious? The Sex Pistols?"

"Oh, him."

"You have no idea who I'm talking about, do you?"

She smiled a little. "Not the least little bit."

"Remind me to play you some songs later. But anyway, if Myrnin said things were spinning out of control, he's not wrong. Amelie doesn't use that power she just pulled out on me, not unless things are really critical. Never just for her own personal amusement." He shuddered, and finally said, in a quiet voice, "She could have killed me, Claire. At least the part of me that isn't pure vampire. She could have made me into—I don't know, her meat puppet or something. She's got power like nobody else."

Claire swallowed, suddenly and sharply uneasy again. "But she didn't do it."

"This time," he said. "What if she decides that's the only way to make me obey the way she wants? I don't want to live like that, if she crushes everything in me that's *me*. Promise me, you and Shane, you'll . . . take care of it. If it happens."

"It won't."

"Promise."

"God, Michael!"

He was silent for a second, then said, "I'll ask Shane." Because they both knew Shane would understand that request, probably far too well.

And that he'd say yes.

"It's not going to happen," Claire said. "No way in hell, Michael. We won't let it happen."

He didn't tell her that it probably wouldn't be a thing she could control, but she already knew it anyway. She just felt better, and more in control, for saying it.

The drive to the blood bank was quiet, and Claire faced toward the blacked-out passenger window. In the aftermath of all the adrenaline, she felt numb, and exhausted, and—weirdly enough—really hungry. Michael went inside the back of the blood bank, through the vamps-only entrance, and came back with a small handheld cooler, which he handed her. She put it on the floor between her feet. "Blood supply's running low," he said. "They'll be sending out the Bloodmobile to collect tomorrow. Is Shane paid up?"

"Is he ever?" Claire rolled her eyes. "I'll get him in voluntarily in the morning. I'll donate, too." Claire, by Amelie's decree, had historically been free of the responsibility of giving blood, which was the tax humans paid in Morganville from age eighteen up; she'd been underage before, but even now that she was legal, she didn't have to contribute. She still did, mainly because the hospitals, not the vampires, were the ones that ran short in an emergency.

Shane had pointedly *not* been excluded from the tax rolls. Probably because of how much trouble he'd historically been in, in Morganville.

Michael sighed. "Do you mind if I . . . ?"

Claire opened the cooler and took out one of the blood bags. It was slightly warm, and heavy, and she tried to pretend it was a bag of colored water, one of those prop things they used in television shows.

But she still looked away when he bit into it.

It took only about a minute for him to drain it dry, and he looked around for a place to put the empty, then let her take it and return it to the cooler. "Sorry," he said. His apology sounded genuine. "I know that's probably not what you needed to see right now."

"All eating is gross," Claire said, "but we all have to do it. Anyway, I'm starving. Is Chico's still open?"

"You know if I get you Chico's, I have to get it for the house, right?"

"I'll pitch in."

Chico's Tacos was a relative newcomer to town, opened by a Morganville resident who'd taken a liking to something he'd tasted out of town in El Paso: delicious rolled tacos, soaked and floating in hot sauce, then topped with shredded cheese. Messy, yeah. Unhealthy, probably. But in taco terms, it was crack. Extra orders were mandatory.

Michael handled drive-through duties, forking over cash and receiving all of the goodies to hand off to Claire. It was still new for them to count *five* housemates; Miranda was only half-time, in that during the day she was insubstantial, but at night she was very much flesh and blood, able to walk around, talk, do chores, eat dinner. . . . It made very little sense to Claire, but the Glass House (like all the remaining Founder Houses original to the town) was capable of doing things that her science couldn't explain, no matter how far out of shape she stretched the boundaries.

When Michael had been killed within its walls, drained by Oliver, the house had preserved him—saved him, literally, like a file, only as a ghost. The Glass home was more powerful at night than during the day, so at night it could create a real flesh-and-blood form he could use to have half a life . . . but when dawn came, it melted away. It wasn't *real*, exactly, though Michael had said he could feel, eat, drink, do everything as if it were real, between dusk and dawn.

But to make that half-life truly permanent, he'd had to make a deal with Amelie and become fully vampire.

Miranda seemed to have inherited the same pluses and minuses. And she had no wish to become a vampire. In life, Miranda had been a lost little girl, cursed with a psychic gift that was as much creepy as it was informative; she'd been shunned all her life by most of the town, and even Eve—her best friend, maybe—hadn't been able to handle her some of the time.

Ghost-Miranda was blooming into a happy young lady, now that she no longer had the psychic powers and was able to have real friends. So Miranda got tacos, too.

"What are we going to tell Shane about what happened? Or Eve?" Claire asked as the familiar crunch of the car's wheels on gravel signaled they'd arrived home.

Michael parked, killed the engine, and spent a moment in thought before he said, "We're going to tell them everything. Anything else wouldn't be fair. And it could put them in a lot of danger if they think Amelie's still somehow got our backs."

It would upset Eve, and it would anger Shane, but he was right; keeping them in the dark was a sure path to disaster. You could protect people from harm, but not from *knowing*.

"Well," Claire said, "at least we have tacos. Everything goes better with tacos."

And the tacos did help. Even Shane, who met them at the door and glared at the cooler in Michael's hand, brightened up at the sight of the grease-stained paper bags Claire held. "You really know the way to a man's heart," he said, and grabbed them out of her hands.

"Between the ribs and angle up?" she said, and gave him a sweet, fast kiss when he looked shocked. "Hey, it's your joke. Don't blame me if I remember it."

"And you look like such a nice girl."

"Fine, if you're not into it, I'll just take those tacos back. . . ."

It devolved into keep-away with taco bags, which Shane of course would have won by virtue of sheer size and agility, except that Miranda sneaked up behind him and stole a couple by surprise, which sent him yelling in pursuit as she dashed off through the kitchen and into the living room. And then Eve was into it, and Claire had to fight to hang on to the two bags she had left.

In the end, it all somehow made it to the dining table. Eve broke out thick paper plates and forks and spoons, and Michael and Shane organized the drinks while Claire and Miranda put little taco boats at each of their place settings. It was all really warm and sweet and *home*, and Claire made sure as they were eating that Miranda got a couple of extra tacos that normally Shane would have grabbed as they passed. He pouted, but in a cute way.

It was when they were finishing up that Shane said, faux-casually, "So I guess everything went okay today?"

Miranda licked the last of the hot sauce out of the bottom of the paper boat and raised her eyebrows. "What happened today? I never get to know anything." She was still physically a frail little thing, and Claire supposed that the girl's delicate, breakable look would never change now; ghosts didn't age, and no matter how many tacos she ate or Coca-Colas she guzzled, she'd never grow an inch or gain a pound. That was something a lot of girls dreamed of, Claire thought. Of course, those girls probably never thought about having to live their eternity trapped inside one house, living half a life, not even being able to shop or see a movie that wasn't brought in, or go out to eat . . . or date.

Miranda was never, ever going to date. That was probably the saddest thing of all. She probably hadn't ever even been kissed. Not once. And what was worse, she was living in a house with two *couples.*

Yeah. Living hell, Claire decided, and she elbowed Shane and gave Miranda the last taco. It seemed the least she could do.

Then she realized that Michael hadn't even started answering the question. Somehow, Claire had expected him to take the lead on it, but since he hadn't, suddenly everyone was staring at her, waiting.

Claire cleared her throat, took a drink of water, and said, "I guess I'll just get it over with. Hannah can't help about getting rid of the ID cards, or the hunting licenses. She's being thrown out of office. Oliver's a jerk. Amelie's turned into a Vampire with a capital V, and she nearly killed Michael to prove how badass she is now. Does that cover it, Michael?"

"Pretty much," he said.

That . . . didn't go over as well as she'd hoped. For a second, nobody said a word, and then everyone was trying to talk at once. Michael tried to put some kind of polish on what she'd said, but there was no changing the truth of it. Eve was sharply demanding to know what was meant by *nearly killed.* Shane was cursing and saying that he'd known it would be like this.

Even Miranda was timidly asking something that was lost in the general chaos.

"One at a time," Claire finally yelled, and that surprised them enough that they all fell silent. Surprisingly, it was Miranda who plunged ahead first.

"Are you feeling all right?" she asked Michael, and there was an edge of anxiety in her voice that surprised Claire . . . and then, didn't. After all, Miranda had never been kissed, and Michael couldn't help being a girl magnet. Claire felt a little relieved, really, because at least the girl didn't moon about Shane. Not that Shane would have noticed, or cared, but still.

Eve, on the other hand, seemed to ignore Miranda altogether; her gaze focused wholly on Michael's face. Her dark eyes were huge, and she'd gripped his left hand tightly with her right.

"I'm okay," he said, not to Miranda, but to Eve, and brought her hand to his lips to kiss it. "Claire might have been exaggerating a little."

"Not much," Claire muttered, but she ate a bite of taco and didn't object any louder.

"She's right, though," Michael continued. "Definitely, there's something wrong with Amelie and how she's handling things. It's not the Founder we've known; this is more the way Bishop acted. Maybe it's something to do with her near miss with the draug."

"Or maybe it's just that Oliver's in her pocket all the time," Shane said. "I'm saying *pocket* because there's a deceased minor present, but by pocket I mean pants."

Claire smacked him under the table on the side of the leg, hard, but she didn't disagree with the substance—just the presentation. "Oliver's a bad boyfriend," she agreed. "And she's listening to him way too much. That's why he's getting rid of Hannah; he doesn't want any disagreements on the Elders' Council. He just wants some rubber-stamping human body sitting at the table, to keep people in line by pretending they still have a voice."

"Can we go back to the issue of Michael nearly being killed?" Eve said. "Because I'm really not okay with that. What happened?"

"I didn't agree with Amelie on something." Michael shrugged. "It's not the first time, right? Eve, seriously, don't fuss."

Eve gazed at him a moment longer, then shifted her attention to Shane. "You buying this no-big-deal crap?"

"Nope."

"Then what are we going to do about it?"

"Oh, I don't know. Kill 'em all; feed their carcasses to chickens? Hell, Eve, what *can* we do? We got by this long because we're lucky and we've had the right vampires on our side. Now the same vamps are on the other side of the line. What've we got going for us?"

"Well, we're all smart, strong, and fashion forward," Eve said. "Except for you."

He saluted her with a fork full of dripping taco and shoveled it into his mouth. "You forgot handsome," he said. "Plus thoughtful, kind, brave . . ."

"Shane, the closest you ever got to the Boy Scouts was when that whole troop of them beat you up in fourth grade," Eve shot back.

"Be fair—they were Brownies, and those girls were soccer-trained. Mean kickers." Shane took a sip of his drink and changed the subject. "We don't have a lot of things counting up in our favor right now, do we? No offense, Mike. You know I love you and Eve, but you two getting married hasn't made life around here any easier; most people avoid us, the pro-human side hates us, the pro-vampire side hates us, too. Now we don't have the Ice Queen on our side, either. Strategically, I guess our whole position boils down to *this sucks.*"

"We've got Myrnin," Claire said. "He doesn't like how things are heading, either. He'll help."

"Oh yeah, because Myrnin's always reliable," Eve said. "Yes, Shane, I said it for you."

"Thanks for reading my mind."

"Thanks for making it so simple."

Shane threw a napkin at her, she deflected it into Miranda's lap, and Miranda threw it to Michael, who didn't even look up as he snatched the wadded-up paper out of the air and lobbed it to Claire.

Who missed, of course.

"Loser does the dishes," Michael said. "New rule."

"Awesome," Shane agreed, and then got less cheerful about it. "Wait—it's all paper plates and stuff."

"Hey, you could have lost if you'd thought about it."

Miranda was the one who spoiled the moment by asking, in a very worried voice, "What *are* you going to do about stopping Amelie? I mean, if she's really dangerous now?"

Eve put her arm around the girl and hugged her. "Claire will have an awesome plan, and we'll all make it work. You'll see."

Yeah, Claire thought gloomily, as she gathered up the trash. *No pressure.*

She was mostly done when she found Miranda standing next to her, handing her stuff. Eve, Michael, and Shane had all moved off, and the younger girl gave her a quick, crooked smile. "I don't mind," she said. "I like to help. Is it okay?"

"Sure," Claire said. "Thanks."

"I wanted to ask you something, actually. I heard Shane say something about those people who came to town. Those people with the TV show."

"Oh, right. Angel and Jenna." And Tyler, who did all the work. "What about them?"

"You don't think they'll, ah, find anything, do you? What if they do? What if they get the word out on Morganville?"

"It won't happen," Claire said. "Even if they do find any-thing—which I really doubt—I don't think they'd be able to get it out of town. Why? Are you worried about their finding out about you?"

"Not—not really." Miranda looked oddly embarrassed. "I

just—they must have met other ghosts before. I just wondered if maybe I could talk to them about it. About what's normal."

"I'm not sure there's any such thing as normal, when it comes to ghosts, especially around here," Claire said doubtfully. "Mir, you're not thinking of trying to get them over here, are you?"

"Well, at night, they wouldn't see anything weird. . . ."

"No. No, definitely no. What if Myrnin comes popping in through a portal in the wall, or some random vamp decides to drop in for a visit? How do we explain that? And Michael? They'd notice something strange about him, wouldn't they?"

"Oh," Miranda said. "Right. I hadn't thought about that. Okay, then. I just—I just wish I could make more friends."

Claire hip-bumped her and grinned. "We're not enough for you?"

She got a smile in response, but it wasn't a very certain one. "Sure," Miranda said softly, and walked away.

Oh dear.

That, Claire thought, might be a problem.

The blood bank in Morganville had odd hours—for instance, they'd instituted twenty-four-hour donations, which meant that Claire was able to shove Shane out of bed and into pants, shoes, and shirt at four a.m., and drag him, half asleep, into the place to drain a pint of blood before he was too awake to protest. She gave a second pint, just to make things even, and took him home to pile back into bed. He refused to go to his own, which was just pure stubbornness, and curled his warm, strong body next to her under the covers for another two hours until she had to rise to go to school. It might have been more sexy, except that he fell asleep within about five minutes, and she held out for only a few ticks more.

Seven a.m. came way too early, but Claire dragged herself yawning through the morning routine: shower, dress, sleepwalk to Common Grounds for a mocha. That was where she picked up the news that Mayor Hannah Moses was "stepping down for personal reasons" and that a write-in election would be held over the weekend.

The college students were, of course, oblivious to what that meant, but there was a stack of the flyers about it near the register, and Claire grabbed one. The press release was boring and dry, and there was a write-in form right on the bottom of the flyer, with instructions to drop it off at City Hall in the appropriate ballot box.

Claire stuffed the flyer in her backpack, grabbed her coffee, and headed out for class. Luckily, she had a different schedule of professors today, ones she actually liked, and sailed through the morning high on caffeine and challenging discussions on condensed-matter physics, which was the study of exactly how atoms combined and recombined to make liquids, solids, and states that, theoretically, hadn't been seen. Except she *had* seen them. Myrnin had invented them, and he used them as transportation hubs around the town. He called them doors, whereas Claire called them portals, but it boiled down to one thing: traveling from *here* to *there* and skipping the in-between.

So she kind of had a head start on that concept, and calculations.

She had a break at noon, and went to the coffee shop on campus. It was Eve's day to work there, instead of at Common Grounds; she was a good-enough barista that she could work anywhere she wanted, and she liked to see different people on the other side of the counter. Plus, Eve always insisted, she liked these little weekly vacations away from Oliver's scowling.

She didn't look especially happy now, though, Claire thought, as she waited in line. As the guy ahead of her walked away with his coffee, Claire leaned her elbows on the counter and said, "Are you okay?" She put the back of her hand to Eve's forehead. "I think you must have a fever."

"What?" Eve looked tired under the makeup, as if she hadn't slept much. "What are you talking about?"

"Mr. Hottie McGorgeous just walking away. He was way into you, and you didn't even smile at him."

Eve held up her hand and tapped the ring on her finger. "Anti-flirting device," she said. "It works."

"Oh, come on—it wouldn't keep you from smiling!"

"I just wasn't feeling it." But that wasn't it, and Claire knew it. There was a piece of paper on the counter, turned facedown, but the water had soaked through in places, and she saw tombstones drawn on it. Before Eve could stop her, Claire reached over and took it.

They were the same four tombstones as on the flyers that kept appearing at the Glass House, only this one was more personal. It had an arrow pointing at Eve's grave, with the words, *Soon, bitch* written above it.

Eve shrugged. "It was on the counter when I got here for work."

"Sorry," Claire said. "People are asses."

"Mostly," Eve agreed. "Mocha, then?"

"Just hot cocoa." Claire took the flyer she'd grabbed at Common Grounds out of her bag and put it on the counter, avoiding the drips of spilled drinks. "Did you see this?"

Eve mixed the cocoa and read the paper at the same time, which was pretty impressive. "Write-in candidates. Well, that's an easy one. They'll just pick whoever they want and write the ballots the way they want them to come out. And we bother voting why?"

"We can't let that be the way things go," Claire said earnestly.

"We have to get people together to demand a free and fair election, counted by humans."

"You have an impressive amount of crazy in that head. How exactly would you do that? Because I guarantee you, if you set up a Facebook page, they'll kill it before you can refresh the screen. And don't even *think* about Twitter."

It was true; the vampires had a headlock on the electronic communications in town, and that stumped Claire for a moment. "Old school," she said finally. "Captain Obvious is still around, right?" Captain Obvious was a little like the Spartacus of Morganville. . . . He was the guy in charge of organizing and leading the human resistance, in whatever form it took. Captain Obvious as an individual usually didn't last long, but a new one was always waiting in the wings.

"Well, in theory, I guess," Eve said. "Last one ran for it before the barriers went back up around town. Last I heard, though, there was nobody in charge of the human underground anymore, so it's pretty much done for . . . not that it ever made any difference in the first place. Bunch of disorganized losers, mostly. Well, except for that one time they saved our lives. But if he's still around, maybe he's the one sending us the die-already notices, so maybe not an asset."

Claire blinked and sipped the hot cocoa Eve handed her. Nobody was in line behind her, so she lingered at the counter. "The old Captain Obvious was outed, anyway. Everybody knew who he was. What if there was a new one? A secret one?"

"Sweetie, I'm pretty sure I'd have heard. I hear *everything*." But Claire wasn't listening now; her brain was firing off a chain of brilliant, random flashes, putting things together, planning—until Eve snapped fingers in front of her eyes and she realized Eve was saying something along the lines of *Earth to whatever planet you're circling.*

"Sorry," Claire said. She smiled slowly. "I think I've got it."

"Swine flu? The answer to cold fusion? An aneurysm?"

"How do we get vampires not to ignore the results of the election?"

"You can't."

"Unless the results are what they want to see," Claire said. "Then they'd just announce them, right? They wouldn't bother to fake anything."

"True." Eve was eyeing her doubtfully. Very doubtfully. "What the hell are you thinking, CB?"

"We write in someone who is exactly what they want: a human connected to an old Morganville family. But one who isn't afraid to get in the faces of the vamps."

"Okay, maybe we need to walk this backward, because you're not making any sense at all," Claire said, and held Eve's stare for long enough that she saw the light begin to—kind of dreadfully—dawn. "Shane?" her best friend said, and covered her ink blue lips with one pale hand. "You can't run *Shane* for mayor. Come on! Shane's the exact opposite of political!"

"I'm not talking about him," Claire interrupted. "But there's somebody else in this town who's perfectly qualified. And perfectly unqualified at the same time. And if anyone knows about causing chaos in this town, it's her."

Silence. Dead, utter silence. Eve blinked, blinked again, and finally said, "What?"

But Claire was already walking away, humming softly under her breath, feeling for the first time in months that she had something actually going the right way in Morganville.

Ironic, really.

FOUR

CLAIRE

)

True to her word, Monica came to the gym ready to work, which was a bit of a shocker; Claire hardly recognized her. No makeup. Dark hair tied back in a plain, thick ponytail. Okay, the tight workout gear was still name brand, and her athletic shoes had a basketball star's name on them, but this was definitely Monica unplugged.

And she was shockingly good at punching things. Even Shane was impressed, after about two minutes of watching her hit the heavy bag with a flurry of well-placed jabs, elbows, and kicks.

"She's not bad," Shane admitted as Monica continued to pummel the target. "Good form. Hell of a right."

"Yeah, she got it beating up other kids, didn't she?"

Shane sent her a slightly embarrassed look. "I'm all for peace and love, babe, but I'm just talking technique, here." He went back to studying Monica with calm assessment, arms folded. "She's been working on it."

She had, no doubt about it. When Monica finished on the heavy bag after the required five minutes, panting and sweating, she sent Shane a triumphant look as she swigged some water. "See?" she said. "Not bad, right?"

"Don't get cocky," he said. "Hey, Aliyah? Got a minute?" He gestured to a tall, rangy girl who was shadow punching in the corner. She turned, and her dark eyes fell on Monica, and widened. "Monica needs a sparring partner."

"Wait," Monica said, and turned to him. "I thought *you* were—"

"I'm the sensei here, and you fight who I say you'll fight," Shane said, with entirely too much relish.

"But she—"

"Problem, Monica?" His smile was brutal, and Monica pressed her lips into a thin line and shook her head. She walked to the roped-off sparring area as Aliyah took her place inside.

"Let me guess," Claire said. "Monica bullied Aliyah."

"You couldn't throw a rock in Morganville without hitting somebody who fits that description," Shane said. "But nobody's bullied Aliyah in, I don't know, at least five years—okay, let's have a clean fight, girls!"

It wasn't.

Aliyah took about ten seconds to lay Monica out. It was a violent ballet of fake, strike, fade—almost surgical, really. Two fast, accurate punches—face and midsection—and a leg sweep, and Monica was on her back, staring dazed at the ceiling while Aliyah danced backward without a mark on her. Aliyah dropped her defense and looked at Shane, who shrugged.

"Thanks," he said. "Tells me what I needed to know."

He climbed in the ring as Aliyah got out, and he crouched down next to Monica, who was making no effort at all toward getting up. "Something broken?" he asked. She shook her head. "Then stand up."

"Help?" She held out her hand, but he straightened up and backed off. Monica groaned. "You son of a—"

"C'mon, you whiner. Up."

She climbed clumsily back to her feet and braced herself against the ropes a moment. "That bitch sucker-punched me." She felt her lip. "If I swell up—"

"You'll deserve it," Shane said, "because your defense was crap. Are you complaining, or training?"

Claire leaned against the pole and watched, mostly; Shane was a good teacher, patient but not kind, and he showed Monica with brutal and cheerful efficiency that bullying didn't really equal fighting. It was a relatively short lesson—about an hour—but at the end of it Monica was a disheveled, staggering mess. When Shane finally said, "Okay, enough for today," she flopped backward onto the floor as if she might never get up under her own power again.

"You," she said between heaves for breath, "are a total *ass*, Collins. You enjoyed that."

"Absolutely," he said, and grinned, but the grin faded fast. "No bull, Monica: you're not bad, you've got strength, but you've never been pushed. Fighting the vamps isn't like taking Jimmy's lunch money in fourth grade. You need to be fast, fearless, and accurate, and you need to understand that there's no giving up, because if they even smell it on you, you're done."

"I can do it," she said. But she said it flat on the floor. "I'm not quitting."

"Good," he said. "Because the opportunity to hit you is pretty much every Morganville kid's dream job. Oh, and you're paying me."

"I'm *what*?" She lifted her head from the canvas and stared at him, and Claire had to choke back a laugh at the look on Monica's face.

"Paying," he said. "For training. What, you thought I'd do this for free? Are we friends?"

"Fine," she said, and dropped her head again. "How much?"

"Twenty an hour."

"You're *kidding* me. You make about seven an hour on your best day!"

"That's when I'm doing honest labor, like cleaning sewers. Working with you means charging a premium."

She wearily lifted a hand and flipped him off, but said, "Okay, fine. Twenty an hour."

"Twenty-five now that you were rude about it."

Monica sent him a filthy glare, rolled over, and limped slowly off to the showers. Shane watched her go with a smile of pure satisfaction. "Gold," he said. "Pure gold."

Claire kissed him. "Don't gloat too hard," she said. "She's going to get better."

"I know. But I can enjoy it while she's not."

Claire took off after Monica for the locker room.

She found the other girl stripping off her workout clothes and examining in the full-length mirror the discolored places that were going to form bruises. Claire immediately felt a surge of awkwardness and didn't know where to look; Monica had an almost perfect body, sculpted and waxed and tanned. Claire flashed back to her awkward early-admission high school years, where showering with the pretty girls had been an exercise in merciless mockery.

But she wasn't even on Monica's radar, except as a second pair of eyes. "Hey," Monica said, without even focusing on her. "Do you think this is going to leave a mark?" She pointed to a red area on her ribs, just under her left breast.

"Probably."

"Dammit. I was going to go to the pool. Now I have to wear a one-piece." She made it sound like a burka. "So, pre-school, did you follow me in here to confess your gay love, or what?"

"What? No. And never you."

"Oh yeah? You got a girl-crush on someone else?"

Claire smiled. "Well, I lost my heart to Aliyah back there when she put you on the floor. . . ."

"Bite me, Danvers. I need a shower." Monica grabbed her soap, shampoo, razor, and a towel, and headed for the open tiled area. Claire followed at a distance and sat out of the range of splashing on the teak bench. "Seriously, are you stalking me? Because you're not doing it right."

"I need to talk to you."

"It's not mutual."

Monica turned the spray on and stepped into the steaming water. Claire waited until she'd foamed up her hair, rinsed it, put in the conditioner, and propped her leg up on the step to run the razor over it before she tried again. "I have a proposition for you."

"Again with the girl love."

"I want you to run for mayor."

Monica jerked, yelped, and blood trickled down her leg. She hissed, rinsed it off, and glared at Claire. "Not funny."

"Not meant to be," Claire said. "I'm really serious. People like familiar names, and there's no name for mayor more familiar than Morrell. Your grandfather was the mayor, your dad, your brother. . . ."

"Look, much as I'd like to be thought of as political royalty, that's not how it works. People have to actually *like* you to vote for you. I'm not stupid enough to believe they do." But she was listening while she soaped her leg again and shaved. Claire had known she would, because there was nothing Monica craved more than power and popular acceptance—and those things came standard with the plaque on the mayor's door.

"I think I can make it work," Claire said. "We could put up signs asking people to write you in on the ballot. You've got people who owe you favors, right? And the vamps would like it. They think you're easy to control."

"Hey!"

"I said they *think* you are. But you wouldn't be here working with Shane if you were all that easy, would you?" Claire cocked her head. "Missed a spot."

"Would you just get to the point?"

"Morganville needs a new Captain Obvious," she said. "And Morganville needs a new mayor the vamps would approve. You could be both."

"What, like a secret identity?" Monica laughed, but it was a dry, bitter sound. "You're such an idiot."

"Shane is already teaching you how to fight," Claire pointed out. "You already know how to target people you don't like. Why not do it for the sake of the town for a change? Captain Obvious has always been kind of a bully, just a bully on the side of the humans."

Monica had nothing to say to that. She simply frowned as she rinsed the last of the soap from her right leg, did the left, and then cleared the conditioner out of her hair. When she shut off the water, Claire threw her the towel. Monica dried off and wrapped up, and finally shrugged. "It'd never work," she said.

"Maybe not," Claire said, "but you owe me. And you're going to run for office."

Monica studied herself in the mirror, then smiled as she met Claire's eyes. "Well," she said, "I *would* make an awesome mayor. I'm very photogenic."

"Yeah," Claire agreed, straight-faced. "Because that's what really counts."

Shane didn't take it well.

"Monica," he kept saying, all the way home. "Wait, let's back up. We're going to campaign for Monica. For mayor."

"Yes," Claire said. "I'm sorry, why is this so hard to understand?"

"Did you trip in the shower and hit your head or something? *Monica Morrell.* I'm pretty sure we still hate her. Let me check my notes—yep, still hate her."

"Well," Claire said, "you're taking money to teach her to fight, so you sort of don't *hate* hate her anymore. And I'm not sure I do, either. She's just sort of annoyingly pathetic now that she doesn't have her position and her posse."

"And you want to turn around and give her back, let's see, a position, with a title and a salary, and the power to make the life of everybody in this town a living hell? She's not that sad a case."

"Shane, I'm serious about this. We need to get someone on the Elders' Council the vampires can't control, and someone who's human, and someone people might vote for. She's a Morrell. She'd get the sympathy vote because of her brother."

He scrubbed his face with both hands as she unlocked the front door of the Glass House. "*Such* a bad idea," he said. "In so, so many ways. Tell me we're not actually helping her."

"Well, I did kind of promise to make signs."

She expected him to kick about that, too, but instead, he got a slow, evil smile on his face and said, "Oh please. Allow me."

"Shane—"

"Trust me."

She didn't.

And sure enough, two hours later, she heard Eve's outraged scream coming from downstairs. She rushed into the living room and saw Shane holding . . . a poster. It was a vivid neon blue thing that read, in block letters, WHY VOTE FOR THE LESSER OF TWO EVILS? VOTE MORRELL!, and it had the saintliest picture of Monica that she'd ever, ever seen beneath it. Honestly, it couldn't have looked more angelic if Shane had Photoshopped a halo on it.

It also had one of those bright yellow callout stars in the corner that read ENDORSED BY CAPTAIN OBVIOUS! HUMAN APPROVED!, plus a copy of the write-in ballot with Monica's name written boldly in marker.

It was simultaneously the funniest thing Claire had ever seen, and the most appalling.

Eve couldn't seem to think of anything to say. She just stared . . . first at the poster, then at Shane, then back to the poster, as if she couldn't imagine a world in which this had happened. Finally, she said, "I really, really hope this is a joke. If it isn't, Monica's going to kill you. And then she'll wrap you in that poster and bury you."

"What's wrong with it?" Shane asked, and looked down at the paper. "I know, blue wasn't my first choice, but I figured hot pink would be overkill."

"Okay, I need a recap. Why exactly are you making a poster to elect Monica for mayor? Did I miss a step, or wake up in Opposite World, or . . . ?"

"It's Claire's plan," he said. "I'm just the graphic designer. She's the campaign manager."

Eve collapsed on the couch and put her face in her hands. "You're insane. You've gone insane. Too much stress. I knew one of us would break someday. . . ."

"Monica's perfect," Claire said. "Eve, really, she is. Think about it. And hey, if you want, you could be Captain Obvious."

"Me," Eve repeated, and gave a dry, strangled laugh. "Yeah, sure. Sure."

"Hey," Shane said. He propped the poster in the corner, and—unexpectedly, at least to Claire—dropped to one knee in front of Eve. He took her hands and dragged them down so he could see her face. "Look at me. You're the original rebel around here, Eve. Hell, you were a malcontent before I was. Before Michael. Before Claire. Most of these Captain Obvious wannabes half assed it because in their hearts they were regular guys, pissed off at not having everything they wanted when they wanted it. That isn't rebellion; it's just selfishness. But you're not like that. If you wanted to be Captain Obvious, you'd be real."

He meant it. No mocking, no digs, no friendly banter; he sincerely meant that, and Eve took in a deep, ragged breath as she stared back. She shook her head, once. "I can't, Shane."

"Yeah," he said. "You could be. But only if you really want to." He said it without drama, without even any special emphasis, just stating a simple fact. "C'mon. Pizza's getting cold."

"Michael's going to kill you both," Eve said, and followed him as he stood up and walked to the table, where Claire remembered what she was doing and set down plates. "Kill you so very, very dead."

But she was wrong, because when Michael showed up—about fifteen minutes later, coming out of the kitchen in that silent vampire-stealthy way he sometimes did, when he forgot his company manners—he took a long look at the poster, cocked his head, and said, "Wrong picture."

Shane cast Eve a look of evil triumph. "Well, I would've used her senior yearbook pic, but she looked like a Spice Girls reject. Anything else?"

"There is no Captain Obvious."

"That's your objection?" Eve said, dropping her half-eaten pizza back to the plate. "Out of everything on the poster, including—oh, I don't know, Monica?—that's your problem with it?"

"He spelled her name right. I actually like the 'lesser of two evils' motto; it really captures the spirit." Michael had brought his own pizza, and one of his opaque sports bottles. Pizza and blood, a combo only a vampire could love; trying not to think about it much, Claire added some crushed red pepper to her slice. "And to be fair, I did object to the picture first. That one makes her look way too sweet."

"I think that was intentional," Claire said. "Everybody knows—"

"There's a new Captain Obvious," Shane interrupted.

"Yeah?" Michael took a giant bite of crust and cheese and meat, then mumbled, "Who?"

Shane silently pointed to Eve, who swatted his hand away. So did Claire. And Michael choked, coughed, grabbed his sports bottle and swigged.

Eve said, "I'm so very not. Ever."

"No," Michael said, and coughed again, so violently Claire wondered if vampires could actually choke to death. Probably not. They didn't really need to breathe, after all; they'd just have to stop talking until they could clear their throats. "Hell no. Not you."

And that, Claire thought, was his first mistake, because Eve, instead of being relieved that he was supporting her general objection, looked at him with a sudden frown. "No? *Por qué,* Miguelito?"

"Because, well . . ." Michael stumbled over putting it into words. "I mean, Captain Obvious . . ."

"Is what, always a guy? That's what you're going with?"

"No, not—it's just that you—uh . . ." Michael leaned back and looked at Shane. "Help me out."

Shane held up both hands in silent surrender. "On your own."

"Look, being Captain Obvious makes you a target, and I don't want you to be—"

Eve interrupted him again, rising her chin in challenge. "Don't want me to be in charge? Out front? Taking risks? Have you *seen* the tombstone flyers people keep leaving us?"

"Yes," he said. "And I'm scared, because I love you. And it's going to be dangerous. You know that without my telling you."

"She knows," Claire said, "but you shouldn't tell her she *can't.*"

Michael was starting to get really concerned. Eve reached over and took his hand.

"Relax," she said, and held his gaze. "I know I *could* do it. But I won't. I know it would put you in a bad position, for one thing. Props for not saying that, by the way."

"It wouldn't matter what happened to me," he said, and brushed the hair back from her face with gentle fingers. "You know that."

"Okay, you're making me lose my pizza," Shane said, and pitched a napkin at him, and a paper war began, flying on all sides until Claire waved the last surviving unthrown one in a sign of surrender.

So it was all okay, then. For now.

One thing about pizza was that it made for an easy cleanup,

again—paper plates and paper boxes, and some glasses dumped in the dishwasher. Miranda had stayed in her room, watching movies; she was still fascinated with their having so many of them, and it was shocking how many of the classics, such as *Star Wars*, she'd never seen before. Claire left Michael to cleaning up, since it was his turn, and considered joining Shane on the couch (he and Eve were bickering over which video game to play, because she was heartily sick of shooting zombies and he never was) but the lure of study was just too much.

That made her weird. She was aware of that.

After an hour or so, she became aware of a faint tapping, and for a moment she thought it was at the door of her bedroom (and that it might, miraculously, be Shane choosing her over zombies), but no, the sound was at her window, the one facing the big tree at the back of the house. It was full dark now, with stars set like diamonds in the dark blue velvety sky; here in the high desert it was so clear, she could even see the faint, cloudy swirls of galaxies. The sky seemed close enough to touch.

So was Myrnin, standing balanced on a tree limb that was far too slender for his weight. If she hadn't known better, she'd have thought he was floating in midair, but not even vampires could accomplish that. No, he was just being incredibly graceful, and ignoring laws of physics that were inevitably going to protest.

"Open," Myrnin said. "Hurry up, girl. Open the window. This branch won't"—he stopped as there was a sharp crack, and the branch sagged under his feet—"hold me for long!" He finished his sentence in a rush as she jerked up the window sash.

He lunged forward through the opening just as the branch broke free and crashed through the leaves to the ground below. Claire got out of his way. Vampires were nimble. He didn't need help, and just now, she wasn't feeling especially like helping him, anyway.

Myrnin hit the floor, rolled, and came with fluid grace back to a standing position. He struck a pose. "I suppose you are wondering what brings me here like this, in secret."

"Not really. But I see you found your shoes, thank God," Claire said. Glancing down at the bright white patent leather loafers on his feet, he shrugged.

"I think they belonged to a pastor, perhaps. All I could locate," he said. "No idea what's carried the rest of my shoes away. Perhaps Bob has developed a taste for footwear, which would be most interesting. Albeit alarming."

"Bob the Spider."

"Yes."

"That's . . . not too likely. Please tell me you washed them."

"The shoes?"

"Your feet. Do you know what kind of diseases are all over alleys?"

He gazed at her with perfect stillness for a second, then said, "I saw the campaign poster on the porch outside. I'm not sure whether to applaud you for your initiative or box your ears. *Monica Morrell?* Really?"

"I know it seems weird."

"Weird? It seems *insane*, and believe me, when I am telling you that, it's worth taking seriously, dear girl. I expected you to put forth a real candidate."

"Can you think of anybody who could really do the job? If Hannah Moses couldn't manage it, nobody else has a shot, anyway," Claire said. "Monica will get the votes, just because, well, her brother died in office. And her father. And she's a Morrell. People mostly just vote for what's familiar, even if it's wrong."

Myrnin gazed at her, and he just looked . . . miserable. Defeated, really. "Unfortunately, I cannot refute your logic. Then we're finished," he said. "The grand experiment is done, and all hope is lost. I suppose I must make preparations to go away, then."

"What?"

"Claire, attend: if this madness proceeds unchecked, there is only one way for this to end, and that is in blood, fire, and fury. Amelie and Oliver have formed what psychologists would call a *folie à deux*, and their indulgences will lead to cruelty, and cruelty will lead to slaughter, and worst of all, slaughter will lead to the discovery of vampires in this modern age. I've seen it before, and I won't be caught up in the inevitable aftermath. Best to flee now, before the pitchforks and torches and scientists come calling. That is, if the two of them don't have a bitter and blackened falling-out first, and destroy the town in their rage."

"Myrnin!"

"I mean it," he said. "There is a reason that I've tried to keep Amelie and Oliver apart. Opposites do not merely attract. A chemist of your skill should know that quite often, they violently explode. Go while you still can, Claire, and take all your friends. In a matter of weeks, it would not be a fit place for you to call home anyway." He seemed almost sad now. "I have liked this home. Very much. It grieves me to leave it behind, and I fear I will never find a place that is as tolerant of my . . . eccentricities."

He really did mean it, and it shocked her. He'd always been a little cavalier about danger, even his own; he wasn't someone who ran away easily. In fact, he'd persuaded the other vampires to stand their ground against the draug, to *protect* Morganville.

How could he want to run away now, from so little?

"Well," she said, "you can go if you want, I guess, but I can't."

"Won't," he corrected primly. "You can leave whenever you like. Amelie has said so, and as far as I am aware, she never countermanded that."

"She said I could go *alone*. As in she insists that Michael, Eve, and Shane stay here. I'm not leaving them behind, especially not if you think it's going to get dangerous. What kind of friend—what kind of *girlfriend*—would I be if I did that?"

"One with a sense of self-preservation," he said, and gave her an off-kilter, fond smile. "And that would be so unlike you. You're always caring about the strays and outcasts among us, myself included. You really are a very odd girl, you know; so little sense of what is good for *you*. Perhaps that's what I find fascinating about you. Vampires, you know, have such an iron-strong sense of self-preservation; we are the ultimate narcissists, I suppose, in that we see nothing wrong with others dying to save us. But you—you are our strange mirror opposite."

"Coming from you, I don't know how to take that, and on the subject of strange and not at all appropriate, could you *please* stop dropping into my bedroom in the middle of the night?"

"Oh, did I?" He looked around vaguely. "I suppose I did. Sorry. Well. If you won't leave this place, arm yourself heavily for as long as you stay," he said. "Don't go anywhere alone. And make alternate plans to flee when that becomes necessary."

"Myrnin—you're scaring me," Claire said, and reached out. "Please, tell me what's going on!"

He took her hand and raised it to his mouth in an old-fashioned gesture that made her skin tingle, especially when she felt the cool brush of his lips against her skin. His eyes were very dark in the dim light of her study lamp, and she didn't think he'd ever looked more . . . human. Crazy, maybe, but so very human.

"I hope I *am* scaring you," he said. "When things seem calmest, that is the time you should fear the most; it's when you have the most to lose. It's not your enemies who are likeliest to hurt you. It is, always, those you trust. And you have trusted Amelie too far."

He hadn't let go of her hand, and she was starting to feel flushed and awkward about it. "I've trusted you, too," she said. And he gave her a sad, slightly manic smile.

"Yes, and that too is a mistake," he said. "As you've known from the first moment you met me, I am not reliable."

"I think you are," Claire said softly. "I really do. Myrnin— please. Please don't go away. You—you matter. To me."

There was just a flicker of warmth, *something*, and for a moment she thought . . . But then Myrnin's face shut down, and he let go of her hand. Where his fingers had touched hers, her skin felt ice-cold.

"Don't," he said. "It's dreadfully unfair to say things like that when this is likely the last time we will speak, and we both know you don't mean what you say. It's pure selfishness that you want to keep me here." His tone had a harder edge than she was used to hearing from him, and his expression was deathly still.

She felt an unexpected surge of anger. "Didn't you just accuse me of not being selfish enough?"

"Don't play at word games with me. I was a master of it before your country even existed."

"You can't just *go*! Where will you—"

"Blacke," he said, cutting her off. "For a start. Morley and I do not get along well, but he and the quite-frightening librarian woman have built a rough approximation of a town where vampires are welcome. It will do until I gather resources to settle elsewhere more congenial. You'd do better to think of yourself. Without me to help protect you, you are likely to end up dead, Claire. I should regret that. You've been the least useless apprentice I've ever had."

"That's it? That's all you're going to say? I'm the *least useless?*"

It burst out of him in a furious, low-voice rush. "Yes, of course that's all I'm going to say, because there's no point in it, no point at all in telling you that I'm *lonely*, that it's been so long since I could discuss books and theories and science and metaphor and alchemy and philosophy, and that is a desperately lonely thing, Claire. Even for someone who has killed to stay alive, there's a point where life—where existence—just seems . . . worthless, without some deeper connection. Do you understand?"

She was afraid to, really, but she gulped down a deep breath, and said, "You're saying that you care for me."

Myrnin froze, staring at her. He really was amazing, she thought; when he had that light in his eyes, it was possible to see past the crazy behavior and clothing chaos and recognize him as just . . . beautiful. The longing in his face was breathtaking.

But he said, in a low voice, "Not as you would understand it. What I admire in you is . . . intellectual. Spiritual."

She actually laughed a little. "You love me for my mind."

He sighed. "Yes. In a sense."

"Then stay."

"And watch you torn apart between Amelie, Oliver, and this town? Helpless to stop it?" He shook his head. "Better I go."

"No," she said, and grabbed at his sleeve. The old fabric of his jacket had an odd texture to it—cloth that had survived a hundred years or more past its makers. He could have avoided her, of course, but he didn't. He simply waited. "You can't go! You fought the draug to save the town!"

"I won't fight Amelie, and for as long as Oliver holds sway over her, she's dangerous to us all. So what do you propose I do? They'll come for me, sooner or later; I've always been a thorn in Oliver's side, and he'll want me dealt with before long. If I'm lucky, he'll do it before he comes after you and your friends, relieving me of the burden of standing by for that."

"Amelie won't let him hurt you."

"Won't she?" Myrnin's face set hard, and he seemed to be re-membering something very unpleasant. "Oliver has a talent for corruption. He had the same skill in breathing life. The atrocities men committed in his name were legion and legendary, and those were mere mortals acting on his behalf. Vampires can be infinitely more cruel. Let enough of us lose our better instincts to that, and there will be a kind of—fever. A madness that sweeps us away, and we won't care about promises of good behavior, or even about our own survival. I've seen it happen to entire towns of vampires. They just . . . break." He snapped his fingers in front of her face in a sharp, dry motion, and the sound reminded her of bones shat-tering. "I don't wish to see it again. And I certainly don't wish to be part of it."

"Then make her listen to you. You're one of her oldest friends!"

"Friends count for little when they cross lovers," he said. "You're old enough to know that. And it is why I can't—" He shook his head. "Why I can't stay."

She felt she would choke on tears, suddenly. He stepped for-ward and took both her hands in his cool ones. For a moment, she thought he intended to kiss her, and for a panicked moment she wasn't sure if she ought to stop him, *wanted* to stop him . . . but then he just touched his forehead to hers and held it there.

"Hush, now," he said, and there was so much sweetness in his voice. "I don't want to see you cry. I'm nothing to cry over."

"I don't want you to go."

He pulled back, still close, very close, *too* close. There was a faint crimson flicker deep in his eyes, like a distant thunderstorm. "Take care," he said. "Promise me."

"I will," she said. "Myrnin—"

He kissed her. It was so fast that she couldn't move to prevent it, even if she'd wanted to; it was also quick, and light, and cool, and then . . .

Then he was gone.

Claire leaned out the window and saw him scrambling in a blur down the tree. He jumped the last ten feet, landed smoothly on his white patent leather shoes, and looked up at her in silence, then held up a pale, long-fingered hand.

She held hers up in response. Tears blurred her view of him, before they broke free of her eyes and rolled hot down her cheeks.

When she blinked, the yard was empty, except for the broken branch he'd been standing on when she'd first spotted him.

Claire gulped in several deep, cold breaths of night air, then slammed the window shut and sat down on her bed. She felt . . . She didn't know how she felt. Just wrong. She wanted to talk, but she couldn't to Shane, not about this; he wouldn't understand, not about this.

Eve. Maybe she could talk to Eve. . . . But she could hear the shouting from downstairs, and Eve's voice was gleefully announcing her victory over Shane in the game. Upstairs felt like a whole world away from that.

Claire stretched out on her bed, closed her eyes, almost ill with how wrong that had been, how guilty she was about that whole conversation. But she'd needed to have it with him; she knew that.

She flinched and bolted upright at a knock on the door, both arms instinctively crossing over her chest. "Who is it?"

"What do you mean, who is it?" Shane eased the door open and studied her. Oh. Of course, that was Shane's knock; she knew it very well. "What's up? You all right? You look scared."

She felt a surge of feeling so fierce that it burned in her cheeks and made her stomach churn, and for a second she didn't even know what it was, until her brain kicked back in.

It was shame.

"No," she said, and her voice sounded shaky. "No, I just—I had a dream. A bad one." *Liar.*

He gave her a grin that made the shame bite deeper, then sank down on the bed next to her. "Shouldn't have come up here and gone to sleep, then. Come on, sleepyhead. It's too early for you to crash out."

He kissed her, and he felt warm and sweet and strong and most of all, *alive* . . . and she fell into it eagerly, almost desperately. The kiss went on, and on, damp and slow, like something perfect in a dream, and she pressed close and into his arms, and all the storm inside her turned into peace, a peace so strong she could feel it glowing in her blood. She sighed onto his lips, into his mouth, and he was smiling, his hair brushing gently over her face like a ghost's caress.

"You make me happy," she whispered. She meant it literally— he'd just led her out of a strange, dark place and into sunlight, and the relief was so great that she felt tears in her eyes. "So happy."

Shane pulled back and looked at her with an expression of absolute focus. His smile was blinding. "I was about to tell you the same thing," he said, and brushed his fingers over her face. "Cheater."

For an awful second she thought he knew about Myrnin, standing here in her room, but then with a wave of icy relief she realized he was talking about her beating him to the punch. She gave him a shaky smile. "Got to be quick."

"Oh," he said, and kissed her very lightly, moving his lips down her throat, "I really don't think I do."

She laughed, because the joy just became a pinpoint of light inside her, bright and searing, and she rolled him over and sprawled on top of him and kissed him again, and again, and again, until everything was a burst of brightness, everywhere in the world.

And when it faded, when it was dark and quiet again, she listened to the strong, fast beat of his heart with her head on his chest, and thought, *I'm sorry.* She wasn't even sure what she was apologizing for, or even to whom it was directed. Myrnin? Herself? Shane? Maybe she'd let them all down, somehow.

But not again.

Never again.

Shane fell asleep next to her, out like a light, but Claire found herself humming with energy and too restless to try to close her eyes. She went out into the quiet hallway, closed the door, and sank down against the wall, turning her phone over and over in her hands. *Might as well,* she thought. It was late, but her parents were used to that, and they were always going on about how she didn't call enough.

Claire dialed before she could think better of it. Her mom answered on the second ring, her tone anxious. "Claire? Are you all right, honey?"

"Fine," Claire said. She felt a deep surge of guilt, because what did it say about her that her mom assumed she was in deep trouble every time she bothered to call? "Sorry I haven't been to see you lately. How's Dad? Is he doing all right?"

"Your dad's fine," her mom said firmly. "Except he worries about you, and so do I. He was hoping you could come home and visit soon. Any chance of that? If you want to bring your boyfriend, I suppose that's okay." She didn't sound so very enthused about *that.* It wasn't that she and Dad disapproved of Shane, exactly, but they were . . . cautious. Very cautious.

"I might do that," Claire said. "So, are you still doing that book club thing?"

"Oh yes; I just read the best mystery novel, *The Girl with the Dragon Tattoo*. Maybe you've heard of it . . . ?"

"Yes, Mom, I've heard of it. And there are movies."

"I didn't think there were any theaters in Morganville."

"There are a couple," Claire said. "But I watched it as a rental. You should do that."

"Oh, I have to do it over the Internet now; it seems so complicated."

"It's not. I could show you—"

"You know me and technology, sweetie. So, how's school?"

"Fine," Claire said. She knew she ought to say something more, something important, but she couldn't seem to come up with anything much. *My vampire boss, who would like to maybe be my boyfriend, just dropped in to tell me he was running away because Morganville's too dangerous.* That was a lot to dump on an unsuspecting parent, on so many levels. "Thanks for the lovely birthday gift." It had really been lovely—Claire had been expecting an out-of-fashion dress or a gift card or something, but instead she'd gotten a hand-bound book that had pictures of her from babyhood on, with space to add more. She'd already put in some photos of her and her friends, and her and Shane. Suddenly it reminded her that she'd never taken a picture of Myrnin . . . and now maybe she never would.

"That's a relief. You know, I think you work too hard at those classes. We'd be so happy to see you, honey. Do you think you might be able to come out this weekend?" Claire's parents lived only a few towns away, in a house that they wouldn't have been able to afford except that Morganville's Founder had bought it for them, in a fit of conscience over their daughter's contributions to vampire survival. Her parents had also once understood about the vampires, but not anymore. Those memories had faded almost to nothing—a deliberate action by the vamps, or by Amelie in particular. And that was okay. Claire preferred it that way—she liked them thinking she was in a safe place, with people who loved her. It was half true, anyway—the second half.

"Maybe I can try," she said. If Myrnin was right, she might not have much choice in getting out of town soon. "Mom—I know you were disappointed at me about not going to MIT when they called me, but . . ."

"I trust you, sweetie. I was just afraid you'd made that decision because of—well, because of Shane. If you really made it because you weren't ready to go, then that's all right. I want you to do things the way that's most comfortable for you. Your dad agrees." There was an indistinct mumble in the background that *might* have been her dad agreeing, but more likely it was just the opposite, and Claire smiled.

"Shane's not in charge of what I do," she said. "But I won't lie. I didn't want to leave him here, either. So maybe there's a little bit of that in there."

"I—honey, I know you don't want to hear this again, but are you sure you're not plunging into something too quickly with him?"

It was a familiar subject, and Claire felt a white-hot stab of annoyance. *Never thought of that, Mom. Wow, what insight!* She wouldn't say it. . . . She'd rarely been sarcastic to her parents, but that didn't stop her from thinking it. Older people so often thought they'd been through everything, experienced everything . . . but it wasn't true. Few of them had ever lived in Morganville, for instance. Or apprenticed to a vampire with poor impulse control.

"I'm not," Claire said. She'd learned that short answers worked best; they made her sound adult and certain. Overexplaining only opened the door for more lectures. "I know you're concerned, Mom, but Shane's a really good guy."

"I know you wouldn't stay with him if he wasn't—you're a very smart girl. But it does concern me, Claire. And your father. You're just eighteen. You're too young to be thinking about spending a lifetime with someone. You've hardly even dated anyone else."

Claire was just about fed up with the *You're too young* litany. She'd heard it from the time she was old enough to understand the words. The format might change, but the song remained the same: too young to do whatever it was she most wanted to do. And she couldn't resist saying, "If you hadn't said I was too young to go to MIT at sixteen, I would never have come to Morganville."

It was true, but it was a little cruel, and her mother fell silent in a way that told Claire she'd scored. *It's not a game,* she reminded herself, but she couldn't help a little surge of satisfaction, anyway.

When her mom restarted the conversation, it was about her new hobby, which had something to do with remodeling the house. Claire listened with half an ear as she flipped pages in her textbook that she'd opened on her lap. She still had another twenty pages of material to digest, and calling home was having the desired effect: it was making her forget all about Myrnin, and what he'd said, and focus back on her studies.

The door to her room opened unexpectedly, and Shane was standing there, bed-headed and yawning. He waved at her. She pointed to the phone and mouthed *Mom.* He nodded, stepped over her, and headed for his own room. Knowing him, he'd be face-down in dreamland in five minutes.

Claire grabbed her stuff and went back into her own room. Mom still hadn't paused for breath, and except for a few noncommittal uh-huhs, Claire was just a conversational spectator.

A second after she settled in on the bed, there was another

knock at the door—not Shane this time, because it was much more tentative. Claire covered the phone and called, "Come in!"

It was Miranda, who stepped inside and looked around with interest. Claire mouthed to her, *I'm on with my mom.* Miranda nodded and went to stare at the large bookcase in the corner of the room. She began pulling out titles.

"Mom, I've got to go," Claire said. "My friend Miranda's here. I told you about her. She's the new one in the house."

"Oh, okay. Love you, pumpkin. Your dad says he loves you, too. Can't wait for you to take a look at the carpet samples. I'm sure you can help us decide on that. Maybe this weekend?"

"Thanks, Mom. I love you, too. Yeah, maybe this weekend."

She hung up and dropped her cell back in her pocket as Miranda wandered over with a couple of books. "Do you mind if I borrow these?" she asked. "I don't sleep anymore."

"Any time," Claire said. "Did you like *Star Wars*?"

"Yes," she said. Miranda sat down on the bed next to her. She was a small-framed girl, and she seemed even more fragile than Claire, who'd at least put on some muscle these past few years, if she hadn't grown much taller. Miranda had the seeming physical strength of a stick insect. That was deceptive, of course; Miranda wasn't really alive in the same way Claire was, and she could draw on the considerable power of the Glass House when she had to, so she could probably break bricks with her hands if necessary.

It was hard not to feel protective, though. The kid just had that look of vulnerability.

"That's it? Yes? People usually have more to say than that."

"It was good?" Miranda tried tentatively, and then shrugged. "I guess I'm not really in the mood for movies after all. You know, I used to think that if I couldn't see the future, it would be terrible, but really, it feels pretty good, not knowing what's coming. It makes it more fun to watch movies and things when you can't guess the ending." She fell silent for a second, then pushed her hair behind her ear. "But it'd be more fun if I did it with you guys."

She'd been coming out of her shell slowly, but steadily; she hadn't quite joined the Glass House gang in full, but she was, at least, an adopted kid who was trying to fit into the family. Claire knew how that felt; she'd come into the house when Shane, Michael, and Eve had already been an established unit of old friends. She knew what it felt like to be an outsider.

Claire hugged her impulsively. "We'll do that," she said. "Movie night. Tomorrow. I've got a bunch of things I think you'd like."

"Michael and Eve are going to move out," Miranda said.

Claire almost fell off the bed as she twisted to get a look at Mir's face. The other girl was staring down, and she didn't look like she was making a bad joke; she seemed serious, and a little sad. *"What?"*

"I know I'm not supposed to eavesdrop, and I try not to, really, but it's hard when you're invisible during the daytime," Miranda said. "I mean, you're drifting around bored and there's nobody to talk to. You can't even watch TV unless someone else turns it on, and then you have to watch whatever they want—"

"Mir, focus. Why would you say they're moving out?"

"Because they're talking about it," she said. "Eve thinks that it's hard to feel married when they're just living the same life, you know? When it's here, with you and Shane. I know she moved into Michael's bedroom, but she doesn't feel like anything really changed. Like, they're married for reals."

Claire had honestly never thought about it. It had just seemed, in her mind, like marriage wouldn't change anything—wouldn't mean any difference at all in the way Michael and Eve felt around her and Shane. They'd already been, ah, together, after all. Why should it matter? "Maybe they just need some time."

"They need *space*," Miranda said. "That's what Michael said, anyway. Space and privacy and nobody listening to them all the time."

Well, Claire could understand the privacy part. She always felt odd about that, too. Even as big as the Glass House was, sometimes it felt very crowded with five people in it. "They shouldn't move out," Claire said. "It's Michael's house!"

"Well, *I* can't move, can I?" Miranda said, and kicked her feet. She was wearing cute sneakers, pink with an adorably weird brown bunny face on them. "I don't want them to go, though. Claire— what happens to me if you guys all leave? Do I just . . . stay here? Forever? Alone?"

"That's not going to happen," Claire said, and sighed. She grabbed a pillow and flopped backward, holding it tight against her chest. "God, this can't happen now. Like everything wasn't complicated enough!"

Miranda lay flat, too, staring up at the ceiling. "I don't feel right tonight. The house feels . . . It feels weird. Anxious, maybe." The Glass House had its own kind of rudimentary life force to it—something Claire didn't exactly understand but could feel all around her. And Miranda was right. The house was on edge. "I think it's worried about us. About what's going to happen to us all."

Claire remembered Myrnin's anxious, determined expression, his insistence that she leave town, and felt a chill.

"We'll be fine," Claire said, and hugged the pillow tighter. "We'll all be fine."

It was as if the universe had heard her, and responded, because all of a sudden she heard the crash of glass downstairs. Miranda stood bolt upright and closed her eyes, then opened them to say, "The front window. Something broke it."

Claire raced her downstairs, with Shane stumbling out of his room in a daze to follow. They found Michael and Eve already there.

The window in the parlor was broken out, and a brick was lying on the carpet in a spray of broken glass. Wrapped around it was another note. Nobody spoke as Michael unfastened the string that held it on and read it, then passed it to Eve, who passed it to Shane, who passed it to Claire.

"Wow," she said. "I didn't think they could spell *perverts.*"

"It's getting worse," Eve said. "They're not going to let this go, are they?"

Michael put his arms around her and hugged her tight. "I'm not going to let anything happen," he said. "Trust me."

She let out a sigh of relief and nodded.

Shane, ever practical, said, "I'll get the plywood and hammer."

FIVE

OLIVER

☾

When Amelie slept, she seemed little more than a child, small and defenseless, bathed in moonlight like a coating of ice. Her skin glowed with an eerie radiance, and lying next to her, I thought she might well be the most magnificent and beautiful thing I had ever seen.

It destroyed me to betray her, but I really had no choice.

I slipped quietly away through the darkness of this, her most secret of hideaways; it was where Amelie kept those treasures she had preserved through years, through wars, through every hardship that had fallen over her. Fine artworks, beautiful clothes, jewels, books of all descriptions. And letters. So many handwritten letters that seven massive ironbound chests couldn't contain them all. One or two, I thought, might have come from my own pen. They would not have been love poems. Likely they had been threats.

I moved silently through the rooms to the door, and out into the jasmine-scented garden. It was a small enclosure, but bursting with colorful flowers that glowed even in the darkness. A fountain played in the center, and beside it stood another woman. I'd have mistaken her for Amelie, at a glance; they were alike enough in coloring and height and form.

But Naomi was a very different kind of woman altogether. Vampire, yes; old, yes. And a blood sister to the Founder, through their common vampire maker, Bishop . . . but where Amelie had the power to command vampires, to force them to her will, Naomi had always wielded her power less like a queen and more like a seductress, though she had little interest in the flesh—or at least, in mine.

Amelie appeared to be made of ice, but inside was fire, hot and fierce and furious; inside Naomi, I knew, was nothing but cold ambition.

And yet . . . here I was.

"Oliver," she said, and placed a small, gentle hand on my chest, over my heart. "Kind of you to meet me here."

"I had no choice," I said. Which was true—she had taken all choices from me. I raged at it, inside; I was in a tearing frenzy of rage within, but none of it showed on my face or in my bearing. None could, unless she allowed it; she had control of me from the bones out.

"True," she said. "And how fares my much-beloved sister?"

"Well," I said. "She could wake at any time. It wouldn't do for her to see you here."

"Or at all, since my dear blood sister believes I'm safely dead and gone. Or do I have you to thank for the attempt on my life, Oliver? One of you must have wished me dead among the draug."

"I organized your assassination," I confessed immediately.

Again, no choice; I could feel her influence inside me, as irresistible as the hand of God. "Amelie had no part in it."

"Nor would she have; we've held our truce for a thousand years. I'll have to think of a suitable way to reward you for betraying that. What does she suspect?"

"Nothing."

"You've gained her trust?"

"Yes."

"You're certain of that?"

"I'm here," I said, and looked around at this, Amelie's most sheltered secret. "And now, you're here. So yes. She trusts me."

"I knew that bewitching you was an investment that would soon pay off," Naomi said, and gave me a sweet, charming smile that made the storm inside me thunder and fury. I hated her. If I'd had the ability to fight, I'd have ripped her to pieces for what she'd done to me, and was doing through me, to Amelie. "She hasn't detected your influence on her decisions?"

"Not as yet."

"Well, she will likely start to question it soon, if she hasn't already; my sister has a nasty streak of altruism that surfaces from time to time. Once the humans begin to complain of their treatment, she may think about placating them once again." She ran her fingers over my cheek, then parted my lips with cool fingers. "Let's see your fangs, my monster."

I had no choice. None. But I tried, dear God, I tried; I struggled against the darkness inside me, I fought, and I won a hesitation, just for a moment, in obeying Naomi's iron will.

And still, my fangs descended, sharp and white as a snake's. There was a single tiny tug of pain, always, as if some part of me even now refused to believe my damned state of being, but I had centuries ago grown well used to that.

The pain she was wringing from within me was much, much worse.

She let me go and stepped back, eyes narrowing. "Your reluctance doesn't please me," she said. "And I can't risk your tearing free even a bit from my side, now, can I? Hold still, Oliver."

And I did, to my shame; I held very still, eyes fixed on the calm flowing water of the fountain as it spilled tears to the stone. She raised my arm to her lips, bit, and drank. She was a true snake, this one, and poison ran from her bite into me; it corrupted, and it destroyed the tiny pulse of will I'd managed to raise. She licked the remains of my blood from her lips and smiled at me.

Defeated.

And then she put her lips close to my ear and said, "I owe you something for that bit of will, don't I? Very well. I want you to feel pain. I want you to *burn*."

It started slowly, a sensation of heat sweeping up from my hands, but it quickly turned into the familiar bite of sunlight beating down on me . . . but where age had given me armor against such pain, I had no defenses from Naomi's witchery. It was like being a newborn vampire again, tied down for the noontime glare, with my blood boiling and burning its way through my flesh, exploding in thin pale flames, flaking my skin to ash and roasting nerves. . . .

I clenched my teeth against the pain, then whimpered softly at the extreme of the agony. *Let me die,* something in me begged. *Just let me die!*

But that, of course, was not her plan. She had done me no physical harm, none at all. It was only the memory of fire, the sense of it; my blood was cool and intact, and my skin unmarked.

I only felt as if I were a torch set afire.

When she finally released me, I fell to my hands and knees on the soft grass, sucking down cold night air in panicked breaths as if I were no more than a human. I didn't need the air, but I craved the coolness; the dew of the grass felt like a balm on my still-sizzling nerves, and it was all I could do to stop myself from pitching facedown to its embrace.

But I would not give her that. Not until she demanded it.

She did not. I calmed myself and climbed to my feet, and wished to heaven I could rip her apart, but I knew better than to even attempt it. And I was rewarded with a slow, calm smile. Above it, Naomi's eyes continued to watch closely for any hint of rebellion.

"Now," she said. "I have a job for you. I wish you to find the vampire Myrnin, and kill him."

Not that I hadn't often wished to do just that, but I hated the thought now, knowing that it was her driving me to it, and not my own will. "Yes, my lady," I said. The response was automatic, but it was also wise.

"That's my lovely knight," she said, and her eyes flashed red. "And inevitably, you will have to do the same to my sister, for my own safety. When we're done, we'll rule Morganville together. You can take your sport where you wish; I care not. That's what you've always wanted."

"Yes," I whispered. *No.* Not at this cost. And not with her.

I had never expected, after all we had endured, to be undone at the lily-white hands of a maiden. Myrnin might possibly have been able to find a way to stop it, and her. That was why Naomi wished him gone, of course.

And why I'd have no choice, none, but to do her bidding, until she finally had no more use for me at all. All vampires had some measure of control of others; it was an instinct that made us effective hunters, but in some—like Amelie—that trait was very strong, a hammer blow that could be wielded against other vampires. Naomi's ability was a whisper, not a shout, but it was just as powerful. I had never suspected she possessed such skills. She had always seemed so . . . innocent. And kind. I ought to have known better; vampires are never kind, not unless that kindness buys us something.

"Tell me," I said. "Tell me why you're doing this. Why now?"

"I did not come after *you*," Naomi pointed out, and raised an eyebrow. "I am not my father, Bishop; I had no need to rule until it became plain that Amelie was . . . incapable. I would have been happy to see her healed and whole again, even then. But *you* had to come after me, Oliver. So it's entirely your fault that I am driven to this extreme."

Naomi's chin suddenly rose, and her eyes dimmed to a pale blue. "It seems I must leave you now, Oliver. She's awake," she said. "You know what to do. And remember, if you fight me, I'll make the punishments I've given you already seem like a caress."

She vanished like smoke. Surviving my attempt to destroy her, in the chaos of the final battle with the draug, had made this one stronger, faster, more coldhearted than ever.

I waited until I sensed Amelie's approach, and then I turned with a false but convincing smile; it ripped at me like razors to betray her so, because even after all our years of rivalry, I had finally come to realize her worth, and now . . . now the smile was no longer mine. It was a lure, a lie, and it sickened me to see her return it.

She walked on bare feet down the path, hands stroking the petals of flowers as she came; her thin white gown blew like mist in the moonlight. She was beautiful, and desirable, and I despaired inside as her hands touched the bare skin of my chest, because I was going to be the death of her.

And there was nothing I could do to stop it. Nothing at all. I wanted to warn her, to tell her how dangerous I was to her now. How destructive.

"You strayed," she said, and kissed me very lightly.

"Yes," I said, and felt myself smile that warm, challenging smile that had charmed her into trust. "But I'll never go far."

Until I kill you. God forgive me.

SIX

CLAIRE

🌙

Claire really wanted to confront Eve about what Miranda had overheard—she and Michael *couldn't* really be considering moving out, could they?—but in the morning, Eve was gone early, and Michael was sleeping late; she wasn't quite gutsy enough to go knock on his door and demand to know the truth. Michael was grouchy in the mornings.

Miranda, of course, had kept Claire up talking into the wee hours; she'd been getting more and more chatty since taking up residence, which was great in a way, because the kid had been so repressed and isolated before, but bad for Claire's sleep cycle. It also cut into the time she could spend with Shane; he tended to steer clear when Miranda was around, and although he wasn't above just moving the girl firmly out of the room when he felt it was necessary, he hadn't done it last night.

So Claire woke up short of sleep, yawning, and a little cranky. Not her best morning ever, but in a matter of minutes it got drastically better; she was still stretching and trying to wearily decide what to wear, when there was a thumping knock on her door, one very different from Miranda's tentative taps.

She grabbed her robe and threw it on as she answered. She didn't open up all the way, just peeked through. There was Shane, balancing one coffee cup precariously on top of another. He'd given her the giant Snoopy cup this morning, which was nice. "What's the password?" she asked him.

"Um, you look hot with your hair standing up?"

"Good enough." She stepped back and relieved Shane of the Snoopy cup as he came inside; then she set it hastily down when he stepped in to slide his free hand around her waist and kiss her. She had morning breath, but it didn't seem to matter to him; he tasted of mint toothpaste and coffee, but she forgot all that in seconds and then it was just all incredibly delicious. Her whole body tingled with warmth.

"Morning," he murmured, his lips close to hers. They were so tasty, she licked them, which made him smile and kiss her again. "Too bad you're dressed."

"I'm not dressed. I just have on a robe."

"Oh?"

"Hey," she said, and put a hand flat on his chest. "None of that, mister. A girl's got to have boundaries."

"You'll let me know when I get there," he said, and untied her robe. "You lied. You've got on jammies."

"Well, yeah, those, too." She was short of breath, and when his hands found their way under the flannel of her pajama top, the air in her lungs rushed away. "You really shouldn't . . ."

"Do this? Yeah, I know." He undid the first button on her pajama top and put a kiss in its place. "But I've been thinking about doing it all night."

So had she, actually, and all the logical objections to why this wasn't a good idea kind of vanished under the heat of his touch . . . until Claire realized he'd left her bedroom door wide-open, and someone was standing in the doorway.

"Your coffee's getting cold," Eve said. She was clearly on her way to the bathroom, arms full of black clothes, hair untied and in a multicolored mess around her pale face. She blew the two of them a kiss.

Claire yelped and jumped away, rebuttoning her top and retying her robe at light speed. Shane hardly seemed bothered at all, but she could feel the hot blush staining her cheeks. "Um, hi, Eve," she said. "Sorry."

"*I'm* not sorry," Shane said, and gave Eve a mean glare. Eve gave Shane a wicked grin. "Don't you have better things to do?"

"Than mess up your morning sexytime? Nope, never. Dibs on the shower! And you might want to remember this thing actually swings shut. Pro tip." Eve slammed the door between them.

Shane picked up a handy book and started to throw it, but Claire grabbed it out of his hands. "Not the advanced calc book!" She searched around and found a history text instead. He shook his head sadly.

"Moment's over," he said, and he wasn't just talking about the opportunity to throw something. He retrieved his coffee and sipped it, and she tried to get her racing heartbeat under control as she tasted hers. It was good and strong, and although it wasn't as good as what *might* have been her morning wake-up, it wasn't shabby. "What was Miranda in here gabbing about last night?"

"Things." Claire shrugged. "You know. She's lonely."

"I know the feeling, believe me." He gave her a puppy-dog look, and she aimed a kick in his direction, which he dodged.

"But she did say something weird."

"Miranda? Go figure!"

"She said—" Should she even repeat this? Somehow, saying it aloud, to Shane, made it more . . . real. But he needed to know. "She said Michael and Eve were talking about moving."

"Moving," he repeated, as if he didn't know the word. "Moving what?"

"I guess out. To another house."

"Why would we move?"

"Not we, Shane. *Them*. Michael and Eve. As a couple. Moving."

"Oh," he said, as if he still didn't get it, and then he did. *"Oh."* He looked as if someone had shot his dog, and he sat down on the unmade bed and stared down into his coffee cup. It was one of Eve's, black with purple bats all over it. "You mean, leave us behind."

He'd just distilled it down to the sharp, hurting point: *leave us.* Because that was what it was, really: not that they needed space, but that Michael and Eve were leaving Claire and Shane behind, in their past.

"They need space, is what Miranda said. Y'know, together-type space."

"They're not the only ones," Shane said. He didn't look up. "Hell. Michael didn't say anything."

"Neither did Eve. So maybe it's just, you know . . ."

"Talk? Maybe. But if they're talking about it, it's real enough to matter." He pulled in a breath and let it out slowly. "I've been thinking about it myself."

"Michael and Eve moving out?" Was she the only one who hadn't seen this coming?

"No. Moving out myself."

Claire couldn't have been more stunned if he'd announced he'd decided to turn vampire. She sat down too fast and just managed not to slop coffee all over herself; even that barely registered as a blip, because her attention was suddenly and completely on her boyfriend, and there was a sick, hurting knot in her stomach. *"What?"*

"It's just—" He gestured vaguely at the door. "We're in one another's pockets around here. Sometimes it'd be nice to just have it be . . ."

"You want to move out," Claire said. "By yourself."

"No!" Shane finally glanced up, startled. "I mean—*we* could . . . find a place—"

The moment froze, with the two of them staring at each other; this was a conversation Claire had never expected to have, and certainly not in the early morning in her pajamas with her hair in a mess. It clearly wasn't something Shane had thought through, either. The whole thing suddenly felt raw, fragile, *wrong*. And she didn't know why. It made the aching lump in her guts hurt even worse.

"Anyway," Shane finally said, in that we're-going-to-pretend-that-never-happened kind of tone, "it's just that this is Michael's house. It ought to be Michael and Eve's, if it's anybody's. I could always—we could—" He couldn't seem to get his words together, either, and she saw the same growing panic in him that she was feeling. *Not ready for this*, she thought. *Really not ready*. It reminded her of what her mother had said, so prophetically, last night on the phone. *Are you sure you're not moving too fast?*

She hated it when her mom was right.

"Okay, clearly, this is crazy talk anyway," Shane said, in a deliberately blow-off tone. "Let us never speak of it again. Wrestle you for dibs on the shower after Eve gets done with it."

"You take it," Claire said. Her lips felt numb. She drank coffee, but that was just to have something to do; she didn't taste it, and her brain felt overwhelmed with all the surges of emotion. Too many things were happening too quickly, none of them in tune. "I'll wait."

"Okay." He wanted to say something else, and even opened his mouth to do it, but whatever it was, his courage failed. He covered up by drinking, and Claire stared at the purple cartoon bats on his cup and wondered if somehow she could reset the morning back to the kissing. The kissing had been so wonderful.

But as Shane had pointed out, that moment was gone, and it apparently wasn't coming back anytime soon.

After an awkward few moments, with the coffee cups drained, Shane finally ventured, "I made up more posters."

"Good," Claire said. "Let's get them up."

She thought they were both relieved to have something to do.

Shane must have made up twenty posters, which was definitely overkill in a town like Morganville. Claire and Eve both had giggle fits over the variety of pictures—mostly wildly unflattering—that Shane had chosen.

"Gotta give it up for Monica," he said, admiring his handiwork. "That girl has a Photobucket album you would not believe. I think it runs to fifteen pages of pics. Even the Kardashians would say it was too much. Lucky for me she likes taking drunk pics."

"Isn't the idea to actually get her elected?" Eve finally managed to wheeze out, then broke out into another uncontrolled burst of laughter. "Oh, my God, *this* one. *This* is my favorite." She tugged one poster out and set it on top. It had Monica in her trademark tight-and-short, standing posed with her hands on her hips, puckering her lips into a duckface. "So many things wrong with this."

"This won't stop her from getting elected," Shane said. "Stupider people get elected all the time. It's America. We love the sleazy. And the crazy."

"I would like to think better of us," Claire said, "but yeah. You're right."

He offered a high five, which she reluctantly accepted, and then they split up the posters between them. They were heavier than Claire had imagined, and she *oofed* a little under the weight. Shane, without asking, redistributed, taking on the rest, and winked at Eve. "Wanna go with?"

"Somebody has to work around here," she said. "I suppose that turns out to be me. Again."

"Have fun with that day-job thing."

"Slacker!"

"And proud of it, wage slave."

Out on the sidewalk, Shane juggled the heavy cardboard until Claire caught up, with her backpack settled on her shoulder. "Did you bring the stapler?"

"Got it," she said. The stapler in question was a giant, ancient, industrial kind of thing, heavy steel that probably could fire its fastener through a car if it had to. "Also brought some stakes in case we need to put things on lawns."

"Like, say, this one?" Shane gazed longingly at the front yard of the Glass House, and Claire laughed out loud. She opened up her backpack and handed him a stake (funny, these had *so* not been meant for putting up signs). He hammered it into the ground and stapled the poster to it, and they stepped back to admire the effect. "A thing of beauty."

Eve opened up the window in the front room and peered out suspiciously. "Hey! You crazy kids, what are you doing?"

"You forgot to say 'Get off my lawn!'" Shane called back.

"Oh no, you didn't put that thing out there!"

"Relax—I used your favorite photo." Shane said to Claire as she zipped up her backpack, "We'd better make a moving target."

The first three signs went up without incident. At the fourth telephone pole, in Morganville's very sparse shopping district, Claire was stapling the sign in place when she heard the squeal of brakes on the street, and then the blare of a car horn. She turned and saw a bright red convertible and a blur of movement as the driver bailed out. Objectively, it was impressive that Monica could maintain her balance on those heels while moving that fast.

"What in the hell are you doing?" she asked, and shoved Claire out of the way as she faced the bright neon poster, which was flapping a bit in the wind. Her face went blank. Not angry, just ... blank. "What is this?"

"What does it look like?" Shane asked. He took the stapler from Claire and finished fastening the poster to the pole, then spun the thing like a very awkward six-gun as he admired the effect from a few feet back. "Looks like you're running for mayor."

Monica's glossy lips parted, and she just ... stared. As if she couldn't think of a single thing to say. *Wait for it,* Claire thought, and readied herself for the inevitable attack. Monica was about to achieve thermonuclear critical mass, and she intended to get to minimum safe distance before she blew.

But instead, a soft, delighted smile curled around Monica's lips, and she said, "Wait a minute. *You* did this?"

"Claire did," Shane said. "I'm just the incredibly awesome graphic designer. Also, head of the entertainment committee. Every campaign needs one of those."

"That's ... incredible," Monica said. "I don't know—okay, well, you know, nobody's probably voting for me. I mean, I'm not

Richard. I haven't gone out of my way to be responsible or anything."

"You're a Morrell," Shane said. "Lots of people figure that's in your blood. Three generations of mayors in your family, right?"

"Well, they'd be wrong."

"We know that," Shane said cheerfully. "But hey, you'll make a hell of a seat-filler, and I *know* you love a good photo op, being such a big fan of yourself." He lost his smile, and all the levity that went with it. "All this comes with one condition, you know," he said. "You do what's good for humans. Not what the vamps say."

Monica arched a single well-plucked eyebrow. "You have that backward, Collins. I don't do what *you* say. You do what *I* say. After all, I'll be the one with the fancy nameplate on the door."

"As long as you don't dance puppet for the vamps, I don't really care," Shane said. "But as to us doing what you say . . . Yeah. Good luck with that."

Monica's attention went back to the poster, and her eyes narrowed. "Wait a second. Is that one of my Facebook photos?"

"Maybe."

"Hmmm." She cocked her head, lips pursed. "Could have picked a better one."

"You always said you can't take a bad picture," he said, straight-faced.

"True." She gave the poster a slow, wicked smile, and said, "Okay, then. Just so long as I don't have to pay for anything, or show up for a lot of meetings. Oh, and make sure people know I can be bribed."

"Deal."

She stared at him for a second, then at Claire. "What exactly are you up to? Don't even pretend that you're into this, because you don't think that much of me."

"We're not," Claire said. "Don't worry about it. It doesn't concern you. All that concerns you is making sure you act nice and wave to people. Pretend it's a popularity contest, because that's what it is."

"You don't win popularity contests by being nice," Monica said. "You win them by making people scared to vote against you. So consider this one in the bag."

She walked back to her illegally parked car, climbed in, and was gone. Claire shook her head as she watched the red convertible screech around the corner, and said, "Only Monica could think *Vote for me or I'll break your leg* is a decent campaign slogan."

"In Morganville, it probably is."

They made another ten stops before grabbing a snack. Reaction had varied from place to place where they'd asked to put up the signs, from laughter to consternation to, at the last stop, outright rage.

Claire had never seen anyone tear a tough cardboard poster apart with such enthusiasm, but the dry cleaner four blocks away definitely wasn't a Morrell for Mayor fan.

"What was that dry cleaner guy so cheesed off about?" she asked Shane as they ate their breakfast burritos sitting outside at a rickety metal table. It was still cool enough outside to do that in relative comfort, though the flies and mosquitoes (new and unwelcome visitors, since the draug's watery arrival) were already dive-bombing them for snacks. They wisely kept the lids on their soft drinks.

"Him? His name's William Batiste. We used to call him Billy Bats. I think Monica might have kissed him once back in junior high. To be fair, she kissed most of the school who stood in one place long enough. Billy's kind of a hard-core resistance guy. Doesn't like the Morrells from way back."

"I suppose not everybody can be a *yes*," Claire said.

"I think we're lucky if she gets the terror and apathy vote," Shane said. "We've still got another ten to put up this afternoon. You still up for it?"

"Sure," Claire said. "It's my free day, anyway. If you don't mind, though, could we stop in at the lab? Just to check on Myrnin?"

Shane wasn't enthusiastic, but he shrugged; he probably figured it was a small price to pay, since he had her all day long. "We just need to be done before dark," he said. "I'm not *that* dedicated a campaign staffer. Especially for Monica."

The town seemed calm and back to normal, and the sounds of construction were everywhere—saws, grinders, hammers. It all sounded industrious and positive. There were more Protection signs visible, too; many shops were displaying them in the windows now, or at least at the counters, and she was seeing more Morganville residents wearing bracelets with their Protectors' symbols on them, too. Morganville was on its way back . . . but to what? Not the same town it had been before the draug. Maybe it was turning the clock all the way back to what it had been in the beginning, with the vampires in iron control.

Not if we have anything to say about it, she thought, and helped Shane staple another poster to a telephone pole outside Common Grounds. They stepped back to admire their work, and Claire became aware of someone standing in the shadow of the awning next to her. She hadn't felt him arrive, but suddenly Oliver was just . . . there.

He was a solid, daunting presence even though he was wearing what Claire thought of as his nice-hippie disguise—gray-threaded hair tied back in a ponytail, a dark T-shirt, and jeans under the long tie-dyed apron with the Common Grounds logo on it. He smelled like coffee, a warm and welcoming kind of scent even though under it he was cold as marble.

He was staring at the poster with an oddly blank expression. "I see," he finally said. "You've all lost your minds."

"Nope," Shane said, and tossed the stapler up in the air in a fine display of both bravado and stupidity; he could have lost a finger to that thing if it had gone off. "Found our calling. We're activists. And hey, Monica takes a decent picture. That's all you really need in a candidate, right?"

Shane got a full-on glare for that one, and Claire felt the burn even from the edges of it. "Don't test me, boy," Oliver said, velvet-soft. "I'm no one you should play games with these days. I've been too gentle with you; I've let you and your friends run riot. No more. You'll take that down."

Shane raised his eyebrows. "Why?"

Because I said so was the obvious answer, but Oliver smiled thinly and said, "It's against code."

Their poster wasn't the only one on the pole; there were flyers for lost pets, missing persons, a new band playing (probably badly) at Common Grounds over the weekend, cheap insurance, baby-sitting.... Claire said, "You never had a problem with it before."

"And now I do." Oliver stepped out in the sunlight, even though his skin immediately began to turn a little pink where the glare touched it, and he began ripping things off the pole without any regard for splinters. His fingernails left gouges in the wood half an inch deep. He shredded Monica's poster in half with a casual swipe, dropped the pieces to the ground, and kicked them back toward Shane. "And now you're littering as well. Pick it up."

Shane didn't move. He didn't speak. He just stood there, stapler in his hand, and it looked . . . dangerous.

"Pick it up or I'll have you arrested," Oliver said. "Both of you.

And no one will be coming to bail you out this time. If Eve tries, she'll join you."

"Michael—"

"I can handle Michael Glass." Oliver's words guillotined whatever Shane was going to say as he stepped back into the shadows. There was a faint wisp of smoke coming off his skin, but it stopped as soon as he was out of the sun, and the burn faded almost as quickly. On the other hand, the glow of his eyes was eerily specific. "Pick. It. Up."

Shane still didn't move, and Claire sensed, with fatal dismay, that he didn't intend to—so she did. She bent over and grabbed up the poster and the other shredded paper, walked over, and deposited it into the Common Grounds trash can next to the entry door. And it might have been okay, except that Oliver just had to purr, "Good girl," at her as if she were his personal pet, and Shane—

Shane punched him.

The vampire never saw it coming, because he was looking straight at Claire, enjoying his little moment of triumph; Shane's fist caught him on the side of the jaw, and the power behind it was massive enough that Oliver actually staggered before turning with supernatural litheness and springing on her boyfriend so fast, it was as if he'd been launched from a catapult. He slammed Shane back into the brick wall next to the window and pinned him there with an arm across his throat. When Shane tried to push him back, Oliver caught his hand and wrenched it hard to the side. Shane froze.

"Nothing's broken," Oliver said, "but it's half an inch away. So please, do that again, boy. I'll crush every bone you have, a handful at a time, and have you pleading for me to finish—"

He cut off abruptly because Claire made him shut up, by the simple expedient of putting the point of a thin-bladed silver knife against his back, just over where it needed to go to reach his heart. "Let go," she said. "I picked up the trash, just like you said. We're even."

They weren't, and she knew it without him even bothering to say it, but Oliver silently released Shane's hand. Claire stepped away, knife still drawn and ready, as Shane pushed Oliver back with a violent shove and picked up the stapler from where it had fallen on the pavement.

"You owe us for a poster," Shane said. "They cost me five bucks apiece. I'll expect a free drink in exchange."

"So will I," Oliver said, "from the vein, the next time I catch either of you in less . . . visible circumstances." He showed teeth, and walked back into the coffee shop.

"I guess that means Monica can't count on his vote, either," Shane said. It sounded like a joke, but he was trembling, and clenching the stapler way too hard. He knew, as Claire did, that they'd just passed over some kind of line. Maybe permanently.

"Why?" she asked him, a little plaintively. "Why did you do that?"

"Nobody talks to you that way," he said. "Not even him."

He draped his arm around her shoulders, picked up the other signs, and they continued on to the next stop.

At the next stop Claire and Shane made to put up Monica's poster, they found someone else there before them stapling notices: a serious-looking older woman and a younger man, probably her son. He was about Shane's height, but thin as a whip. He nodded to Claire as if he knew her (and she didn't think they'd ever met), then fixed his gaze on Shane. "Hey, man," he said, and offered his hand. "What's up?"

"Nothing much. How are you?"

"Good, good. You remember my mom, Flora Ramos, right?"

"Mrs. Ramos, sure, I remember the burritos you used to make for Enrique in grade school," Shane said. "He used to trade them to me if I gave up my M&Ms. I always made the deal; that's how good they were."

"You gave away my burritos, 'Rique?" Mrs. Ramos said, and raised her eyebrows at her son. He spread his hands and shrugged.

"You gave 'em to me every day," he said. "So yeah."

"They were delicious," Shane said. "Hey, he made a profit. He used to cut them in half and trade each separately."

"Enrique."

"I was an entrepreneur, Mama." Enrique gave her a devastating grin. "What, you want my M&Ms now?" In answer, she handed him a small letter-sized sheet of paper, and he held it against the telephone pole as she stapled it in place.

The flyer said, CAPTAIN OBVIOUS FOR MAYOR, and it had a big question mark underneath the caption where a picture ought to go. The slogan said, VOTE HUMAN. That was all.

"What the hell?" Shane asked, and pointed at the blank picture. "Mrs. Ramos, Captain Obvious left town. You can't ask people to vote for somebody who isn't even here."

"Maybe an empty seat is better than one filled by another useless bootlicker," she said, and as friendly as she seemed, her eyes were chilly and dark all of a sudden. "I've seen these Morrell posters. How can *you* of all people support such a thing, Shane? I know what that evil *bruja* did to you and your family!"

"It's not . . ." Shane took a step back, frowning. "It's not what it looks like. Look, Monica's a whole lot of things, but a bootlicker? Not so I've ever noticed. She's more likely to be wearing the boots, and kicking with them. Weak, she's not. And we need somebody on that council who will stand up to the vampires for us."

Anger flared in Mrs. Ramos's lined face. "She is part of the cancer that eats at this town. She and her whole disgusting family! I thank God that her father and brother are gone——"

"Wait a second," Shane interrupted, and it was his serious voice now, the one that meant he wasn't going to let it go. "Richard Morrell was okay. He tried. Don't——"

"He was a corrupt man from a corrupt family." Her voice had gone hard now, as unyielding as the flinty distance in her eyes. "Enough. I've finished talking with you."

Claire tried a different approach. Emotion clearly wasn't getting them anywhere. "But——they won't let you write in someone who doesn't even exist!"

"Captain Obvious does exist," Flora said. "He always has, always will. Until he stands up again, I'll stand for him."

"You," Claire said. "*You're* the new Captain Obvious?"

Enrique had gone quiet now, and when he wasn't smiling and being friendly, he looked a little bit dangerous. "Why? You got a problem with that? My mom's not good enough for you?"

"No, I just——" Claire didn't know how to finish that.

Shane did. "Dude, she's your *mom*. She used to throw bake sales. She made cookies. How can she be Captain Obvious?"

"How can any mother not want to be against the evil that lives here?" Flora said. "I raised kids in this town. Enrique, Hector, Donna, and Leticia. You tell me, Shane. You tell me what happened to three of my kids."

He just looked at her mutely for a long few seconds, and then away. "That wasn't anybody's fault. It was an accident."

"So they said."

Claire cleared her throat; she felt——as always——as though

someone had failed to fill her in, and here she was standing in the middle of a scene clearly full of tension, and she didn't understand any of it. "Uh, sorry, but . . . what happened?"

Mrs. Ramos didn't reply, and Shane didn't seem to want to, now that he'd tripped over the land mine. So Enrique finally sighed and dived in.

"My sister Donna was driving," he said. "She was seventeen, just got her license. She was taking my brother Hector to work— he was nineteen—and my sister Letty to school. It was the middle of winter, a little icy like it gets sometimes. Black ice, the kind you can't see. She hadn't ever driven on it before. They hit a pole." He didn't finish the story, but Claire guessed how it would end: in funerals. That was confirmed by a sideways glance at Shane. He had that quiet, closed-in look he got when people talked about their lost friends and relatives; he'd had so much of it himself, losing his sister, then his mom, and finally his dad. He always seemed to guard against emotion, even when it came from other people.

"That wasn't all of it," Flora Ramos said, with a suppressed anger that made the hair shiver at the nape of Claire's neck. "My children were out there lying hurt and alone, and *they* took their lives. I know they did."

"Mama, it was an accident. They bled out; you know what the doctors said."

"The doctors, the doctors, like they don't work for the monsters just as we all do? No, Enrique. It was the *vampiros*. It wasn't an accident. You should know that!" She sounded weary and furious at the same time; whenever it had happened, it was still fresh in her mind. "I have one child left they haven't taken from me. And they won't. Not while I have breath left in my body."

"You could leave town," Shane said quietly. "You had a chance."

"And our house? Our life? No. My husband is buried here, and my children. This is our *home*. The monsters must leave it before we do." She raised her chin, and Claire saw that despite the wrinkles, the gray hair, she was determined, and dangerous. "Don't play these games, Shane; politics here means our lives. I will not let you make it a joke."

Shane stared at her for a long moment. He felt sorry for her; Claire could see it. He knew how it felt, to blame the vamps for the loss of people he loved. But above all, Shane was practical. "You can't win," he said. "Don't do this. We've got a plan. Trust us."

"*You* two?" Flora laughed. "Your girlfriend, she's a vampire's pet—the Founder's pet. And you, you are too much in love to see it, and too much of a child. She's with *them*, not you." She dismissed them both with a flip of her hand. "Enough. Enrique. *Vámanos.*"

He sent Shane an apologetic look and lifted his hands in a what-can-you-do? kind of gesture. "She's my mother," he said. "Sorry."

"It's okay." Shane nodded back. "But you should talk her out of this. Seriously. It's dangerous."

"I know, man. I *know.*"

Enrique hurried to catch up. His mother was already half a block away.

Claire stood with Shane, staring at the poster promoting Captain Obvious, and Shane finally took Monica's bigger, brighter poster and firmly stapled it right over the top.

"Let's go," he said. "I guarantee this isn't over."

SEVEN

CLAIRE

It wasn't over, not by a long shot, but at least they were left alone to put up the rest of the posters; that didn't mean people weren't glaring at them, or saying mean things, but nobody actively tried to hurt them. Claire did wonder if Mrs. Ramos would be tearing down posters behind them—and if she'd approve of Oliver doing the same thing. Maybe they'd meet in the middle. That would be an interesting thing to witness.

By the time they'd stapled the last cardboard to a pole, in front of Morganville High ("Go Vipers!"), Claire was thoroughly worn out. This, she thought, had to be the worst day off ever.... They hadn't even stopped for much of a lunch, though they'd wolfed down some cookies between stops and had a couple of Cokes. Morganville wasn't a very big town, but they'd been down almost every street of it, and that was just about enough for one day in her opinion. She was going to voice it, but she didn't have to, because Shane gave her a look that told her he was just as tired, and said, "Can we skip the lab and go home?"

"Home," she said, and slipped her arm through his. The only weight now was the stapler dragging down her backpack (and the anti-vamp knife and extra stakes that she rarely left behind) but it still felt like a ton. Shane took it from her and slipped it on one shoulder, and she envied those muscles—and admired them, too. They felt so warm and firm beneath her fingers, and it made her a bit light-headed, never mind the exhaustion. "What do you think Monica's doing right now?"

"Bullying someone to make her a crappy Web site and some buttons?"

Claire groaned, because he was almost certainly right. "We created a monster."

"Well, no. But we're enabling one."

By common unspoken consent, they avoided the street Common Grounds was on, which put them on a different, less traveled avenue; it was one that held some bad memories, Claire realized, and wished they'd risked Oliver's wrath one more time.

This was the street where Shane's house had once stood. There was nothing in the spot now except a bare, weed-choked lot, a cracked foundation, and the crumbling remains of what would have once been a fireplace. Even the mailbox, which had been leaning before, had given up the ghost and fallen to pieces of random, rusted metal.

"We don't—maybe we should—" She couldn't think how to say it, or even if she should, but Shane just kept walking, eyes fixed on the pavement ahead.

"It's okay," he said. She might have even believed him, a little, except for the slight hunch to his shoulders, and the way he'd lowered his head to let his shaggy hair veil his expression. "It's just an empty lot."

It wasn't. It was full—full of grief and anger, anguish and terror. She could almost feel it like needles on her skin, an irresistible urge to slow down, to stop, to *look*. She wondered if Shane felt it, too. Maybe he did. He wasn't walking quite as quickly as they approached the silent empty spot, which was choked with trash, scattered fire-blackened bricks, and the snarled balls of tumbleweeds.

It was the spot where Shane's family home had once stood, before it had burned down, taking his sister away with it.

Just as they took their first steps in front of it, Shane stopped. Just . . . stopped, not moving at all, head still down, hands in his pockets. He slowly looked up, right into Claire's startled eyes, and said, "Did you hear that?"

She shook her head, confused. All she heard was the normal, constant background noise of daily life—TV sets whispering from distant houses, radios in passing cars, the rattle of blown tumbleweeds against chain-link fences.

And then she heard something that sounded like a very soft, but clear, whisper. She couldn't have said what it *meant*, couldn't make out the word, but it didn't sound like distant conversation, or TV dialogue, or anything like that. It sounded very . . . specific. And very close.

"Maybe . . . a cat?" she guessed. It could have been a cat. But she didn't see anything as she glanced over the ruins of Shane's childhood. The only things still recognizable about it having been a home was the foundation—cracked in places, but still there where it wasn't hidden by weeds—and the jumbled outline of what must have once been a brick fireplace.

Shane didn't look toward the lot at all. He kept looking at

her, and she saw his eyes widen just as she, too, heard what he was hearing.

A voice. A clear girl's voice, very, very soft, saying, *Shane.*

His face drained completely of color, and Claire thought for a second he was going to hit the pavement, but he managed to hold on, somehow, and turned toward the lot to say, "Lyss?" He took a tentative step toward it, but stopped at the edge of the sidewalk. "Alyssa?"

Shane.

It was very clear, and it did *not* sound like a real person's voice—there was something eerie and cold and distant about it. Claire remembered the draug, the vampires' enemies who lurked in water and lured with song; this held something of that quality to it—something just not right.

She grabbed Shane's sleeve as he started to step onto the lot's dirt. "No," she said. "Don't."

He stared at the tumbled wreckage of his house, and said, "I have to. She's here, Claire. It's Alyssa."

His sister, Claire knew, had died in the fire that had wrecked this house—and he hadn't been able to save her. It was the first, and maybe the biggest, trauma in a life that had since had way too many.

She didn't even try to argue that it was impossible for his sister to be here, talking to him. There were far crazier things in Morganville than that. Ghosts? Those were no more unusual than drunken frat boys on a Friday night.

But she was scared. Very scared. Because there was a vast difference between ghosts who manifested themselves in the Founder Houses—like the Glass House, in which they lived—and one who could talk from thin air, powered by nothing at all. The first kind she could explain, theoretically at least. This?

Not so much.

"I have to do this," Shane said again, and pulled free of her. He stepped into the weeds, into what had once been the carefully tended front lawn of a relatively stable family, and walked steadily forward. The broken remains of a sidewalk were hidden under those weeds, Claire realized; it was buckled and broken into raw chunks, but it was recognizable when she looked for it. Shane kept going forward, then stopped and said, "This used to be the front door."

Claire devoutly did *not* want to do it, but she couldn't leave him alone, not here, not like this. So she stepped forward, and instantly felt a chill close in over her—something that didn't want her here. The pins-and-needles feeling swept over her again, and she almost stopped and backed up . . . but she wasn't going to let it stop her.

Shane needed her.

She slipped her hand into his, and he squeezed it hard. His face was set, jawline tight, and whatever he was looking at, it was not the rubble in front of them. "She died upstairs," Shane said. "Lyss? Can you hear me?"

"I really don't know if this is a good—" Claire caught her breath as the pins and needles poked again, deeply. Painfully. She could almost see the tiny little stab marks on her arms, the beads of blood, though she knew there was no physical damage at all.

"Lyss?" Shane stepped forward, over the nonexistent threshold, into what would have been the house. "Alyssa—"

He got an answer. *Shane.* It was a sigh, full of something Claire couldn't really comprehend—maybe a sadness, maybe longing, maybe something darker. *You came back.*

He sucked in a deep, shaking breath, and let go of Claire's hand to reach forward, into empty air. "Oh God, Lyss, I thought— how can you still be—"

Always here, the whisper said. So much sadness; Claire could hear it now. The resentment she felt was that of a baby sister hating that someone else had taken her brother from her; it might be dangerous, but it was understandable, and the sadness brought a lump into Claire's throat. *Can't go. Help.*

"I can't," Shane whispered. "I can't help you. I couldn't then and I can't now, Lyss. . . . I don't know how, okay? I don't know what you need!"

Home.

There were tears shining in his eyes now, and he was shaking. "I can't," he said again. "Home's gone, Lyss. You have to—you have to move on. I have."

No.

There was a wisp of movement at the edge of Claire's vision, and then she felt a shove, a distinct shove, that made her take a step back toward the sidewalk. When she tried to move toward Shane again, the pins and needles came back, but it felt more like a pinch now, sudden and vicious. She hissed and grabbed her arm, and this time when she looked down, she saw she had a red mark, just as if someone had physically hurt her.

Alyssa really didn't care for the idea that her brother had found a girlfriend, and Claire found herself skipping backward, pushed and bullied back all the way to the sidewalk.

Shane stayed where he was. "Please, can I—can I see you?"

There was that faint hint of movement again, mists at the corners of her vision, and Claire thought that for a second she saw a ghostly shadow appear against the still-standing bricks of the fireplace . . . but it was gone in seconds, blown away.

Please help me, Alyssa's whisper said. *Shane, help me.*

"I don't know how!"

Don't leave me alone.

Claire suddenly didn't like where this was going. Maybe she'd seen too many Japanese horror movies, and maybe it was just a tingle of warning from generations of superstitious ancestors, but suddenly she *knew* that what Alyssa wanted was not to be saved, but for Shane to join her.

In death.

She didn't know what Shane might have done, because just as she came to that breath-stopping conclusion, she caught sight of a shiny black van pulling around the corner. For a second she didn't connect it to anything in particular, and then she recognized the logo on the van's door.

Great. "Shane—we've got company," she said. "Ghost-hunting company."

"What?" Shane turned and looked at her blankly, then at where she pointed. Not only had the ghost hunters arrived, but the two hosts—Angel and Jenna—were already out and walking toward them. Jenna had something in her hands that looked like an electronic metering device; it was making strange, weird noises like a frequency tuner. Angel had what looked like a tape recorder. And behind them, following with a bulky handheld camera on his shoulder, was Tyler.

"—Activity," Jenna was saying in an intense voice. "Definitely some significant signs here. I got a huge spike from the van, and it's even bigger now. Whatever's out here, it's definitely worth checking into."

"Where?" Angel sounded tired and more than a little irritated. "We've had a lot of false alarms already. If I didn't know better, I'd think the local residents were trying to screw us up—oh, hello. Look, it's the kids from the courthouse. Where's your pretty friend?"

Claire didn't know which to take offense at more—the implication that she wasn't pretty, or that Monica might be considered a friend. She was saved from answering by Shane, who walked up to her and kept walking until he was blocking the path to the vacant lot completely. "Get lost," he said flatly. "I'm not in the mood."

"Excuse me?" Jenna said, and tried to move around him. He got in her way. "Hey! This isn't private property. It's a public sidewalk! We are fully within our rights to be here."

While she and Shane were facing off, Claire heard Angel mutter to Tyler, "Make sure you're getting all this. It's great stuff. We can use it in the teasers. The town that didn't want to know."

"You," Shane said, and pointed past Angel, at Tyler and the camera. "Turn it off. Now."

"Can't do that, bro. We're working here," Tyler said. "Relax. Just let us do our job."

"Do it somewhere else. You don't do it here."

"Why?" Jenna was staring at him intently, and past him, at the empty lot. She held out her meter gadget, and Claire could hear the tones it gave off. She didn't need to be an expert in ghostology to know it was pinging like mad. "Something you don't want us to see, perhaps?"

"Just back the hell off, lady. I mean it——"

"We'll see about this," Angel said, and pulled out a cell phone. Theatrically, of course. "We *do* have a permit to film direct from the mayor's office!"

"Let's see it," Shane said. "Go ahead; call somebody. I'll wait." He stared Angel down until the other man put the phone away. "Yeah. Thought so. Look, just do us all a favor, okay? Call it a day, get in your van, and head to some other town where they don't mind your making fun of dead people, all right?"

"That's not what we're doing!" Jenna said sharply. "I'm very committed to trying to locate those who are lost and stuck, and finding a way to bring them some peace. How dare you say—"

"I don't know—because you arrange all this crap for ratings, advertisers, and money? Maybe that?" Shane stepped forward, and he was using all his size and attitude this time. "Just *go*. Get off this street."

The device that Jenna was holding gave a sudden shrill alarm; she jerked in surprise and stared at it, then turned it to Angel. Tyler angled in to get a close-up of the meter.

"What?" Shane snapped.

"We got a huge electromagnetic spike," Jenna said. "It's coming from that vacant lot behind you. I've never seen anything like it—"

Shane. It was a very clear, cold, longing whisper, and it came from right behind them. And it just froze everyone right in place. Claire had a vivid, clear snapshot of them: Tyler, mouth open behind his camera; Angel, stunned silent; Jenna, eyes wide.

And Shane.

Shane's lips parted, but he didn't speak. His face had gone blank and pale, and he actually took a long step backward, pulling Claire with him. She didn't mind. That voice had a scary, otherworldly quality that didn't sound human.

Angel almost dropped his recorder, but he gained his composure and moved in to the camera to get a close-up. "Did you hear that?" he asked Tyler, then turned to Jenna. "That was no EVP. That was a *voice*."

"Someone's messing with us," Jenna said in annoyance. "Cut, Tyler."

"I don't think so," he said. "Rolling. Keep going."

"Tyler!"

"Rolling, Jenna, keep rolling!"

"I'm telling you, the locals are having us on. We'll probably find some kind of EM transmitter out here, and some giggling high schooler with a megaphone. . . ."

"Rolling!"

"Okay, okay, it's digital. At least you're not wasting film. . . ." She took in a deep breath and said, in her tense ghost-hunting voice, "We may have gotten an actual spirit contact! I can't even begin to describe how incredibly rare this is!"

"Can you speak to us again?" Angel said, and if possible, he got even more pompous. "You said a name. Can you say it again?"

Nothing.

"I think it said *shame*," Jenna said. "Is it a shame you're gone? Are you ashamed of something?"

"Oh, for the love of—" Claire couldn't bite back her exasperation. "Come on. We have to go, now." She very deliberately didn't use his name. They didn't seem bright enough to make the connection, but even so . . .

"That's Alyssa," Shane said. "I'm telling you, it's her. My sister is *right there.*"

Dammit. Well, there went her entire *nothing to see here, move along* plan.

"No such thing as ghosts," she said, and pointedly looked at the camera. Shane, recovering from the shock, finally got back on script enough to nod. "I think someone's messing with you. Really. You need to just—chalk it up to locals being stupid."

"Or," Shane said, "you could poke around in the dark. That's fun. There might be fewer annoying visitors if you tried it."

"Excuse me?" Jenna said. "Are you threatening us?"

"No, just making an observation. I mean, wandering around in the dark isn't a good idea, lady. Ask anybody." He shrugged. "Meth. It's a cancer around here. So I've heard, anyway."

"Oh," she said, and seemed to take it seriously for the first time. "It is a problem in a lot of places. I should have thought of that. Guys, maybe we should pack it in until later."

"But we *heard that*," Angel protested. "We should at least do EVP in the vacant lot, just in case!"

Shane started to object, but Claire tugged at his arm, urgently. *Let them*, she mouthed, and he finally shrugged and stepped out of the way. "Knock yourself out," he said. "Try not to get bitten by any rattlesnakes or anything."

"Snakes?" Tyler suddenly sounded very, very nervous.

"Or, you know, scorpions," Claire said cheerfully. "And tarantulas. We have those. Oh, and black widows and brown recluse spiders—they love it out here. You'll find them all over the place. If you get bitten, just be sure to, you know, call 911. They can most always save you."

"Most always," Shane echoed.

They walked on, leaving the three visitors—no longer quite so eager to delve in—debating the risks. As they did, Shane pulled out his phone.

"What are you doing?" she asked.

"Texting Michael," he said. "He needs to get to somebody in the vamp hierarchy and get these idiots off the street before this becomes really, really public and a big PR problem. . . ." He paused and looked up. "Oh hell. Twice in one day? Who did I piss off upstairs to make that happen?"

He meant that Monica Morrell had just crossed their path, again. She was standing against the side of a big, trashy-looking van, tongue wrestling her current boy admirer, just around the corner from where Shane's home had once been. Like most of Monica's boyfriends, her current beau was a big side of beef, sporty, with an IQ of about room temperature, and she was climbing him like ivy up a tree.

"Excuse me, Dan," Shane said as they got closer. "I think you got something on you—oh, hey, Monica. Didn't see you there."

She broke off the kiss to glare at him. "Freak."

"Any particular reason you're hanging out here, exactly? Not your usual territory. I don't see any stores within credit-card distance."

Her boyfriend—Dan, apparently—looked like a varsity football jock; he had the muscles, the bulk, and the jarhead hairstyle. Monica tended to attract the big-but-dumb ones, and this one, from the questioning look he sent toward them, seemed to run to type. "She said this was the right place," he said, "to set up the—"

"Shut up," Monica said.

"Set up the what?" Shane asked. "Would you maybe be planning to mess with our ghost-hunting friends?"

"Aren't you?" she shot back. "Yeah. We've got this thing in the van, totally guaranteed to screw up their—what is it?"

"Screw up their shit," Dan said, earnestly. "You know, their monitoring shit. It's going to play Black Sabbath backward and really freak 'em out. I read it on the Internet."

"Jesus, Dan," Shane said. He almost sounded impressed. "You are just . . . landmark stupid, aren't you? Has Guinness called yet about that world record?"

Dan growled and came at him, and that was of course a mistake; Shane balanced lightly on the balls of his feet, avoided his rush, dodged back toward the van, and as Dan lined up to rush him again, sidestepped like a matador and sent Dan crashing like a bullet headfirst into the metal.

Dan didn't go down, but he definitely thought about it. He leaned heavily on the metal and stared blankly into the distance for a minute. His forehead had a vivid red mark on it, and Shane said, "You probably ought to get some ice on that, man."

"Yeah," Dan said. "Yeah, thanks, bro." He didn't dare come after Shane again, so he turned on Monica with a glare. "Well? Brilliant plan, *Mayor.* What else you got?"

"Oh, Dan, don't be like that—"

"Play your own stupid pranks for a change."

Monica gave him a searing glare of disappointment, and he shrugged and got in the van. In seconds, it fired up and drove away in a belch of smoke.

Leaving Monica behind. She shot Claire a look of fury mixed with outrage. "I was trying to help get those jackasses out of town. Being proactive and all mayorlike! What the hell were *you* two doing? Auditioning for starring roles in their stupid show?"

They'd attracted attention, of course. It wasn't from surrounding houses, since no one bothered to look outside at mysterious fighting in the streets for entirely sensible reasons, but from the team from *After Death* that had come charging over with cameras, microphones, and gadgets. Angel immediately fixed his model's smile straight on Monica. "Are these two bothering you, lovely lady?"

"Please," Claire muttered, but it was too late; Monica was batting her eyes and putting on her best wounded-butterfly act as she crowded up next to her newly arrived knight in shining leather shoes.

"Oh yes," she breathed. "Did you see? He beat up my boyfriend!"

"Call the police," Angel ordered Tyler, who was still recording, but Tyler was distracted by Jenna, who was whacking her electronic meter device in obvious irritation.

"Hey, hey, hey, it's technology, not a drum!" he said, and took it from her. "What? What's wrong with it?"

"I had a strong signal!" she said. "It was there, I swear it was, but it just vanished about thirty seconds ago. I think they scared it off."

"You were reading something wrong."

"I saw it! It was maxed out in that vacant lot—I'm telling you. . . ."

"Oh—um, that was my boyfriend," Monica said, and brought the overlapping chaos to a dead halt. "He had the van that just took off? He was broadcasting a signal to make you think it was some kind of ghost. He thought it was kind of funny."

Angel was looking at Monica with a heartbroken expression. "Why would you do that?"

"It was Dan, not—"

"Why do teenagers do anything?" Jenna snapped. She stepped into Monica's space, looking for the world as if she was feeling just as strong an impulse to slap the girl as Claire was. "Get lost, before I call the cops."

"It's not against the law!"

"You're right. Get lost before I do something that *is* against the law, like putting my fist in your face."

"Hey!" Monica stepped into *Jenna's* space now, cheeks flushing a bright, hectic pink. "Do you know who I am?"

"Last year's high school queen bee who's no longer relevant but still thinks she is?" Jenna shot back, and Claire's eyes widened at the accuracy of the thrust. So did Monica's. "Look, sweetie, I've seen a dozen one-stoplight towns just like this, and there's always somebody just like you who thinks you're . . . well, somebody."

Monica opened her mouth to reply, but didn't. She was remembering that she was, in fact, nobody, at least by her own standards; she was just another bully now, with nothing to back it up. She didn't even have her best friends to enable her. Even her Cro-Magnon boyfriend had bailed on her at the first sign of trouble.

And it hurt. In that moment, though she shouldn't have, Claire felt a little twinge of sympathy.

"I'm running for mayor!" Monica rallied enough to snap back. "So careful what you say, because my first official act would be running you three out of town on a rail!"

Jenna shrugged and glared at Angel, who was still looking gravely disappointed, and said, "Come on, let's retake that last bit over in the vacant lot. We can still save some of the footage." She set out at a rapid pace around the corner, heading for the vacant lot. After a hesitation, Tyler followed her.

Angel shrugged and said, "I'm sorry, but you see how it is. We have work to do." This time, there was no hand kissing, and not much flirting, either.

"Wait," Monica said as he started to walk off. "You're just going to leave me here? Alone? With *them*?"

Angel flashed her a perfect smile but kept walking. "I'm sure they'll see you get home safe."

"Oh yeah," Shane said. "On my to-do list, right after discovering Atlantis. Enjoy your walk, Princess Mayor." He put his arm around Claire and tipped her chin up to look into her eyes. "You okay? Not hurt?"

"No," she said. "You?"

"The only way Dan can actually hurt me is to try to have a conversation. He may be on the college football team, but trust me, he's just barely junior varsity on street fighting."

Monica looked from the departing television people back to the two of them, then at the empty street. Looking for some kind of third option, Claire thought. "You could just go it alone," Claire said, with a little too much sweetness. "I'm sure you'll be safe. After all, *everybody* knows who you are."

"Thanks to our posters," Shane put in.

"You know, it's your fault my life is such a hell, anyway, so spare me your little gestures!"

"So now you're blaming us for your life falling apart, after a lifetime of earning it? Interesting."

"My life was fine before you came here!" Monica spat.

Shane gave her a long, level look. "You know whose life wasn't so fine? Pretty much everybody else's. Including the vampires', not that I'm counting that for a plus, but you get the idea."

She ignored Shane. Oddly, because those two were almost always gasoline and a match. "I need an escort home," she announced to the air somewhere between the two of them. "Tell me you're going that way."

Shane shrugged when Claire glanced at him. "Well, I guess we'd better. How can she be mayor if she's dead in a ditch?"

"She just taunted you with the voice of your *dead sister!*"

"No," Monica said.

"What?" Claire snapped; she was getting really angry now, angry enough to do or say something she couldn't take back. And Shane, oddly, wasn't.

"I didn't do that," Monica said, and met Shane's eyes. "I wouldn't do that. Dan and I were messing with their electronics, and we were planning to sneak over and make some rattling noises. But I swear, I didn't pretend to be your *sister.*"

"She wouldn't," Shane said softly. "Not after Richard, anyway." There was, Claire realized, some kind of understanding between the two of them now, something she didn't quite get but could see; it wasn't affection, and it sure wasn't a crush, but a kind of mutual . . . caution. As if they understood each of them had a place that could be hurt, and neither was willing to go there anymore.

"Then what *was* that? Was it really—really—" She couldn't finish the thought. She was feeling a little unstuck now, as if the world were bending around her. . . . She thought she'd seen enough of Morganville that something like that would never happen again.

"I don't know," Shane said, "but I intend to find out."

Walking Monica home was just exactly as fun as Claire expected, which was not fun at all. She complained about having to walk in her heels (to which Shane, proving he was not *totally* off the Let's Hate Monica bandwagon, suggested she mount her broom and fly home); she complained about the hot weather, and sweat ruining her outfit; she complained about the lack of cab service (Claire had to agree she had a point there—Morganville desperately needed cabs).

Claire had begun to tune her out by that point, since they were within sight of Monica's luxury apartment complex (the only one in Morganville, in fact, with ten apartments that cost more than most of the town could even think about paying). Monica had sold the Morrell family home, which had mostly survived all the troubles of the past few years intact except for party damage, and made a tidy bank account to allow her to not work for at least a couple of years, though it probably wouldn't last at the rate Monica blew through designer shoes.

And then Monica said, "I heard people talking around town today. Your friends ought to be watching their backs, 'cause the knives are out."

That got Claire's attention, fast. Shane's, too. They both stopped walking, and Monica clomped on a few more steps before coming to a halt and saying, "What? Like you didn't know?"

"What are you talking about?" Shane closed the distance toward her, fast. "What did you hear? Spill it!"

"Hey, hey, hold on!" She tried to back up, but she overbalanced on her precarious heels and almost went down; Shane grabbed her arm and steadied her, and didn't let go. "Look, I don't know why you're so surprised and all! Let go!"

"Not until you answer the question. What about Michael and Eve?"

"Oh, come on. A vamp marrying a human gets the fanged ones all upset, and Eve made herself look like the ultimate fang-banger to all the humans by putting a ring on one, so what did you expect, exactly? Flowers and parades? This is Texas. We're still figuring out how to *spell* tolerance."

"I said, what do you know about it? Where? When? Who's involved?"

"Let go, jerk!"

He didn't say anything, but Claire was almost sure he squeezed, because Monica made a funny little sound and went very still. "Okay," she said. "Okay, jackass, you win. It's just general talk as far as I know, but some people are saying an example should be made. Michael and Eve are just handy targets standing in the middle of the war zone. Come to think of it, so's your girlfriend, what with all her cozying up to Amelie."

Shane let her go. "You're one to talk."

"Yeah, I am. I know what it's like to think you're secure and safe and all of a sudden be standing all alone. You think you and your friends are the only ones in the crosshairs? Do you have any idea how many people want to hurt *me*?"

Monica was more self-aware than Claire had ever given her credit for. She knew how things were—maybe better than Shane, surprisingly enough. She'd probably had to learn how to protect herself fast, once the town had stopped being cowed by her status as Self-Crowned Princess.

"Then you shouldn't be pissing off the only ones who might listen to you when you scream for help," Shane said. "Get me?"

Monica finally nodded, a little unwillingly. She shot a quick, unreadable look at Claire, and then turned and strode up the walk to her apartment. They watched as she produced a key (though where she'd kept it on that skintight dress was a mystery) and unlocked her door. Once she was inside, and the lights were on, Shane put his hands in his pockets and extended an elbow to Claire, who threaded her arm through his.

"You're super nice to her, all of a sudden," Claire said.

"Ha. If I was super nice to her, she wouldn't have bruises on her arm right now," he said. "But I'm willing to forget to hate her, every once in a while. She's had it rough these past couple of years."

"So have you."

He flashed her a smile. "I never did have much, so having it rough came with the territory. I was conditioned for it. And you're forgetting the most important thing that's different."

"You don't have a fashion addiction to skintight clothes?"

"I have you," he said, and the warmth in his voice took her breath away. She let go of his arm and crowded in close as they walked, and he hugged her close. It was awkward making progress that way, but it felt so sweet. "Okay, and I don't have a fashion addiction. Valid point."

"You don't think she knows something about a plot to hurt Michael and Eve, do you? The way she said that back there . . ."

"I don't know," Shane said. "I don't think she'd hide it; she'd really like teasing us with it, but she'd give it up. She'd want to, I think. It's not as if she wants Michael dead, anyway. She always had a little bit of a thing for him."

"And you," Claire said, and elbowed him. "More than a little bit."

"Ugh. Please don't say that or I'll lose my will to live."

"I love you." It came out of her spontaneously, and she felt a little jolt of adrenaline, then a little burst of fear right on the heels of it. There had been no reason to say it now, walking down the street, but it had just seemed . . . right. She was a little afraid that Shane would think it was clingy, or fake, but when she glanced over at him, she saw he was smiling—an easy, relaxed smile, uncomplicated and happy.

It wasn't something she saw very often, and it made her feel glorious.

"I love you, too," he said, and that felt like some kind of milestone to her, that they felt easy enough with each other to just say it whenever they wanted, without feeling awkward about it, or afraid.

We're growing up, she thought. *We're growing up together.*

He put his arm around her, and they walked close together, all the way home. The setting sun was lurid reds and golds, spilling into the vast and open sky, and it was as beautiful a thing as Claire had ever seen in Morganville.

Peaceful.

It was the last of that, though.

EIGHT

AMELIE

)

I knew of no one, vampire or human, who could detour Myrnin from a course once he had decided on it, whether it was mad, manic, destructive, or simply single-minded. So when the guards informed me that he had refused to stop at the checkpoint to the hallway of my office, I did not bother to order them to try to detain him. It might have been possible for a few moments, an hour, a day, but Myrnin wouldn't forget. He would simply start again, and sooner or later, he'd succeed.

I pressed the button on my phone—still such an awkward and common device, to my mind, nothing attractive about it—and informed my assistant that upon his arrival she should not stand in his way. Poor thing, she had taken enough abuse lately, from humans as well as from vampires.

Only I could handle Myrnin with any measure of success.

He exploded through my doorway with the force of a tropical storm, and indeed the riot of colors about his person reminded me of that . . . so many shades, and none of them complementary. I did not bother to catalog all the offenses, but they began with the jacket he had chosen. I had no name for that particular hue of orange, other than *unfortunate.*

"This is my last attempt at making you see sense," he said. Shouted, actually. "Damn you, how long have we worked, how many sacrifices have we made? To see you throw that all away for *him . . .*"

I had already decided, well before his grand entrance, what my first move would be, and with an economy of motion, I slapped him full across the face. The force of it would have felled a strong mortal; it certainly made Myrnin pause, with the mark of the blow blushing a very faint pink in the shape of my fingers.

He blinked.

"You may save your well-rehearsed speech," I said. "I'll hear none of it. This ill-advised intrusion is at an end."

"Amelie, we have been friends for—"

"Don't presume to tell me how many years. I can count as well as you, or possibly better on the days when you're insane," I snapped back. "Sit down."

He did, looking oddly watchful. I paced. I'd been doing that more frequently than was my normal habit, but I put it down to raw nerves. Morganville lately had seemed exasperating, a broken toy that would never be put right no matter how much time and love I lavished on the repairs.

Myrnin said, "You even move like he does now."

"Silence!" I whirled on him, snarling, and knew my eyes had gone deep crimson.

"No," he said, with an eerie sort of calm. Myrnin was many

things, but he was rarely calm, and when he was, it was time to worry. "There are some people who may say this is a good match for you, that you needed a strong right arm to calm the fears of the vampires and subdue the human population. I am not one. Sam gentled you, Amelie. He made you feel more a part of the world you rule. Oliver will never do that. He feels no responsibility for those he crushes, and—"

"Foul his name again and we're finished," I interrupted. I meant it, and it dripped from every syllable I spoke.

Myrnin sat still for a moment, staring into my eyes, and then he nodded. "Then we are indeed," he said. "I just had to be certain that you were beyond my hope, and my help. But if he has you tied this close, he will have you do as he wishes. Whomever it hurts."

"Do you think I am so—so stupid? So utterly weak that I would allow any man to—"

"Not just a man," Myrnin said. "He swayed a nation to kill its king, once. He persuades. He influences. Perhaps he doesn't even intend to do so, but it's in his nature. And while you are more powerful than he by far, once he has your trust, there is no saying what he might be able to accomplish, through you."

His words left me cold inside, a chill I'd not felt since the moment I'd finally acknowledged the aching need for Oliver's regard, for his loyalty, for his attention. I had been alone for so long; Michael's grandfather Sam Glass and I had loved, but save for a few precious times, always carefully, and from afar. Oliver had come at me like a storm, and the fury of it was . . . cleansing.

But was Myrnin right? Could I be falling victim, as so many had, to Oliver's deadly charm? Was what I was doing here right, or simply convenient to his ambitions?

I slowly sat down in a chair across from my oldest living friend, the one who—in the end—I trusted more than any still walking the earth, and said, "I know my own mind, Myrnin. I am Amelie. I am the Founder of Morganville, and what I do here, I do for the good of all. You may trust that. You *must*."

He had a sadness in his eyes that I could not understand, but then, who ever had understood Myrnin fully? I couldn't make that claim, and neither could Claire, the girl he trusted so much. And then he stood, and with the ease of thousands of years of experience, he made a graceful, ages-old bow, took my hand in his, and kissed it with the greatest of love and respect.

"Farewell," he said.

And then he was gone.

I slowly drew my hand back to my chest, frowning, and became aware that I was cradling it, rubbing the spot where his lips had pressed as if they had burned me. *Farewell.* He'd thrown tantrums many times, threatened to leave, but this—this seemed different.

It was a calm, ordered, and above all *sad* departure.

"Myrnin?" I said softly into the silence, but it was too late.

Far too late.

NINE

CLAIRE

⚬

Shane preceded Claire into the house by a couple of steps as she shut and locked the door behind them; apparently that was a lucky thing, because as she was turning the dead bolt, she heard him say, "Oh, crap," in a voice that was choked with laughter, and then a startled yelp from Eve, followed by the sound of scrambling and flailing. Shane backed up next to Claire and held her back when she would have moved forward.

"Trust me," he said. "Wait a second."

Michael and Eve were in the parlor, the front living area that was so rarely used, except for dropping coats and bags and miscellaneous stuff, and from the hasty whispers and rustles of clothes, Claire quickly figured out exactly why Shane was holding her back.

Oh.

"I guess I should have said, *Put your pants on*," Shane said, loudly enough that they could hear. "Alert, there's a barely legal girl out here."

"Hey!" Claire swiped a hand at him, which he easily avoided. "What were they doing?"

"What do you *think*?"

Pink-faced, Eve leaned around the frame of the doorway and said, "Um . . . hi. You're early."

"Nope," Shane said with merciless good cheer. "It's sundown. Not a bit early. You got clothes on?"

"Yes!" Eve said. Her cheeks burned brighter. "Of course! And you didn't see anything anyway." There was a bit of worry to her voice, though, and Shane made it worse with a big, utterly unsympathetic smile.

"Married people," he said to Claire. "They're a menace."

Eve eased out of the door, zipping up her blouse—it was one of those with a front zip—and cleared her throat. "Right," she said. "We really need to talk, you guys."

"You know, my dad sucked at most things, but he did give me the birds and bees Q&A when I was ten, so I'm good," Shane said. Man, he was enjoying this way too much. "Claire?"

She nodded soberly. "I think I understand the basics."

Eve, still blushing, rolled her eyes. "I'm serious!"

Michael finally appeared behind her. He was dressed, kind of; his shirt was unbuttoned, though he was doing it up as quickly as he could. "Eve's right," he said, and he wasn't kidding at all. "We need to talk, guys."

"No, we don't," Shane said. "Just text me or something next time. We could go grab a burger or a movie or—"

Michael shook his head and walked inside the parlor. Eve followed him. Shane sent Claire a look that had a little bit of alarm in it, and finally shrugged. "Guess we're talking," he said. "Whether we want to or not."

Michael and Eve hadn't taken seats, when the two of them came in; they were standing with their hands clasped, for solidarity, apparently.

"Uh-oh," Shane murmured, and then put on a cheerful smile. "So, Mikey, what up? Because this looks like more than just a 'how was your day' kind of discussion."

"We needed to talk about something," Eve said. She looked nervous, and—for Eve—she'd dressed super plainly, just a black shirt and jeans, not a single skull or shiny thing in evidence, except for the subtle glimmer of her wedding ring. "Sorry, guys. Sit down."

"You first," Shane said as Claire dumped her backpack with a heavy *clunk* by the wall. Michael exchanged a look with Eve, and then sat beside her on the old velvet sofa, while Claire settled in the armchair and Shane leaned on the top of it, his hand on her shoulder. "If we're playing guessing games, I'm going to go with— you're pregnant. Wait, can you be? I mean, can the two of you . . . ?"

Eve flinched and avoided looking at the two of them. "That's not it," she said, and bit her lip. She twisted her wedding ring in agitation, and then finally said, "We've been talking about getting our own place, guys. Not because we don't love you, we do, but—"

"But we need our own space," Michael said. "I know it seems weird, but for us to feel really together, married, we need to get some time to ourselves, and you know how it is here; we're all in one another's business here."

"And there's only one bathroom," Eve said mournfully. "I *really* need a bathroom."

Claire had suspected it was coming, but that didn't make it feel any better. She instinctively reached up for Shane's hand, and his fingers closing over hers made her feel a little steadier. She'd gotten so used to the idea of the four of them together, always together, that hearing Michael talk about moving stirred up feelings she'd thought she'd outgrown . . . feelings that hadn't been on her radar since she'd first walked in the door of the Glass House.

She suddenly felt vulnerable, alone, and rejected. She felt homesick, even though she was home, because home wasn't the way she'd left it this morning.

"We want you to be happy," Claire managed to say. Her voice sounded small and a little hurt, and she didn't mean it that way, not at all. "But you can't move out—it's your house, Michael. I mean, it's the *Glass* House. And you two are . . . Glass. We're not."

"Screw that," Shane said immediately. "Sure, I want you two crazy kids to be happy, but you're talking about busting up something that's good, really good, and I don't like it, and I'm not going to be all noble and pretend I do. Together, we're strong—you've said that yourself, Michael. Now all of a sudden you want more privacy? Dude, that's about as logical as *Let's split up* in a horror movie!"

Michael gave him a look as he finished buttoning his shirt. "I think it's pretty obvious privacy's an issue."

"Not if you don't decide to get crazy in a room without a locking door. Or, you know, a *door.*"

"It's just that we were waiting on you guys, and we were nervous, and . . . it just happened," Eve said. "And we're *married.* We have the right to get crazy if we want to. Anywhere. At any time."

"Okay, I get that," Shane said. "Hell, I'd like a little spontaneous sexytime, too, but is it worth putting us all in danger? Because Morganville ain't safe, guys. You know that. You go out of this house, or make us leave it, and something is going to happen. Something bad."

"Have you taken up Miranda's fortune-telling?" Eve asked. "I could say something about crystal balls. . . ."

"Don't need a psychic friend to tell me it's nasty out there and bound to get worse. Michael, you're on Team Vampire. Are you saying you don't think it's going toxic with Amelie and Oliver in charge?"

Michael didn't try to answer that one, because he couldn't; they'd all agreed on it already.

Eve jumped in, instead. "We could get a house in the vampire quarter," she said. "Free. It's part of Michael's citizenship in town. It wouldn't be a problem except—"

"Except that you'd be living in Vamp Central, and the only thing with a pulse in a couple of square blocks, surrounded by people who think of you as an attractively shaped plasma container?" Shane asked. "Problem. Oh, another problem: Mikey, you said yourself that being around us, meaning *all* of us, helped you cope with your instincts. Now you're talking about isolating yourselves with a bunch of also-deads. Not smart, man. It'll make you more vamp, and it'll put Eve in more danger, too."

"I never said we were moving to the vampire quarter," Michael said. "Eve was just pointing out we could, not that we would. We could find something else, something close. The old Profit place is still for sale down the street. Amelie gave me a bequest, so I've got money to put down."

"Michael . . . We are *not* moving into that pit," Eve said. It sounded like an old argument. "It smells like cat urine and old-man clothes, and it's so ancient, it makes this place look like the house of the future. I don't think it has phone lines, never mind Internet. Might as well live in a cardboard box."

"Always an option," Shane said cheerfully. "And you'd have a huge bathroom. Like, the entire world."

"Ugh, gross."

"It's what you pay me for."

"Remind me to give you a negative raise."

"This isn't getting us anywhere," Michael interrupted, and shut them both down, hard. "Besides, it's not just the four of us anymore. It's Miranda."

The conversation came to a sudden and vivid halt, and they all waited to see what would happen. It was night; that meant Miranda had physical form.

But it didn't necessarily mean she could hear everything.

Claire lowered her voice to an instinctive, fierce whisper. "Hey! Don't be that way!"

"Look, I'm not saying I don't have sympathy for her; I do, a lot. I used to *be* her," Michael whispered back. "I know what it feels like being trapped in here. It drives you half crazy, and the only way you can survive it, the *only* way, is to be around people who think of you as . . . normal. But she doesn't have that. We know what she is. We know she's around all the time, and that means she tiptoes around us, and we tiptoe around her, and—it's just not good, okay? It's not."

"So, what do you want me to do?" Miranda asked. They all flinched and turned. She hadn't been there before, but now she'd appeared in the doorway to the hall, just like the spooky ghost she sometimes was. Claire was almost sure it was deliberate. "Leave?"

"You can't," Michael said. He did it gently, but there wasn't any doubt in it, either. "Mir, you knew when you came here that last time"—when she'd been killed here, he meant—"that there'd never be a way to leave again. The house saved you, and protects you, but you have to stay inside."

"Just because you did?" Miranda said. There was something different about her now, Claire realized; she was wearing a definitely not-Miranda outfit. No dowdy oversized dresses this time, or cheap fraying sweaters; she was wearing a skintight black sheer shirt with a black skull printed on it, and beneath that, a red scoop-neck that somehow managed to give her cleavage—just the suggestion, but still. For Miranda, that was . . . quite a change. "I'm not you, Michael."

"Maybe not, but do you have to become Eve?" Shane asked. "Because I'm pretty sure you raided her closet."

"I bought those for her!" Eve protested. "And anyway, she looks cute in them."

She did. Miranda had also gathered her hair up in two thick ponytails on either side of her head, and used a little of Eve's eyeliner. It was a little Goth, but not full-on, either. It suited her.

"It's me, isn't it?" Miranda said, ignoring both Eve and Shane this time. She was totally fixed on Michael, her eyes steady and wide. "It's about me, being here all the time. You feel like you can't hide from me. Well, that's true. You can't. I'm sorry, but that's just how it is, and you know it better than anyone. You can't just . . . turn off, like some kind of light. You're here, and you're bored."

"I know," Michael said. "Mir—"

"That's why you don't want to stay here. Because I'm here. It's not about them at all."

"No, honey, it's not really—" Eve bit her lip and glanced from Michael to Miranda and then back again. "It's not that, I swear. . . ."

"Don't swear," Miranda said, "because I know I'm right."

"She is," Michael said. When Eve turned toward him, he held up a hand to stop the outburst. "I'm sorry, but like I said, I've been there. I know how it feels. I can't just . . . ignore her. And I can't enjoy life in here knowing how miserable she is, or at least is going to be."

"You were miserable?" Eve said in a small voice. "Really? With us?"

"No—I didn't mean—" He made a frustrated sound and plumped down in one of the chairs, elbows on his knees. "It's hard to explain. Being around you, the three of you, was all that made things bearable, most days. The world just keeps getting smaller and smaller until it smothers you like a plastic bag over your face. With her here, I—I remember how that feels. I dream about it."

"So what am I supposed to do?" Miranda demanded. "I saved Claire's life, you know! I *died* for her!"

"I know that!" Michael snapped back. "I just wish you'd done it somewhere else!"

Even Shane sucked in a breath at that one and said, softly, "Bro—"

"No," Miranda said. Her chin was trembling, and she blinked back tears, but she didn't fall apart. Claire felt an aching urge to hug her, but Miranda looked as if she might break if anyone touched her. "It's not his fault. He's right. I made this happen, and it isn't fair. Not to him, not to me, not to anybody. It's a mess, and I did it. I thought—I just thought that it was perfect. That I'd finally have a real home, real family, people who—" Her voice broke and faded, and she shook her head. "I should have known. I don't get those things."

"I didn't mean that—," Michael said, but she turned and walked off.

None of them reacted at first. Claire thought nobody quite knew what to think, or to do, and then she saw Michael flinch and rise to his feet. She didn't know why until she heard the front door opening.

"No!" he shouted, and flashed at vampire-speed out of the room.

"The hell?" Shane blurted, and rushed after him, followed by Eve and Claire. "What—"

Claire pushed past him as he stopped, and she sucked in a deep, startled breath.

Because Miranda was *outside.* On the porch. And Michael was standing there, holding on to her arm as she fought to pull free. He was holding on to the doorframe, stretched fully out, and Miranda must have had a tiger's strength in that small body, because he was clearly having trouble keeping his grip. "Stop!" he yelled at her. "Miranda, I'm not letting you do this!"

"You can't stop me!" she screamed back, and there were tears streaking her face now in uneven trains of running eyeliner. She looked horrified and tragic and very, very upset. "Let go!"

"Come back inside. We can talk about it!"

"There's nothing to talk about. You don't want me here, so I just need to go!"

"You can't go—you'll die!" Claire blurted. She pushed past Michael and out onto the porch and grabbed Miranda in a bear hug. She could feel the girl's not-quite-real heart pounding against her forearm, out of terror, anger, or sheer adrenaline. "Miranda, *think.* Come back inside and we'll talk it over, all right? None of us wants you to die out here!"

"I'm dying in there, if you all leave! This way you can stay; you can be happy again—"

"It's not you; I never meant that!" Michael was afraid, Claire thought, really and starkly afraid that this was all his fault. "You can't do this. We'll work it out."

Miranda went very still for a second, though her heart continued to race uncontrollably fast, and she let out a deep, surrendering sigh. "All right," she said. "You can let go."

Michael said, "If you come inside, sure."

"I will."

Claire loosened her grip, just a little.

And it was just enough for Miranda to twist like a wild thing, ponytails whipping in Claire's face, and when Michael yelled and tried to pull her in, Miranda grabbed hold of his arm and bit him, hard enough to make him let go.

And then she stumbled backward, free, down the steps, and sprawled on the ground in the yard.

They all froze—Miranda, Claire, Michael, Eve, and Shane who had lunged out as well. The only thing moving was a single fluttering moth circling the yellow glow of the porch light.

Miranda slowly got up.

"Um . . . ," Shane said, when no one spoke. "Shouldn't she be, I don't know, dissolving?"

Michael took a step down toward her, and Miranda skipped backward. He held out his hand, palm out, as if she were a lost child who might bolt out into traffic. "Mir, wait. *Wait.* Look at yourself. Shane's right. You're not—going away."

"I'm still on the property."

"It doesn't work that way," he said. "I couldn't leave the doorway, let alone get down into the yard. Claire?" He looked at her as she stepped down next to him, because she'd had a brief period trapped in a ghostly state, too. She nodded.

"I couldn't leave, either," she said. "Miranda, how are you doing this?"

"I'm not!" She took another step backward down the sidewalk, toward the fence. "I'm just trying to—to get out of your hair, okay? If you'll just let me go!"

It seemed so quiet out tonight. The houses of Lot Street were sketched out in broad strokes of grays; the sky overhead had turned the color of lapis, and the stars were bright and cold. There were no clouds. The temperature had already fallen at least ten degrees, as was typical for the desert; it'd dip down almost to freezing before dawn.

"How did it feel? Going outside?" Michael asked.

Miranda gave a little shudder. "Like . . . pushing through some kind of plastic wrap, I guess. It felt cold, but it's colder out here. Much colder. Like I'm moving away from a fire."

"But you feel okay? Not coming to pieces?" Eve said. She was watching with wide, scared eyes. "Miranda, please, don't go any farther, okay? Just stay where you are. Let's—think about this. If you don't want us to go, we'll stay, okay? We'll all stay in the house. We'll all be friends and be a family for you. I promise. We won't let you down."

"It's better if I go." Miranda shuddered again. She looked pale now, but not exactly ghostly. Just cold. Claire wondered if she should get her a coat, but that was stupid; the idea was to get her back *in*, not help her stay out.

That plan didn't seem to be working so well, because as Claire tried to take a step closer, Miranda opened the front gate in the leaning picket fence, which was badly in need of paint.

"No!" the four of them said, in chorus, and Michael took a chance, a big one. He rushed the girl, at vampire-speed, hoping to get hold and pull her back inside before she stepped out onto the public sidewalk, off Glass House property altogether.

But he didn't make it.

Miranda ducked and ran all the way to the street.

To the *middle* of the street, where she stopped, shuddering almost constantly now, and looked up at the wide Texas sky, the moon, the stars.

"I'm okay," she said. "I'm going to be okay. See? I don't have to be inside all the time. I can go out. I'm fine. . . ."

But she wasn't fine; they could all see it. She was milky pale and her teeth were chattering. It wasn't that cold outside; Claire's breath wasn't even steaming, but from the way Miranda was shaking, it might as well have been below freezing.

"You're not fine," Eve said. "Mir, please, come back. You've proven your point. Yeah, you can leave—" She glanced at Michael and mouthed, *Why?*, but he only shrugged. "You can leave anytime you want. So let's go inside and celebrate, okay? Besides, it's dark. You're vamp bait in the middle of the street like this."

"What are they gonna do—bite her?" Shane asked. "She's *dead*, Eve. I don't even think she has blood."

"Yes, she does," Michael said. He was watching Miranda with a concerned expression now. "She's got a living body, for the nighttime, just like I did. She can be hurt at night. And drained. It just wouldn't kill her permanently; at least I don't think it would. . . . I think she'd come back."

"Renewable blood resources," Eve said softly. "There's a nightmare for you. We can't let them find out about her. We need to get her back inside and figure out how she's able to do this."

"How? She won't let any of us get close!"

"Surround her," Eve said. "Michael, Shane, get on the other side. Claire and I will come in from this side. Box her in. Don't let her run. We'll just herd her back inside."

"She's strong," Michael warned. "Crazy strong."

"She won't hurt us," Eve said. Michael glanced down at his arm, which was still healing and showed bite marks. "Well, not much, anyway."

"You and your strays," he said, but Claire could tell there was love behind it. "All right, we'll do it your way. Shane?"

"On it."

Michael and Shane spread out, right and left, circling around

Miranda and leaving her a wide berth in the middle of the road as Eve and Claire closed the distance from the front. Claire supposed it looked weird, but if anyone was watching from the other houses, no one made a sound. Not a curtain twitched. Not only did the town of Morganville not care; it didn't even notice when a tweener was stalked by four older teens.

Even if they had good intentions.

Miranda wasn't trying to get away, though. She had wrapped her thin arms around her body and was shuddering in continuous spasms now, and her skin looked less real, more like glass with mist behind it.

"Miranda," Claire said softly, "we need to get you inside. Please."

"I can do this," Miranda said. She was staring down at herself with a blank expression, but there was a stubborn set to her chin, and she wiped her cheeks with the back of a hand and squared her shoulders. "I can live out here. I can. I don't need to be in there."

"You do," Eve said. "Maybe it's a gradual thing. You need to work on it a little at a time. So we can try again tomorrow night. Tonight, hey, come inside; we'll watch a movie. You get to pick."

"Can we watch the pirate movie? The first one?"

"Sure, honey. Just come inside."

Shane and Michael were making steady progress coming up from behind Miranda, and Michael nodded to Claire as she got into position. "Let's all go in," he said. Miranda shuffled awkwardly in place, as if her legs didn't want to move, and turned to look at him over her shoulder. "We don't want anything bad to happen to you, Mir."

"Well," she said, "it's a little late for that, but I appreciate the thought. Did you know? I can't tell the future anymore? It's as if all the power I had went somewhere else." She gestured down at herself. "Into this."

That . . . might make some weird kind of sense, Claire thought, that Miranda's powerful psychic gifts—the same ones that had led her to die inside the Glass House to save Claire's life—had become a kind of life-support system for her, after death.

"But it means I don't know anymore," Miranda said. Her voice was fainter now, almost like a whisper. "I don't know what's going to happen. I'm scared."

"You don't have to be," Claire said, and stretched out her hand.

Miranda hesitated, then reached out.

But the second their skin touched, Miranda's cracked like the thinnest ice, and an icy fog spilled out, searing Claire's fingers with chill. She drew back with a cry, and there were cracks all over Miranda's body now, racing through in lace black lines, and then she just . . .

She just broke.

For a few seconds the fog held together in a vague girl shape, and Claire heard a cry, a real and surprised and scared cry . . .

And then she was gone. Just completely gone, except for empty clothes lying in the street.

"Mir!" Claire felt the pressure in her hand vanish, and lunged forward, scissoring the air, hoping for something, anything . . . but there was nothing—just empty space.

Miranda had vanished completely, and her last word seemed to echo over and over in Claire's mind.

Scared.

"Oh God," she said in a whisper, and felt tears sting her eyes. Miranda had been dealt raw deals her whole life, up to and including dying in the Glass House at the hands of the draug, but it had felt like, finally, she was getting *something* going her way. A place of safety. A life, however limited, that she could call her own.

It was just . . . very sad—so sad that Claire felt tears choking her, and she fell into Shane's arms, clinging to his solid warmth for a long few moments before he whispered in her ear, "We have to go back. It's not safe out here."

She didn't want to go, but there wasn't any point in risking their lives for someone who was already gone. So she let him guide her back toward the Glass House. Michael and Eve were already there. Eve, uncharacteristically, hadn't shed a tear, from the flawless state of her mascara; she was usually the one prone to bursting into tears, but not this time. She just looked blank and shocked.

"Maybe she's okay," Eve said. Michael put his arm around her. "Maybe—oh God, Michael, did we make this happen? We started this, with all the talk about moving. If we hadn't said that she was bothering us, maybe she wouldn't have . . . have . . ."

"It's not your fault," Shane said quietly. "She was bound to try it, sooner or later; once she figured out she could make it out the door, she was going to keep pressing her luck. And anyway, you could be right. She might still be okay. Maybe she's just not anchored anymore. It could be harder for her to get back or let us know she's still around. Maybe she'll be back tomorrow."

He was trying to put the best face on it, but no matter what, it was grim. They'd lost someone, out here in the dark—a scared little girl, left on her own. Maybe for good.

And from the look in his eyes, even Shane knew they were all to blame.

Claire had been looking forward to spending the night in Shane's company, in all the shades of meaning that might hold, but Miranda's disappearance had taken all the joy out of it for them both. Michael and Eve seemed to be just the same. They all ended up sitting on the couch together and watching a DVD that none of them particularly cared about—something about time travel and dinosaurs—just because Eve had mentioned that it had been Miranda's favorite out of their little store of home videos. Claire closed her eyes for most of it, leaning her head on Shane's chest, listening to his slow, strong heartbeat, and allowing his steady strokes of her hair to soothe the grief a little. When the movie ended and silence fell, Michael finally asked if anybody wanted to play a game, but nobody seemed willing to take up the controllers—not even Shane, who had, as far as Claire could remember, never turned it down. That split Michael and Eve upstairs to their room, and left Claire and Shane sitting by themselves.

It felt chilly. Claire found herself shivering, but she didn't want to move away from Shane's embrace; he solved that by taking the afghan from the back of the couch and wrapping it around them both. "Well," he finally said, "I guess the issue of moving is off the table, at least for right now."

"Guess so," Claire said. Tears threatened again, but she wiped her eyes with the back of her hand in an angry swipe. *Enough.* She knew she wasn't really crying for Miranda at the moment; she was just feeling sorry for herself, for losing another brick in the wall of her zone of safety, for more change when she just wanted everything to stay the same. "But the issue's not going away. And we can't let our friends just . . . leave, Shane. It's not right. It's not safe."

"It's Morganville," he said, and kissed her gently. "Safety isn't something we get guaranteed."

"They do." She really meant, *He does,* because Michael was the one with the exemption to human rules, but surely that extended to Eve now that she was his wife. *Wife*—what a weird word; it still didn't sound quite real to Claire's mental ears. Eve was a *wife.* And Shane had raised the even weirder possibility that someday Eve might be a *mother.* Maybe that shouldn't have been quite so strange to her, but she hadn't had any other friends who'd gotten married; it was still a foreign concept when applied to an actual person, and she didn't altogether understand why Michael and Eve, who'd been so easy with sharing a house when they were all single-but-committed, would be so weird about it now that there'd been an actual church ceremony.

"Well, you might have a point. The Glass family's had special consideration for a long time," Shane agreed. "Probably because as a rule they weren't douche bags. But Eve's family . . ." He hesitated, as though wondering whether this was something he should share. Then he must have decided it was, because he said, "Eve's family had a bad rep, going back generations."

"For . . . ?"

"Some people suck up and stomp down, if you know what I mean. Eve's family was like that: sucking up to the vamps at every opportunity, stomping on the heads of everybody they thought beneath them. Bullies. Kind of like the Morrells, only on a much smaller scale. That didn't get them respect from the vamps, or the humans; they didn't have money to buy people off, or the power to make them afraid. So I wouldn't say Eve was born with the immunity idol or anything. Not like Michael was, when he was human. Everybody liked the Glass family."

Claire had known Eve's dad was bad, and her mom was pretty much wallpaper, but the knowledge that it had gone on for generations was revolting. Generation after generation, pandering to the vampires for favors, and giving up their children when the vampires got interested—as Brandon, the Rossers' Protector, had ordered Eve to be given to him. Eve hadn't played along, which was part of why she'd ended up in the Glass House with Michael in the beginning. She'd been so willing to rebel that she'd risked death to do it.

"So, you're saying that Eve could be hit from both sides if she leaves this house."

"I'm saying I think it's pretty much certain. She's got nobody but Michael to look after her, and he can't be there all the time. She wouldn't want him to be. It just . . . makes me worry." Shane smiled a little and gave her a sideways glance. "Don't get jealous. You're still my number one girl."

"I'm not worried," she said. She really wasn't. "I'm scared, too. And what happens when Michael and Eve aren't there for *us?* Because we're in the same boat, right? I have some respect from the vamps, but your family . . ."

"Yeah, the Collins family went out of its way to make itself unwelcome around here. And vampires don't forget. Ever." He sighed and snuggled her closer against him. "You know, we really should get some sleep. It's almost three in the morning, and you've got class today, right?"

She did. Her heart wasn't in it, but she couldn't afford to blow off any more lectures; the old days of professorial indulgences were over. Her newly minted grade B was enough to prove that. "Just a little longer," she said. "Please?"

"Can't say no to that."

And they fell asleep, spooned together on the couch and wrapped in the afghan, until a crashing noise—shockingly loud—brought Claire awake with a flailing spasm.

She couldn't get her breath to ask, but Shane vaulted over her, landed cat-footed on the wood floor, and ran to the hallway. He was gone only a second before he came back at a dead run. "Fire!" he yelled, and slammed through the kitchen's swinging door as Claire fumbled on her shoes. He came back in seconds, toting the big red extinguisher. "Get Michael and Eve up, and get out of the house through the back door!"

"What happened?"

He didn't answer her; he was already gone, pelting back down the hall. As she flew up the stairs, she heard him opening the front door, and she smelled acrid smoke.

Michael, dressed and ready, already had the bedroom door open, and Eve was belting a red silk kimono around her body. She took one look at Claire's face and slipped her feet into untied Doc Martens. "Let's go," she said, and led the way down the steps. Michael split off from them at the bottom, heading for the front; he grabbed up a heavy rug, yanking it like a magician right out from under the couch, and ran to join Shane in fighting the fire.

Claire and Eve went out the back. "What happened?" Eve asked as she flipped the locks open. "We heard something, but—"

"I don't know," Claire said. "Whatever it was, it was loud."

She started to plunge outside, but Eve held her back, craned her head out the door, and took a careful survey of the dark yard before saying, "Okay, go."

It was a mistake. A bad one.

Because they didn't look *up.*

The vampire dropped down behind them, cutting them off from the house, and Claire didn't even notice his appearance until she heard Eve give a little surprised gasp. That was all she had time for, because in the next instant he was already right behind them, with his hands closed around Claire's shoulders . . .

But only to shove her violently out of the way.

She fell and rolled, fetching up with a painful slam against the bark of the old live oak tree that Myrnin had climbed to get into her bedroom. It wasn't Myrnin who'd dropped in this time. This was Pennyfeather, a pallid, long-faced friend of Oliver's who reminded her of a skeleton held together with string and a covering of flesh. He wasn't interested in Claire. Not at all.

He had hold of Eve, fingernails shredding the red silk of her robe. She screamed and tried to break free, but he was too strong; Claire could see the gouges in Eve's arms that his claws left as she struggled to get free.

"If you want to be one of us," Pennyfeather said with a dreadful grin, "one of us really should oblige you. Your husband seems incapable of doing his duty."

That sounded awful, and as the implication sank in, Claire gasped and tried to get up. She didn't have anything to fight him—no stakes, no knives, not even a blunt object—but she couldn't just let him . . . do whatever he was going to do. As she scrambled up, her hand fell on a tree branch—broken, with curled-up, dried leaves along its length.

It was sheared off in a sharp, angular point toward the thicker end. The break looked fresh, and it took Claire a moment to realize that it was this branch that had broken under Myrnin's feet as he launched himself through her window the night before.

She grabbed it and launched herself into a run at Pennyfeather, yelling at the top of her lungs. It was a war cry, coming from someplace deep and primal inside, and she should have been afraid, she should have felt awkward or tentative or stupid, but she just felt filled with red, red fury, and determination.

She'd already lost Miranda tonight. She wasn't losing Eve, too.

Eve saw her coming, and her dark eyes widened. Pennyfeather was too intent on pulling Eve's head to the side and prepping his fangs for the bite to notice, and Claire had an instant of clarity to realize that if she kept going, heading straight for them, she was likely to skewer Eve along with the vampire.

So Claire changed course, ran *past* them, whipped around, and lunged, full extension, just like Eve had taught her to do when they'd been messing around with fencing foils. She put her whole body into it, the straight line of her back continuing the same angle as her stiffened left leg, and her right arm extended up, out, and she slammed her weapon into Pennyfeather's back, neatly to the left of center.

The branch was too thick to make it completely through the ribs, but it shocked him, and he gave a shriek that made the hair stand up on Claire's arms. He let go of Eve, and she toppled forward in a heap of tattered red silk, crouched, and spun to face him with a look on her face so murderous that Claire was momentarily shocked. Pennyfeather didn't notice. He was too busy trying to claw the wood out of his back, but even when he grabbed hold, the springy wood bent, and he only managed to scrape it partly free before it snapped out of his hand.

"Get the bag," Eve snapped to Claire, and she nodded and dashed back into the kitchen. In seconds, she had hold of one of the black canvas totes they kept ready, but by the time she'd made it back outside, Pennyfeather had yanked the branch free, ripped it to pieces, and was stalking toward Eve with a low, furious growl and one piece still held as a club in his clawed hand.

There was no time to get to Eve. Claire did the next best thing; she spun around and flung the bag. It arced through the air and hit the grass at Eve's feet, spilling out a confusion of objects, but Eve didn't hesitate over choices. She grabbed a small bottle, popped the plastic cap, and threw the contents in Pennyfeather's face.

Silver nitrate.

His growl turned to a howl, rising in volume and pitch until it hurt Claire's ears, and he sheared off from making his run at Eve to claw at his face. The liquid silver clung like napalm, and burned about as fiercely. Claire grabbed the bag, stuffed items inside as fast as possible, and grabbed Eve's wrist. "Come on!" she yelled, and they ran around the side of the house, feet sliding on the loose white gravel.

Michael and Shane were at the front, and between the last blast of the fire extinguisher and smothering flaps of the rug, they'd put out a fire that had blackened a ten-foot section of the exterior of the house. Broken glass lay around the base of it, and as they got closer, Claire smelled the sharp, almost-sweet stench of gasoline.

There was something pinned to their front door, too, fluttering pale in the night breeze.

Michael dropped the rug and flashed at vampire-speed to catch Eve in his arms. He must have smelled the blood from her cuts, Claire thought; she could see the faint, iridescent shine of his eyes. "What happened?" he asked, and touched the claw slashes on her kimono. "Who did this?"

"Pennyfeather," Claire said. Now that the adrenaline rush was passing, she felt weirdly shaky, and she was beginning to realize how many things she'd done that could have gone badly wrong for her. For Eve, too. "It was Pennyfeather. He was—he was going to bite her."

Michael made a hissing noise, like a very angry and dangerous snake, and blurred out of sight toward the backyard. Shane's gaze followed him, but he didn't go along; he reached instead for the bag that Claire held and sorted through the contents. He handed Eve a knife, gave Claire another of the bottles of silver, and for himself, a baseball bat—a regular bat, except that the last six inches of the business end were coated with silver plate. "Been dying to try this out," he said, and gave them both a tight, wild smile. "Batter up." He swung it experimentally, nodded, and rested it on his right shoulder. "You good, Eve?"

"This was my favorite robe," she said. Her voice was unsteady, but it was from rage as much as from fear, Claire thought. "Dammit. It was *vintage!*"

Shane was still watching the side of the house, around which Michael had disappeared. He was clearly wondering if he ought to go back him up. Claire put a hand on his arm and drew his focus, just for a second. "Eve got Pennyfeather with a face full of this," she said, and held up her bottle. "He's got a handicap, and Michael's really pissed off."

That eased some of the tension in Shane's back and shoulders, at least. "I don't want to leave you two alone out here," he said. "The fire's out. Get back inside and lock the doors. Go."

"What about you guys?"

"If you hear us crying for our mommies, you can come rescue us, but hey, Eve's kinda half naked and bleeding out here."

Shane had a great point, and as Claire looked over at her, she saw that Eve was gripping the knife in a white-knuckled hand and shivering badly. It was cold out, and the shock was setting in.

Claire took her arm and steered her up the steps. Shane watched them until they reached the door, and then nodded to her and dashed away into the dark, bat held at the ready. She pushed open the door and hustled Eve inside, then paused and looked at what was pinned to the wood.

She supposed it was Pennyfeather's writing, because it was hard to read, spiky, and had a nasty brownish color to the ink that might well have been blood.

It said, *Done by Order of the Founder,* and it was pinned deeply into the wood by a giant knife, like a bowie knife on steroids.

Claire worked it back and forth until she could pull it out of the door's surface, folded the piece of paper, and locked up with trembling fingers.

Eve was standing there watching her, an unreadable expression on her face. She was still shaking. "It's a death sentence, isn't it?" she said. "Don't lie, Claire. You're not good at it."

Claire didn't even try. She held up the knife. "On the plus side," she said, "they left us another weapon. And it's sharp."

Truthfully, that was cold comfort indeed. And in the end, after Michael and Shane came back in without Pennyfeather, who'd managed to run for his life despite taking a pretty good battering from both of them, nobody much felt like celebrating.

Or sleeping.

Morning brought light and warmth, but not much in the way of reassurance; the cops came and took statements, looked over the damage to the house, and photographed the slashes on Eve's arms (which, upon inspection at the hospital, fortunately turned out not to be as deep as they'd looked).

The police declined to include the destruction of her vintage robe as a separate charge of vandalism. They also played dumb about who Pennyfeather was, or even that vampires existed at all, even though both men were plainly wearing Protection bracelets in full view. Typical. Once upon a time, Claire could have called on some Morganville police detectives who had reputations for impartiality . . . but they were all gone now. Richard Morrell had been police chief before he'd been mayor, and he'd been fair about it; Hannah had been great in the same role, but now Richard was dead, and Hannah was helpless to act.

Done by Order of the Founder. That said . . . everything, really. It meant that whatever tenuous claim the four of them had to safety in Morganville was officially cancelled.

Claire stayed with Eve as long as she could, but classes were calling, and so was her in-jeopardy grade point average; she grabbed her book bag, kissed Shane quickly, and dashed off at a jog to Texas Prairie University. Nothing was going to happen during the day, at least from the vamp quarter. Morning was well advanced over the horizon, and she had to skip her normal stop for coffee and flat-out race the last few hundred yards to make it into the science building, up the stairs, and down the long, featureless hall to her small-group advanced study class. Today was thermodynamics, a subject she normally loved, but she wasn't in the mood for theory today.

It was more of an applied sciences day—such as the amount of fuel required to burn down a house. Claire slipped into her classroom seat, earning a dirty look from Professor Carlyle, who didn't pause in his opening remarks.

Pennyfeather had been the one who'd attacked them, but that didn't mean he'd been acting alone; he *could* have thrown the Molotov cocktails at the front of the house and then jumped up on the roof to wait for them to exit the back, but somehow, Claire thought there was more to it. Someone in the front, and Pennyfeather waiting for Eve, specifically. And while it was a little bit of a relief not to be the main target, it was unsettling. Eve wasn't helpless, but somehow she was more vulnerable. Maybe it was just that Claire wanted desperately for Michael and Eve to somehow work out, and for the town to stop hating them, and . . .

"Danvers?"

She looked up from consideration of her closed textbook; she didn't even remember getting it out of her bag. She'd lost track of time, she guessed, and now Professor Carlyle—a severe older man with a close-cropped brush of gray hair and eyes the color of steel—was staring at her with a displeased expression, clearly waiting for something.

"Sorry?" she said blankly.

"Please provide the equation for the subject on the board."

She focused behind him. On the chalkboard, he'd written *Harmonic Oscillator Partition Function*.

"On the board?"

"Unless you'd like to perform it in interpretive dance."

There was a stir of laughter and smirking from the ten other students, most of whom were master's candidates; they were at least five years older than she was, every one of them, and she wasn't popular.

Even here, nobody liked a smart-ass.

Claire reluctantly rose from her desk, went to the chalkboard, and wrote $zHO = 1/(1-e-a/T)$.

"Where?" he asked, without a trace of satisfaction.

Claire dutifully wrote down *where a=hv/k.*

Carlyle stared at her in silence for a moment, then nodded. Apparently, that was supposed to make her feel insecure. It didn't. She knew she was right; she knew he'd have to accept it, and she waited for that to happen. Once he'd given her the signal, she put down the chalk and walked back to her desk.

But Carlyle wasn't done with her quite yet. "Since you did so well with that, Danvers, why don't you predict the following for me?" And he scribbled on the board another equation: $K_p = P_b/P_a - [B]/[A]$. "What happens if T is infinitely large?" T was completely missing from that equation, but it didn't really matter. T was an implied variable, but that was misleading. It was a trick question, and Claire saw many of the others open their books and begin flipping, but she didn't bother. She met Carlyle's eyes and said, "K_p equals two."

"Your reasoning?"

"If T is infinitely large, all the states of energy are equal and occupied. So there are twice as many states in B as A. K_p equals two. It's not really a calculation. It's just a logic exercise."

She was taking advanced thermodynamics purely to help her understand some of what Myrnin had accomplished in building his portal systems in Morganville. . . . They were doorways that warped space, and she knew there had to be *some* explanation for it in physics, but so far, she'd found only pieces here and there. Thermodynamics was a necessary component, because the energy produced in the transfer had to go somewhere. She just hadn't figured out where.

Carlyle raised his eyebrows and smiled at her thinly. "Someone ate her breakfast this morning," he said, and turned his laser focus on another hapless student. "Gregory. Explain to me the calculation if T equals zero."

"Uh—" Gregory was a page flipper, and Carlyle waited patiently while he looked for the answer. It was blindingly obvious, but Claire bit her tongue.

It took Gregory an excruciating four minutes to admit defeat. Carlyle went through three other students, then finally, and with a sigh, turned back to Claire. "Go ahead," he said, clearly irritated now.

"If there isn't any T, there isn't any B," she said. "So it has to be zero."

"Thank you." Carlyle glared at the others in the class. "I weep for the state of engineering, I truly do, if this is the best you can do with something so obvious. Danvers gets bonus credit. Gregory, Shandall, Schaefer, Reed, you all get failing pop quiz scores. If you'd like to solve extra-credit equations, see me afterward. Now. Chapter six, the residual entropy of imperfect crystals . . ."

It was a grim thing, Claire thought, that even when she got the high grade *and* dirty looks from her fellow students, she still felt bored and underchallenged. She wished she could go talk to Myrnin for a while. Myrnin was always unpredictable, and that was exciting. Granted, sometimes the problem was to just stay alive, but still; he was never boring. She also didn't have to sit through the incredibly dense (and wrong) explanations from other students when she was at his lab. If he'd ever had assistants that dumb, he'd have eaten them.

Somehow, she made it through the hour, and the next, and the next, and then it was time to run to the University Center and grab a Coke and a sandwich. It wasn't Eve's day to work the counter at the coffee shop, so after gulping down lunch, Claire—done at school for the day—walked to Common Grounds, just to check in on her.

It was only lightly occupied just now, thanks to the vagaries of college schedules; there were a few Morganville residents in the house, and a group of ten students very seriously arguing the merits of James Joyce. Claire claimed a comfortably battered armchair and dumped her bag in it; the chair and everything else smelled like warm espresso, with a hint of cinnamon. Common Grounds, for all its flaws, still had a homey, welcoming atmosphere.

But when she turned to the counter, she saw a sullen young man in a tie-dyed apron and red-dyed emo hair, who glared at her as she approached. He yawned.

"Hi," she said. "Um, where's Eve?"

"Fired," he said, and yawned again. "They called me in to take her shift. Man, I'm fried. Forty-eight hours without sleep—thank God for coffee. What's your poison?"

At Common Grounds, that *might* be literal, Claire thought. "Bottled water," she said, and forked over too much cash for it. Nobody drank Morganville's tap water. Not after the draug invasion. Sure, they'd cleared the pipes and everything, but Claire—like most of the residents—couldn't shake the idea that something had once been alive in there.

Better to pay a ridiculous amount for water bottled out of Midland.

"So, what happened this morning to get her fired? Because I know she was planning to come in."

Counter Guy wasn't chatty enough to come up with an answer; he just shrugged and grunted as he rang up her purchase and handed over the cold bottle. He had tattoos running up and down his arms, mostly Chinese symbols. Claire considered asking him what they meant, but in her experience he probably didn't have a clue. He did have one thing in common with Eve: black-painted fingernails.

"Is Oliver here?"

"Office," Counter Guy said. "But I wouldn't if I was you. Boss ain't in a good mood."

He was probably right, Claire thought, but she knocked anyway, and received a curt, "In," a command she followed. She shut the door behind her. Counter Guy and the other residents out there wouldn't come to her rescue if things went badly, and she didn't want the clueless students involved. They were having enough trouble with James Joyce.

Oliver didn't even glance up, but then he didn't need to, she thought; he'd probably identified her before she'd come anywhere near the office, just by her heartbeat or the smell of her blood or something. Vampires were an endless source of creepy. "Pennyfeather attacked Eve last night," she said. "Did you tell him to do it?"

He *still* didn't bother to look up from whatever piece of paper he was reading. He picked up a pen and scribbled down a note, then signed the bottom. "Why?"

"He left a note pinned to the door, 'Done by Order of the Founder.'"

"I am not the Founder," he said. "And Pennyfeather is no longer my creature. He does as he pleases. Though I would say his attitude is an accurate weather vane of public opinion among our kind, if that is what you're asking." Oliver didn't ask how Eve was, or what had happened, and that, Claire thought, was different. He'd kind of grown a bit more human since she'd first met him, but now he was back to the bad old vamp, unfeeling and utterly careless of human lives. He wouldn't go out of his way to hurt Eve, probably, but he wouldn't bother to help her, either, if it meant he had to make an effort. "Do you have some valid reason for disturbing me, or are you simply trying to annoy me?"

"I know what's happening," Claire said softly, and his pen stopped moving on the paper. The sudden silence made her feel breathless, as if she were standing at the edge of a bottomless pit full of darkness. "You've wanted to rule Morganville ever since you found out it existed. You came here wanting to get Amelie out of power and make yourself king or something. But she didn't let you, so you had to get . . . creative."

Now he looked up at her, and although his face was human, softened by loose, curling gray hair, the expression and the focus were purely those of a predator. He didn't say anything.

Claire plunged ahead. "Amelie trusted you. She let you get close. And now you're playing her to get what you always wanted. Well . . . it's not going to work. She may like you, but she's not stupid, and when she wakes up—and she will—you're going to be sorry you tried it."

"I don't see that my relationship with the Founder is any of your business."

"You can influence other vampires," she said. "You told me so before. And you're subtle about it. Whatever you're doing to her, stop it before this all goes bad. The humans won't stand for being cattle, and Amelie won't let you go as far as you think. Just . . . back off. Oliver—maybe I'm crazy for saying this, but you're not like this. Not anymore. I don't think you really want all this deep down."

He stared at her with empty, oddly bright eyes, and then went back to his paperwork.

"You may leave now," he said. "And count yourself lucky you are allowed to do so."

"Why did you fire Eve?" she asked. It was probably a mistake, but she couldn't help but ask it. And surprisingly, he answered.

"She accused me of trying to have her killed," he said. "Just as you did. Unfortunately, I'm unable to fire *you*. And my patience is now at an end. Begone."

"Not until you tell me—"

She never even saw him move, but suddenly he was around the desk and slamming the pen into the wood of the door behind her. It was just a simple ballpoint, but it sank an inch deep, vibrating an inch from her head. Claire flinched and came up hard against the barrier at her back. Oliver didn't move away. This close, he looked like bone and iron, and he smelled—ironically—like coffee. She was forcefully reminded that he'd been a warrior when he was alive, and he wasn't any less a killer now.

"Go," he said, very softly. "If you're wise, you will go very, very far from here, Claire. But in any case, go from my presence, *now*."

She opened the door.

And as she did so, she had the blurred impression of someone standing a few feet away on the other side, of people scrambling and exclaiming, of Counter Guy yelling "Hey!" Then she zeroed in not on the figure standing before her, but on what the tall, dark figure was holding.

It was a crossbow with a silver bolt.

And before Claire could take a breath or react, the crossbow was raised and fired.

Claire felt a burning brush against her cheek as the bolt zipped past, and she clapped a hand to the bleeding scrape as she turned to see what had happened.

The arrow had slammed home in Oliver's chest, but it was up and to the right of his heart. Claire stared at it with a feeling of unreality; the silver glint, the slowly spreading crimson circle around the shaft, the bright red feather fletching, and Oliver, pinned in place with surprise as much as pain.

Then he staggered back against his desk. Claire didn't think; she just acted, reaching out for the crossbow bolt.

He swatted her hand away with impatient fury, hard enough that he could have broken bones, and said through gritted teeth, "You can't pull it out from the front, fool. Take it through my back!"

He said it as if he had no doubt at all that she'd obey, and for a fraction of a second, Claire was tempted to obey him; that might have been her natural tendency to want to help, or it could have been Oliver exerting his will.

She paused, though, and looked through the still-open doorway.

The attacker was calmly loading up another bolt in the bow. She didn't—and couldn't—recognize the person; it was just a blank figure in some kind of black opaque mask, a zipped-up black hooded jacket, and plain, well-worn blue jeans. Black boots. Gloves. Nothing to betray any personal identification at all, not even gender.

The figure looked up and saw her standing there, and she felt a chill, unmistakable and indefinable. Then it pointed to her and jerked a thumb at the door. *You. Out.*

"Claire!" Oliver snapped. His voice sounded ragged now, and full of fury. "Pull the bolt out!"

"Did you have Pennyfeather try to kill Eve?"

The wound around the silver was starting to smoke and blacken, and it must have hurt a whole lot, even if not immediately fatal, because he tried to snarl at her, but it came out as more of a moan. He collapsed down to a sitting position on the floor, leaning one shoulder against the desk. She almost caved in, almost, because he really looked bad just then . . . vulnerable and damaged.

But then his eyes flickered bright red in fury, and he said in a poisonous hiss, "I'll have him kill *you* if you don't do as I say, girl. You're a pet, not a person."

"Funny," she said, "seeing as I'm the only thing standing between you and a guy with a crossbow." Literally. The masked figure was still standing behind her, ready to fire. She was just in the way. "Did you?"

"No!" he roared, and convulsed over on his side. The poison was working on him, and working fast.

Claire turned to face the would-be assassin, who was pointing the crossbow now at her. Directly.

Move, the figure gestured once again, impatiently. Claire shook her head.

"Can't." She didn't try to explain, and she wasn't sure she actually could; there was not a reason in the world why she shouldn't walk away from Oliver and leave him to whatever fate was bringing. Clearly the rest of the coffeehouse population had fled, including the students; Counter Guy's red hair and tats had left the building, too. It was just her, standing between Oliver and death.

She guessed that she was doing it because it didn't matter that it was Oliver, after all. She'd have done it for anyone. Even Monica.

She hated bullies. She hated anyone being kicked when he or she was down, and Oliver was most definitely down.

Whoever the figure holding the crossbow was, he or she considered taking her out to get to Oliver. She could see that, even if she couldn't see a face, and she knew that in this moment she was in as much danger as she'd ever been in Morganville. She was utterly at the mercy of whatever this person decided. No one could, or would, help.

She smelled the acrid tang of burning flesh behind her. Oliver was bad, and getting rapidly worse.

The masked head nodded, just a little, as if in acknowledgment of what she hadn't said. The figure lowered the crossbow, stowed it in a black canvas bag, and backed away toward the front of the store. She lost sight of it in the glare of daylight silhouetting the form, though she had the impression that the attacker had stripped off the mask before running out into the street.

Claire didn't try to follow. She stood there for a few seconds, then turned and looked at Oliver.

"If I do this for you," she said, "you're going to owe me. And I'm going to collect."

He was beyond making a bitter comeback. He just nodded, as if he couldn't summon up the strength to do more, and managed to roll a little farther over onto his stomach. The sharp, barbed end of the bolt was sticking out of his chest about three inches below his shoulder blade. The edges were wicked, like razors. That might actually be a good thing; it wouldn't have done quite as much damage that way.

But she needed to get it out before the silver poisoning got much worse—either that, or leave it in for good—which she could just hear Shane saying was still a perfectly valid option.

With gritted teeth, she wrapped the loose fabric of her shirt around the razor-sharp arrowhead, grabbed the shaft just below that, and pulled, hard and fast. She almost stopped when Oliver convulsed again, and his mouth opened wide in a silent scream—silent because he couldn't draw in breath to fuel it—but she didn't dare quit. Better it was painful now than deadly later.

It seemed to take forever, but it must have been just a few seconds before she yanked it completely free. She dropped the arrow to the floor with a ringing clang and tried not to think about the blood staining her shirt where she'd pulled it out of his body. Or whose blood it might have been, because it wasn't really *Oliver's* blood, was it? It was borrowed, or stolen, from others.

She stood up, breathing heavily and trying not to feel nauseated by what she'd just done—not just the blood, or the pain she'd caused, but the fact that she'd just saved Oliver's life. Shane would have been so angry with her, she realized; he'd have walked away and called it karma. Or justice, at least.

But right now, that wasn't the smart play. If Amelie was out to get them—if she really had sent Pennyfeather, and Oliver hadn't—then she needed Oliver on their side.

For now.

Oliver rolled over on his back, eyes tightly shut. The wound in his chest was still smoking, and clearly he was in pain, but he'd heal. Vampires always healed.

"You'd better not have lied to me," she said. "And remember, if you come after Eve, you come after all of us. That's going to be a lot more dangerous for you than some random dude with a mask and a crossbow."

He didn't move, and didn't speak, but his eyes flicked open and studied her with odd intensity. She couldn't really decide what he was feeling, but she did decide that she really, truly didn't care.

She shut the office door on her way out.

TEN

CLAIRE

)

"Well?" Shane demanded. "Who was it?" Claire was on the phone with him as she headed home. Wherever he was, it was machine-shop noisy, metal grinding and whining, and he had to shout to make himself heard. "Who tried to hit Oliver?"

"I don't know."

"C'mon, Claire. Take a guess."

"No, really, I don't. Whoever it was had a mask and jacket and gloves and everything. Kind of tall, maybe a little on the skinny side. Good with a crossbow, though. Seriously good." She remembered the cut on her cheek and touched it with tentative fingers. It didn't really hurt, and the bleeding had stopped, but there was a definite slice. For the first time, she actually wondered how bad it looked, and whether it might leave a scar. "Um, anyway, I didn't get a look at him without the mask. It wasn't *you*, was it?" That last was teasing. She knew better; Shane wouldn't have fired with her in the way, not unless he had no choice. This was someone who wasn't quite as . . . involved.

"Hell, girl, if it had been me, he'd be dead on the floor right now, because I wouldn't have missed. Make my day. Tell me he's hurting."

"Oh yeah, he's definitely hurting," she said. "And I don't think he was behind Pennyfeather last night. But there's something weird about him, Shane."

"When isn't he weird?"

"No, I mean—" She couldn't put her finger on it, really. "Did Eve tell you what happened this morning?"

"What?" Shane instantly sounded on guard again, braced for the bad news. "What now? Damn, hang on . . ." He retreated from what sounded like a car being crushed in the background, until he found a relatively calm space. "Go on."

"Oliver fired her from Common Grounds. I guess he got kind of pissed when she accused him of trying to kill her. You know Eve. It probably wasn't subtle."

"Might have involved trying to hit him with something, like an espresso machine," Shane agreed. "She's home, but she's not talking. Went straight to her room. She had that look, like she was going to cry, so I didn't get in her way."

"Coward."

"*Crying*, so yeah. Are you on your way home?"

"Yes," she said. "I need to make a stop, though. See you in about an hour."

Shane knew her way too well. "You're going to see Myrnin, aren't you? Claire—"

"I need to see what he's doing," she said quickly. "He was strange the last time I saw him."

Her boyfriend mumbled something that might have been *He's always strange*, but he mostly kept his dissatisfaction to himself. "Say hi to my dad while you're there. You know, the brain in the jar? Frankenstein? That guy."

"You could come and—"

"No," Shane said flatly. There was a second's pause, as if he'd surprised himself by the vehemence of his reply, and when he spoke again it was in a softer tone. "Be careful out there. If you want me to come along . . ."

"To Myrnin's lab? That's just asking for trouble and you know it. I can manage. I've got resources." And silver-coated stakes, in her backpack. She had resolved to never leave home without them, after the events of last night. "If I'm not home before dark, though—"

"Yep, rescue has been calendared. Got it," he said. "Love you."

She heard the effort it took him to say it—not because he didn't mean it, but because boys just didn't like admitting it over the phone. He even lowered his voice, in case someone—Michael?—could overhear him.

Honestly.

"Love you, too," she said. "Watch out for Eve, will you? There's something funny about all this. I think Pennyfeather really did come for her, not for any of the rest of us. I think there's something going on in vampireland that has to do with her and Michael."

"Copy that," he said. "Collins out." He made a kissing sound into the phone before he hung up, which was way more embarrassing than saying *Love you*, but probably amused him more, and she smiled so much on her walk to Myrnin's lab that her face hurt—especially around the cut.

The street that held the entrance to Myrnin's lair—she always thought of it as a lair, as much as a lab—was a pretty much normal Morganville residential neighborhood; more run-down than some, better than others. The houses were mostly cheaply built clapboard, thrown up forty or fifty years ago, though there were a few standouts. Two houses had burned down or been otherwise trashed during the recent draug invasion, and those were busy with swarms of hard-hatted workers scrambling over piles of bricks, lumber, and tile. The skeletons of new houses were up already. Claire wondered what it might be like to move into a new place, one that had never had anyone else in it, one that was fresh and unhaunted. That would be odd, probably. She'd gotten so used to houses with history.

At the end of the street loomed the old Day House. It was a Founder House, built almost exactly like the Glass House where Claire lived; it had been freshly painted a blinding white, and the trim had been done in a dark blue. As always, there was a rocking chair on the porch. Claire expected to see Gramma Day's ancient little form there, rocking and knitting, but instead, the woman sitting there was tall, long-legged, and she wasn't knitting.

She was cleaning a gun.

Claire veered off from the alleyway that was the entrance to the lab, and paused respectfully at the gate that blocked the Day House sidewalk. "Hi, Hannah," she said.

Hannah Moses looked up, and the sunlight threw the scar on her face into sharp relief; it was hard to read her expression, but she said, "Howdy, Claire. Come on up."

Claire unfastened the gate and came up the steps to the porch. There was another chair sitting across from the rocking chair, and a low table in between where Hannah had laid out the parts of her weapon with straight-line military precision.

"Grab a seat," Hannah said, and blew dust off the part that she held in her hand. She examined it critically, buffed it with a cloth, and put it down in its place on the table. "Where you headed, Claire?"

"Myrnin."

"Ah." Hannah's gaze fastened on the cut on her cheek. "Something interesting happen?"

"Depends on how you feel about Oliver, I guess. Someone all in black tried to shoot a silver arrow into his heart."

Hannah paused in the act of sliding a piece onto the frame of the handgun. "Tried," she repeated. "I assume, not successfully?"

"It was pretty close."

"I can see that. Apparently, whoever tried didn't much care if you were in the way."

"Cared enough to miss, I guess."

Hannah nodded and went back to reassembling her gun with graceful, practiced efficiency. It took a breathtakingly short period of time, and then she loaded the weapon, chambered a round, and checked the safety before laying it back on the table. "Claire, we both know I'm sidelined by the vampires, and I won't have much opportunity to help in an official capacity. So I want you to do something for me."

"Sure!"

"I want you to leave Morganville."

Claire fell silent, watching her. "I can't just run away."

"Yes, you can. You always could have done it."

"Okay, then, I won't do it. My grades—"

"You can't use a good grade if they're carving it on your tombstone. Pack up and get out. Go find your folks, get them to pack up, and go somewhere else. Far away. An island, if you can manage it. But get the hell away from the vampires, and keep away."

"But you're staying?"

"Yes," Hannah agreed, "I'm staying. This house has been in my family for seven generations. My grandmother's too old to go, and they've still got my cousin locked up somewhere in their dungeons, if she's not dead and drained. I was like you. I wanted all this peace and love and cooperation to work, but it's not going to happen. The vampires are ripping up the agreements. That ain't on us. It's on them."

When Claire didn't speak, Hannah shook her head, leaned over, and picked up the weapon. She seated it in a holster under her arm. "There's a war coming," she said. "A real war. There's not going to be any room for people like you standing in the middle, trying to make peace. I'm trying to save your life."

"You always wanted peace."

"I did. But when you can't have peace, there's only one thing you can aim for, Claire, and that's winning the war the best and maybe the bloodiest way you can."

"I don't want to believe it. There has to be a way to make Amelie listen, to stop all this—"

"It's too late," Hannah said. "She set up the cage in Founder's Square again. It's a clear message. Cross the vampires, and you'll burn. Everything you worked for, everything I worked for, is going away. You pick a side, or you go. Nothing else to do."

Claire cleared her throat. "How's your grandmother?"

"Ancient," Hannah said, "but she's been that way as long as I can remember. She's a hundred and two years old this year. I'll give her your respects."

There wasn't anything else to say, so Claire nodded and left. She closed the gate behind her and glanced back to see Hannah stand up, lean against the porch pillar, and gaze out into the street like a sentry watching for trouble on the horizon.

Anybody who decided to go up against Hannah Moses had to

have a death wish. It wasn't just the gun she'd so expertly assembled and loaded—heck, gun toting in Texas was practically normal. It was in her body language: calm, centered, ready.

And deadly.

If there really was going to be a war, being on the side against Hannah would be a very dangerous place.

Claire headed down the alley, away from the normal world of construction and power tools and Hannah standing sentry. As the wooden walls rose on either side of her, and narrowed from a one-car street into a cart path into a claustrophobic little warren, she hardly noticed; she'd made this walk so many times that doing it in broad daylight held no terrors for her at all.

But something was different when she got to the end of the alley.

The shack, the ancient, leaning thing that had been there ever since Claire had first come here, was just . . . gone. There was no sign of wreckage, not even a scrap of wood or a rusty nail left in its place. There had been stairs going down into Myrnin's lab inside the shack itself.

Now, there was a slab of concrete. It was almost dry, but it had been poured only a day ago, Claire was certain of that; concrete dried fast in the Texas desert heat, and this was still just a tiny bit cool and damp to the touch. Someone had left a handprint at the corner of the slab. She put her own hand in the impression; it was a larger hand, longer fingers, but still slender.

Myrnin's hand, she thought.

He'd sealed up the lab.

Claire felt an odd wave of dizziness pass over her, and she lowered her head and breathed in deeply to combat it. He'd told her that he was going to leave, but she hadn't really believed it. Not like this. Not this fast.

But sealing your lab with concrete was a pretty definite sign of intent.

Claire left the alley at a run. She blew through the Day House gate and up the steps, and said breathlessly to Hannah, "I need to use your portal."

"Our what?"

"C'mon, Hannah. I know you've got a portal in your house. It's in the bathroom. I used it to get to Amelie before. I need to see if I can still get into the lab that way." Hannah's face remained tight and guarded. "Please!"

The front door creaked open, horror-movie style, and the tiny, wizened form of Gramma Day appeared in the gap. She studied Claire with faded brown eyes that still held the same sharp intelligence that Hannah's did, and held out a palsied, wrinkled hand. Claire took it. The old lady's skin was soft as old, fragile fabric, and burning hot, but beneath it was a wiry strength that almost pulled Claire off-balance. "You get in here," Gramma Day said. "Ain't no call for you to be standing out on the porch like some beggar. You, too, Hannah. Nobody's coming today for us."

"You don't know that, Gramma."

"Don't you tell me what I know or don't, girl." There was a firm tone of command in the old lady's voice as she led Claire down the hallway. There was an eerie sense of déjà vu to it—the same hall as the Glass House, the same parlor to the left, the same living room opening up ahead. Only the furniture was different, and the march of family portraits on the walls, some of them going back to the mid-1800s, of earnest-looking African American people in their Sunday best. As they shuffled down the hall, it got more modern. Color portrait photos of people with heavily lacquered bouffant hairdos, then thick, luxurious Afros. Toward the very end, Hannah Moses looking incredibly neat and imposing in her military uniform, and a framed set of medals beneath it.

There was one important difference between the Glass House and the Day House: there was a downstairs bath. It must have been added ages ago, but Claire envied it, anyway. Gramma swung open the door and shooed her inside.

"You going to see the queen?" Gramma asked her.

"No, ma'am. I'm going to see if I can find Myrnin."

Gramma snorted and shook her trembling head. "Ain't no good gonna come of that, girl. Trap-door spider's not a safe thing for you to be running after. You ought to go home, lock your doors, get ready for trouble."

"I'm always ready," Claire said, and grinned.

"Not like this," Gramma said. "Never seen a time when the vampires weren't scared of something, but now, they ain't afraid of anything, and it's gonna go hard for us. Well, you do as you like. Folks always do." She swung the door shut on Claire, and Claire hastily felt for the light switch, an old-fashioned dial thing on the wall. The overheads clicked on. From the look of the bulbs, they might have been original Edisons.

It was an altogether normal sort of bathroom, and although she kind of needed to go, Claire didn't dare use it. Only Myrnin would have ever been thoughtless enough to build a portal in a bathroom, she thought. The people in the Day House must have a lot more fortitude than she did, because she'd never be able to take down her pants in a room where anyone with the secret handshake could walk right out of the wall and stare at her. Granted, that was a smallish circle of people . . . Amelie, Oliver, Myrnin, Claire herself, Michael, a few others (and even Shane had managed once or twice).

Oh, and a couple of would-be serial killers who'd gotten their hands on the secret. Ugh.

Claire cleared her mind, closed her eyes, and focused. She felt the answering tingle of the portal, lying dormant and invisible, and when she looked, she saw a thin film of darkness forming over the white-painted door. It was misty at first, then as dark as a velvet curtain hanging in midair, rippling gently in an unfelt breeze.

She built the image of Myrnin's lab in her mind: the granite worktables, the art deco lights on the walls, the chaotic mess of books and equipment. Then there was Bob the Spider's tank in the corner, larger than ever and thick inside with webs, along with the battered old armchair sitting next to it where Myrnin sat and read, when he was in the mood.

The image flickered in the darkness, ghostly, and then flared out. No, it was still there, Claire thought, but the lights themselves had been turned off. To keep her away?

Screw that. Claire reached into her backpack and pulled out a small, heavy flashlight. She switched it on and stepped through the portal into the dark.

It was not just dark in the lab. It was profoundly, elementally black. This far below ground, and with the entrance sealed anyway, it felt like being sealed into a tomb. Claire felt the portal snap shut behind her, and for a moment she was tempted to turn around and wish herself home, immediately, but that wouldn't help. She still wouldn't *know*.

There was a master switch to the power, and by carefully watching her footing (Myrnin hadn't bothered to clear up the leaning piles of books or the scattered trip hazards), she found her way to the far wall, next to a musty old mummy case she'd always assumed was a genuine thing—because it was Myrnin's. She'd never opened it. Knowing Myrnin, there could be anything inside, from a body he'd forgotten about to his dirty laundry.

She threw the master switch up, and lights flared on. Machines started up around the lab with a chorus of hums, pops, crackles, and musical tones. The laptop she'd bought for Myrnin booted up in the corner and glowed reassuringly. At least one beaker started bubbling, though she couldn't see why.

But there was absolutely no trace of Myrnin.

She stopped at the table where she'd left the device she'd been working on; it was still there, covered over with the sheet. Myrnin hadn't taken it with him, and he hadn't made any more of his suspiciously accurate adjustments to it, either. For a moment, Claire debated sticking it in her backpack—she couldn't leave it here, gathering dust, not when she was close to it actually starting to work—but the weight was pretty extreme, and she needed to look around more.

She'd come back, she decided, and flipped the sheet back into place.

Claire edged past a pile of boxes and crates in the corner and opened the door in the back—or tried to. Locked. She rooted around through drawers until she came up with a set of keys, which contained everything from ancient, rusty skeleton models to modern gleaming ones. She sorted through, eyeing the lock, and tried likely candidates until she found one that fit and turned. The door swung silently open on Myrnin's bedroom. She'd stayed in it before (without him, of course) when she'd been confined to the lab on punishment duty, so she was well familiar with the contents. Nothing seemed different. The bed had been mussed, pillows tossed to the floor, and drawers were hanging open, but she couldn't tell—as always—if it was normal, or some kind of panic-packing frenzy.

There was no note. Nothing to tell her whether Myrnin was just temporarily out, or gone for good. She couldn't believe that he'd just . . . leave. Just like that.

"Frank?" Claire walked out of the bedroom into the main lab. "Frank, can you hear me?" Frankenstein, Shane called him. Frank Collins had, once upon a time, been Shane's dad—maybe not a good one, but still. Then he'd been turned vampire, against his will. Then he had died, and Myrnin had decided to scavenge his brain and use it to power the town's master computer.

Maybe Frankenstein wasn't too bad a name for him, after all.

There was a buzzing sound that seemed to come from all around her, and it coalesced finally into a distorted, drunk-sounding voice. "Yes, Claire," it said.

"Are you okay?"

"No," it said, after a long pause. "Hungry."

Claire swallowed hard and clenched her fists. Frank—Frank Collins, or what was left of him—was hardwired into a computer downstairs, an area that Myrnin hadn't wanted her to venture into. "I thought your nutrients were delivered automatically."

"Tank dry," he said. He sounded terribly tired. "Need blood. Get blood, Claire."

"I—I can't do that!" What was she supposed to do—order up a gallon drum from the blood bank? Somehow magically haul it all the way down there herself? She had no idea how Myrnin did these things; he'd never included her on any of that maintenance activity. But she strongly suspected the only one who'd be able to manage it would be a vampire. "Is Myrnin gone?"

"Hungry," Frank said again, faintly, and then just . . . stopped talking. The buzz under his voice shut down. She thought he was the equivalent of offline, like a laptop drained of battery shutting down.

If she wanted him to survive, she really did have to figure this out. Clearly, Myrnin wasn't here to do it.

Claire went to the glass enclosure in the corner. It was hard to see under all the webs, but when she took the top off the tank, Bob the Spider crawled up eagerly to the top of his wispy multilevel construction. He was a big fuzzy spider, and somehow impossibly cute, although part of her still screamed like a little girl at the thought of touching him.

He bounced up and down in his web, all eight eyes staring right at her.

"You're hungry, too," she said. "Right? Myrnin didn't feed you, either?"

That was really strange. Myrnin might neglect Frank, because he and Frank really weren't a marriage made in heaven (and Frank could be faking it; he had a cruel and weird sense of humor), but leaving Bob on his own and starving wasn't like her boss at all. He was ridiculously fond of the thing. She still remembered Myrnin's utter panic the first time Bob had molted. It had been like a normal person freaking out over the birth of a child.

It was not like him to leave Bob behind if he was really leaving.

Something was wrong here. Very wrong.

Claire pulled out her phone and dialed Myrnin's speed dial. It rang on the phone, and suddenly she heard an echo in the lab, a ringtone composed of scary organ music. She'd given him the phone and had put the ringtone on it herself.

The phone was lying in the shadows next to a stack of books. It had a cracked screen, but it was still working. Claire picked it up and felt stickiness on her fingers.

Blood.

What had happened?

"You shouldn't have come," Pennyfeather said from behind

her. His voice, like the rest of him, was colorless, and his odd, lilting accent only made him seem less human, somehow. "But don't worry. You won't be leaving."

Claire stumbled backward in surprise, catching her heel on a pile of discarded volumes, which overbalanced and rained down dusty, heavy tomes on top of her. She yelped and ducked, and realized she had an opportunity as Pennyfeather paused to survey the chaos; she jumped, slid over the top of the nearest lab table, sending books and glass beakers flying, and hit the floor running. She heard soft noises behind her, and in her mind's eye she saw Pennyfeather leaping effortlessly onto the same table, touching down, and racing after her.

She felt human, solid, clumsy, and utterly outmatched against his eerie grace. Claire was accustomed enough to running from vampires not to be utterly terrified—she'd done it often enough here, in this lab—but Pennyfeather was different from the others. Oliver, Amelie, Myrnin . . . They all had some kind of humanity to them, some hints of mercy, however hidden. They could be reached.

Pennyfeather was pure vampire-fueled serial killer, and a human, any human, was no match for him.

Claire grabbed for the silver-coated stake in her backpack, but it had rolled to the side, and running and hunting around in a bag and watching treacherous footing weren't exactly complementary activities. It was inevitable that just as her fingertips brushed the cool metal, her foot would come down on a book that slid greasily to the side, and she'd tumble, off-balance, to the floor.

As she did.

She got a grip on the stake just as Pennyfeather landed on her chest, nimble and startlingly heavy. He easily pinned her arms down. All she could do was rattle the stake ineffectively against the tile. No way could she get leverage to stab him, or even scratch him. She bucked, trying to throw him off, but he rode it out easily.

It came to her, with cold clarity, that she wasn't getting out of this. No last-minute brainstorms. No clever little science applications to solve the problem. In the end, she was just going to be another Morganville statistic. Score another one for the vamps.

"Hey," a scratchy, electronic voice barked over Pennyfeather's shoulder, and a grayscale, two-dimensional image flickered into existence there. Frank Collins, Shane's absent/abusive dad, looking scarred and scary, was wielding a tire iron, which he swung at Pennyfeather's head.

Pennyfeather reacted to the thing coming at him from the corner of his eye, jerking out of the way and letting go of Claire to stop the swing of the blunt object . . . but his hands went right through Frank's insubstantial arm, and Pennyfeather pitched forward, off-balance. Claire seized the chance to roll away, and Frank flickered between her and Pennyfeather, confusing the issue.

"Out of my way, spirit!" Pennyfeather snarled, fangs out.

"I'm not a spirit," Frank countered, and his fangs descended, too, as he returned the snarl. "I'm your worst damn nightmare, Skeletor. I'm a vampire killer with fangs and a grudge."

That sounded so much like Shane that Claire was actually startled. So was Pennyfeather, as a sudden blaze of fire shot up from one of the Bunsen burners nearby. Claire barely glimpsed it before scooping up the rolling stake and her book bag, and lunging for the dark doorway of the portal. *Concentrate!* she begged herself, shaking all over with adrenaline. She had seconds, at most, before Pennyfeather reached her no matter what kind of distractions Frank might be trying; he didn't have any actual, physical force to wield on her behalf, even if he was inclined. She needed out of here, fast.

She couldn't mentally reconstruct the Day House bathroom under this kind of pressure, or anywhere else that Myrnin had established one of his teleportation thresholds. The only one that leaped clearly and instantly to her mind was home—the living room of the Glass House, with its comfy couch and armchair and barely controlled chaos. . . .

It formed in front of her as she plunged forward, trusting somehow, desperately, that she could make it happen.

Pennyfeather lunged forward and caught her foot just as she pushed through the plastic-wrap pressure of the doorway, and she was stuck, mostly out but with her left leg held in a grip so iron-strong, she knew he'd drag her back through.

Or worse. If she was stuck in the portal when it closed, she'd be cut apart.

"Help!" Claire shrieked.

Michael, Eve, and Shane were all in the living room. Michael and Shane dropped the game controllers they'd been holding and twisted around on the sofa to look blankly at her, as Eve—already facing her—clapped hands to her mouth in shock.

"Help me! Pull me out!"

All three of them broke out of their momentary freeze at the same time. Michael scrambled over the back of the sofa and got to her first, grabbing her arm just as Pennyfeather yanked backward, and although Michael held on, they both slid toward the portal.

Claire couldn't get her breath. "He's got me; he's got me; I can't—!" she shrieked as Pennyfeather yanked hard on her leg, and she felt the strain in her muscles. He was still playing with her. She'd seen an angry vampire rip limbs off a person, and it was frighteningly possible just now.

Shane took hold of Claire and wrapped his arms around her in a grip so tight it felt as if she'd be crushed. "Go, Mike. I'll hold her here! Get the bastard off her!"

"It's the lab!" Claire blurted, "He's in the lab!"

She wasn't sure Michael could make it through at all—there wasn't much room—but she twisted over to the side in hopes of making more space. At least Michael knew what he was doing. He paused for a moment, fixing the lab's location in his mind, then nodded at her and plunged through in a rush.

Claire felt the disturbance of the thin membrane still holding her leg at the knee like a strange tidal wave, and Pennyfeather's grip tightened. He started to yank her steadily backward, and all of Shane's strength wasn't enough to keep them from sliding forward. If anything, Pennyfeather just seemed to be more intent on taking her with him, not less.

Claire screamed and buried her face in Shane's chest as she felt the strain on her leg increase, going from painful to intensely agonizing, and in one more second she knew she'd feel muscles tearing loose. . . .

But then a second later, the crushing hold on her ankle released. Shane had braced himself and was pulling with all his strength to counterbalance, and when the pressure let go, they both went crashing to the wooden floor with her on top. She was breathless and frightened, but it was still nice to be body-to-body with him, and she saw the pleasure fire in his eyes, too, just for a moment. He brushed her hair back from her face and said, "Okay?"

She nodded.

"Then let's do this again later," he said, "but right now, Michael needs backup. Stay here." He rolled her off him, got to his feet, grabbed the black canvas bag that Eve threw to him from the kitchen door, and dived into the dark.

Eve hurried to her side as Claire tried to bend her leg, and winced at the shooting pains that went through it. "Don't," Eve ordered, and dropped down next to her to run her hands over Claire's knee. "Damn, I can't believe Myrnin did that to you. I'll stake his ass myself, if there's anything left when the boys get done teaching him manners."

"Myrnin?" Claire asked, and then realized what she'd done. *"It's not Myrnin!"*

With a horrible sense of doom, she realized that she hadn't told them it was Pennyfeather.

And neither of the boys was prepared for that.

ELEVEN

MYRNIN

)

I t was so dark. Dark dark dark dark dark dark. *Darkdarkdark-darkdarkdarkdarkdarkcan'tbreathedarrrrrrrrrkkkkkkkk . . .*

I gained control of my clattering, chattering mind with an effort that left me trembling. Had I been still human, still breathing—as I was sometimes in dreams—I thought I would have been drenched in the sweat of fear and gasping. I dreamed that sometimes, too, the sticky moisture on my skin, dripping and burning in my eyes, but in the dreams it wasn't dark; it was bright, so bright, and I was running for my life, running from the monster behind. . . .

So many years running blackness turning red nothing nothing safe no havens no friends lost all lost until Amelie until this place until home but home was gone gone dead and gone . . . I gagged on the taste in the back of my mouth, the excruciating spike of hunger, and sagged against the wet, slick wall. *Don't remember,* I told myself. *Don't think.*

But I couldn't stop thinking. Ever. My mother had beaten me for fancies when I watched the stars and drew their patterns and forgot the sheep while wolves ate the lambs and my sisters with their cruel and petty wounds when no one saw and my father penned up like an animal as he howled all the *thinking never stopped never never never a howling storm in my head until the heat burst through my skin and devoured me.*

Stop. I shouted it inside my head until I could feel the force of it hammering against bone, and for a blessed moment, I gained the space of silence against all the pressing weight of memory and terror that never, never went away for long.

There was time enough to think where I was and to remember my present situation . . . not my past.

The prison was familiar to me, familiar not from Morganville but from ancient and heavily unpleasant years past. . . . My enemy was still a great fan of the classics, because he had dropped me into an oubliette—a round, narrow hole in stone that was deep enough, and smooth enough, to thwart a vampire's attempts to jump or climb. In less civilized times, one would be dropped in to be forgotten entirely. Humans lasted only days, generally, before the confinement, darkness, hunger or thirst—or simple horror—took them. Vampires . . . well. We were hardy.

It's a sad thing for a vampire to confess, but I have always hated the bitter, choking dark. It's useful to us to hide and stalk, but only when there is a hint of light—a glimmer, something that will define the shadows and give them shape. A blood-hot body glows, and that, too, is a comfort and a convenience.

But here, there was no glimmer, no prey, nothing to relieve the inky and utter black. It reminded me of terrible, terrible things *like the grave I had dug my way out of more than once, the taste of dirt and screams in my mouth, vivid and sour, and that taste never went away, leaving me gagging on*

*it, gagging and unable to fight past the choking, awful sense of burial only blood
could wash out, blood and searing light. . . .*

DarkdarkdarkdarkdarkdarkdarkdarkdarkdarkdarkohmyGodwhy . . .

When I came to myself, I was doubled over and retching, my
hands flat against the wall. I was on my knees, which was even less
pleasant than standing. I sagged back and found the cold, wet
stone of the wall only a few inches behind me. I could sit, if I did
not mind waist-high filthy water, and my knees to my chin. Well,
it made for a change, at least.

It was my fault that I was here, entirely mine. Claire always
chided me for my single-mindedness and she was right, right, always right, even Frank had told me to go but poor, surly Frank,
starving for lack of nutrients no one to change out the tanks and
care for him properly, and Bob, what to do about Bob, I couldn't
leave him behind all on his own how would he catch his flies and
crickets and the occasional juicy beetle without assistance he was
so very much my responsibility and Claire Claire Claire vulnerable now without Amelie without pity kindness mercy no no no I
could not go should not . . .

Chilly skeletal Pennyfeather, with his acid eyes and killer's smile . . .

Frank warned me warned me warned me . . .

*Pennyfeather dragging heretics to the flames, hunting me, digging me out of my
last safe nest and into burning sunlight where Oliver laughed and then the oubliette
the darkness dark darkdarkdarkdarkdarkdark . . .*

I opened my eyes again, eventually, with my screams still ringing back at me from the stone walls. What a noisy chorus I was. It
was still complete and utter darkness—the rock I leaned on, the
water, my hand in front of my face, all bleak and black, not even a
spark of light, life, color.

That was because I was blind. I remembered it with a sudden,
guilty shock; it was odd that one would forget something that sig-

nificant. But in my defense, one doesn't tend to wish to remember such things (Pennyfeather's awful pale grin, the flash of the knife, the pain, the fall).

You've healed from worse, I told myself sternly. I pretended to be someone clear, someone practical. Ada, perhaps, in her better days. Or Claire. Yes, Claire would be quite practical at a time like this.

Blind blind three blind mice see how they run who holds the carving knife where is the cat Dear God in heaven the cat *and I am only a mouse, a blind and helpless mouse in a trap cheese if only someone would drop down a bite of cheese, or another mouse . . .*

The oubliette, I was not a mouse, I was a vampire, I was a blind vampire who would heal, of course, eventually, and see again. *Stop,* I told myself. I drew in a deep breath and smelled ancient death, crushed weeds, rotting metal, stone. I had no idea where the oubliette was located. I was simply at the bottom of it, standing in cold, filthy water and thinking that this time, my favorite slippers were well and truly ruined. Such a pity.

All the whimsy in the world won't help you now, fool. I could hear Pennyfeather saying it; I could feel the cold clench of his hands on my shoulders. *This town belongs to the strong.*

And then the fall.

Well. I was strong. I had survived. I always survived. *Not this time never no one to rescue me no one to know I was so alone alone alone darkkkkkkkkkkkkkkkkkkkkkkkkkkkkk.*

The panic took some time to subdue; it lasted longer each time, it seemed; from a purely scientific perspective, I supposed I ought to have been taking notes. *A monograph on the subject of terrors of the dark, with additions for the blind.* I could write volumes, should I ever see again to be able to write.

Your eyes will heal, the rational part of me—a tiny part, at best, and by no means the best of me—whispered. *Delicate tissues take longer to regenerate.* I knew this, but the animal, instinctual part of me still shrieked in panic, convinced that I'd be left in this, choking nothing forever, doubly blind, unable to even make out the blank walls that confined me.

The evil tide of panic rolled over me again, and when it finally passed and my screaming brain stilled, I was crouched low in the water, huddling to the chilly walls and shaking in a near fit. My throat felt odd. Ah. I'd been screaming, again. I swallowed a trickle of my own precious and scarce blood and wondered when Claire would seek me out. She would; she *must.* I desperately believed she would. Surely she was not so angry with me that she'd spurn me and leave me here, in this awful place.

Please. Please come. I can't survive this I can't alone no no no not alone not blind no . . .

I was not used to feeling this horror, which combined all the fears of my mortal life in a toxic elixir; the closeness of the walls, the darkness, the filthy water, the knowledge that I might never leave this place, that I'd starve here to rags and bones until thirst robbed me of all shreds of the mind I'd struggled so hard to preserve, gnawing my own flesh until it was drained dry.

I have become my father after all.

My father had gone mad when I was only a very young boy, and they'd confined him . . . not in a well like this, but in a hut, a lightless and chained hovel, with no hope or memory of daylight. When I had nightmares—daily—that was my hell, that I woke dressed in my father's filthy rags, chained and alone, abandoned to the screaming in my head.

In the dark.

And here it is, nightmare come real, in the dark, alone, abandoned.

Nonsense. Pennyfeather has always worked for Oliver. I tried to focus on logic, anything to prevent myself from sliding over that muddy slope down into the pit of despair again. *Ergo, Oliver wished that I be removed. Why would he wish it? Because Amelie trusts me?*

It did not feel right. Oliver was not randomly cruel; he enjoyed power, but mostly for what power could do. He'd had many opportunities to remake Morganville in his own image, but he'd refrained, over and over; I'd thought there was genuine respect, even an odd and grudging love, growing between him and Amelie. Yet he'd changed, and through him, so had Amelie. For the worse.

Amelie, my sweet lady, so small and shy and quiet in the beginning when your master and mine had met, when as fledgling vampires we had learned the joy of the hunt, the terror of being owned. I rescued you from your vile father, and lost you, and found you again. Do you remember me at all, as that young and tentative vampire, full of fear and vague notions?

Amelie wasn't herself. Oliver should not have done this to me; he should not have been able to, without her consent. There was something missing, something I did not yet understand.

It was a puzzle, and I liked puzzles; I clung to them, here in the dark, a shield against all the pieces falling apart, crashing together in my head, crashing and cutting. . . .

Another panic attack swept over me, hot as boiling lead and cold as the snows that piled waist high in my youth, and what little mind I had dissolved in an acidic frenzy, thoughts rushing as fast as modern trains crashing through stone, veering wildly from the tracks, turning and burning into chaos *closedarktoodarktooclose smoothwallsnonono.* . . .

It was harder this time, coming back. I ached. I trembled. I think I might have wept, but water dripped cold on me, and I wasn't sure. No shame in tears. No shame at all, since there was no one to see me, no one ever ever ever again.

Come for me. Please, the lonely and lost part of me wailed. But no one did.

Hours crawled slowly, and I began to feel something odd . . . a pressure, a strange sensation that made me want to claw at my injured eyes . . . but I held off, hands fisted into shaking lumps, and pounded the hard, smooth walls until I felt bones shifting beneath the skin. It healed faster than I would have liked; the distraction didn't last, and the pressure in my eyes built and built and suddenly, there was a breathtakingly lovely burst of *light.*

The glare burned so badly I cried out, but it didn't matter. I could see, and suddenly, the panic wasn't quite so desperate or overwhelming. I could manage this. I *would* manage it. As everything in my life, there was a way out, a single slender thread of hope, however insane. . . .

Because that was, in fact, my secret. In an insane world, sanity made very little sense. No one expected me to live, and therefore, I did. Always.

I looked up, and saw a depressingly narrow tunnel closing into a tiny, dim hole far, far above . . . and the gleam of a silver grate above, a circle enclosing a cross. Pennyfeather hadn't just thrown me blinded into a pit; he'd thrown me into one of the levels of hell, and locked me in with silver, on the terribly unlikely chance I might scale the heights to crawl out. And who knew what lay beyond; nothing good, I was sure. If it had been Oliver giving the order, he'd left little to chance when he was determined in his course.

Still. At least it's not dark now, I consoled myself. I looked down, and in the faintest possible sliver of light I saw my legs—bare below the knees, since I had perhaps unwisely worn a pair of ancient velvet knee britches, and as pale as I had ever seen my skin. It was the color of dirty snow, and wrinkled to boot. I lifted one foot from the brackish water, and the bunny slippers were soaked and drooped pathetically. Even the fangs seemed robbed of any charm.

"Don't worry," I told it. "Someone will pay for your suffering. Heavily. With screaming."

I felt I should repeat it for the other slipper, in case there should be any bad feelings between the two. One should never create tension between one's footwear.

That duty done, I looked up again. Water dripped cold from the heights and hit my face in sharp, icy stabs. It was cruel, since it could only irritate me, not sustain me. Still, there must be rats. Every dungeon had rats; they came standard issue. Rat blood was not my favorite, but as the old saying goes, any port in a storm. And I was most definitely in a storm, a true tempest of trouble.

Water. Water water water falling cold in gray skies drowning the land gray dirt gray ashes gray bones of houses falling slowly into ruin gray eyes of a woman staring down with pity and tears so many tears mother so much disappointment in her face, and what I was now was not what I had been when she'd last seen me . . . the screams, the slamming door, no family left now, no one to care . . . my sisters, screaming at me to go away, go away . . .

I pulled myself sharply away from the memory. No. No, we do not think of those things. *You should think of them, think of your sisters, think of what you did,* something whispered in my ear, but it was a bad whisper, a vile and treacherous worm with the face of someone I had once loved, I was sure of that, but I didn't want to remember who might have warned me. I hadn't listened, in any case. I never listened.

I lifted up the right slipper again and addressed its soggy little head. "I'm afraid I might have to leave you behind. And you, too, twin. It will be difficult enough to climb without you hampering me. And your fangs aren't very sharp."

They didn't respond. A small bolt of ice-cold clarity swept

over me, and I felt ashamed for talking to my shoes, and especially for apologizing to them. Clarity confused me. It was far less forgiving and kind than the general state of disconnection in which I liked to live.

Nonetheless, sanity—however brief—did force me to look again at the walls. The surface wasn't perfect, after all; it was pocked with tiny imperfections. Not built, but bored out of solid stone, and while whatever drill had made it had polished the sides clean, it hadn't quite removed every hint of texture.

It wasn't much, but it was something, and I sighed at the prospect of just how unpleasant this was going to be.

Then I grimly jammed my fingernails into the wall and began to scrape tiny handholds.

Come and find me, I was still begging Claire, because I knew all too well that my nails—however sharp and sturdy—would be worn to nubs long before I reached the silver grate above. And said silver would be impossible for me to break from below, with no leverage and a chancy hold. And, of course, it would take days to scrape myself a ladder to the top, even assuming my nails could hold out so long.

But the least I could do would be to try. Pennyfeather might come back, after all; he might not be done with me. Perhaps I had been gifted to him as some macabre toy. If that was the case, I certainly needed to be ready to kill him, quickly, before he could invent new horrible things to do to me.

It might be the only chance I had to survive.

TWELVE

SHANE

◡

At least the lights in the lab were on; that was something. I hadn't thought to ask Claire if I needed a flashlight—I mean, there was a lot going on, and no time for leisurely Q&A—but when I squeezed through that icy/hot darkness that Claire called a portal, and I called *wrong*, it was decently lit up on the other side.

Myrnin's lab was, as usual, a wreck, but I thought it was worse than before . . . probably because there were two vampires fighting the hell out of each other, and at the speed they were moving, it was hard to be sure which one was my friend. All I got was impressions as they shoved each other up and down the crowded aisles made tricky with spilled and slaughtered books. Claire would hate that—all the mutilated pages.

I was more worried about the blood, because there were smears of it here and there, and it looked like someone was getting the worst of the fight.

And my guess that it was Michael was confirmed when suddenly the fight ended. It went from speed of light to full stop in one cold second, and Michael was on the floor with the creepy, androgynous Pennyfeather kneeling on his chest, eyes red and claws dripping the same color.

Oh, holy crap. It wasn't Myrnin. In a straight-out fight, Michael could have probably taken Claire's boss, but Pennyfeather was something else—something worse.

Pennyfeather drew back for a blow that would probably have decapitated Michael, except that I leaped forward and planted a boot in his side, slammed him off-balance, and shot him with my newest, sweetest toy. It had been made to tranquilize big game animals, like lions and tigers, and I figured it would do just fine for vampires. Especially if, instead of using sedatives, the darts were filled up with silver in suspension.

And it worked. Pennyfeather thought he had me; he rolled up and focused his rage right in my face, and yeah, that was scary, but I saw the first flicker as it passed over his face. Confusion. Then pain. Then shock.

"What—?" he said, and then he collapsed to his knees. He grabbed the dart I'd buried in his neck and yanked it out. I saw a wisp of smoke curl out from the blackened hole in his skin. "What did you—"

"You tried to kill my girlfriend *and* my best friend," I said. "Suck it, fangboy."

There wasn't enough silver in the dart to kill him, but it was more than enough to make him deeply unhappy for a long time— and, most important, stuck right there, unable to move.

Just the way I wanted him.

I held out a hand to Michael, who hadn't moved from where he'd landed, and he took it and managed to stand. His leg was broken, and I winced when I saw how not-straight it was, but he just shook his head, hopped on one foot, and kicked out, hard. The bones slid back together. He managed not to scream. I would have. A lot. But he did clamp his hand on my shoulder and hold on with brutal strength.

"You good?" I asked, which was a weird thing to say, admittedly; he'd just reset a broken leg, vampire-style, which was gross and cool at the same time.

"Nothing that can't heal," he said. "Damn, he's fast. I mean, *really* fast. I was expecting Myrnin gone wild. Not him."

"Want to go kick him a few more times?"

"With a broken leg?"

"Okay, fair point." I made sure he could stand on his own, then went back to my dropped bag. It was full of interesting things. I sorted through, slowly, because I knew Pennyfeather was still conscious and watching me. "Hmmm. So, should I go with something fast, like the silver stake through the heart? It's a classic, I'll admit, but I was hoping for something he'd really appreciate. One thing I know about this jackhole is that he really likes his quality pain."

"He's not getting out of here again," Michael agreed. "But you don't have to go all Marquis de Sade on him, either. Just kill him. Or let me."

"You're not a killer," I told him. "Fangs aside, I know you, man. You've got a nice-guy streak a mile wide. Now me..." I pulled out a big silver-coated knife, suitable for skinning deer, presuming I ever hunted any vampire deer, and held it up so it caught the light. "Me, I'm more of a 'Welcome to the dark side' kind of person."

Michael's leg was fixed well enough that he hobbled over to me and took the knife away. I let him, of course. "You're not a stone-cold murderer," he said. "And Pennyfeather's just lying there waiting for it. You'll kill somebody in self-defense, or defending someone else, but not like this."

"And you will? Give me my knife."

"Are you going to use it, or just pose for pictures? Because you know we can't leave him alive." Those last words were said quietly, in a voice that was a whole lot darker than the Michael Glass I'd known most of my life, the one who'd always had my back and been ready to kick ass if necessary.

But neither one of us *killed*. Not in the sense of cold-blooded murdering.

"He tried to kill Claire," I said. "I guess——"

"He tried to kill Eve, too," Michael said, "and wife trumps girlfriend just a little. So it's my job." His blue eyes looked dark now, almost like a night-sky color, and I would have actually felt better if he'd been vamping out in some way. But he wasn't. It was just regular Michael, talking about murder, with my knife in his hand.

I didn't know what to say to that. I stood up slowly, watching his face, and he nodded.

"Guess I'll get it done."

"Dude——"

Ignoring me, he limped over to Pennyfeather, who was still lying prone on the floor where the tranquilizer had taken him out. I had to admit, that one had worked way better than I'd expected.

Which raised the important question of why it had worked better than expected—because nothing ever did. In fact, I was always surprised when any of the things I invented worked at all. And Pennyfeather was one hard-to-kill fanger.

All of a sudden, I had a black, sick feeling in the pit of my stomach.

"Michael—"

"I've got this," he said. He looked pale but determined. "He tried to kill Eve, and Claire, and if we let him go, he's going to do worse. You know that."

"Watch—"

Out, I was going to say, but I didn't get the chance, because Pennyfeather wasn't all that tranquilized after all. He wasn't fully healed, though, and that was all that saved Michael from having his arm ripped off as the other vamp came up off the floor, grabbed his wrist, and yanked hard enough to break the knife free. It clattered to the stone floor and bounced, and I scrambled after it as Michael punched Pennyfeather in the face a couple of times to try to break his grip, without success. Pennyfeather's eyes had gone full-on red, and his fangs were down; he was trying to pull Michael down into biting range, and managed to score a long red scrape down his forearm before Michael wrenched backward. I grabbed the knife and headed back, and Pennyfeather knew the rules had changed; maybe it was the look on my face, and the fact that however much I might hesitate at knifing a helpless enemy, I wasn't even going to hesitate when he was a threat to my friend.

He shoved Michael hard into a table behind him, but Mike was ready for it; he bounced *forward* again, directly into Pennyfeather, and body-slammed him flat into the floor.

"Shane!" he yelled. "Hurry up. I can't hold him!"

I was hurrying, and that was a mistake, because one of Myrnin's stupid always-scattered books slid under my foot and threw me off-balance, and during the second or two it took me to grab my balance again, Pennyfeather heaved Michael off him and almost levitated up to a standing position. He was by no means well; he was swaying in place, but somehow that made him seem more menacing, more inhuman, like some sinister demonic puppet with glowing eyes.

Instead of coming for me, he leaped backward, up onto a table, where he sent glass crashing and flying to the ground, and full-on hissed at us. He was still woozy, and maybe he really would come down for good from the silver, but not yet. Obviously.

Attacking a vampire who had the higher ground wasn't smart, and I slowed my rush and stood shoulder to shoulder with Michael. If he decided to come at us from up there, we'd be fighting for our lives in earnest, and although the knife would help, it wasn't enough. Not nearly.

"You know," I said to Michael, "my girlfriend took him down with a broken tree branch."

"Too bad she isn't here," he said. "Watch—"

He was probably going to say *out*, but Pennyfeather did something neither of us was ready for: he backflipped off the table to the floor, and ran, zigzagging through the land mines of Myrnin's lab, off into the shadows.

"Dammit," I said. "What the hell do we do now? We can't leave him here, not if the portals still work. He could show up in our house. And where the hell is Myrnin?"

"I don't know," Michael said, "but definitely not here. We have to get him. Once and for all."

"We may not have much time." I pointed toward the black doorway, which was still shimmering. Maybe Claire was holding it open for us, but it was starting to get an uneven look to it. I looked toward the stairs, where the other, non-magical exit was, and for a long moment couldn't figure out why I was seeing a wall. "Um, Mikey?"

"What?"

"Where's the regular door out of here?"

He turned and looked, too, and saw exactly what I did: a rough-poured mass of concrete that filled and blocked the stairs that led up and out.

"What the——?" He didn't waste time on it, though, just turned back to the portal. "That's our way out. Our *only* way."

"Like I said, time's ticking, man." I was watching the portal nervously, because it seemed to be vibrating, rippling like silk in a strong wind. Not good, or at least I assumed it wasn't good. "Either we go now or we're stuck here, and my odds aren't so good with two hungry vampires and no blood bank."

"He's not going to be easy to catch with what we've got here. We need something else!"

I looked around. There was surely no shortage of crap here that could be dangerous, but it was all a hopeless jumble . . . and as I opened up the first drawer I came to, Pennyfeather glided out of the shadows about twenty feet away, and pounced.

I almost got the knife in place, but he slapped it away, and it took everything I had—and Michael leaping on the other vamp's back—to wrench free of his grip before he could start ripping pieces off me. I grabbed blindly and wrapped my hand around a heavy, solid piece of—well, something. It looked a little like a fancy camera, only really cumbersome. I didn't try to do anything clever with it, just whacked it into the side of Pennyfeather's albino head as hard as I could. It was substantial enough that it didn't even bend, and he weaved as if I'd done some damage, which I followed up with a kick that doubled him over.

And we *still* couldn't get him, because he dodged free of Michael and circled around, and Michael stalked after him, intent and focused and with his eyes glowing with vampire power. He was more concerned for me, and I appreciated that, but I got the distinct feeling that Pennyfeather wouldn't mind adding Michael's death to his scorecard, either.

I guess in trying to swing the thing I was holding at the attacking vampire again, I hit some kind of a switch, because I felt a heavy surge of energy crawl up my arm, and then I must have accidentally turned it on Michael, because he flinched as if something had hit him . . .

And then he just went *maniac*. He moved in a blur at Pennyfeather, screaming in fury, and Pennyfeather went down hard. Next thing I knew, Michael was holding him on the floor, punching him with vicious fury like I'd never known he was capable of feeling before. It was . . . scary.

I stared down at the machine humming in my hands and quickly, clumsily felt around for an off button. I pressed something that seemed switchlike, and the hum died.

Michael stopped, breathing hard, staring down at Pennyfeather with eyes that glowed so red they seemed to be swimming with hellfire. Pennyfeather wasn't moving.

"Jesus," I whispered, and put the weapon—because that was what it was, some kind of weapon—down fast on the nearest available table space. "Michael?"

"I—" His voice sounded rusty and strange, and he looked up at me with those fury-filled eyes, and I almost wished he hadn't. "Give me the knife."

"Um . . . dude . . ."

"Knife."

I shook my head and put it away. "It's not because I don't want him dead. It's because I don't trust what you're going to do with it right now."

"He tried to kill Eve." There was a kind of terrible eagerness to the way he said it that made me want to shudder.

"Okay, man, it's great you got in touch with your inner serial killer and all, but no way." I was serious. I wanted Pennyfeather dead; that was no problem at all. What I earnestly didn't want was for Michael to wake up from this—whatever it was—and have the memory of what he was about to do. Besides, in the event he suddenly took an unhealthy interest in me, I wanted to be the one holding the knife.

It took another few seconds, but finally the glow faded out of his eyes to a more-normal bloody color—I hated that I could say it was normal—and he sat back, shaking all over. "What the hell was that? I just—"

"Went all evil superhero? Yeah. I don't know. One of Myrnin's fun little gadgets, I guess." I poked at it, frowning, and it slid on top of a pile of books and nearly toppled to the floor until I grabbed it and settled it in place again.

Michael was still holding out his hand to me, and I realized he was still waiting for the knife. Calmly, now. Our eyes met and held, and I said, "Are you sure, man?"

"No," he said. "But it's got to be done."

I handed it to him. Pennyfeather's eyes were shut, and he looked lifeless already, stunned unconscious by Michael's furious attack. Lying there silent, he seemed a lot . . . smaller. And with that androgynous bone structure, he could have just as easily been a strong-featured woman as a man, and that made the whole thing even more unsettling. I wasn't sure I could have done it at all, honestly.

And just to make matters worse right then, the portal shimmered, shivered, and belched out Claire. My girlfriend was still running on adrenaline; it was obvious in her too-wide brown eyes, the color burning in her cheeks. She had a longbow in her hand that was almost as tall as she was, and an arrow nocked and ready to pull. The arrow had a barbed silver tip.

She skidded to a halt, but she didn't drop her guard. "Is Pennyfeather—" She spotted Michael kneeling over the fallen vamp, and the knife, and she sucked her breath in hard.

"Has to be done," I said. She bit her lip, but she didn't try to argue. "Look, we need to get out of here. Myrnin did something crazy and filled in the exit, so we're now relying on the goodwill of my Frankendad keeping this portal thing open, and I'm not feeling good about the plan."

"Feel worse," she said. "Frank's starving. I don't know if he can even keep this up at all. We need to get out of here, *now*."

"Not if we leave Pennyfeather behind and he has a way out that leads through our house."

Eve burst through just then, having apparently stopped to load up a rapid-fire crossbow that she held with frightening competence. She checked the corners for threats, too, before letting her guard down and starting to head toward Michael.

"Wait," I said, and got in her way. "Just—give him a minute."

She took a step back and considered me silently a second, then said, "I'm the one Pennyfeather came after. It's my job, right?"

"No!" Claire and I both said at the same time, but Claire went on, earnestly. "Eve, it's not killing him in a fight. It's—murder."

"So?" Eve said. Her eyes had gone flint-hard. "How many murders has he committed? You don't think he has it coming?"

"I don't think that's something any of us should decide!"

"Oh, honey," Eve said, and smiled just a little. "You really aren't from Morganville yet." She looked at me. "What's your objection, Collins?"

I shrugged. "Michael can handle him if he wakes up. You can't. Logistics."

Claire seemed shocked, but hey, Eve was right; Morganville kids understood this better. It might seem cruel and harsh, but when it came down to living and dying, we knew which side we wanted to end up on. Having Pennyfeather continue to stalk us was not an option.

Eve nodded. She walked over to Michael and put a gentle hand on his shoulder, and he looked up at her and took in a deep, steadying breath.

"He can't," Claire said. "He *can't*, Shane—"

I stepped in, and she dropped the bow and arrow with a clatter as I wrapped my arms around her and turned her back to what was going to happen. "Hush," I said, and nodded to Michael over her shoulder. "It'll be fast."

"Stop."

The voice seemed to come from everywhere, all around us, from hidden speakers and the tiny little one on my phone, too. It was scratchy and pale, and sounded exhausted, but it was all too familiar.

"Frank," I said. Facing down my dad was something I'd done a lot over the past few years, but it always seemed to have a new sting in the tail, every time. I wondered what it would be today. I swallowed what felt like a mouthful of acid, and said, "Just leave us alone, okay?"

"You don't need his blood on your conscience," Frank said. "Trust me, kids, you don't. Let me do it."

"You? Dad, hate to break it to you, but downstairs there's a computer, and in the middle of it there's a brain floating in a jar with wires running into it, and that's *you*. As in, you're not doing jack to Pennyfeather, however badass you think you are."

"I only have to do one thing, Son," he said. "I just have to die. I'm dying anyway; the nutrient tanks are dry, and there's nothing left for me. If you leave him here, I'll hold the portals shut until I'm gone. He's not going anywhere."

I turned and looked at Michael and Eve, and they seemed just as surprised as I was. And a little bit relieved. "Well," Eve said, "maybe it's the best—"

"Think about what you're saying," Michael said. "Because if I put this in his chest right now, he's finished. If we walk away, what if your dad screws up and lets him out?"

"Worse," Claire said, "what if he doesn't? You don't want Pennyfeather's death on your conscience, but you have no problem with leaving him here to starve? How would that be, Michael? Fun? Easy?"

He looked away. He knew, and I knew, that vampires didn't go easy from starvation; they lived a long, long time. And suffered. "Maybe he deserves it."

"Maybe," I agreed. "But if he does, he damn sure deserves the knife, too. And I don't want to wake up thinking of him down here screaming, do you?"

Pennyfeather took the decision out of our hands, because he opened his eyes, and snarled, and lunged up, claws outstretched.

And Michael acted completely out of reflex, defending himself and Eve. Quick and smooth and deadly accurate.

Pennyfeather hit the floor hard, and the silver began eating through his skin. His eyes stayed open. I didn't know if he was still alive, but I hoped not; either way, it didn't take long.

Frank's voice came back, weaker this time. "Time to leave," he said. "You need to go, now."

Michael left the knife in Pennyfeather's chest, took Eve in his arms, and led her to the portal. It rippled as they passed through without pausing.

That left just Claire and me staring at each other.

"Hey, Dad," I said to Frank. My voice sounded unexpectedly husky, and I cleared it. "Maybe this is wrong, but I think you tried to help me when the draug had me in their tanks. They were killing me and making me dream while they did it, only someone—someone kept trying to make me wake up. Was that you?"

Nothing. Silence. I listened to the distant drip of water for a while.

"Well, if it was, thanks, I guess. It made me fight."

That summed up me and my dad perfectly. He made me fight, whether I wanted to or not, and whether it was for a cause I believed in or not. He'd made me tough, and strong, and a survivor, and yeah, that was worthwhile, especially now that I had things to really fight for. Claire had quoted a writer named Hemingway to me, not so long ago: *The world breaks everyone, and afterward, some people are strong at the broken places.* I don't think my dad ever read Hemingway, but he'd have liked him.

I spent another couple of seconds waiting for—I don't know, something—and then I turned to go.

And a grainy, shadowy, two-dimensional figure formed in front of me.

My father had chosen a younger version of himself than the age he'd been when he'd died, but it was still him—him from the last of the good times of my childhood. Relatively speaking. We stared at each other for a moment, and then his lips moved. I could just barely hear the scratchy words hissing out of an ancient speaker on the side of the machine across the room.

"I knew this day would come, Shane. That's why I sent you back here. To be here when everything went bad."

"The vampires," I said. It was always about the vampires with him. He blamed them for everything—for my sister's probably accidental death, for my mom's probable suicide, for his own drinking and bitterness and anger. And yeah, okay, maybe he was right, because Morganville was a toxic place. "They're out of control."

"Always were," he whispered. "Always will be. Stop it. No matter what it costs. Burn the town around them if you've got to."

That was my dad. Always kill-'em-all-let-God-sort-'em-out. If a few innocents got caught in the inferno, well, collateral damage.

"Claire, go," I said. She was crying, I realized, silent tears that ran in silver drops down her cheeks. I couldn't sometimes fathom all of the goodness inside of her, because who cried for my dad, for a brain in a jar who'd hardly ever been good for anybody?

Claire did. She was probably crying for Pennyfeather, too.

"Go," I said again, gently, and kissed her on the lips. "I'm right behind you."

She picked up her bow and arrow and—after a hesitation, grabbed the bulky machine thing that had affected Michael so strongly. Before I could wonder about that, she headed for the portal, but she paused there, looking back. "Come on," she said. "We go together."

I headed for the exit, walking right through Frank's image. It felt like a curtain of pins and needles, but I was used to pain, especially where it came to my dad.

He re-formed ahead of me, blocking the way to Claire. I kept walking, and he kept backing up, traveling smoothly as the ghost he was. "Son," he said, "I want to tell you one thing. Just one."

"So do it."

"I'm proud of you," he said.

I came to a sudden and complete halt, staring at him—at the man I'd never really known, because he'd never let me know him; he'd treated me like a useful tool and potential enemy my whole life.

"You're different," he said. "You're better than I ever was. And I'm proud of you for being so strong. That's all. I just needed to tell you, before the end."

He dissolved in electronic smoke. Gone.

"Dad?" I turned on my heel, my voice echoing through the cool, silent lab. "Dad?"

Nothing. Just . . . silence. That told me he had no further energy to spare, and we were out of time. The lights flickered, warning me of the same thing.

Claire suddenly said, "Oh no—Bob!"

"Bob?" I stared at her blankly, and she pointed across the lab.

Oh. The spider. I shook my head and jogged over to pick up the tank—which, except for the glass content, was light—and made damn sure the lid was on it tightly before carrying it to the portal. Claire waited anxiously as the lights continued to flicker, faster and faster.

I paused on the edge of the portal as she stepped through. I wanted to say something profound, but I'm not that guy, so I just said, awkwardly, "Okay, Dad. See you."

"See you." His voice sighed, and there was something wistful in his electronic voice.

I stepped through the portal into the cool, familiar air of the Glass House, and felt the thing snap shut—utterly shut—behind me. There was an almost physical sensation of disconnection, of the whole system just . . . dying.

I put my hand on the blank wall and concentrated, for a moment, on just breathing. *You've lost him before*, I told myself. *He wasn't really there anyway.*

But it had felt real to me when he'd said he was proud. Maybe I'd always craved that, needed it. Maybe he'd known it.

But despite the surge of sadness, there was something good about leaving him this time—something that felt final, and complete.

Maybe this was what all those TV psych doctors meant when they talked about closure.

I put Bob's tank down on the dining room table, to Eve's

muttered distress, and Claire quickly dumped the heavy, clunky machine on the coffee table, along with her bow and arrow. I noticed vaguely that it was pointed in my direction, but at the moment, that didn't mean anything—and neither did the prickly feeling that raced through me.

"You're all right?" Claire said, and stepped closer with an expression of pure concern. She looked . . . I can't explain it, exactly, but all of a sudden I felt a bolt of heat go through me like fire out of heaven, and, man, did I want her in all kinds of ways—right and wrong. She'd grown over the past year—filled out in curves that begged to be held and stroked, and this definitely wasn't the time, but all of a sudden I was considering not minding what was appropriate behavior.

"Fine," I said through a suddenly dry throat. "I mean, I will be, anyway."

"I'm so sorry," she said. "I wish we could've done something."

"That's why I love you," I said, and reached over to brush her hair back from her face. "Because you care so much." Her gaze came up and hit mine, and more heat exploded through me like a bomb. I saw the shock wave of it in her eyes. *Oh.*

I really could not explain what was going on in my head and ricocheting around my body, but it was . . . good. Great, in fact. I fitted my hand around Claire's cheek and bent to kiss her. Her lips tasted like cherries and salt, sweet and tart together, and I growled somewhere deep and leaned in, pulling her close. She was mine, *mine*, and that was all that mattered. Myrnin had gone, vanished, and he wasn't any threat now. Some traitorous little whisper told me I could have asked Frank about him, about what had happened, but I hadn't wanted to know. He was gone.

And I had Claire, body and soul, and *man*, did I want her, right now. In so many ways.

"Hey," Michael said from somewhere behind me. "That's really sweet and all, but we just killed a guy and your dad—are you sure you want to be doing this *now*?"

He was dead right about that, but I couldn't take my hands away from her—or my lips. I'd somehow worked my thumbs under the tight knit of her shirt and found skin beneath, and I didn't want to let that go. The sensation of her fine, soft flesh, even that much of it, made me feel as if my head were on fire.

And then Claire gasped, coughed, and fought her way free of me. I instinctively reached for her and got air, and stumbled after . . . and as soon as I did, I sucked in a sharp, cold breath of air and felt something like sanity start to come back.

Oh. *Oh.* The machine. It lay on the coffee table, glowing a faint green, and the business end was pointed toward where Claire and I had been standing. It had gotten turned on when she'd dumped it there, I supposed.

And then, ha ha not funny, it had turned *me* on.

Claire, blushing a furious and gorgeous shade of red, circled around the table and flipped some kind of switch on the back. The glowing died, and so did the humming, and I felt . . . not normal, but less crazed. "Sorry," she said, and bit her lip. They were still damp and swollen from our kissing, and I shook myself out of focusing on them with a real effort. "It's—kind of an experiment."

"Myrnin's making a lust ray," I said. Of course he was, because . . . why not? I had to admit, I'd probably see some value in that myself. Hell. I just *had.* "Wait a second. I accidentally pointed that at Michael, and it made him—"

"Angry," Michael said. "Hyper-angry. Ready to kill."

"No, no, it's not—" Claire swallowed and visibly tried to calm herself. "It's not a lust ray. It just magnifies what you're feeling. And it's not Myrnin's. It's mine. I was just—experimenting."

"I know I'm not a scientific peer review or anything, but I have to say I think it works. If that's what you were going for, anyway." I skipped over the whole issue of why it had decided to focus on that particular impulse in me. She'd take it as a compliment, hopefully, but I wasn't too sure about that. My track record of guessing what might offend girls wasn't exactly perfect. "What were you thinking of using it for? Because the way it sent Michael into rage overdrive . . ."

The blush just wasn't getting any less red, or—even without the ray—any less interesting. "The idea is that once I can exactly amplify a feeling, I can also cancel it out," she said. "It was supposed to just work with vampires, not humans. I don't know why—why it worked on you, Shane. I'm so sorry."

"Well"—I shrugged—"I'm not, particularly. That was a little bit fun."

"I hate to admit it, but it was when it was pointed at me, too," Michael said. "Kind of like it took away all the inhibitions."

"A drunk gun," I said. "Awesome."

"Not," Claire said, and frowned. "It's dangerous." She picked it up and stuck it in her backpack, engaging some kind of safety switch I hadn't noticed before. "I'll find someplace to keep it where it won't hurt anybody until I can destroy it. It was probably a dumb idea, anyway."

Eve disappeared into the kitchen, ever practical, and came out with a blood bag that she tossed to Michael, who snatched it out of the air and bit into it with a frightening level of enthusiasm. He drained it in about, oh, ten seconds or less, the same way a human would chug water after a really aggressive workout. And it had about the same effect; he got a little weak-kneed and had to brace himself on a wall, but after the shock passed, he seemed almost immediately better. His eyes faded back to simple blue, and his skin coloring went from dead-guy pale to more like ivory. Wounds started shutting faster, too.

"Thanks," he said to Eve. She raised a cocky eyebrow.

"You'll make it up to me later," she said, and winked. That got a really different kind of smile from Michael, and I found something else to look at, fast. Now I was the one feeling like an intruder on something personal, like I guessed Mikey had earlier, what with all the passionate groping and tongues.

Funny how just the way they smiled at each other could be intimate. Or maybe I was just turning into a girl, living with two of them in the house. That was frightening. Not that I don't like girls. I just preferred to be plain old insensitive me.

"One down," I said. "But Frank gave me a warning. This town's really going to go crazy. We need to be ready."

"Always," Eve said, and high-fived me.

But I wondered if we really, truly were.

THIRTEEN

CLAIRE

The portal system had gone completely, utterly dead. The next morning, Claire started trying each of the entrances she had mapped out, and she found each of them just as inactive as the ones in the Glass House. Even Amelie's emergency escape, the one upstairs in the secret attic room, was gone.

She had known that was coming, but it was still ... weirdly sad. She shuddered, and tried not to think about Frank dying slowly in his silent tomb as she exited the abandoned warehouse—portal number twelve on the map—and headed back toward the center of town. This side of Morganville was mostly left to rot and rats—had been for years, slowly falling into ruin as the businesses closed or relocated. The porch had finally fallen down at the front of the old hospital building where she and Shane had once run from both his father and Oliver, blocking it to even the hardiest urban explorers. There were likely lots of other ways in, but nobody sane wanted to go in there. It was a great place to go permanently missing—not just because of the vampires, but because there were some serious drug trade people who had claimed it for their own property. They could have it, as far as Claire was concerned. The place wasn't just haunted; it was *evil*.

I could have spent the morning working on the machine—what am I going to call it? The Vampire Power Cancellation Device? VPCD, for short? Fine, how about the Magic Thingy? She was fantasizing too much about what it could do, she thought, but she couldn't shake the idea that if she could just get a perfect amplification signal to match what the vampires were sending out, she could somehow cancel it . . . and perfectly nullify the effect.

Not that it would have stopped Pennyfeather from trying to rip her throat out, of course. Drawbacks.

This area of town was *really* run-down. Claire cursed under her breath as she tripped over another fallen fence. The vampires really could have done some urban renewal around here, but they liked having some ruins around; maybe it suited their Gothic sensibilities, or maybe it was just practical, having places where they could stalk around after dark in private. She wondered why they hadn't shut down the meth trade, though. Maybe—likely—they just didn't care enough.

As Claire was walking away, she saw the black ghost-hunting *After Death* van turn the corner and pull to a stop right in front of the building. *Oh, no. No. Don't* . . . But there they were: Jenna, Angel, and Tyler, getting out of the van, pulling out all kinds of equipment, cables, boxes. They were clearly going to stage some kind of spirit investigation in there. *Such* a bad idea.

Claire took out her phone and dialed the Morganville police department's nonemergency number. They weren't fast responders, generally, and it took at least ten rings before someone finally picked up. "Hi, it's Claire Danvers," she said. "You know who I am?"

"Yes. What do you want?" The voice on the other end was professional and cold. No clues as to who it was she might be talking to, or how the individual really felt.

"I'm standing in front of the old hospital building, the abandoned one? And those stupid ghost-hunting people are here. I just thought—maybe you could send a car over, tell them to move on?" She hesitated for a second, then plunged on. "Why are they still here, anyway?"

"We're waiting for a decision as to how to handle them," the voice said. "Until then, we're letting them poke around. People know to avoid them. The hope is they'll just lose interest and leave."

People meaning, Claire assumed, *vampire people.* The cops seemed to have it handled. "Okay," she said. "But that hospital's not safe. You know that, right?"

"We'll send a car," he promised, and hung up on her.

So much for being civic-minded. Claire watched the activity over at the van for a while, until she saw them actually ducking through a cut in the chain-link fence around the building. They were going inside.

Not good. For them.

She crossed the street, hoping to hear an approaching siren, but there was nothing except the hissing, constant desert wind and the rattle of tumbleweeds against the fences. In places, there were so many of the balled, thorny plants tangled in that it looked like a barricade. One skipped across open ground and bumped against her pants leg, and she had to stop to pull the burred tips free; her fingertips tingled and itched afterward.

Tyler had already gone inside. Angel was sliding through the fence now, with Jenna holding it open.

"Hey," Claire said, and they both turned to look at her in surprise. "Sorry, didn't mean to scare you, but this isn't a good place. It's unstable in there. The floor's all rotten."

"Ah, it's—Claire, right?" When she nodded, Angel smiled—with far less wattage than he would have used for Monica, she thought. "Well, we thank you for the warning, but we're very used to working in dangerous spaces. Remember the asylum, Jenna? The one in Arkansas?"

"The floors were completely gone," Jenna said. "We had to walk on the beams or we'd have dropped at least three stories straight into the basement. Got some great stuff, though. It was a huge ratings winner." She pushed a box through to Angel, then a second one. "Don't worry, we're trained for this kind of thing."

"There are snakes in there," Claire said. "Rattlers. And black widow spiders. It's *really* not safe."

"And we're *really* okay with it," Jenna said. "You go on, Claire. We've got this." Jenna studied her with curious pale eyes. "You seem pretty eager to keep us out of there. What's your real reason?"

Claire shrugged and kicked a random rock. "Nothing," she said. "Just I hate to see you get in trouble in there, for nothing. You're wasting your time around here, anyway."

"You'd be surprised what we've picked up already around here," Jenna said. That sounded ominous. "My personal opinion is that this town is a hotbed of paranormal activity. I believe we'll get dramatic footage out of what we find inside. It's almost as if—as if we're being guided."

"Guided," Claire repeated. "By what?"

"By whom," Angel corrected. His smile held just a touch of

indulgent doubt. "Jenna believes that she's made contact with a lost spirit."

"I have," Jenna said, and it sounded like the embers of an old argument, flaring up again. "Maybe you might recognize her. It's a young girl—"

Not Alyssa, Claire thought, stricken. *Please don't say it's Shane's sister.* Because there was no doubt in her mind, now, that Alyssa's spirit lingered, trapped in the lot where she'd died, even though the house had tumbled down.

"Miranda," Jenna finished. "At least, that's what I've been able to make out from the EVP recordings. We have quite a lot of them. She's very talkative."

"Miranda," Claire repeated, and drew in a deep breath. She'd survived out here, somehow; she'd latched onto the ghost-hunting crew in the hopes of getting help. But that was *so* dangerous. "Um . . . no, I don't think I recognize that name. Probably before my time."

"Huh," Jenna said, but Claire didn't like the look in her eyes. It was far too shrewd. "Funny how she knows *your* name, then. And a whole lot more."

She was saved by the distant wail of a siren. It was coming closer. Jenna and Angel looked at each other, eyebrows raised, as it became clear it was heading into their area, and both called, at the same time, "Tyler!"

Tyler backed out of the tumbled, brick-strewn doorway of the hospital. "Yeah, what? I'm going to have to climb over all this crap to get in this way. Maybe we should check the side—"

"Did you clear the location with the PD?" Angel asked.

"Didn't you?"

Jenna sighed. "Dammit, Tyler—"

Claire made a quick, tactical retreat as the Morganville police cruiser pulled up behind the van, lights and siren still going, and left them to sort it out.

Miranda was still around, and she was working with the ghost hunters in some way. Well—that was good that she'd found a way to survive, but still, Claire had a terrible feeling that it was also a complication.

Maybe a big one.

Claire felt better after leaving the neighborhood and starting to see open businesses again, ragged as they were; most of them were scrap yards and places that repaired appliances, maybe a couple of "antique shops" that were where you took things a step above the scrap yard. A secondhand clothing store Claire sometimes visited, though it was mostly Morganville natives who shopped there; the store over by campus was the one with stuff in her size, and from out of town generally, because of the college students who shed their clothes by season. It was terrible to be thinking of clothing just now, though; she'd just eliminated any possibility of searching Myrnin's lab for clues to where he'd gone. It deeply sucked. Not to mention that it would take a jackhammer and a backhoe to dig through the concrete sealing the entrance if she ever intended to rescue Myrnin's books, which were mostly irreplaceable.

She saw the first mayoral campaign sign stapled to a light pole—one for Captain Obvious—and remembered, with a shock, that the election was *today*. She hadn't cast a ballot yet. Well, the day was still young; she had time. And it was kind of her duty, since it had been her brainstorm in the first place, to vote for Monica, though she'd have to hold her nose to do it.

So she headed to City Hall, and ran straight into a mob scene. The noise was a dull roar about a block away, and she thought it was some kind of construction work, maybe a giant bulldozer or grinding machine or something . . . but as she got closer, she heard that it wasn't mechanical at all. It was voices—yelling voices, all blending into something that sounded like a collective insanity. People were running *toward* the noise, and she found she had the same impulse to go and see what was going on. Though there'd been some attempts, nothing that big had ever happened in Morganville, in her experience. People just didn't have the heart to riot in those numbers.

Until now.

As Claire turned the corner, she saw there was a flatbed tractor trailer parked on the curb in front of City Hall, decked out with some sad-looking patriotic streamers and ribbons, and on it stood Flora Ramos, with someone in a black leather jacket, black pants, gloves, and a motorcycle helmet with a dark, opaque faceplate. His—at least, Claire assumed it was a man—arms were crossed. Flora was at the microphone next to a big pair of speakers.

The posters that people had on poles and held up over their heads were the CAPTAIN OBVIOUS FOR MAYOR signs.

And clearly, the guy standing on the dais next to Flora was . . . the new Captain Obvious? It could have been the same guy who'd fired at Oliver in Common Grounds; he'd been wearing a black hood then, instead of the helmet, but the jacket looked similar.

Flora Ramos held up her hands and stilled to a dull mutter the approving roar of the thousand or so people crammed in the street.

"We've had enough," she was saying. "Enough of the oppression. Enough of the death. Enough of the inequality. Enough of losing our homes, our lives, our children, to things we don't control. And we won't be silent. If Mayor Moses couldn't make our voices heard, we will make them heard on every street, in every building, and on every corner of Morganville until things change! Until we *make* them change! We built this town with our sweat and blood and strength, and it is *our* town as much as that of those who pretend to own it!"

She was, Claire had to admit, a *great* speaker. She was angry, full of passion, and it arced out of her like lightning to sting the crowd into more yells, chants, and shouts. Claire slowed down. She was a little afraid, suddenly, of the power of that mob, and of Flora's eloquence. So were the Morganville cops, she realized. They were out in force, all twenty or so, forming a solid cordon between the crowd and City Hall.

No telling how the vampires felt about it, but Claire had no doubt, none at all, that they were well aware of this. And if they'd been unhappy about Monica seeking the office, how pissed off were they now? Plenty, she imagined. From the crowd that had gathered, Captain Obvious was going to win in a landslide, and if the vamps thought they could ignore the ballots and pick their own candidate, it was going to get very ugly, very quickly. Nobody would be fooled, and clearly, the humans were in no mood to take it lying down.

Flora was still talking, but it was hard to hear her over the constant, fevered applause and cheering. Claire stared hard at Captain Obvious. Hard to tell anything about him, underneath the disguise, but he had a hell of a lot of guts coming out here in public and standing as a free target after putting a crossbow bolt in *Oliver.*

So she could have predicted what came next.

It started calmly enough. Claire was used to looking for vampires, so she picked up the smooth, subtle movements from the shadows well before most other people. It started with one or two coming out, well swathed in long coats and scarves, hats and gloves, but it didn't stop there. Soon it was ten. Then twenty. Then too many for Claire to count.

And like the police, they fanned out, but not to cordon off the crowd.

They were making for the stage, and Captain Obvious.

He saw them coming about the time that most others did. Vampires didn't need protection, even in a crowd like this; Morganville natives had it bred into them to back up, get away, and that was exactly what they did. Cries of alarm went up, and little islands of space formed around the vamps as they pushed forward.

Captain Obvious's helmet turned toward Flora, and she nodded. He backed up to the edge of the trailer, dropped off and out of sight, and one second later Claire heard the roar of a motorcycle. He came roaring out from concealment on the other side of the truck, spraying smoke as he fishtailed around. The crowd cleared for him, too, or at least for the snarling bike, and he leaned into the handlebars and hit the thrust hard.

A lunging vampire tried to take him off the machine, but he ducked low and weaved expertly, and she went rolling. When another tried it ten feet later, someone in the crowd—more daring than the rest—ran forward and knocked the vampire's hat off. The vampire turned with a roar of fury and slapped the broad-brimmed coverage back over his smoking head, but his second was lost, and Captain Obvious accelerated away, leaning into a sharp turn with his knee almost on the ground. It was someone with training, Claire thought, someone with a lot of skill.

The vampires largely gave up on him, though a few tried chasing him; the rest bolted forward, swarmed onto the stage, and two grabbed Flora Ramos. A third cleanly severed the microphone cord with a single pull, robbing her of her soapbox.

But when they tried to take her down from the platform, people surged forward, shouting. They'd lost their fear, all of a sudden. It made sense. Flora was a popular lady, a widow, who'd lost kids to the vampires. She was everybody's mom, all of a sudden, being dragged off into the dark—not in the middle of the night, but in public, in broad daylight, in a blatant show of vampire force.

Amelie and Oliver must have approved this. They must be watching, Claire thought with a sudden twinge. She turned and looked behind her, and saw a long blacked-out sedan idling at the corner. She walked that way. Walked right up to the car and rapped on the backseat window.

It glided down to reveal the pale, sharp face of Oliver. He didn't speak. He just gazed at her with cool disinterest. Next to him, Amelie was looking straight ahead, a slight frown grooved between her brows. She looked flawless, as always, but Claire knew her well enough to think she was bothered by what she saw before her.

"Let Mrs. Ramos go," Claire told Oliver.

"She's preaching sedition and breaching the public peace," he said. "She's ours by law."

"Maybe. But if you take her off that stage, you lose. Not just now, but for a long time. People won't forget."

"I care not what they remember," he said. "The only way to stop a rebellion is to crush it with blood and fire, and to wound them so they'll never dare to raise a hand again."

He sounded as if he almost *liked* it. Claire shuddered, and looked past him, to Amelie. "Please," she said. "This isn't right. Stop it. Let Flora go."

It took forever for the Founder to speak, but when she did, her voice was soft, even, and decisive. "Let the old woman go," she said. "It gains us nothing to make her a martyr. Our goal is to find this new Captain Obvious. He can't hide for long. Once we have him, we make an example of him and make it clear that this kind of disruption won't be tolerated. Yes?"

Oliver scowled and sent Claire a murderous glance. "My queen, I think you are listening too much to your pets. The girl's soft-hearted. She'll lead us all to ruin." He lifted Amelie's pearl white hand to his lips and kissed it, lips lingering on her skin, and she finally looked at him. "Let me guide you in this. You know I have the best interests of Morganville at heart. And *you* are Morganville."

The frown between Amelie's perfectly arched brows relaxed, smoothed, and she kept her gaze fully focused on him. "I fear your way will bring us more trouble, Oliver."

"And this chit's way will bring us death," he said. "Mark me, compromise is no answer. We would compromise ourselves into a pyre of ashes. Humans have no pity for us, and never have; they'd kill every one of us. Have you forgotten that one of them just yesterday tried to put a silver arrow in my heart?"

"And I pulled it out," Claire said. "Or you'd be dead now, you jerk. What exactly is a *chit*?"

It was a rhetorical question, but Amelie's gaze tugged away from Oliver's for a moment, and Claire got the full force of the Founder's attention. "A disrespectful young woman," she said. "Something I was called more than once. Something every woman of quality is called, sooner or later, by a man who feels they do not know their place. As we do not, because our place is as lofty as we may aspire to climb. It is the language of men who fear women." There was something weird about Amelie's eyes; they seemed darker than normal, and Claire couldn't figure it out until she realized that the pupils were inordinately large, as if she'd had some kind of dilating drops in them. Was she being drugged? "Which brings up a good point, Oliver. I believe you've called me a chit, upon occasion. Yet suddenly you call me your queen."

"You've ever been queen in my heart," he said, which made Claire want to gag. His voice was smoky, soothing, and way too seductive. "Can we not agree on this one thing, my liege? That the survival of what few vampires remain must take precedence over the legions of humans who roam this earth in their billions? If we trust to their good graces, we will die."

"He is not wrong in that, Claire," Amelie said. "Mankind is not known for its charity toward those it fears. If we're not torn apart as demons, we'll be dissected in your laboratories, for science. Or worse, put on exhibition, no better than those ragged lions and exhausted bears in your zoos. Who will protect us, if we don't protect ourselves?"

Claire wanted to say that she was wrong, that it wouldn't be like that, but she'd read enough history and knew enough about the grudges and fears that people held close to their hearts to realize that Amelie was probably right, in principle.

"Let her go," Claire said. "And people will see you're not afraid to be part of this town and listen to them. Trust me. Please. I don't want this to explode, and neither do you, but it will. You make Mrs. Ramos disappear, and it'll never stop exploding. Vampires will take out humans, humans will take out vampires, and sooner or later, we're all dead or you're discovered."

"I cannot let her go. Not an option." But Amelie seemed to consider things, and suddenly she pulled her hand free of Oliver's hold, opened the other side of the limousine, and stepped out into the sun.

Unlike the other vampires, she didn't bother to try to cover herself; she was old enough that the sun wouldn't do more than give her a painful but mild burn. The sight of her in full daylight was startling. She wore a white silk suit, expertly tailored, and her short stature was concealed with tall white pumps. Her pale gold hair, wrapped in a coronet around her head, was almost the same shade. The only color on her was a bloodred ruby necklace and a matching ring, and as she walked off toward the mob, she looked every inch a queen.

Oliver slammed his door open, grabbed Claire by the arm, and shoved her back against a brick wall. "Stupid girl," he said, and ran after Amelie. She didn't seem to be moving fast—drifting, almost—but he had trouble catching her.

She reached the crowd before him, and it parted in front of her like smoke before a strong wind. The vampires paused on stage, suddenly aware of her presence, and silence swept over the chaos to the point that Claire imagined she could almost hear the click of Amelie's heels as she moved up the portable stairs to the stage.

Oliver scrambled behind her, impassive in expression, but she could see the anger and frustration in his body language. He was too late to stop whatever she intended to do.

"Release the woman," Amelie said to the two vamps holding Flora. They let go, immediately, and stepped away with their heads bowed. Amelie advanced to stand in front of her. "Are you injured?"

Flora shook her head no.

"Then you may leave this place, if you wish. Or you may stay here, on this stage, and accept the very difficult and thankless job of mayor, a position to which I believe you are uniquely suited."

Whatever Flora was expecting, it wasn't that. Neither were her supporters. A confused babble started up, and Claire jogged back over so she could hear more clearly over the confusion. The microphones were dead, so only the first few rows were likely to hear what was going on.

"I'm not running," Flora said. "It's Captain Obvious the people want."

"And Captain Obvious they will not get," Amelie replied with perfect calm. "One cannot elect a man too cowardly to show his face. You, Mrs. Ramos, have courage enough for both, quite clearly. And so *you* are my nominee. What say you? We have enough residents here to win you the day, simply by voice. Yes or no?"

"I can't——" It wasn't a refusal, though; it was a confused and reluctant argument. "I'm not a politician."

"Neither is Captain Obvious, else he would not have run away at the first sign of trouble," Amelie said coolly, and got a ripple of chuckles from a few in the crowd. "I come to stand before the people of Morganville as the Founder. Unafraid. Can he say as much? You stand before them as well. And I say you will uphold their trust. I ask you for nothing but honorable service. Will you accept?"

Claire didn't hear the answer, because the roar that went up from the crowd was deafening.

There really wasn't any question of refusing.

Amelie had outmaneuvered Captain Obvious *and* Oliver, and she had regained the equilibrium of Morganville, at least temporarily—all in a mere thirty seconds.

Claire shook her head in wonder, and went home to tell Shane that, despite their hard work—and glitter—Monica was off the ballot.

He'd be *so* disappointed.

Claire wasn't the first one to get the news to the Glass House, even though she called as she jogged away from City Hall. Eve answered on the first ring and said, "Are you at the riot?"

"It's not really a riot. More of a rally."

"Because the underground talk is that it's a riot. Are they beating people with signs? Is there pepper spray involved? Details!"

"Not that I saw," she said. "I really thought I had breaking news, but you beat me to it."

"Not so much, sugar pie. Is it true that they almost got Flora Ramos? Man, I wish they had. It would have just destroyed whatever high ground Amelie had left. I mean, *Flora Ramos*—everybody knows about her kids. . . ."

"They didn't take her in," Claire said, and talked fast, in case Eve was refreshing the Web page. "Amelie declared her mayor."

"Wait—*declared?* How is that fair? Wow, Monica is going to be *pissed* that she didn't even get to properly lose. . . . Okay, that's an upside, actually."

"She wouldn't have gotten much of a vote. There was about half the town rallying out there—you know, the half that breathes? And they weren't carrying any 'Monica Morrell' signs. Everybody was Team Obvious out there."

There was a rustle on the other end, and then a confused blur of voices arguing. "Hey!" Eve came into focus again. "Hell no, Shane, call her yourself. I got her first. . . . Oh, all right. Shane says to tell you he worked hard on those signs, and they were way better than Captain Obvious's signs." Eve covered up the speaker, but Claire still heard her muffled exchange with him. "Really? You had to try to steal my phone to say that? Loser!" Shane's comeback was indistinct, but probably insulting. Eve frostily ignored it and said, "You were saying, Claire?"

"No matter how great they were, all our posters got torn down or . . ."

"Or? Claire? Hellllloooooooo?"

"Gotta go," Claire said hastily, and hung up, because Monica's red convertible was pulled in at the curb up ahead, and she was standing there, staring at one of her posters that *hadn't* been pulled down. Claire could see the blank expression on her face, which made her curious, and she hurried over to stand at an angle where she could see the poster.

She covered her mouth to hide an appalled gasp, because someone had gotten downright artistic on Monica's poster—more than one person, obviously, from the ink-color variations and styles. One had written, in bold Sharpie, *Burn in Hell*, which was really the nicest thing anyone had said. The additions to her half-drunk duckface picture were interesting, too, and mostly pornographic.

Not that Monica didn't deserve it. She did. This was nothing but retribution, but from the look on the girl's face, she hadn't seen it coming, not at all.

"They hate me," Monica said. Her voice was quiet and a little hushed, and her eyes were wide. There were spots of high color on her cheekbones under the spray tan. "Jesus, they really do hate me."

"Um . . . sorry. But what did you expect?"

"Respect," Monica said. "Fear. But they're not afraid of me. Not anymore." She reached out, took hold of the poster, and yanked it down. It ripped in the middle, and she tore the second half down with even more vicious fury. The cardboard was tough, but she managed to reduce it to vivid neon scraps and toss it defiantly to the sidewalk in a shattered heap. "Their mistake! And *yours*, bitch! I know you and Shane set this up. You always wanted to see me humiliated!" She advanced on Claire, fists clenched. Claire stood her ground calmly, and Monica stopped coming when she realized she wasn't going to make her back down, but rage still boiled through her whole body. At the slightest opportunity, the least little sign of weakness, she'd pounce.

"We thought you might pull it off," Claire said. "It's not our fault you have more baggage than an airport at Christmas. Maybe instead of getting even, you ought to be thinking how to improve what people think about you."

"I think *you* have about ten seconds to get out of my face!"

Claire shrugged. "Enjoy your outcast life, then. You'll get used to it. The rest of us do just fine."

"Bitch!" Monica yelled at her back, but it was just words, and it was a sign of just how much things had changed between the two of them that Monica didn't dare attack her with anything else, not even when her back was turned. "I'll get you for this—I swear!"

Claire just waved and kept walking, though the area right between her shoulder blades kept itching until she heard Monica's car door slam and heard the roar of the engine. Even then, she stayed ready to jump out of the way should the Mustang mysteriously jump the curb, but once it had flashed past her, burning rubber in a thin, bitter mist on the still air, she relaxed. A little.

But only for a moment.

It was a sunny morning, quiet; the sun hung warm in a cloudless sky the color of faded denim, and a couple of big hawks kited overhead, circling for prey. It wasn't the time or place that she would have expected to sense a threat, and yet . . .

Yet something was wrong. She could just . . . feel it.

It took her a few seconds of quick analysis to figure out that what had tripped her alarm switch was the dusty college bookstore she had just passed. Instead of opening up, someone had been sliding the curtains closed in the window . . . and now a hand reached through the curtain and turned the OPEN sign to CLOSED. That wasn't right. It was a regular workday, and the store wouldn't have been open for very long. *Well, he could have just wanted to grab breakfast. Or an early lunch.*

She couldn't be sure, because it happened very quickly, but she could have sworn that the hand flipping the sign had taken on a vivid red sunburn even in that brief exposure to the sun.

Vampire.

Claire slowly backed up, staring at the store. She thought back to what was happening while she'd been talking to—well, been taking abuse from—Monica. Had someone gone inside the place? Yes, one person; she'd seen him out of the corner of her eye. And, now that she thought of it, that person had been Professor Carlyle, he of the utterly unearned B on her physics paper, so obviously not a creature of the night, even if he was evil.

Someone had been in the store already, like a spider waiting in a web.

Not my problem, Claire told herself, but something deep down argued with her. Maybe she'd spent too much time around Shane, who was always throwing himself gleefully into one fight after another. Maybe she was just still angry at Amelie and Oliver's arrogant attitude toward the mostly defenseless human population of Morganville. Whatever.

She slipped her backpack off her shoulder, tugged free a silver stake, and tried the door, and despite the sign, it was still unlocked. She was committed then—the vampire would have heard her anyway, however distracted he might have been. So she charged inside, let the door bang shut behind her, and landed solidly on her feet, ready for the fight.

Good thing she was, because the vampire came at her fast out of the shadows, a white distorted face and a red snarl, and she struck out and got flesh, but not his heart. He screamed and darted off, clearly not prepared for a fight with someone who could hurt him, and in the brief respite Claire glanced around the shop. The lights were on, which was helpful. Typical college bookstore, with loads of shelves crammed with dog-eared, highlighted-over textbooks; the whole place had a run-down, cheap look to it that probably was exactly what the average TPU student liked about it—that, and the low, low prices. (Claire had tried it out once, but the book she'd bought at pennies on the dollar also had significant issues, such as missing about a dozen crucial pages in the middle.)

The shopkeeper, whose name she vaguely remembered as Sarah something—Sarah Brooke, that was it—was sitting on the floor. Her wrists and ankles had been tied together, and her eyes were so wide that she was likely screaming under the duct tape that covered her mouth.

Professor Carlyle was kneeling beside her. He'd been blitz-attacked, apparently; he had a cut on the side of his head that was bleeding freely in shocking red streams, and he was holding a trembling hand to his neck. More blood trickled out of that wound, but it wasn't gushing. "Danvers?" he said, in blank astonishment.

"You okay, sir?"

"He—he bit me—but I'm Protected!" He held up the hand that wasn't clamped over his throat, and Claire saw the silvery glint of a bracelet. "This can't happen!"

Sarah was Protected, too—she was wearing a similar bracelet that guaranteed her safety from vampire attack, at least theoretically. Obviously, it wasn't a magic shield.

The vampire, who'd backed away from Claire temporarily, took another run at her, and this time, she skipped backward and ripped down the curtains over the big front window, framing herself in bright daylight. "Come on, if you're coming," she said, but the vamp skidded to a halt right at the edge where shadow met sun.

And she got her first good look at him. "Jason?" she blurted in horror.

The vampire who was trying to kill her—and Sarah, and Professor Carlyle—was Jason Rosser, Eve's brother.

He'd wanted to be a vampire—had actively campaigned for it—and she'd been afraid he'd be even worse as a person if he grew fangs; here it was, proof positive, that if you had creepy violent tendencies as a human, you felt free to indulge them as a new vampire. The only good thing about the situation was that he was *really* new, and super allergic to the sun. In fact, today's attack might have been his first try at hunting.

If so, it wasn't going extremely well.

"Get out of here," Jason said. His voice was low, rough, and ugly with fury. "I don't want you. *Get out.*"

"Too bad, you've got me, jackass. What the hell are you doing?"

"What does it look like, bite bait?" He flashed his teeth at her, which might have scared her, oh, years ago.

"Failure? And don't drop fang at me, Jason. It's not polite. Ah! Watch it!" He'd made a move, and although she didn't think he'd charge into the sunlight to grab her, she wasn't assuming anything. She brought the stake to an easy-stabbing position. He already had a blackened, sizzling hole in his side that wasn't healing fast. He wasn't eager to take another hit. "These people are Protected, idiot. They're off the menu. Go to the blood bank if you need your fix of B positive or whatever it is you're jonesing for." *Besides causing pain and terror,* she thought, but didn't say. Clearly, that was a big part of it for Jason. Most of the other vampires were more clinical about their feeding, but he'd brought all his weird, twisted baggage over with him.

In some ways, he and Eve were mirror images of each other—both fascinated by the darkness. Only Eve had chosen to manifest hers outwardly, and Jason . . . Jason had taken it all deep inside. For a while, Claire had been convinced there was something in him more than that. Something better. But over time, he'd proven her wrong.

And now, here he was, bloody-mouthed, grinning at her like Batman's Joker, if the Joker had fangs.

"Protection's a joke," Jason told her. He prowled the line of shadow, staring at her with dark, angry eyes that looked unsettlingly like his sister's. "Always has been; it's a racket, and the vampires laugh about it over their drinks. You know what the penalty is for me draining these two? I have to pay a *fine*. It's like a note in your file at school. I can do what I want. Nobody's going to care. Nobody's going to stop me."

"Oliver might. Or Amelie. They kind of like vampires to stay in line around here. Makes things easier for everyone."

He made a harsh buzzer sound. "Sorry, wrong answer," he said. "Old pioneer days, Claire. You're not keeping up. We've got privileges now. You can't keep us walking around on leashes anymore like tame dogs."

His pacing reminded her of a caged animal, too. Creepy. "Don't make me stake you, Jason. I'd have to tell your sister, and I don't want to do that."

"As usual, it's all about Eve. Why is it her business what I do?"

"She still cares about you, you know."

"She never really cared. Don't try that on me. If she'd been any kind of a stand-up sister, she'd have watched out for me. She just ran off and left me behind to take my punishment and shacked up with her precious *Michael*." Jason singsonged the name like a grade-schooler. *He's just trying to scare you,* Claire told herself, somewhat unconvincingly. *You've dealt with Myrnin all this time; you can handle this stupid kid.*

But she wasn't so sure. She'd counted on a vampire who'd back down, not one who was the poster child for unbalanced. Time for a shift of strategy.

Claire put down the stake. She needed both hands as she unzipped her backpack and reached inside to the inner pocket.

Jason decided it was the perfect time to make his move. He was fast, she had to give him that, but so was she, and she'd known he'd take the bait; he wasn't the cautious sort. So when her hand came up out of the bag holding the canister, he laughed, and his hands closed on her shoulders with crushing force.

"What're you going to do? Perfume me?"

She sprayed liquid silver in his open mouth.

Jason's shriek almost burst her eardrums, and, coughing and gagging, he staggered backward, smoke pouring from between his lips. His skin was burning from the sunlight. Claire shoved him backward into the shadows, and he stumbled a few steps, kept gagging, and sank down to his hands and knees to cough convulsively.

"It's just a little," she told him. "Consider it breath freshener. The next time, I spray it in your eyes, Jason, so keep the hell off me if you like your face."

He was too busy retching to try to speak, even if he could have managed it. Claire bypassed him and went to Sarah, tugged the ropes free, and let her pull the tape off her mouth. It must have hurt. The skin beneath it looked red and abraded, and Sarah whooped in a deep breath of relief. She fixed a poisonous glare on Jason. "You just wait, you little piece of crap," she said. "My Protector's not going to stand for this."

"Neither will mine," Professor Carlyle said. He looked pale and shaky, but righteously angry. Claire found paper towels behind the bookstore's counter and folded some into a thick pad, which she gave him to apply to his head wound. "Thank you, Danvers."

"You're welcome," she said. "So . . . can we talk over that B on the last paper? Because it was really an A effort. I'd take a B if I deserved it, but—"

"Yes, yes, fine, A it is. As far as I'm concerned, you have an A for the rest of the class," he said. "Sarah, would you like me to call someone, or—"

"Nope," the woman said, and climbed to her feet. She was small but had a wiry strength that probably came from bench-pressing boxes of textbooks all day. "I'm calling the pound to see if they can come get this damn rabid dog—"

Before she could finish the thought, Jason had scrambled to his feet and was running for the back door. Alleys, Claire thought. Shaded alleys, with sewer access. He'd be gone before anyone could catch him.

"Might want to keep that back door locked from now on," she said to Sarah as she returned the silver canister to her backpack and picked up the stake to slide it into the holster next to it. "Professor."

They both nodded, clearly still off-balance from the encounter with their own mortality; Claire felt it, too, a hissing tension running through her body that made her realize how much she'd just taken on herself. Shane would have been livid that she'd tried it without backup.

She went outside and walked fast, all the way home.

Where she was going to have to tell Eve her brother had gone full-on Hannibal Lecter. Fun.

She spotted the shiny black van of the ghost hunters—clearly driven off from their targeted hospital visit, thankfully—cruising slowly down the street. Jenna and Angel were arguing (there was a shocker) and Jenna was consulting a street map. There weren't many maps of Morganville that the vampires hadn't, ah, edited, so if the team members were trying to find some "haunted" location, they wouldn't be finding anything more exotic along the way. Except maybe Jason, who could be on the rampage after not getting his afternoon snack.

Claire swallowed her pride, dialed Amelie's number, and got the brisk, Irish-accented voice of her assistant, Bizzie. "Please tell Amelie that Jason Rosser's out here biting people, in public. Protected people. And if she wants those ghost hunters to get a good story, he's a great way to do it." She didn't wait for an acknowledgment. Amelie would shut Jason up; she might shut him up permanently, but that wasn't Claire's concern. She was more worried about the ghost hunters.

Nobody had said so, but it had seemed obvious from her conversation with the police that the decision the vampires were considering about the strangers had two outcomes: wiping their memories and dumping them out of town somewhere, or planting them somewhere deep, where no one would ever find the bodies. If they were still here, it was almost as if Amelie (or Oliver) had decided to toy with them, with no intention of letting them ever leave town alive.

Despite herself, Claire admired the ghost hunters' determination, a little. She recognized the curiosity, and the blind stubbornness; she had loads of that in her own character. She hated to see them punished for it.

But that, like so much in Morganville, was probably out of her hands.

Claire's adrenaline had finally stopped buzzing in her ears by the time she walked up the steps to the front door of the Glass House, and luckily, it seemed there was no emergency in progress. There was lunch being contemplated, and as she walked into the kitchen, Eve, Michael, and Shane were arguing the relative merits of hot dogs versus grilling hamburgers outside.

"Hot dogs are faster," Michael pointed out. "Microwave."

"Ugh, that's disgusting. Also, we don't make mac and cheese in there, either. That's just wrong," Eve said, and poured herself a tall glass of Coke. "Hey, college girl. Drinky?"

"Yes." Claire collapsed into a chair at the kitchen table. Eve gave her a quick look that let her know she'd picked up on her tension, then got down another glass from the cabinet. "The Apocalypse must be near, because a guy is arguing against grilling. That's just un-Texan, Michael."

"Vampire," he pointed out. "If I went out there, the only thing barbecuing would be me. And hot dogs are all-American. All-American trumps Texan."

"You're brainwashed by commercials about cars and baseball," Eve shot back, and handed Claire a fizzing glass. "Hot dogs are made of pig butts and the parts nobody in his right mind would eat. Yes, I used to like them. Don't judge me, okay?"

Shane was clearly Team Grill; he'd already gotten out the burger-flipping utensils and put them on the counter, and now he was digging sauces out of the fridge. "We're not even having this discussion," he said. "Eve's unemployed. The least she can do is help me grill burgers. And you two can chop veg—" He paused, looking straight at Claire. "What the hell happened?"

"Monica got creamed in the election?"

"We'll throw the party later. And?"

She really didn't want to say it. "I saw Jason. He was kind of . . . attacking people. So I stopped him. By the way, the silver pepper spray? Works great."

Eve had gone completely still. She stared at Claire for a moment, then said quietly, "Is he okay?"

"I didn't get him too badly. He's okay. Just less bitey for a while. Eve—he's not, ah—"

"Not wound too tight," Eve supplied, and lowered her gaze to fix on the bubbles in her Coke. "Yeah, copy that. He's always been off. You know that."

Off didn't really describe the feeling she'd had with Jason today. "I think it's worse than that," she said, as gently as she could. "He's really—vicious."

Michael stepped in, then. "It's not unexpected that would happen," he said. "Look, becoming a vampire—it's complicated, what it does to you, but it does kind of amplify whatever bad impulses you already had. It's tough to hang on to the good stuff, but easy as hell to bring the bad with you. I knew he'd be . . ." Michael shook his head. "Anyway. I'll let Oliver know. He's in charge of Jason."

"From what Oliver's doing now, he won't really care," Claire said. "He's gone a little power crazy. You might have noticed."

"Okay, so Jason Rosser is evil, and Oliver's power hungry. This is not breaking news that should keep us from grilling burgers," Shane said. "Can I get an amen?"

Eve and Michael chimed in, but Claire kept her head down. She was feeling pretty low. She'd spent a lot of energy this morning running down the portals and coming up empty, and then there had been the excitement of the rally, and Jason. . . . She was drained—not even hungry, actually, which was surprising.

She was also worried, *really* worried, about Myrnin. She'd thought that by now she'd have gotten some word from him. Bob was sitting upstairs in her room, contentedly spinning webs around flies that she'd caught for him, and she couldn't believe that even at his craziest, Myrnin would have left his pet to starve. He was careless of assistants, but never of his spider.

So . . . where was he? And if he couldn't communicate, how was she supposed to even begin to find him? It made her head hurt, and her stomach churn, and suddenly all she wanted was to finish her cold, sweet soda and crawl upstairs to sleep.

"Hey," Michael said as he took out tomatoes, lettuce, onions and pickles from the refrigerator. "Hand me a knife, would you?"

She pulled one off the magnetic strip Shane had installed on the wall—easier access, he'd said, in case it came down to that kind of a fight. Shane always thought ahead that way. She gave the blade to Michael without comment and watched as he chopped stuff up. He was neat, fast, and accurate. Vampire senses apparently made for great prep cooks. "Michael," she said as he finished slicing pickles into quarters, "do you know what bloodline Myrnin comes from?"

"I'm guessing you don't mean Welsh," he said. "Vampire bloodline?"

She nodded.

"No. Why?"

"Because I need to track him, and I remember Naomi could, you know, drink a sample of another vampire's bloodline to find him. She did it with Theo. Maybe—maybe you could do it to find Myrnin?"

"Maybe," Michael said, but he sounded doubtful. "I heard there's a blood record somewhere, but I have no idea where it is. Or if Myrnin's in it. From what I heard, he's the only one still living out of his line. It's pretty ancient, and he didn't make any others who survived long, so there may not *be* a record."

"But could you ask? Maybe look around? I need to find him, Michael. I think—I think he's in trouble."

"Why?" He put down the knife and looked at her directly. "Did he say something?"

"Only that he didn't like the way things were going in town," she admitted. "And that he was planning to leave. But you know how he is. I don't think he really would have run away. Not like that. You saw the lab!"

He shrugged. "The lab's always a mess; you know that. It's impossible to tell whether there was a struggle, or he just didn't like the latest newspaper he read and decided to trash the place."

"He left Bob! And how did Pennyfeather get in? He didn't have authorization."

"You don't know that. And maybe he just forgot about Bob. It's not like he's an exciting pet."

"Bob's cool, and Myrnin loves him like any other pet. He'd never just abandon him to starve," Claire said. "But . . . I just have the feeling, okay? So would you? For me?"

Michael ruffled her hair. "Yeah, sure. For you. Here. Chop some onions."

"Hey!"

"Consider it prepayment."

Lunch cheered her up—as did Michael's promise—and Claire actually enjoyed the burgers, which Shane had cooked pretty much to perfection. Eve and Shane got into it over the age-old mustard versus mayonnaise debate, but they had a nice time, even with that controversy devolving to tossing packets of condiment at each other. Even better, since it was Shane's turn to clean up.

After lunch, Claire went upstairs to her room while Michael and Shane settled in to try out a new first-person shooter game, and Eve shopped online; she stretched out on the bed and fell immediately, deeply asleep.

For a while she was too tired to dream, but finally she dreamed, and it was . . . odd.

At first, she didn't really understand. She was someplace dark and very, very quiet, except for the steady hiss of water dripping. She was cold and felt a gnawing, desperate hunger.

Then she heard a voice out of that dark whisper, "Claire?" It was as if she were torn out of her body and thrown violently up through the dark in a blur, and everything in her wanted to scream but she didn't actually have lungs or a body to use to do that, only a pure, condensed feeling of real terror. . . .

And from a great height, she looked down into a very deep, narrow pit, and far below, a starkly pale face upturned to her in the moonlight.

The voice.

It had sounded like Myrnin's voice, but it couldn't have been; it couldn't. There was no sense to this dream, because what would Myrnin be doing at the bottom of a hole, and why wouldn't he just jump out?

"Help," he said, from very far below, very far away. "Help me."

"I don't know how!" she called down, at least in the dream, and because it was just a dream, it made sense that he could hear her, somehow, and that even though she was very far away, she could see the desperation in his expression.

"Come for me," Myrnin said, and it sounded like a ghost, like Shane's sister whispering out there in that eerie vacant lot, like Miranda being torn to shreds of fog.

It sounded like someone who was already gone.

She woke up with a pounding heart and a nauseating headache bad enough to drive her to the medicine cabinet for ibuprofen, which she washed down with handfuls of bottled water in frenzied gulps. Somewhere in there, she noticed she'd managed to sleep away the rest of the day; it was already approaching sunset. *What the hell was that?* she wondered. She'd had anxiety dreams before, lots of them, but they usually involved being naked in a crowd, or running in slow motion, or taking a test unprepared. Nothing like this.

This was awfully—suspiciously—specific. If she was going to dream about Myrnin, why have him stuck deep in a hole in the ground?

Trap-door spider, something whispered in the back of her mind. *Gramma Day always called him that. So did you, once.*

Yes, but she hadn't meant it literally.

Maybe you just want him to need you, that awful, calm voice said. *Maybe you just like it that he depends on you so much.*

The thought unsettled her. She decided to put it out of her mind, all of it, especially the dream, because it was just her imagination working out her anxieties, just as it ought to do.

Maybe.

She went downstairs and found the video game amazingly still in progress, but on pause, as Michael and Shane argued the finer points of how the weapons array worked, and which would be a smarter choice with which to attack some kind of fortified position. It was confusing, and she still felt weird and sick. Downing a glass of milk helped settle her stomach, though, and she was just rinsing out the glass when the doorbell rang. The ring was followed up by knocking.

Michael had gotten up from the sofa, but Shane, still locked in his game world, was not paying much attention to anything else. Claire came out of the kitchen and met Eve coming down the stairs.

"Mail call?" Eve guessed.

"Not unless the postal service is starting night runs," Michael said. "I'll get it." The unspoken implication of that was that if it was something bad, he'd at least have a decent shot at fighting it. He went down the hall and opened the door. Beyond it, the sunset was burning the horizon a bright orange, but it wasn't quite evening yet.

"Who is it?" Claire asked, and craned to look.

"Can't tell," Eve said. "Oh, wait—it's—" She didn't finish the sentence. She broke free and raced down the hall.

Claire, instantly scared and imagining all kinds of mayhem, pelted after her. She almost immediately skidded to a halt in the suddenly crowded hallway; Shane had somehow managed to cut in front of both her *and* Eve. Being shortest sucked; she couldn't see over Eve's shoulder, never mind Shane's broad back.

But she heard a frantic, female voice say, "Close it—please close it, fast!"

Miranda's voice. But Mir was *gone*—disappeared out in the darkness. Dissolved into mist.

And now, apparently, she was back.

And, from the sound of it, very, very scared.

Eve turned, ran into Claire, and shooed her backward; Claire took several steps down the hall, and the party spilled out after her and into the living area. Between Shane and Michael came—yes!—Miranda, but a different one than before. This Miranda was translucently pale as a glass copy of herself, and she seemed terrified.

Everybody was trying to talk at once, except her. Ghost-Girl leaned up against a handy wall (why didn't she fall through?) and closed her eyes as if she were exhausted (could ghosts even get tired?). Eve finally got the upper hand, conversationally speaking. "What happened to you? Where did you go?"

"Away," Miranda said faintly. "So tired. Need energy." But the fact she was visible at all, before sunset, was odd and impressive. "I feel better here." She was looking better, too—already taking on a bit more form and substance. It wasn't a real body, but it had faint traces of color in it now. "They were after me. I had to keep running, find a safe place."

"Who was?" Shane asked. She'd just said the magic words to make him really pay attention. "Vamps? Why would vamps want a ghost?"

"She's not a ghost all the time," Michael said. "Remember, when she has a body, it comes complete with blood. Just like mine did. And since she can't be killed . . ."

"Oh, right," Eve said faintly, and her eyes widened. "They could keep her and keep, ah, draining her dry. . . ."

"Not the vampires," Miranda said. "I can handle the vampires. It's the rest of them. They won't leave me alone. They keep—" She was interrupted by *another* doorbell chime, followed by knocking. "Don't!" she said, and grabbed at Michael's sleeve, but her hand swiped through him. "Don't answer it yet—not yet!"

"It'll be okay," he said. "I'm just going to look. Relax. You're safe now." He pointed to Shane. "Stay with them."

"You suck!" Shane called after him as Michael went back to the door. Underneath, though, he was taking it seriously. Miranda wasn't the most reliable source of information, but Shane never underestimated a warning. "If it's Jason out there, no problem. If it's somebody worse, I don't know if Michael can hold his own."

"Then we'll handle it if it gets by him," Claire said, and surprisingly, she meant it. Between the four of them, nothing was going to overwhelm them. Not like it used to.

She thought that right up until the freaking ghost-*army* arrived.

The first indication she had that something was very, very wrong was Michael's outcry; he wasn't that kind of boy, generally, much less that kind of vampire. It was surprise, and definite worry—the kind of cry you made when you found a spider on a doorknob, or a snake in the toilet. A that-shouldn't-happen kind of sound.

Claire exchanged a look with Shane, and Miranda said, wearily, "I'm sorry I brought them here, but it was the only place I could think of that might keep them out. Maybe . . . maybe the house won't let them in."

But it turned out that the house did.

The first ghost to drift past—no, *through*—Michael was an old man, no one Claire recognized. He was just barely a visible shape, more a trick of the eyes than an actual presence; she saw him better in her peripheral vision than straight on. He walked down their hallway in a zombielike state, staring straight ahead. Shane backed up, but then stood his ground and tried to wave the phantom off. It ignored him and flowed around him like smoke over glass, and Shane shuddered and moved away, fast. "Okay, that was—unpleasant."

And there were more. Lots more. Some were just shadows, ominous and strange; some were almost-visible people. Claire only caught a glimpse of them because Michael let only a couple of them inside before he stepped back and slammed and locked the door . . . and that, surprisingly, worked. No more came inside.

But the ones already in were bad enough. One was an almost-visible man, but Claire couldn't make out his face as he moved toward them, until suddenly a trick of the light and shadows came together and showed her it was Richard Morrell, Monica's dead brother. She gasped and grabbed Eve's arm, and Eve nodded as she bit her lip. Richard slowed and looked at them, and Claire saw his mouth open and close, but he couldn't seem to speak. After a few seconds, he flowed on, heading for . . .

For Miranda, who was retreating from the oncoming old man, and Richard following behind. She looked miserably terrified. "Make them stop," she said, and looked at Michael. "Michael, *make them stop!*"

"I don't know how!" he said. It was ominous and eerie how the old man had zeroed in on Miranda, as if the little girl were the last cupcake left in the world and he had a sweet tooth. "What do they want?"

"Me!" She looked more real now, and she'd taken on a faint blush of color in her face and clothes. Miranda, in fact, looked way more real than any of the other ghosts. "They want me!"

"Shane . . . ?" Claire looked for him, but he wasn't beside her. That was surprising, but then she saw him, and she knew, with a sickening sense of horror, why.

He was standing motionless a few feet away, facing a ghost—a small ghost in the shape of a girl barely into her teens, with her hair in two long braids.

Claire knew immediately who it was he was staring at, even before she heard the small, pallid voice whisper, "Shane."

"Lyss," he said. There was a world of emotion in that name— pain, guilt, longing, love, horror. "Oh, my God, Lyss."

She reached out for him, and Shane raised his hand.

"No!" Miranda yelled. "No, don't touch her! You can't touch her. Don't you know *anything*?" She scrambled around the barrier of the sofa, playing keep-away with the shambling old man who was still chasing her. Richard was stalking her, too, now, but at a distance, as if he were irresistibly drawn toward her but didn't want to be. It was more of a slow circling. *Like a shark*, Claire thought, and shuddered.

She took Miranda at her very urgent word, and launched herself at Shane, slapping his hand away as he tried to touch his dead sister. He let out a harsh sound of surprise, and she saw his hand clench into a fist, but it relaxed almost immediately, and he pulled in a deep breath.

"Don't," Claire said. "Please don't."

Alyssa was still holding out her ghostly hand, but she wasn't trying to come at Shane. She was just waiting. Maybe—whatever Miranda was afraid of, maybe it had to be his decision to touch her, and it wouldn't count if Alyssa touched him first.

Though what would happen if he did do it was an entirely different question, and Claire really didn't want to know the answer. Not even as a scientist.

"Lyss?" Shane asked. "Can you hear me?"

She didn't move or speak again. She just kept holding out that ghostly, smoking hand toward him. Shane stared at it, and Claire knew he wanted to try, wanted it with everything inside him.

"Don't," she whispered, and took his hand in hers. "Please stay away from her."

Shane sucked in a deep breath. There were tears shimmering in his eyes, but he blinked them back and nodded. "Sorry, Alyssa," he said. "I can't." His voice shook. His whole body shook. But he meant what he said, and Alyssa clearly understood, because she dropped her hand back to her side and drifted back a few feet, then turned and joined the old man in stalking Miranda.

"Help me!" Miranda screamed. With ghosts on three sides, she was rapidly being cornered. It was only a matter of a minute or so until one of them had hold of her. "Do something!"

"What?" Michael asked, and then his eyes widened, as if something had finally occurred to him. "Can I make them leave? As head of the house?"

Normally Shane would have chimed in with something like *Who says he's head of this house?* but Shane's attention was riveted completely on his little sister's ghost, and it was Eve who said, "Maybe. Try!"

Michael closed his eyes and leaned against the wall, as if drawing strength from the house itself, or at least trying to communicate with it. Claire felt a flicker of energy around her, as if the connection were *almost* there, and then it died.

"All of us!" she shouted, and waved Eve to the wall, too. She put her hands flat on the old wallpaper and concentrated. *Come on, house. I know you're there. I know you're still alive; I can feel you. . . . Come out, come out, wherever you are. . . .*

Shane didn't join them. Claire didn't think he could. He was almost as fixed on his sister as the ghosts who stalked Miranda were on her . . . but luckily, that didn't seem to matter. Three of them together seemed to complete some kind of circuit, and Claire felt a surge of raw power whip through the room. "Hold on, Miranda!" she said, and the ghost-girl took hold of the arm of the sofa as a wave of force swept through the room in an almost-liquid ripple. It passed over Claire, leaving her skin tingling and raw, and when it hit the nearest ghost—Richard—he blew apart into mist. Alyssa was next, and then the old man, just seconds away from touching Miranda with his outstretched hand.

Miranda wavered and went pale and smoky, but then she stabilized as the wave passed her by, into an almost-real transparent form. She slowly let go of the sofa and straightened to look around.

"What did you do?" Shane said. He turned in a circle, frantically looking. "Where's Lyss?"

"Outside," Miranda said. "She's okay, Shane. She just isn't welcome here anymore. The house put her out."

"This is insane," he said, and sank down on the couch with his head in his hands. "Insane."

Eve sat beside him and put her hand lightly on his back. "I know," she said. "I'm sorry. I'm so sorry."

Before Claire could go to him, too, there was a thundering volley of knocks on the door, loud as gunshots, and all of them jumped. "What the hell now?" Michael said.

"Whatever it is," Eve said, "just leave it outside. Please."

"No," Miranda said. She took a deep breath,and pulled herself up to her full height—which wasn't very much, but she looked suddenly very adult. "The house is looking out for us now, looking out for *me*. And it isn't just ghosts out there, anyway. They can't make noise like that."

The knocks came again at the door, and Michael took a few steps in that direction before turning to look at her again. She nodded.

"Please," she said. "It's okay. Now that the house is paying attention, it's not as bad. I think I might be able to . . . able to help them. It was just so overwhelming, out there alone. In here, I don't feel as bad."

Michael didn't seem convinced, but he didn't seem to know what else to do, either. He flipped the locks on the door and swung it open during the third round of knocking, and outside there were dozens of ghosts, maybe hundreds, a mass of misty waving forms crowded together like zombies on the attack, and standing in the middle of them on the doorstep were Angel, Jenna, and Tyler.

The ghost hunters.

Who apparently couldn't see any of the ghosts. Ironic.

Angel Salvador stiff-armed a very surprised Michael Glass out of the doorway and rushed up the hallway, followed by Jenna Clark and Tyler, with his camcorder light glowing red. "Hey!" Michael said. "Hey, wait a minute. I didn't say—"

"Keep rolling, Tyler. We can cut that," Jenna said. "I know she's here; I can feel her. Angel, are you getting anything there?" She seemed almost frantic, and there were spots of color high on her cheeks. "Hello, little girl. Are you here? Anywhere?"

"Hey!" Michael shut the door, though for the moment the house itself seemed to be barring the ghosts from drifting inside the opening, and darted around them—not *quite* vampire fast—and got in their way again. "Hold up. What the hell, man? This is our house!"

"Congratulations," Angel said. He continued staring at the handheld device he was clutching. "The readings are remarkably strong. I think we've found her. It looks like this is her home location." He looked up at Shane, who was right in front of him, blocking the hallway, and said, "How long has your house been haunted?"

Shane looked past him, to the camera, and then at Michael. Claire would have given odds that he'd punch him out, but instead, Shane turned beet red and burst into uncontrollable laughter.

"Hey!" Eve said, and pushed him out of the way with an irritated glare. "You people, out! Out of our house, right now!" She tried to push Tyler, but he danced backward, clearly used to people going for that move.

Angel cut her off. "Wait, wait, not yet. Let us at least document these readings—do you know the history of this house? Was there anything violent that happened here, perhaps a famous murder? Who were the previous owners? How long have you lived here?"

The blizzard of questions was confusing, and all the time Angel was firing them off, he was moving relentlessly forward. It wasn't so much that Eve backed off as she was swept out of his way by the force of his momentum, and the rest of them just followed along.

Tyler focused on Eve, evidently liking her Goth look in connection with a haunted house, which Eve didn't approve. "Hey, get your camera out of my face before I put it in yours!"

"Easy, babe," Michael said, and grabbed her by the shoulders to pull her back. "We're fine. It's okay." He leaned over to Claire and whispered, "Find out what the hell Miranda wants us to do." Then he turned the full glare of his smile on the camera. "So, do you want me to show you around, or . . . ?"

"We just need you to get out of the way," Jenna said. "You kids are what, under twenty, all of you? You've got no idea how this kind of thing can turn bad. One careless session with a Ouija board, messing around with tarot cards, you're inviting spirits to contact you. Once they're here, you might not be able to get rid of them . . . even when they start hurting you. I know. It happened to me."

There was, Claire sensed, a backstory that the show's viewers would probably all know. Jenna's face was tight and sober, and there was a feverish believer's light in her eyes. Claire had an eerie memory of the vindictive ghost of the house's original owner, Hiram Glass, tearing at her with hatred, and wondered exactly what a younger Jenna might have gone through. She was right. Ghosts could be vicious.

Miranda knew that better than anyone, apparently.

Despite Michael's winning personality and movie-star smile, it wasn't working. Michael had a definite effect on girls, when he was really trying . . . and *boy*, was he trying. Claire could feel the tingle from five feet away, and it wasn't even directed at her. He'd always had charm, but lately she'd realized that as a vampire, he was fully capable of wielding it like a weapon—a kinder one, but powerful in its own right.

But Jenna seemed immune.

Claire couldn't see Miranda, and she had the sinking feeling that maybe she'd lost her nerve and run, but then she saw a ghostly face peeking out from behind the bookcases. Claire headed that way, trying not to look obvious about it. She leaned in next to her and muttered, "Michael needs to know what you're doing."

"Waiting," Miranda said.

"For what?"

Miranda was looking past her, Claire realized—looking at the window that faced west, toward twilight.

Toward the sun slipping steadily below the horizon.

"For sunset," she said, and stepped out from behind the bookcase. Clearly a ghost. Clearly a walking dead girl.

There was a sudden, vivid silence as Michael, Jenna, and Angel all stopped talking, and everyone focused right on Miranda. Claire could even hear the tiny mechanical whir of Tyler adjusting the focus on his camera.

"Hello," Miranda said. "My name is Miranda. I'm a ghost."

And then she vanished.

"No!" Jenna screamed. "No, please, come back! I want to help you. *We* want to help. Don't run!"

And that was the exact moment the sun completely set outside, and Miranda fell out of the ceiling, going from mist to solid in midair, and thumping flat on her face on the floor in the middle of the rug.

She said, in a muffled voice, "Ow."

No one said anything else for a moment. And then Jenna said, in a flat, odd voice, "Tyler? Please tell me you got that."

*   *   *

For what felt like minutes, nobody seemed able to move. The three ghost hunters looked like wax statues, frozen in their poses, unable to process what they'd just seen. Tyler finally moved the camera away from his eyes and blinked, as if not sure exactly what had gone wrong with his eyes.

"Well, that was awkward," Shane finally said, and crouched down next to Miranda. "You okay, kid?"

She wasn't. She stayed facedown for a long moment, shuddering, and Claire remembered with a shock that when Michael had been trapped as a ghost, he'd reexperienced how he'd died, every day. That was particularly awful for Miranda, who'd been killed by the draug—not a pleasant way to go.

Shane helped her sit up, and Miranda gave him a grateful, brave little smile. "Sorry," she said, "but I needed to get their attention."

"Well, you've got it," Jenna said, barking out a laugh. "We *can't* leave. We have the biggest thing that's ever been recorded in ghost hunting. Hell, not just ghost hunting. Science. This isn't just huge, it's—it's world-breaking! It changes everything!"

Angel clearly didn't know what to say. He was staring down at Miranda with a curiously blank expression, as if he really didn't know how to handle this at all. He was more of an actor than someone who really believed, Claire thought, and unlike Jenna, who saw it as vindication, he saw it as upheaval. When Miranda plunged out of the air, his world had definitely broken, and it looked as if he'd be a while trying to put it all back together again.

Tyler hadn't said a word. He was still recording, as if too frozen to stop, but Claire heard him muttering under his breath, "Holy crap, holy crap, holy crap, what the hell!"

She'd felt the same way, the first time she'd seen Michael coalesce out of thin air. But by then, she'd already known about vampires. Her world had already been spun off its axis; the ghost team was having to make a whole lot of adjustments pretty damn quickly.

Jenna leaned in toward Miranda as she climbed to her feet. "You've been speaking to me, haven't you? Trying to help us?"

"No, I——" Miranda looked tired, and very worried. "I wanted to warn you. You were getting them all upset. It was going to get you hurt."

"Who?"

"All the ghosts."

"But that's why we're here, to talk to——"

"Morganville isn't like any other town," Miranda said, cutting her off, and met her eyes with an intensity that made Jenna blink. "You came here looking for ghosts, and they heard you. And that's dangerous. There's—okay, I can't explain so much of it, but there's power here. Old power. And sometimes the dead can use it if you give them access. You opened up the tap, I guess. And now we need to shut it off before something worse happens."

"This is insane," Angel said, and stood next to Jenna. "Clearly, this is the most sophisticated hoax I've ever seen, but . . ."

"Shut up," Jenna said. She was staring intently at Miranda, and suddenly she reached out and took the girl's hand in hers. "You feel real. You look real."

"I am," Miranda said. "Half the time. But it's because I'm like you. I had power, and the house could use that to save me—not all the way, but this way. During the day, though, I'm mostly invisible. It was hard to make you see me just now, even inside the house. I'm getting better, though."

"You're—you're a real spirit."

"Yes," she said, and shook Jenna's hand. "Pleased to meet you."

Jenna burst out in a delighted laugh and kept shaking Miranda's hand until the girl finally pulled free.

"It's a hoax," Angel said again. "Jenna, you can't believe any of this. It's obviously . . ."

"It's okay," Miranda said to him. "It'll take time to sink in. I know."

"Shut up!" he growled at her.

"Hey!" Eve said, and took a step forward. "She's a *kid*. Watch your mouth. Miranda, you don't have to talk to them. If that's going to be their attitude, they can shove that camera up their—"

"Eve," Michael said, and shook his head. "Not helpful." He got behind Tyler and tapped him on the shoulder. "I'm going to need that thing."

Tyler jerked forward, crowding protectively shoulder to shoulder with Angel. "Oh *hell* no, man. You're not taking this away."

"You don't think so?" Michael's eyes had little random flickers of red showing. Claire waved at him behind their backs and pointed toward her own eyes, then at him. He caught the message, and she saw him calm down with an effort. "Look, whatever you think you saw, you just didn't understand. There's nothing supernatural going on here. It's a trapdoor. She came from the next floor up."

Tyler and Angel both craned their necks to look up at the totally smooth ceiling . . . and Michael, vampire fast, snatched the camera away and backpedaled when Tyler came after him. "Don't make me crush it," he said. "It looks expensive."

"It is, man. Give it back!"

"Sure. Hang on." Michael looked it over, ignoring Tyler's attempts to grab it away again, and found the memory chip, which he ejected. He held it up, and handed the camera back. "No problem."

"You can't keep that!"

"Not planning to," Michael agreed. He snapped it in half, then tore the halves into smaller pieces. Then he put the pieces in his jeans pocket. "Done. Sorry, Mir, but you know they can't walk out of here with that footage."

She nodded in agreement, but Claire sensed something was wrong, especially when Tyler exchanged a fast glance with Angel and Jenna. "You asshole," Tyler muttered, but it sounded like something he felt he ought to say, not that he deeply felt. He backed off. "Maybe we should go, guys. Next thing, they'll be breaking our necks. Angel's right. This is some hell of a hoax."

Jenna looked at Miranda again. "You can talk to me," she said gently. "You really can. I'm not afraid of you."

"No," Miranda said. "I know. But I'm afraid of you. And what you can do. You made them hungry, and now they're dangerous. Don't you understand that?"

"Maybe," Jenna said. "My twin sister died, and she stayed with me for the longest time. Not real, like you are, but—there. But she changed. Turned evil. I had to . . . I had to get rid of her, send her away."

"You don't understand," Miranda said. "It wasn't something else. It was *you*. You changed her. You made her see a way back, and that makes them—us . . . *ghosts*—desperate. Desperate enough to do anything. It's you that's making it happen."

"You're not one of them, those lost people. You're loved here. Loved. Protected. And that's good; that's really good. I just want to be sure you're protected from the things your friends can't see and fight." Jenna took in a deep breath and blew it out. "I think that you and I together could—could fix whatever it was I did wrong. You could show me how."

"You need to leave," Miranda said. "You need to go before it's too late and everything goes completely wrong. I'm sorry."

"But—"

"I'm going to need the rest of the recordings," Michael said to Tyler. "Sorry, man."

"We don't have anything else," Tyler said. "You just broke the crap out of our whole show."

Shane looked at Michael, eyebrows raised, and Michael shook his head. "Lying his ass off," he said. *Heartbeat*, Claire thought. He could hear them. He might not be able to always tell when one individual was lying, but it was easier for him if there were three people all in on the same falsehood. More people meant more data, like a triangulation of the truth.

And most likely, all three of the ghost hunters knew Tyler had backups.

"I read people really well," he said. It was an obvious lie, but he didn't give Tyler time to argue. "All right, all three of you, out the door. If you want me to take your whole van apart next, I'll be happy to do that, too."

"Or, you know, punch you," Shane said cheerfully. "This is Texas. We have the right to do that when you break into our house."

He left it to Eve to say, "Or worse," in a voice so low and dark, it qualified as Goth all by itself.

Jenna shot to her feet. "Fine. If you want to doom this little girl to an eternity of pain and torment, you're doing exactly the right things. You're not prepared for what's going to happen to her. I am!"

Maybe that was kind of true; it was very hard to tell. But in any case, Claire was fed up with half-truths and aggression, especially when her head was pounding so very hard. "Just get out," she said wearily. "She's our responsibility. We'll take care of her. If she's right, you've done enough damage already around here."

That was when Jenna turned and focused on her, really focused, and Claire saw something familiar in her cool, pale eyes. It was the same distant look she'd seen so often in Miranda . . . here and not here at the same time. "You dreamed it," she said. "It's true. I see . . . water. A hole. A silver cross in a circle. Someone's trying to reach you."

"Yeah, yeah, save the Vegas act, lady," Shane said, and pushed her forward toward the door. Angel and Tyler were already making their way out ahead of her. "If we want professional help, we'll call the Ghostbusters. At least they have matching uniforms. Ciao."

Miranda followed them, looking anxious. "Claire," she said, and caught her arm. "*Claire!* It's dark out there."

"It's okay. They have a van," she said. She wasn't feeling particularly charitable toward the *After Death* team just now. If Michael was right—and she honestly figured he was—then Jenna's interest in stirring up the dead had brought back Shane's sister, and that, that was unforgivable. "They'll be fine. Don't worry about them."

"The ghosts know what she is. They'll follow her, eating little bits of her. She won't feel it at first, but then she'll get tired and sick, and they could kill her, Claire. Worse: they could get strong enough to do other things. Dangerous things. She's really powerful."

"I think she's full of it," Claire said, but now that her anger was fading a bit, she ran what Jenna had said to her through her head. *Water. Hole. Silver cross in a circle.* That fit with her dream about the hole in the ground, and the water around her legs. *Someone is trying to reach you.* "I think she was just making it up, Mir. Listen, you stay here. We're going to make sure they leave, okay?"

Miranda shuddered. "I can't go out there again."

Even so soon after sunset it was dark outside, darker than

Claire had expected; the orange bands on the horizon were already fading, being painted over by shades of purple and blue. The biggest, bravest stars had already made appearances overhead, but there was no moon, not yet.

The *After Death* van was parked on the street, two houses down; they'd probably had trouble finding the place. Claire remembered seeing them checking maps. They'd probably been looking for the Glass House already. *Ugh.* To think she'd thought Angel was kind of greasily charming in the beginning. Now, she never wanted to see him again.

There was no sign of the mass of ghosts she'd seen before when they'd been in the house, which seemed weird; she could feel something out here, an uneasy sensation on the back of her neck, a phantom whisper on the wind. On instinct, Claire stepped back over the threshold into the house, and as she did, she saw the mists come into focus again. All the ghosts crowded now around Jenna as she headed for the van.

Inside the house, the ghosts were visible. Out there, in the real world, there was nothing.

Shane was already down the steps, and Claire hurried down to join him. "They're leaving too easily," he said. "Didn't it seem to you like they just let that thing with the memory card go too fast?"

"What choice did they have?" she asked. "Michael had it and broke it before they could do much."

"Yeah, but . . ." Shane shook his head. "I expected more drama out of them. They're on TV. It's kind of what they do for a living."

"The camera was off."

"For people like them, the camera's never off. . . ." His eyes suddenly widened, and he dashed forward to take the camera out of Tyler's hands. Tyler resisted, yelling for help, and suddenly it was a tangle of guys—Angel, Tyler, Shane, and Michael, all wrestling for control of the thing. Not too surprisingly, given the players, Michael won and tossed it to Shane.

"You wanted this?" he asked.

"Hey, you can't do that!" Tyler shouted. "That's expensive pro equipment, man! I'll sue your ass!"

Shane jogged back up the steps and held it under the porch light. "Dammit," he said. "Michael—you got the memory card, but this thing was broadcasting straight on broadband, too. The memory card was just backup. They've rigged it so it can record without the light coming on."

Michael rounded on Tyler, whose face had gone pale. "Where did it broadcast to?"

"Dude, you're wrong. Yeah, sure it's got the capability, but I didn't even switch it on—"

"That's a lie," Michael said, and grabbed him by the collar. "Tell me another one; go ahead."

"Let him go." Jenna's voice was cool, calm, and focused, and they all looked at her. Michael let go of Tyler, because Jenna was holding a gun. It was something semiautomatic; Claire couldn't tell the caliber, but it didn't really matter. Michael wouldn't be scared of it, but getting holes put in him and healing up would be just as damning, if not more so, than what they already had recorded on Miranda. So he held his hands up and stepped back.

"That's not going to look so good on camera," Michael said. "Better rethink it."

"I'm just defending my friends from some scary people," Jenna said, "and besides, by the magic of editing, they'll never see I was armed, anyway. Now let's all just calm down, okay? This doesn't have to get any crazier." She jerked her head at Tyler. "Get the camera and get your ass to the van. We have editing to do."

"We could stream it live," Angel suggested.

"Don't be stupid, Angel; you don't waste a revelation like this on a couple of thousand people who stumble over it on the Web. This is a major TV event, maybe even pay-per-view. We're going to tease the hell out of it for weeks before we put a single frame of it out. Tyler!" She raised her voice to a whip crack, and the camera monkey scrambled up the steps and took the recorder out of Shane's unresisting hands. "You don't know what you've got here. Or what's coming. You're going to need us, trust me. *Miranda* needs us. This whole town is going to be famous."

She was probably going to say more, but she never got the chance, because a dark-clothed figure came out of the shadows behind the trees, and before Claire could draw a breath, the figure knocked Jenna out of the way, spinning her to the ground. The gun tumbled away, lost in the sparse, weedy grass.

The intruder showed a flash of a pale face, red eyes, a young woman's crimson smile, and in a heartbeat more, she had hold of her target.

Not Jenna, after all.

Angel. The vampire clapped a hand over his mouth when he tried to speak and said, "Hush, now, pretty. What will all the neighbors think if you make a fuss?"

Tyler mumbled out a curse, and ran for the van. He made it as far as the fence before another vampire ghosted out in front of him.

Jason.

Eve's brother looked just as demented as he had earlier, and Claire shuddered at the smile he turned first on Tyler, and then on his sister. "Hey, Eve. You don't write, you don't call . . . but at least you brought us dinner. That's nice."

"No!" Eve dashed forward and put herself between Tyler and

Jason. "No, Jase. What the hell are you doing? They're not from here! You can't just—"

"I hate that word. *Can't.* Fact is, I can, big sister. I can do anything I want. So can Marguerite, here. And Jerold, he's back there somewhere. . . . Wave to my nice sister, Jerold." Claire turned. There was a vampire crouched on the edge of the steep roof, staring down at them with a knowing smile. He waved. "See, we have privileges now. We get to hunt if we want. And we really do want. So if you don't choose to be on the menu, turn your ass around and walk back in the house and shut the door. Hell, you were just arguing with these fools. Why do you care?"

"I—" Eve didn't really have a comeback for that. "It's not about them. I don't want to see you . . . be this. God, Jason. Is this how it's going to be? You weren't bad enough already?"

"No," he said, very rationally. "I've never been bad enough to keep the bad stuff from happening to me. Until now." He waited. Eve didn't move. "Okay then. I'm going to be kind this time. We can share just this one. You can keep the other ones." He snapped his fingers, and Marguerite, the one who had Angel, nodded. She picked Angel up in her arms—quite a feat, because the man was bigger, taller, and panicked—and before any of them could draw breath, she just . . . disappeared.

Michael started to run after her, but he came up short when Jerold dropped off the roof into his path. In one gloved hand, he held a glass bottle that swirled with silver. "We learned this from you," Jerold said. "You started fighting your own kind, and we're going to fight back. You like this stranger enough to burn for him, Michael?"

"No!" Eve looked pleadingly at her brother—who, whether she liked it or not, clearly was in charge. "No, come on, please—Jason, don't. Don't hurt him."

"If he stays out of our way, he'll be fine," Jason said. "Ditto for you, and Claire, and Shane; I'll leave you alone. But it's a new day around here. Our day. And the sun's never coming up to spoil it for us."

Somewhere out in the darkness, there was a pained cry. Angel. Claire tried desperately to think what to do, but there was nothing. They had weapons but Michael had just been outflanked; Shane just had stakes, and although Eve had a crossbow, she didn't seem inclined to use it on her own brother.

I need to do something, Claire thought. *Anything. I need to save him.*

"Jason, if you let him go, I think we can make some kind of deal," she said, talking as fast as she could. She didn't even know what she was saying. "Look, I'll even let you bite me—two pints for the guy you just took. Come on, it's a good deal. I'll get it witnessed at Common Grounds, we can put it in writing, and—"

"Shut up," Jason said, still smiling. "I don't want a measly two pints, like I'm out for a beer with the guys. I want to *hunt*. Button it if you don't want to play the rabbit, little girl."

She shut her eyes and tried to think what to do. There were three vampires, and even though she and her friends outnumbered them, it would be a tough fight, and probably one of them would be badly hurt, maybe killed. She'd never hated math so much in her life.

Shane put his arm around her. "Don't," he said quietly. "You can't, Claire. You can't save everybody."

And God, he was right; he was right and she hated that, too.

"All right," she said. "Eve—call the cops. Hurry."

Eve nodded and ran into the house. Jason laughed out loud.

"Good call," he said. "And nice counter, but the cops ain't gonna catch us, and you know it. They know better than to try. Nice doing business with you folks." He touched a finger to his forehead in ironic salute. "Catch you later."

"Wait!" Jenna blurted. "Wait, what about Angel, what—"

"Pretty lady really doesn't get it, does she?" Jason said. "Explain it to her. I'm starving."

And then he and Jerold were just . . . gone. Like smoke on the wind. And Angel had stopped crying out, though whether that was due to being gagged or being dead, Claire couldn't tell and didn't want to imagine. Her whole body ached with strain, and she wanted to throw up. *What did I just do?* Nothing. She'd saved the life of one of her friends, probably. At the cost of Angel's.

When she tried to take a step, she staggered and almost went down. Shane caught her and held her up. "Hey," he said. "Hey, it's okay. We're okay. The cops will be on the case."

Claire knew he didn't believe that any more than she did. The cops wouldn't be on the case; they wouldn't dare, unless Amelie or Oliver directed them to stop the hunting. After all, Jason—like Michael—had *privileges*.

And Angel had technically been fair game . . . unProtected, a stranger.

It meant, though, that there'd be some necessary cover-up with Jenna and Tyler. Either their memories would be altered to explain away Angel's disappearance or death, or they'd face the same fate. *Ten minutes ago you were throwing them out of the house,* she reminded herself. *They were going to go public about Miranda. About Morganville.*

"Check the van," she said to Shane. "See if Tyler was telling the truth. If they streamed that video to a server in their van . . ."

"Got it," he said, and jogged away to the vehicle. It was unlocked—trusting bunch—and he slid back the cargo door to climb inside.

"Hey!" Tyler snapped out of his stunned trance, and color flooded his face. "Hey, get the hell out of there—there's delicate equipment in there!" He charged for the van, but Michael caught

up and stopped him with nothing but a look. That didn't, however, stop Tyler from talking. "We have rights, you know. You
touch anything in that van and I'll sue your asses off!" It was obviously something he could seize on, something real and reassuring
in a world that had drunkenly upended on him. He had to know
Miranda was the real thing, but that was at least partly in his
comfort zone, or he wouldn't be doing the *After Death* show. But
being stalked and preyed on by vampires—even if nobody had
said they were vampires—was different. And there was a fever-
ishly bright light in his eyes that reflected as much fear as it did
anger.

"Easy," Michael said. "Wait." He kept a hand outstretched,
palm out, to ward Tyler off if he continued his rush forward, but
Tyler just paced, staring past Michael at the van.

And then at Shane, who stepped out of it about half a minute
later. "Video's on their server, Mike. What do you want me to do?"

This time, when Michael focused on Tyler, he wasn't playing
around. Red swirled in his irises, and Claire felt a force coming
out of him—what it was, she couldn't say, but it was powerful. "Is
that the only copy left?" he asked Tyler. Even his voice sounded
different, somehow. Less human.

"Yes," Tyler said, and blinked. "I mean, no! It streamed to the
Internet already. . . ."

"Yeah, that's a lie." Michael glanced back at Shane and nodded. "It's the only copy. Wipe it."

"No!" Tyler's cry was furious and agonized, but he didn't try
to go up against Michael, either. He must have sensed how dangerous it was to try.

Jenna didn't even protest. She slumped down on the ground,
sitting cross-legged, and put her head in her hands. "He didn't believe," she said. "Angel never really believed. God. I shouldn't have

gotten him into this. I should have made him go home. . . ." She sounded tired, and Claire remembered with a chill what Miranda had said. All around her, invisible here in the real world beyond the Glass House, ghosts were crowded around Jenna, breaking off pieces of her in some strange psychic way and consuming the tasty strength she'd brought to town.

Making themselves stronger.

Silence. Profound silence, broken by the distant, frantic barking of a dog.

"Come on," Michael said, and took Tyler by the arm. "Let's get inside."

Claire went to Jenna and offered her a hand. She looked at it, then her, and finally nodded and rose. "This is crazy," Jenna told her.

"I know," she said. "Come inside."

She paused on the doorstep to watch as Shane jogged back to join them. Nothing loomed out of the darkness to menace him . . . this time. Once he was in, she closed and locked the door, and took a moment to lean her head against the wood.

I'm sorry, she told the vanished Angel. In his way, he'd been charming. *I wish . . .*

But she didn't even know how to finish the thought.

FOURTEEN

MYRNIN

☽

The trick to doing the impossible, I've found, is to simply never think past what is at your fingertips. Do the thing in front of you. Then the next. Then the next. In such ways have men built the pyramids, or climbed mountains, or raced to the moon on rockets.

And that is how I had carved, inch by painful inch, the niches for my hands and feet in the stone wall of the oubliette. I did not look up; I did not look down. I looked only at the task before me, and ignored the pain as a side effect. I'd had enough practice at that, certainly.

With enough concentration, the panic attacks faded into a running babble at the back of my mind, like a fast-rushing river that became background noise I didn't feel the need to heed. In a way, it was a comforting sort of distraction. It was a bit like not being alone, even if my only real company was my own horribly distorted, screaming mind.

I found out just how far I'd ascended the hard way, when I lost my concentration, and losing my concentration was *not my fault*. I was remarkably centered, but when suddenly there was a sensation inside my mind that felt like cold, icy fingers shuffling through my thoughts, and . . . well. One does tend to get distracted when something like that happens.

My fingers slipped, then my bare toes, and as I fell—counting the feet on the way down, my goodness, nearly ten steps completed—I saw Claire's face. Just a flash of it, pale and worried. And another face, a woman's, with pale gold hair and light-colored eyes. It was not Amelie, though in some ways the resemblance was there. . . . It was someone I didn't know.

Someone human. More remarkably, a human whose mental fingerprints were clear on my mind. A seer, a true one, like the girl Miranda—someone who could see the future, but not only that; one who could reach and touch the minds of others. I doubted she had enjoyed the experience any more than I had, but I had the conviction that through her, Claire had been told *something* of me.

Come for me, I begged her again, just as my fall abruptly ended in ice-cold water, and the even-colder stone beneath. Bones broke, of course. I stayed there, jammed in awkward discomfort at the bottom of hell, until I had enough focus and strength to heal, and then to start considering the climb again.

Claire, I thought. *Come for me. Please.*

Because the doubt had begun to creep in to inform me that ten feet was barely a beginning, and I had a very, very, very long way to go . . . and hunger was already nipping my heels. Soon, the clarity and focus I had managed to achieve thus far would be difficult.

And then impossible.

You won't make it, some coldly logical part of me declared, which was just not at all helpful. I wanted to cut that part of my brain out and leave it floating in the water, but perhaps that might not have been a very sane response.

So I locked the logical part of me up in a prison made of mental bars, focused on the next thing in front of my nose, and began to climb.

FIFTEEN

CLAIRE

The police took notes, sounding professionally skeptical of the idea that a strong young man might have vanished in full view of his friends. *Because that never happens here,* Claire thought cynically, but she knew that in a way they were right to be doubtful. . . . The vampires picked off strays; they didn't run at the herd. It wasn't smart, and they'd always been very careful not to involve strangers who might have been easily missed.

Angel was as high-profile a visitor as Morganville ever got, if you didn't count a drive-through by the shiny-haired governor two years before. That guy hadn't even stopped for gas, just whipped through town in a whirlwind of blown sand and shiny cars, though he'd reportedly rolled down the window at a stoplight and waved to people who hadn't really cared.

Carrying off Angel was almost as likely as vampires stopping the governor's caravan, ripping off his sedan door, and dragging him off in the middle of the afternoon.

They'd all provided statements—Eve, Michael, Shane, Claire, Jenna, and Tyler. Miranda had sensibly stayed inside. Tyler's story had morphed itself into an attack by a gang of teens bent on robbing the van—*armed* teens—and Jenna had just said she hadn't seen much except for one of them grabbing Angel and taking him off.

Shane had straight-out asked Eve before the first sirens and lights pulled to a stop, "Do you want us to snitch on your brother, or not? Your call, Eve. Personally, I don't think the little monster needs any more breaks, but—"

"Yes," she'd interrupted him. "Do it. I'm going to tell them everything."

So the four of the Glass House residents had all identified Jason by name and provided the names of the other two vampires as well; Claire certainly felt a bitter sort of validation in doing that. She'd trusted Jason, for a while, but he'd spun wildly out of control, and he had to be stopped. Even Eve acknowledged that now.

The cops had called it in, and gone on their way; no one seemed to have much of a sense of urgency about the whole thing. Tyler and Jenna sat together on the front steps, clearly numb and unsure what to do next, so Claire asked them inside, organized coffee, and—after consultation with the others—bedded Jenna down on the sofa in the living room, and Tyler in the parlor. Nobody slept very well, and when Claire came downstairs before dawn to make coffee, she found that the two visitors were up and sitting together at the dinner table, holding hands.

Claire paused on the stairs, watching. It was an odd kind of scene, and there was something definitely weird about it. For a moment, Claire didn't catch what Jenna was saying . . . and then, with a chill, she did.

"... Close," Jenna said in a distant, drugged voice. "I can sense him out there; he's coming.... Just a moment ... It's hard for him to get through the barriers around this place...."

Claire cautiously descended a step, then another. The room was dark, except for flickering candles on the dining table to add sinister mood lighting. *What are you doing?*

It became very clear in the next second, as Angel's pale, insubstantial ghost drifted through the walls.

Tyler stiffened in his chair, but Jenna held on to his hand and made him sit down again. Angel hovered there, glowing with the eerie dim light of phosphorescence. He looked lost and distressed.

Claire's legs felt numb. She sat down fast on the stairs, watching with her lips parted on a fast-drawn breath. *What the hell is going on?* Angel was clearly, well, dead—no doubt of that; you don't get to be that kind of ghost without going all the way over the line. There was a dark smudge around his throat, and Claire winced seeing it. No doubt it evidenced what Jason had done to him. Or his friends. Whether Angel's body had been recovered or not, he was a victim of Morganville's growing vampire problem.

And Jenna—Jenna had been able to summon him up, and even get him past the house's defenses to appear.

Jenna let go of Tyler's hands, and Claire expected the ghost-Angel to vanish, but he stayed, drifting closer and closer to Jenna as if some kind of gravity were pulling him toward her. "Angel," she said, "I am so sorry. So sorry."

Claire realized that she was reaching out toward the ghost, and she remembered Miranda's stark fear. "Wait!" she blurted, and came down the stairs at a run. "Wait, don't. Don't touch him."

But it was too late. Jenna had already done it, and when their hands connected, Angel took on form, weight, even a little color—almost a kind of reality.

And Jenna sagged back in her chair, clearly exhausted.

"It's true," Angel said. His voice sounded as if it came from the bottom of a deep well. "It's all true what you said. So many spirits here, Jenna. So lost. So angry."

"I'm so sorry we couldn't help you," Jenna whispered.

"I know." He included Tyler in that, with a sideways glance, and the younger man flinched. He'd probably hoped to be ignored completely. As Ghost-Angel's gaze moved past him to brush across Claire, she knew how Tyler felt. There was something really, truly terrifying in that empty gaze. "And you," Angel said to Claire. "Not your fault. I know you blame yourself."

Claire shivered. The air in the room was feeling icy cold, as Angel's spirit drew in energy from the world around him. "I'm sorry we lost you."

"Angel's not lost," Jenna said. "I've got him. He can help us."

"I don't—" Claire took in a deep breath, and it felt like breathing in winter. "I don't think it's a good idea, Jenna. You know what Miranda said. . . ."

"Miranda's not here, and I'm certainly not abandoning our friend."

"You should," said a soft voice from the kitchen door, and Claire turned to see Miranda standing there with a mug in her hand that steamed fiercely in the chill. "You need to let him go. The longer he stays here, the hungrier he will be. And after a while he won't be your friend anymore, Jenna. Just like your sister."

"Don't talk about her!"

"You have to let him go," Miranda said. She walked to the table and set down her mug—the contents smelled like hot chocolate— and took a deep breath. "I can show you how to make him go on to where he needs to be."

Jenna's eyes widened, then narrowed. "How do I know you can do that?"

"Because I was there, and I came back. He's confused and scared. I can take him there if you'll let me. But I can only do it in the morning." Miranda looked out the window. It was still dark, but there was a strong glow to the east. "And I can only do it if he wants to go with me. The more you make him want to be here, with you, the harder that is. You have to let go of his hand, right now."

Jenna frowned, but she pulled her hand away from Angel's, and he immediately began to lose color and substance, taking on the wispy, foggy character of a ghost just barely together. The change, along with the obvious pain and horror on Angel's face, was so alarming that Jenna immediately tried to reach out again for him.

Miranda pulled her hand away. "No," she said. "You can't. Understand? You just can't. He's okay. What he feels . . . It isn't pain like you know it. It's confusion. I'll take him once the sun comes up. It'll be okay."

"Mir?" Claire asked softly. "Is this—is this okay for you to do? Is it dangerous?"

The girl sighed and shrugged, just a little. "It's hard," she said. "But I'm not ready to go, so I can come back. Not everybody can. And not every time. You remember, don't you? That feeling?"

Claire *did* remember, though she earnestly tried not to. . . . She'd died here, briefly, in the Glass House, and there had been this sensation, when the house's protections had collapsed, that had given her the feeling of being sucked up somewhere, thrown into chaos. And maybe that would have turned out all right, but it was genuinely terrifying.

She nodded.

"I can do it," Miranda said quietly. "I just don't like it. That's why they were all following me, before. Because they know I can help. I just . . . I just don't want to."

"Can you talk to them?" Claire asked.

"I can," Jenna said, and Miranda nodded as well. "I guess we both can."

"I was thinking . . ." She really hesitated on this, because it seemed like such a selfish use of what she'd just learned. "I was thinking maybe, if it was possible, you could ask them to find out something for me."

"What?"

"About Myrnin," she said. "Jenna, you had a vision of him, before. I think he's being held somewhere against his will. I need to help him, but I need some idea where to look. Can you help me? Can *they* help me figure out where it is?" She was trying not to make the desperation in her voice sound obvious, but she probably failed hard in that. "Please?"

"It's too dangerous for her," Miranda said, and nodded toward Jenna. "She shouldn't be trying to talk to any more of them. I will, though. As long as she stops making them excited, I should be able to get out and see them. . . ." She looked toward the window suddenly. "The sun's coming up. Angel and I have to go now. Sorry."

Miranda walked to Angel and took his hand, and he seemed to give a sigh of deep relief that he wasn't alone anymore. They were both fading. Tyler, who had been sitting in silent, dumb amazement the whole time, jumped back from the table, sending his chair flying; Jenna scrambled away, too, as Miranda threw her head back, closed her eyes, and her very real body seemed to just . . . dissolve, along with Angel's.

Then they were both gone.

Claire gulped back the instinctive fear, and said, "Mir? You still around?" She got a cold pulse that moved through her, and she understood that to mean *yes.* "It's okay. She's still here; we just can't see her right now. She'll get Angel where he needs to go, I guess."

Tyler looked about to cry. "Who *are* you people?"

But Jenna wasn't looking like that at all. She seemed . . . focused. There was a light dawning in her eyes, and her shoulders went back and squared up. "This is why I was led here," she said. "This is what I was meant to do. Meet this girl. And help her."

"Yeah?" Tyler shot back. "What about *me*, Jenna? What am *I* supposed to do, exactly? How am I supposed to go back to having a normal life now? Jesus, this was just a job, a stupid *job*. I never was some true believer, not like you. . . ."

But now he was, clearly. And he didn't like it. He tugged at his messy hair as if he wanted to pull it all out, then flopped facedown on the table, utterly spent.

"I can never leave here, can I?" His muffled voice floated up, almost as ghostly as Angel's had been. "Dammit. I had season tickets to the Red Sox. Good seats."

Claire heard footsteps behind her, and Eve appeared, Doc Martens clunking heavily on the stairs. She paused, yawning. There was something weird about her hair—it was sticking up like a cockatoo's crest. Probably not on purpose. She still had on an adorable pair of pajama pants, a giant White Stripes concert T-shirt, and she hadn't put on her makeup yet. "What'd I miss?" she asked.

"You'd better sit down," Claire said, "and I'd better make coffee."

☆   ☆   ☆

The police finally called after breakfast—breakfast meaning Pop-Tarts and arguments over whether it would be a good idea to knock Jenna and Tyler over the head and lock them in a room until they could decide what to do with them, which was Shane's idea. Claire half expected the cops to want the two surviving *After Death* crew members, but no, they wanted Eve down at the station. Just Eve, which was good, because Claire had to head off to class; she was aching to talk to Miranda again, and see if her ghostly connections might be able to find Myrnin, but hanging around the house demanding answers wasn't going to get her anywhere. And neither would blowing off classes.

"I have a jam session in five minutes at Common Grounds," Michael said, shifting as he checked his watch. Eve was sitting at her dressing table, applying eyeliner.

"And?" she asked. Claire was fascinated, watching her; she had so much concentration and precision, it was eerie. Claire wasn't good with eyeliner. It took skill.

"And I need to get moving," he said. "Are you coming?"

"Sweetie, true beauty can't be rushed." Eve switched to mascara. "You go ahead. I'll be fine."

"Not on your own," Michael said. "New rules. None of you walks alone. Not even Shane."

"Gee, Overprotective Dad, you probably should have told him that before he left this morning."

"Where was he going?"

"Job interview—he didn't tell me what it was for, so maybe it was something embarrassing, like flower arranging or male stripping," Eve said. "Relax; he's fine. And anyway, I can drive. The Car of the Dead is finally ready to go again." She meant her custom hearse, which had seen so many repairs and replacements, it was almost a brand-new vehicle again. "Besides, I'm seeing the cops, not hunting for vamps in dark alleys. I've got all the vampire I need." She blew him a kiss.

Michael leaned over and kissed the top of her head—now that her hair was tamed again, not such a dangerous proposition—and said, "Be careful."

"Always am."

He left in a hurry, carrying both his acoustic and electric guitars. Eve smiled serenely and did her other eye with the mascara in careful, even strokes.

"Can you give me a lift?" Claire asked. "I've got classes. And what *are* we going to do about our visitors, anyway?"

"Nothing," Eve said. "It's not our business."

"But—what if Jenna decides to go public? Or Tyler? They know too much, way too much."

"They've got no proof now. And that's what I'm going to tell the cops," Eve said. "It's not a Glass House problem anymore. It's a Morganville problem, and it needs to be officially handled. Hell, Jason is the one who made all this happen, not us."

It still felt wrong; Claire was afraid the official Morganville solution would involve two more bodies in a car crash, the end of the *After Death* story. But she had to admit, she couldn't see any way out of it without telling the cops, or Oliver, or Amelie. Things had gone a little too far. And, she had to admit, she was carrying around a staggering load of guilt over Angel's death. She had the nagging feeling that she could have done something to stop it . . . even though, in practical terms, she knew she couldn't have.

It was a tangled mess, and it would take time to sort it out, but one thing was certain: they couldn't afford to let Jason get away with it. He was already dangerous. If he thought he had a free hand, who knew what he'd do? Well, Claire knew; she knew that eventually, he'd come after Eve. And there was no way she could let that happen.

Eve *did* look beautiful, in a very Eve-ish way; she'd toned down the skull-themed clothes but kept the Goth color scheme of black, black, and some accent color. Her jewelry remained edgy, and her makeup was something normally seen only on fashion ads and outer-space movies.

She kept the clunky work boots, though, and Claire had to admit that it suited her.

The Car of the Dead looked shiny and new again, and Eve had added a bobblehead Grim Reaper to the front dashboard, complete with scythe and glowing red eyes that flashed when his head bobbed. She'd also swapped stuff for a kickin' stereo that she cranked up to twelve and a half on a ten-point scale, the better to advertise for Florence + The Machine in a town that, Claire thought, had probably never heard of the band at all.

The music was too loud to talk, and that was okay; Claire was in a brooding mood anyway. She hadn't slept well, and she was increasingly anxious about Myrnin. The day, by contrast, was a typical hot Texas day, low on humidity and high on sunburn potential. She kept the window rolled down for the arid breeze, such as it was.

Heads turned as they cruised past. Some, mostly older people, of course, were annoyed by the noise; some seemed neutral until they spotted the hearse. It was easily recognizable as Eve's car; nobody else in Morganville, except the Ransom Funeral Home, owned anything even vaguely like it, certainly not with Death as a dash ornament. Claire, suddenly nervous, reached over and turned down the music.

"What?" Eve asked. She was in a surprisingly sunny mood, considering the events of the night before and her brother's suddenly murderous turn, but then, Claire imagined she was relieved to be taking some kind of positive action against him for a change. "C'mon, it's not *that* emo."

"No, it's cool. I just—" Claire couldn't explain what her unease was, really, except that she definitely had a weird feeling. Maybe it was just all the flyers that they'd seen, and the fact that their front window was still shattered and braced up with plywood.

But it definitely felt personal, the glares they had coming these days.

The car cruised past Common Grounds, and in a glimpse through the front window, she saw that Michael was setting up his guitars. He didn't get to play as much as he liked, so this was a special event for him. Becoming a vampire might have modified his rock-star ambitions a little, but there was no denying that he was really, really, really good. He'd even had an offer of a recording deal, but he'd turned it down, since touring seemed like a bad idea (and, of course, Amelie had forbidden it). After all, he had a substance problem that even major record labels wouldn't be able to keep quiet about.

He didn't say much about that, Claire realized; about how his whole life had been centered on music, and then it had changed without warning, and without his permission. He never complained about how unfair it was—at least not out loud. And not to her.

"He should have more people there," Eve said.

"What?"

"A crowd. Michael *always* draws a crowd, but—look back there. Do you see a line of people?" Eve sounded shocked at first, then angry. "Those idiots. They're not mad at him, are they? Why?"

Because he's a vampire married to a human, Claire thought, but didn't say. Eve knew that. She just couldn't accept that people could hate Michael on principle, without counting who he really was.

"It'll break his heart if they don't come to hear him play. It's all he ever wanted, to play and make people happy. If they take that away from him..." Eve bit her lip, and tears shimmered in her dark eyes. Claire reached over and grabbed her hand, and squeezed, and her best friend sucked in a deep breath and tried for a smile. "Yeah. He'll be okay. We'll be okay. Right?"

"Right," Claire said, and felt the hollow ring of saying something she didn't quite feel. She covered it with a big smile.

Eve paused at one of the town's few stoplights, waiting for a few beat-up pickup trucks to crawl through the intersection, and said, "You in a big hurry to get to TPU?"

Claire checked her watch. "My class is in twenty minutes."

"Oh. I was thinking maybe a coffee at Common Grounds..."

And making Michael feel better by their support, Claire guessed. She hated to do it, but she said, "Aren't the police waiting for you, though?"

"Yes. Like there's anything else I can tell them they don't already have in the five-inch-thick file on my brother."

"I guess they want to know who his friends are now, things like that."

"Like I'd know."

True. Jason and Eve had gone very separate ways from an early age. Claire wondered sometimes what it would be like, having brothers and sisters, but considering how bad Eve's experience with it was, maybe she ought to be grateful to be an only child....

"Hey!" Eve said sharply. "What are you doing?"

Claire jumped, thinking she'd directed it at her, but no, Eve had rolled down the window and was yelling *out.* As Claire started to turn her head, she heard a high-pitched screeching sound, metal on metal, and Eve yelped, threw open her car door, and jumped out. Claire fumbled at her seat belt and finally got it loose, then exited after her. "What happened?" she asked, but it was immediately obvious, because a group of teens stood there on the sidewalk next to the intersection, and one of them had keys out and was scraping out *letters* into the paint of Eve's car. He had a B and an I already incised. Claire guessed the T-C-H were coming.

"God, it's like high school all over again!" Eve said, and shoved the boy away from the hearse. "Get your hands off my car, Aaron!"

"How about you get your hands off *me*, fang-banger?" he sneered, and shoved her back to slam hard against the scratched paint. "What goes around comes around."

"You know, you weren't the brightest crayon in the box even before you flunked out of school, but those were your glory days, weren't they? You really want to get into it with me, dumbass? Biggest mistake of your life!" Eve, color managing to burn bright in her cheeks even through the Goth makeup, was furious, her body tight and shaking, her fists clenched.

"You think you've got some kind of magic shield, what with your hot vampire boyfriend?" one of the girls said from the curb. "You don't."

"Not boyfriend. Husband," another one said, and made a retching sound. "God, don't you have any self-respect? *Marrying* him? That's just gross. It's like a cow marrying a butcher. They ought to throw you both in jail for being sickening."

Aaron laughed. "Oh, sure, you'd say that, Melanie. You dated the guy in junior high."

"Sure, before he turned into one of them!"

"My dad says you're a traitor," said another boy, and he had a very different tone—quiet, sure, dangerous. "My uncle Jake

disappeared the other night. Just another casualty in a town full
of them, right? And you helped. You helped put the vamps right
back on top where they've always been. Just like all the Founder
House families. You're nothing but whores giving it up to the
vamps for money."

Eve lunged at him. Claire darted around the end of the limo
with a sinking conviction that she'd never be fast enough to stop
her, and she was right: Eve landed a solid slap right across his face.
"Don't you *ever*, Roy Farmer!" Eve shouted at him. "Don't you—"

He hit her back, clocking her, hard, right on the point of her
jaw, and before Claire could even draw a breath. It was as if some
invisible signal had gone out to all the other kids—her age or just
a couple of years older—to attack.

"No!" Claire screamed as Eve was grabbed, dragged forward,
and thrown to the ground. It all happened so fast, and in such
chaos, that she didn't know where to aim a shove or a punch to get
to her friend's rescue. Everyone was moving all at once, and Eve
was in the middle of it, and it was all just *insane*.

It seemed as if it went on forever until Claire grabbed hold of
one girl by the hair and yanked. The girl, foot raised to deliver a
furious kick, lost her balance and fell backward, and Claire
dragged her a few feet away as she screamed and twisted and
clawed. Whatever the girl was screaming, it involved a lot of curse
words, and Claire wasn't paying attention. She shoved the girl into
a thorny shrub and lunged back toward the circle of attackers.
Stopping one hadn't put an end to the beating. The weapons she
had were for vampires, not humans, and she couldn't use them on
people who couldn't heal . . . though if this went on any longer, she
might have to inflict real and lasting damage to save Eve's life.

Deep breath. She let herself take a second's pause, and identified
the ringleader, the one Eve had slapped; he was the one laying into

her with real viciousness. Claire quickly stepped up behind him, tried to channel Shane as hard as she could, and did two moves he had taught her: first, a hard, fast punch to the kidneys; second, putting the toe of her shoe in the bend of his knee as he twisted in her direction.

It worked. He broke off the attack and fell to his knees; then he got up, staggering, and turned on her. The others were still going after Eve, but as he came after Claire, they began to break off and follow.

She danced backward, screamed for help (probably uselessly), and tore off, running.

They followed.

Everybody in Morganville was pretty good at running, of course, but Claire had motivation; she slowed down just enough to make them believe they could catch her, and still stayed out of easy grabbing range. The ringleader of the group—what was his name? Roy something?—Roy was fast, and she had to work to stay just a few inches past his lunges. If he caught up with her, she had no doubt he'd take out his rage on her just as he had with Eve.

Let her be okay. Please, let her be okay!

Her legs were starting to burn; Claire could run a fair distance, but adrenaline and fear were taking their toll, and she knew that the kids baying like hounds behind her weren't going to get tired as fast—they had mob mentality to urge them on. There was another intersection ahead, but she didn't see anyone on the street. No, wait—there was a car, cruising up to the stoplight.

A red, flirty sports car with an open roof.

Monica Morrell's car.

Monica had a scarf looped over her head to prevent the dry wind from blowing her glossy dark hair all over the place, and she was wearing big rock-star sunglasses; when she turned toward the noise of Claire's pursuit, it was impossible to read her expression.

Claire took a chance. Jumping over the door of the car and into the passenger seat, she narrowly missed flattening Monica's expensive designer purse.

Monica stared at her for a second in silence, then looked past her as Roy Farmer skidded to a stop a foot away from the car, breathing hard and crimson with fury.

"What?" Monica demanded. "Touch my car and die, Roy Toy." And then, without turning her head to even *look* at the light, or oncoming traffic, she gunned the convertible straight through the intersection with a burning squeal of rubber. The mob—well, it wasn't actually a mob, Claire realized, so much as six teens fired up with rage—fell behind fast, even though they took a couple of steps in pursuit. Monica watched in the rearview for a couple of seconds, speeding up to a limit-breaking sixty miles per hour and blasting through two more stop signs without slowing down, then said, "Any particular reason for that? Not that I care, except somehow trash blew into my passenger seat."

"Thanks," Claire said, because regardless of the insult, Monica really had just done her a solid. She was having trouble catching her breath both from the run and from real worry. "Right turn!"

"Not heading that way, sunshine. I'm going shopping."

Claire grabbed the wheel and forced it, and Monica swore—honestly, she knew words Claire had never heard of, in interesting and colorful combinations—and smacked Claire's hand away to manage the turn carefully. "I swear to God, if you make me dent this car, I will *end you!*"

"They got Eve," Claire said. "Right turn! Make the block!"

"Why should I?"

"They beat her up. She's hurt. They could go back!"

"And I care because . . . ?"

"Monica, they could kill her! Just do it!"

Monica hesitated just long enough to make Claire consider diving out of the car while it was speeding, but then she hit the brakes and fishtailed into a hard right, then another one, then U-turned to squeal to a halt in the intersection where Eve's hearse still idled.

Monica didn't say anything at all. Claire took one look at Eve lying on the pavement in a pool of her own blood, time just seemed to freeze into a block of ice for a long breath. Then it shattered, and Claire scrambled out to kneel beside her. Eve's eyes were closed. She was breathing, but her skin looked ashen, and she was bleeding freely from cuts on her head; Claire didn't dare move her, but she could see the livid red marks on her arms where she'd been kicked and stomped. There could be internal injuries, broken bones. . . .

Ambulance, she thought, but even as she reached for her phone, she heard Monica saying, "Yeah, 911? There's somebody bleeding all over the sidewalk at Fifth and Stillwater. Just look for the hearse."

Claire looked up at her as Monica shut off her cell phone and tossed it into her purse. Monica returned the glance, shrugged, and checked her lipstick in the mirror. "Hey," she said. "Never let it be said I'm not civic-minded. That sidewalk might stain."

Then she drove off with a roar of the convertible's engine.

Claire was right about Roy leading the others back, but by the time they arrived, half of his friends had come to their senses, and the ones still with him weren't enough to really work up a good frenzy. They were further held back by the sound of the ambulance siren piercing the air and moving closer. Claire sat back on her heels as she stared at Roy. He was a nondescript boy, nothing really—an okay kind of face, neutral hair, standard high school clothes. The only thing that really made him stand out at all was the blood on his hands, and even as she noticed, he must have, too, because he pulled out his shirttail and scrubbed the skin clean, then tucked the fabric back into his pants. Evidence gone, except for the bruises on his knuckles.

He pointed at Claire as the ambulance pulled to a stop, siren winding down, behind the hearse. "This ain't over," he said. "Captain Obvious says vamp lovers get what they deserve. You do, too, for sticking up for her."

She had an almost-uncontrollable desire to scream at him, but she could see it wouldn't do any good. They were all looking at her as if *she* were the monster and as if Eve were some kind of pervert that deserved to die. Shane might have known what to say, but Shane wasn't here. Michael wasn't here. It was just her, alone, holding the limp and bloody hand of her best friend.

She met his gaze squarely and said, "Bring it, Roy Toy."

"Later," he promised, and jerked his head at his posse. They headed out at a jog and split up.

It was only as the ambulance attendants asked her to move back and started evaluating Eve's condition that she realized exactly what Roy had said.

Captain Obvious says . . .

Captain Obvious.

Oh God. Claire remembered the flyers, the brick, the gasoline thrown on their house, and the paper with the tombstones on it, and their names.

All their names.

Maybe Pennyfeather hadn't used the gas at all; he'd just taken advantage of the distraction. Maybe *humans* had already tried to kill them all.

She tried Michael's phone, but of course it was turned off; it would be, if he was playing. She dialed Shane, instead. He picked up on the fifth ring. "Hey," he said, "kinda busy trying to get an actual job here. . . ."

"Eve's been hurt," she said. "Get to Michael. Captain Obvious has us on some kind of hit list. And watch your back."

"Jesus." Shane was quiet for a second; then he said, "Is Eve okay?"

"I don't know." For the first time, the reality of it was hitting her as the adrenaline rush faded away, and she felt panic choke her up. "God, Shane, they were kicking her so hard—"

"Who?" She could read the fury in the single word.

"I don't know. Roy Farmer, some guy named Aaron, a girl named Melanie—three others. Shane, please, get to Michael. He's at Common Grounds. . . ."

"On it," he said. "You safe right now?"

"I'm going to the hospital with her," Claire said. "Watch your back—I mean it."

"I will."

He hung up, and she had an insane wish to call him back, to hear his voice saying her name, telling her it would all somehow, impossibly, work out, that he loved her and she didn't have to be afraid of the humans of Morganville, too, instead of just the vampires. But Shane would never say that last thing.

Because he'd known better, and always had.

Eve had disappeared into an emergency room treatment area, and Claire wasn't allowed to follow; she ended up sitting on the edge of a hard plastic chair in the waiting room, rubbing her hands together. They felt sticky, even though she'd washed them twice. When she closed her eyes, she kept seeing the avid delight on the faces of the kids—people Eve knew—as they kicked her when she was down.

She'd faced down Monica and her friends, but that had been a cold, calculated kind of violence. This was . . . This was sickeningly different. It was a blind, unreasoning hate that just wanted blood, and she didn't understand *why*. It left her feeling horrified and shaky.

The first she knew of Michael's arrival was Shane putting his hand on her shoulder and crouching down in front of her. When she looked up, she realized that Michael had just walked straight past her, past the nurse who'd tried to stop him, and stiff-armed open the emergency room PATIENTS ONLY BEYOND THIS POINT door.

Shane didn't say anything, and Claire couldn't find the words. She just collapsed against him, and let the tears boil out of her. It wasn't all grief; part of it was a sharp-edged ball of fury and frustration that kept bouncing around in her chest. First Myrnin had disappeared, and then Pennyfeather had come at them, and Jason, and Angel, and now *this*. It was as if everything they'd known was going wrong, all at the same time. Morganville's bricks and mortar were back together, but its people were coming apart.

Shane made boyfriend noises to her, things like *Hush* and *It's okay*, and it did soothe that deep, scared part of her that had felt so alone. She gulped back her sobs and got enough self-control that she asked, "Was everything all right with Michael?"

"Nah, not really," Shane said. "While we were leaving, some guy taunted Michael about Eve getting what she deserved. We might have trashed the place a little bit. Oliver's going to be pissed. That was a bonus, though. I had to keep Michael from ripping the idiot's head off. He had some kind of Human Pride thing going on, and you know I don't exactly disagree with that, but . . ." He shrugged. "At least I got to hit somebody. I needed that."

She dug in her backpack and found a sad little crumpled-up ball of tissues, blew her nose, and wiped the worst of her tears away. "Shane, I couldn't stop them. They were just—all over her. I tried, but—"

"Knowing you, you did more than try," he said. "I heard a rumor that Captain Obvious had put out the word we were no longer off-limits, but I didn't take it too seriously; hell, he just got started up again, I didn't think he had real juice yet." He sat beside her and took her hand in his. "Eve's tough. She's okay."

"She wasn't," Claire said, and felt tears threaten again. "She couldn't even try to fight them. They just—"

He hushed her and tipped her head against his shoulder, and they sat together, in silence, until Michael came back. He was moving more slowly now, but his face was tense and marble-pale, and he wasn't bothering to try to keep the vampire grace out of the way he walked, like a prowling animal. His eyes looked purple at a distance, from the flickering red in them.

He stopped in front of them, and Claire started to ask about Eve, but something in him kept her quiet and very still.

"I need you," he said to Shane. Shane slowly rose to his feet. "You know who it was?"

Shane glanced at Claire, then nodded.

"Then let's go."

"Bro—," Shane said, and for him, his voice sounded almost tentative. "Man, you've got to tell us something. We love her, too."

"She has a concussion and a broken rib," Michael said. "I can't be here. I need to go, right now."

Shane gazed at him for a long few seconds before he said, "I'm not letting you kill anybody, man."

"I have the privilege to hunt. If you want to stop me from using it, you'd better come along."

Shane cast a quick look of apology at Claire, and she nodded; there was no doubt that Michael was in a mood to get more violent than she'd ever seen him, and having Shane as wingman might actually save lives. "Stay here," he said to her, and gave her a fast, warm kiss. "Do *not* leave without me."

"Don't let him do anything stupid," she whispered. "And don't *you* do anything stupid, either."

"Hey," he said with a cocky grin, "look who you're talking to!"

He left before she could tell him—as if he didn't know—that she loved him, so much, and Michael never even glanced back at her. Maybe he blamed her, she thought miserably. Maybe he figured she should have been able to stop it, to save Eve.

Maybe she ought to have been able to, after all.

She sat in silence, miserable and aching with guilt and grief, for hours. It was long enough that she got thirsty and bought a Coke, downed it, had to find the restroom, went through all the ancient magazines piled on the table, and actually napped a little.

It was almost eight o'clock when the doctor finally appeared from the treatment area. He looked around, frowned, and then came to her. "You're here for Eve Rosser?"

"Yes." She shot to her feet and almost stumbled; her legs had gone a little numb from sitting for so long. "Yes!"

"Where's her immediate family?"

"He's"—she tried to think of something more clever than blurting out *Getting his revenge*, and shifted uncomfortably from one foot to the other—"gone to tell her mom."

That seemed to do the trick, because the doctor looked more satisfied with that. "Well, when he comes back, tell him she's in recovery. We've got her stabilized, but we'll have to keep her for a couple of days and make sure there's no brain trauma. She's lucky. The surgery went well."

"Surgery?" Claire covered her mouth with her hand. "*She had surgery?* For what?"

He stared at her in silence for a moment, then said, "Just tell him she's stable. I don't anticipate more than one night here for her, unless there are complications we can't foresee right now. But the internal bleeding is under control."

He walked off before she could ask him if she could see Eve. He got all the way to the door, then turned back to see her settling miserably back into the plastic chair. "Oh," he said. "If you want to see her, she'll be waking up soon. I warn you, she'll be in some pain."

Claire climbed to her feet again and followed him to the recovery room.

He wasn't kidding about the pain, and Claire was in tears trying to soothe Eve as she moaned and tossed and whimpered, but they finally gave her some kind of a shot that quieted her a little. Claire followed as they wheeled her into a room and hooked her up to machines, and this time, when Claire dozed off in a chair, it was a little more comfortable, and she pulled up to Eve's bedside.

When she woke up, Morganville had gone still and dark, bathed here and there in the soft glow of porch lights and streetlamps. Car headlights crisscrossed the grid of streets. There were, as always, more out at night. Vampire vehicles.

She was still staring out at it when she heard a rustle of sheets, and Eve said, in a shockingly small voice, "Michael?"

Claire went to her side as Eve woke up. She had bruises on her face—red right now, but starting to turn purple at the edges. Both eyes were puffy. "Hey," she said in as soothing a voice as she could manage. She took Eve's hand, carefully, and held it. "Hey, you scared the hell out of me, sweetie."

"Claire?" Eve blinked and tried to open her lids wider, then winced from the effort. "Crap. What car hit me?"

"You don't remember?"

"Did someone run into us? Is my hearse—" Her voice faded off, and she was quiet for a moment, then said, "Oh. Right. They jumped me, didn't they?"

"Yeah," Claire said. "But you're okay. You're in the hospital. The doctor says you're going to be fine."

"Son of a—" Eve tried to lift her hand, but it had tubes coming out of it; she looked at it, then lowered it slowly back down. "Where's Michael?"

"Ah—"

"Please don't tell me he went after them."

"I won't," Claire said. "Look, you just need to rest, okay? Get your strength back after surgery."

"Surgery? For what?" Eve tried to sit up, but she groaned deeply and sank back down in the pillows. "Oh *God*, that hurts. What the hell . . . ?"

The nurse came in just then, saw Eve was awake, and came to lift the bed up to help her sit. "You can sit up for a while," the nurse said, "but if you start feeling sick, use this." She pressed a bowl into Eve's hands. "The anesthesia could make you vomit."

"Wow. Cheery," Eve said. "Wait—what kind of surgery did I have?"

The nurse hesitated, glanced at Claire, and said, "Are you sure you want me to tell you with your visitor present?"

"Claire? Sure. She's like—like a sister." Eve paled a little as she shifted. "It hurts."

"Well, it will," the nurse said, without much sympathy. "They had to remove your appendix. It was bleeding."

"*It what?*"

"You were kicked in the stomach," the nurse said. "Your appendix was badly damaged. They had to remove it. So it's best if you stay still for a while and let yourself heal. The police are coming to interview you about what happened."

"Good."

The nurse smiled. There was something a little ominous about it, a little disturbing. "I'd advise you to refuse to give a statement. Might be healthier for you, all things considered. The people who hurt you might have friends. And you don't have very many."

Claire blinked. "What did you just say?" The nurse turned away. "Hey!"

Eve put a hand on her arm as Claire tried to get up. "I understand," she said.

The nurse nodded, checked the readings on a couple of machines, and said, "Don't keep her awake long. I'll tell the police to come back later. Give you some time to think about what you're going to say to them. You're a smart girl. You know what's best."

The message, Claire thought, was chilling and clear: don't tell the cops the names of the people who attacked you. Or else. And an "or else" from a medical professional was pretty nasty. If Eve wasn't safe here . . .

Captain Obvious had always been a little bit of a joke, in most Morganville resident circles, but Claire was starting to think that this new, more aggressive Cap was something else entirely. He was inspiring people. And leading them into frightening extremes.

Like the vampires, with their identification cards and hunting licenses.

If both sides kept escalating, nobody could stand in the middle for long without having a price on his head—and it sounded as though that had already happened. Eve was the first, but any one of them could be next.

The nurse left. Eve watched her go, then closed her eyes and sighed. "Figured that would happen," she said. "Humans first, and all that crap. They've gotten stronger. And now Captain Obvious is back. It's a bad time to be us, Claire. I have to tell Michael to back off. . . ."

Eve tried to sit up, but the effort left her pale and exhausted. "He never should have gone after them. That's what they *want*; don't you get it? They came after me to get to him. I'm not important. He is. He's Amelie's blood—kind of like her son. If they can hurt him, kill him—Claire, go find him. Please. I'll be okay here. Just *go*. The worst thing they're going to do to me is give me crap Jell-O."

Claire hesitated a long moment, then leaned over and hugged Eve, giving her a gentle and awkward kind of embrace that made her aware of just how fragile the girl was—how fragile they all were.

"Love you," she said.

"Yeah, whatever, you, too," Eve said, but she smiled a little. "Go. Give him a call. He'll listen to you—or at least Shane will."

And for the love of her, Claire tried, but the phone kept ringing, and ringing, and ringing, straight to voice mail.

And the day slipped away as they anxiously waited.

SIXTEEN

MICHAEL

The anger that had hold of me made me ache all over, especially in my eyeteeth; I'd rarely experienced the urge to bite somebody in pure rage, but *damn*, I wanted to sink my fangs deep in someone now. Roy Farmer, that little son of a bitch, to start, and then the rest of his murderous little crew.

Eve had looked so broken, lying in that bed. So unlike the bundle of strength and energy I loved. I really hadn't known, deep down, how much she meant to me until I'd seen her like that, and known, really and deeply *known*, that I could lose her.

Nobody hurt my girl and got away with it.

Shane was angry, too, but—and this was a reversal of our usual roles as friends—he was the cautious one, the one telling me to play it smart and not let anger drive the bus. He was right, of course, but right didn't matter so much just now. I wanted blood, and I wanted to taste it and feel the fear spicing it like pepper. I wanted them to know how *she'd* felt, helpless and terrified and alone.

And yeah, it probably wasn't fair, but I was angry at Claire for leaving her, even for a moment. I knew she'd done the right thing, drawing off the mob, but that had left Eve lying bleeding on a sidewalk. Alone. And I couldn't get that image out of my head. She could have died *alone*.

I understood how Shane felt when he drove his fist through a wall. Some things, only violence could erase.

"Roy lives over on College Street," Shane said, "but he won't be there. He lives with his parents. He's a punk, but not so much of one that he'd run home to his mommy."

"Where, then?" We were in Eve's hearse, and Shane was driving; I was sitting in the blacked-out back area. Shane had verbally kicked my ass about risking sunburn when I'd wanted to walk; he'd made me stop off and grab a long coat and hat and gloves, too, just in case. "You know the guy, right?"

"Kinda," he said. "Roy's one of those vampire-hunter-wannabe types, came to me a couple of times for pointers on things, and showed me things he was working on as weapons. He hero-worshipped my dad, which tells you a little bit about how screwed-up he is. I never thought he'd do this, though. Not coming out for Eve, or any of us. Didn't think he'd have the guts."

"It doesn't take guts to kick a girl half to death," I said. Shane said nothing to that, just gave me an uneasy look in the rearview and tightened his grip on the wheel. "Where would he be?"

"Probably at the 'Stro," Shane said. "He has a sick hand-built Cadillac he likes to show off there. He's probably getting back-slaps from his buddies about how awesome he is."

The Astro was an abandoned old drive-in on the outskirts of

Morganville, just barely within its borders; it had a graying movie screen that tilted more toward the desert floor every year, and the pavement had cracked and broken in the sun, letting sage and Joshua bushes push up through the gaps. The concession stand had fallen down a couple of years back, and somebody had touched off a bonfire there for high school graduation.

It went without saying that the place was a favorite of the underage drinking and drugging crew.

Shane drove out there. It was close to twilight now, and sunset had stacked itself in bands of color on the horizon; the leaning timbers of the Astro's screen loomed as the tallest thing around in the flatland, and Shane circled the peeling tin fence until he came to the entrance. The cops made periodic efforts to chain it shut, but that lasted only as long as it took for someone to cut the lock off—and most of those who hung out here had toolboxes built in the beds of their trucks.

Sure enough, the entrance stood gaping, one leaf of it creaking in the fierce, constant wind. Sand rattled the windshield as Shane made the turn, and he slowed down. "Got to watch out for bottles," he said. "The place is land-mined with them."

He was right. My eyes were better in the dark, and I could see the drifts of dark brown bottles, some intact, most broken into shards. The fence line was peppered with shotgun blasts, and I got the feeling that a lot of the empties had been used for target practice. Standard drunken-country-teen behavior; I couldn't say I hadn't done some of that myself, before I'd been forced to adapt to something different.

I didn't miss it, though.

Shane's headlights cut harsh across dusty green sage, the spiked limbs of mesquite pushing up out of the broken pavement, and, in the far corner of the lot, a gleam of metal. Cars, about six of them.

Most were pickups, the vehicle of choice out here in Nowhere, Texas, but one was a sharply gleaming Caddy, painted electric blue, with shimmering chrome rims. Shane was right. It *was* a sick car.

A bunch of kids—about twenty of them—were sitting on the hoods of the vehicles, passing bottles, cigs, pills, whatever else they had to share.

They watched the slow approach of the hearse with the wary attention of people who might have to run for it at any moment. The only reason they hadn't scurried already was that it wasn't a standard vampire sedan, or a cop car.

Roy Farmer was sitting on the hood of his Caddy with his arm around a plump blond girl. They were both wearing cowboy hats and boots. She must have been cold in her tank top and torn jeans shorts, but from the looks of her, she was too drunk to care. Roy watched as the hearse pulled to a stop, and he took a long pull out of the brown bottle in his hand.

"Mike," Shane said as I reached for the door. "Seriously, man, slow your roll. He wouldn't just be sitting there like this if he didn't have something up his sleeve. He has to know you'd be coming for him. Let me check it first."

I didn't bother to answer. I wasn't letting Shane, or anyone, do *this*. If Roy had come after Eve, he'd come after me, and I couldn't let him see it any other way. Maybe it was loyalty; maybe it was possessiveness. I don't know; Eve wasn't there to set me straight on the difference. But I knew that it was my job, not Shane's, to make Roy regret it.

Maybe that was part of being married. Or maybe it was just me, discovering for the first time that I really, truly wanted Eve to look up to me and believe that I could—and would—protect her. She'd probably laugh and call me a Neanderthal, but secretly, deep down, she'd be pleased.

I got out of the hearse and walked over toward the other cars. The teens fell silent, watching me. Nobody ran, nobody reacted overtly, but they were all ready; I could see it in the tension of their bodies. Even the stoners put down their drugs of choice to pay attention.

I knew how it was. I'd rarely been one to come hang out here, but I was a Morganville kid. We'd all been taught to watch vampires with complete attention when one was in the area.

"You," I said, and nodded at Roy. He stayed where he was, one arm draped over his girlfriend's shoulders. "Just you. Everybody else gets a free pass tonight."

"Hey, look; it's the big man off campus," he said. "I'm busy. Screw you."

I felt a growl building inside me, the beast clawing on its chain. Eve's smile flashed in front of my mind's eye, and I wanted so badly to wipe the grin off his face. "Careful," I said softly. Just that. His girlfriend must have sensed the menace coming off me, because she straightened up and cast Roy a worried look; the others were slipping quietly off the hoods of their own vehicles, stowing their drinks and smokes. No loyalty here. Nobody was willing to stand up for Roy, not even the girl he still held clamped under his arm as if he intended to use her as a human shield.

I waited until the other vehicles started their engines and began heading for less hostile places to get high. Once they were all gone, the Morganville night was cold, silent, and very, very heavy around us.

"Why Eve?" I asked him. I was aware of Shane standing somewhere behind me, ready and most likely armed; I didn't need him. Not for this. "Why did you go after my wife?" *Wife* still sounded strange in my mouth; she'd been *girlfriend* or *friend* for so many years. But it was a heavy word, an important one, and he must have heard it, because his grin got tighter and more predatory.

"'Cause it's evil," he said. "Anybody stupid enough to marry a vampire deserves to die before she contaminates other people."

"She wasn't hurting you."

"Man, it makes me want to vomit just looking at her, knowing *you* had your hands all over her. She's better off dead." That grin— I kept staring at it, wanting to rip it off his face. "Is she? Dead?"

"No," I said.

"Too bad. Maybe next time. 'Cause you know there's gonna be a next time, fanger. You can't get us all."

"Maybe not," I said, "but I can damn sure get you."

I moved, and he caught it and moved at the same time, shoving his girlfriend into my path. She screamed and rolled off the hood, tripping me, but I landed easily on the other side of her and grabbed Roy by the arm as he tried to jump behind the wheel. His shirt tore as he jerked free, and he backed up, still grinning, but it was more like a snarl now.

He had a spray can in his hand. I didn't need to ask to know it was silver. The downside of all the weapons that Shane and Eve had developed to help us survive was that now all of the humans of Morganville had the recipes; he'd made his own anti-vamp pepper spray, and if he nailed me with it, it wouldn't just hurt; it might blind me for days. It would certainly put me down hard enough that he could stake me with silver without breaking a sweat.

Except that I heard Shane, still standing behind me, pump a shotgun. Roy's eyes slid past me to focus on him, and his snarl faltered.

"Looks like somebody brought a can to a gunfight," Shane said. "Just to be clear, if you tag my friend, I get to spray you right back. Seems fair."

"You won't shoot me," Roy said. "I'm like you. I'm resistance."

"Then the resistance is scraping the bottom of the DNA barrel," Shane said. "And you're going after my friends. That trumps anything else." I wouldn't have doubted him, in that moment. Eve was like his adopted sister, and I knew how Shane felt about her.

So did Roy. He stepped back, eyes darting side to side. He finally dropped the spray can and held up his hands. "Okay. Okay, fine, you got me. What you gonna do now, vamp? Kill me?"

"I could," I said.

"He's got a card that says he can, and everything," Shane said. "But he's not going to." I sent him a look. Shane shrugged. "You're not, man. I know you. Anyway, it ain't the Roys of this thing you have to worry about. You need to talk to the head man."

"Captain Obvious," I said. Roy's face drained of color. "You're going to tell me where to find him."

"No way."

His girlfriend was getting to her feet behind me. I didn't even look at her, but I grabbed her and pulled her closer, my arm around her neck to hold her still as she struggled. "We'll start with her," I said. "And if she's not important to you, then I'm pretty sure saving your own neck will do the trick. You kicked my wife when she was down, Roy. You're not that brave."

"Michael," Shane said, very quietly.

"Shut up," I said, and let my fangs come down. "Captain Obvious. Now."

It took only about a minute for him to give it up, but for me to feel I was done with him, it took four more.

"You have something to say?" I asked Shane. I was in the front now, since it was no longer daylight. He cut his gaze toward me for a second, raised his eyebrows, and shook his head. "Too little or too much?"

"I'm not you, Michael. I don't know. It's really too bad about the car, though. That was a really nice car."

"If it were Claire—"

"It nearly *was* Claire." He paused for a moment, then shook his head. "I don't know. I'd want to kill the little bastard. Hell, I still want to."

"I could," I said. "And nobody would say a thing about it. Do you know how scary that is?"

"Yeah," he said. "And I think it was damn nice of you to just break his arm. But the next vampire, they'd kill somebody for staring at them too long, spilling their coffee, whatever. That's why it can't be like this, with every vampire getting some kind of free pass to murder. For every Michael, there are three Jasons. Get me?"

I nodded. I understood that better than he did, probably; I'd been around more vampires over the past year or two than he ever had. "We have to fix things," I said. "You're right about that. First Captain Obvious, and then—"

"Then Oliver," Shane said. "Because that crusty old bastard is getting his way, and if he does for much longer, we're not going to have a town left. The only way we're going to survive here is if we make everybody show respect."

The drive—like every drive inside the city limits—was short, and when we pulled to a halt in front of a plain, everyday house— it was a little weather-beaten, a little run-down—Shane and I sat for a moment, assessing it. "What do you think?" I asked him. He shrugged.

"Looks okay," he said. "But if Roy wasn't shining us on, and it *is* Captain Obvious's place, he's going to be prepared for the vampire apocalypse in there. You walk in there all fangs and red eyes, and you're done."

"You want me to let you go in by yourself."

"Seems safer," Shane said. "After all, I'm the poster child for anti-vamp, right? He's going to hear me out."

"Maybe," I said. "But the point isn't to talk, Shane. It's to kick ass and make sure he never comes after Eve again. Or you. Or Claire. If he wants to nail a target on me, fine, I've earned it along with the thirst for blood. But there's a line, and he's crossed it."

"I know," Shane said. "Believe me, I know."

"No, you don't. You haven't seen Eve yet."

Shane considered that, then nodded, opened his door, and got out. He left the shotgun behind, on the rack behind the seat. "You hear me yell, get in there," he said. "Otherwise, wait here. Promise me."

I didn't, and he didn't insist on it; after a second's hesitation, he shook his head and walked up the cracked steps to the front door. He tried the bell, then knocked, and after a few long moments, the curtains in the front window twitched, and the door swung open.

I sat very still, watching. Listening. And, I realized, I wasn't the only one. There was another vampire in the shadows, almost invisible except for a quick shimmer of red eyes. Vampires had no scent, unless they'd recently fed, and out here in the yard, with all the smells of grass, manure, dirt, wood, metal, there was no chance to detect one that way at all. I wondered who it was. No point in a confrontation, anyway; I needed to focus, in case Shane ended up needing me.

The vampire disappeared just seconds after I noticed his presence.

Shane didn't yell for help. He opened the front door and gestured; I got out and walked up toward him.

"Take it slow," he advised me. "Think of it as visiting the

Founder's office. He's just about as ready to kill you if you put a foot wrong."

I'd defied the hell out of Amelie already, I thought, but Shane didn't necessarily need to know that. I walked up to the door and ... stopped, because the house had a barrier. Most Morganville houses didn't, unless they were really old or Founder Houses, but this one was different.

And it was strong.

"Come in," Shane said, but that didn't change anything. I was a vampire, and I wasn't getting inside until the house resident altered the rules.

Enrique Ramos appeared in the hall behind my friend, and stared at me for a moment before he said, "Yeah, come on in."

I passed a pile of black clothing, a mask, a leather jacket, and paused to look at them. There was also a motorcycle helmet. "Yours?"

"Sure," he said, and threw me a cold smile. "Everybody saw me in them at the rally."

"Then you're not Captain Obvious," I said.

"Why not?"

"Too obvious."

And I was right; he was probably one of three or four decoys out there, playing the captain, leading the vampires around on goose chases. This was his house, and a good place to hold a neutral headquarters, since it had been in his family a long time; his mother had moved to a new place and left it to her son, and he'd made it a kind of secured, fortified meeting place.

The war council of Captain Obvious was in session at the dinner table in the kitchen, and as Enrique and Shane walked me in, I realized just how much trouble we were in. There were several of Morganville's most prominent businessmen at the table, including the owner of the bank, but that wasn't the issue.

There was a vampire sitting at the Captain Obvious table. *Naomi.* A blood sister to Amelie, she was a pretty, delicate-seeming vampire who looked all of twenty, if that; she had a gentle manner and sweet smile, and it concealed depths that I hadn't understood for a long time. She wasn't just ambitious; she was calculating, backstabbing, and determined to win.

"I thought you were dead," I told her. I'd been informed she'd been killed by the draug, in the final battle; there'd been a whisper that it wasn't the draug who'd done it, but Amelie, by proxy, getting rid of a credible rival for leader of Morganville.

Naomi lifted her shoulders in a very French sort of shrug. "I have been before," she said in that lovely, silvery voice, and laughed a little. "As you know, Michael, I am hard to keep that way." She sent me a smile that invited me to share the joke, but I didn't smile back. For all her graces and kind manners, there was an ice-cold core to her that most didn't ever see. "Sit and be welcome."

"*You're* not Captain Obvious," I said, and stared at each of the human men at the table in turn. Then I turned to the woman seated across from her. "*You* are."

Hannah Moses nodded. Her scarred face was still and quiet, her dark eyes watchful. "I knew you'd be impossible to fool about this. Sit down, Michael."

I didn't want to sit down at the Captain Obvious table. I was still angry, yeah, but I was also more than a little bit shocked, and betrayed. Hannah had been a friend. An ally. She'd protected all of us, at one time or another; she was a solid, real person, with a solid set of values.

That made it so, so much worse.

But anyway, I sat, because the alternative was to go full throttle, and I wasn't quite there. Not yet. Shane kept standing, leaning against the wall, arms folded. He was watching Enrique, who was doing the same thing; bodyguards, I guessed, facing off in silence and ready for the other to make a move. There was muttering among the business leaders, and at least one of them got up to leave the room in protest.

"Sit down, Mr. Farmer," I said without looking at him. "We're going to have a conversation about your son and where he gets his funny ideas."

Roy Farmer's dad got an odd look on his face and sank back in his seat. "Is my son alive?"

"Yep," Shane said, with false cheer. I wouldn't have been quite so quick to reassure him. "Hope you don't mind the fix-up on his car. Oh, and his arm."

"You bloodsucking parasite son of a—"

I moved, then, slamming my palm on the table hard enough to leave a crack in the wood. "I didn't kill him," I said. "Shut up and take it as a gift."

He did, looking white around the mouth. Then I looked at Hannah. "You put us in the crosshairs. You put *Eve* in the crosshairs," I said to Hannah. "Why would you do that?"

"Why did you have to put her in the middle?" she asked me, in a frighteningly reasonable tone. "You know that the vampires won't let her stay there for long; they'll have her killed before they let humans gain power in this town through her status as a legal consort. You knew that when you married her. By putting pressure on her from the human side, we were hoping we could save her life and make her leave you. Get you to understand how dangerous this is for her, and for you. We don't hate you, Michael. But you're in the way."

"Wait," Shane said, turning his head toward her. "You had Roy Farmer beat her up to *help*? That's what you're telling us?"

"It's hardly our fault. Roy was never supposed to do more than frighten her," Naomi said, with that charming little way she had. "I assure you, he was never supposed to harm her badly. He was only to make it clear that she would not be accepted as Michael's wife. As the vampires have also made it clear. I have heard that Oliver sent Pennyfeather to make that same point."

"Eve's not a pawn you can move around the board," I said, spearing Naomi with a glare, then Hannah, then the others. "And neither am I."

"But that is exactly what you are, Michael. You, Shane, Claire, Eve—all of you. You are played for one side or the other at every turn, and you fail to see it." Naomi shook her head in what I was sure was fake sadness, but it was very convincing. "Mistakes have been made, but no one intended permanent harm to your lover. You may take my word for it."

"My *wife*," I said, pointedly. "Call her that."

Naomi inclined her head. *"D'accord."*

I looked at Hannah. She hadn't said much so far, and left Naomi to try to make the justifications. She watched me, and Shane, with calm and careful attention, hands loose and relaxed on the table in front of her.

But she was afraid. I could feel that, hear it in the rapid beat of her heart. All of the humans were afraid. *They ought to be,* I thought. They were allied now with a traitorous vampire, and they'd just made an enemy of someone who by all rights should have been their friend and supporter.

"You should never have touched Eve," I told Hannah.

"I'm sorry for what happened," she said. "But, Michael, you all made your choices, and your choices have consequences. If you want Eve to be safe, you should allow her to come back to her own side. With us."

"Why do there have to be sides? We're *people*, Hannah."

She shook her head. "You *were* people. You like to think you still are, but you're a killer at heart. And there are always sides. If you can't give her up just because you love her, then you're selfish, and you're the one putting her more at risk every day—from your own kind."

"So what am I supposed to do?" It burst out of me in anger, and all of a sudden I was on my feet, eyes blazing, rage bringing out my fangs and my fury. "*She's my wife!* This isn't you, Hannah. It's not like you at all, bringing innocent people into this, getting them hurt, maybe killed!"

Hannah didn't move, and she didn't reach for a weapon. Enrique pushed off the wall, and so did Shane in a match move, but I was the only one showing any threat.

Hannah said, "Gentlemen—could you leave me, Naomi, and Michael alone, please?"

The Morganville businessmen all got up and left the room without argument. Enrique stuck around.

"I will if he will," Enrique said, and nodded toward Shane, who nodded right back.

"Maybe you guys can go have a stare-off in the other room," I said, and got a challenging frown from Shane. "If something was going to go sideways, it already would have happened. Right?"

"Probably," Shane said. "But I don't like this."

"It's better if we do this alone," Hannah said. "You, me, and Naomi. There are things we need to keep private, even from our advisers."

I studied them, then jerked my head at Shane. He made an

after-you motion to Enrique, then followed the other man out of the room.

The door to the kitchen shut tightly behind them.

From the moment the door closed, Hannah said nothing. It was as if she'd just ... powered off. It was Naomi who stood up and walked the perimeter of the kitchen, apparently fascinated by the countertops, the appliances, the drawer pulls.

"The solution to your problem is perfectly commonplace," Naomi said finally. "Let Eve think you have ceased to care for her, and her safety will be assured. Your marriage is the problem, and it's the marriage that must be ended. You may choose the timing of the legal actions, of course, but it's imperative that you make her leave you *now*."

"I can't do that." The anger wasn't helping me, and all too soon, it drained away, leaving me feeling empty and hollow. "I can't just push her away. Hannah—"

Hannah wasn't looking at me, or at anything. I had a visceral sense of sudden danger, and I turned on Naomi. "Why are you here? You're not Captain Obvious; you can't be. How did you get them to even let you in the door?"

"I was wondering when you'd ask that," she said, and smiled at me from under her long eyelashes. "I can be *very* persuasive. It's been my strength. Once I realized that Hannah Moses made such an excellent leader for the human resistance, it was clear I should ally myself to it. How else am I to bring down my sister?"

I glanced at Hannah again, eyes widening, because it wasn't right that she was sitting so quietly, like a doll that had been switched off ... or a *puppet*.

The distraction was all Naomi needed. If my nerves hadn't been strung guitar-tight, I'd never have seen her move; even with that much warning, though I didn't understand what she was going to do. I thought she was going to stake me, and I raised my hands in defense, but she darted past me, behind me, grabbed me, and pulled me off-balance. I felt her hands snaking cold around my chest, then pushing my chin high—

And then she bit me before I could yell for help.

Her fangs slid into my throat, and it felt like being stabbed with ice; all the warmth began to flood away from me, into her, and in its place I felt a terrible dark influence sliding through my veins. Naomi, like Bishop, her vampire father, had the power to subvert other vampires—and now, she had me. Just as she'd taken control of Hannah, and through Hannah, the entire human resistance.

We were all just puppets now.

It didn't take long, and there was absolutely nothing I could do to fight it. When she let me go, I collapsed to my hands and knees on the tile, mouth open, fangs extended, and Naomi walked calmly back to take her seat again at the table. She looked at Hannah. "Then that's finished," she said, and tapped her fingers on the wood of the table in a complex, musical rhythm. "Michael. Stand."

I did. I wanted to lunge at her, kill her, rip her apart, but I knew that none of it was showing on my face or in my body language. Just as nothing showed in Hannah's. The reason it hadn't fit for Hannah to have put Eve at such deadly risk was that it hadn't been her choice. It was Naomi's decision—all of it, tracing back to Naomi. And it was way too late for me to do anything about it. I couldn't even try to warn people.

"This is what you will do, Michael," Naomi said. "You will go back to see your lovely wife and tell her you've had second thoughts. You'll do whatever is necessary to destroy all trust between you. And then you will pack your things and come back here, to me. You'll make an excellent soldier. Best of all, no one will suspect you. Amelie's bloodchild? You are a perfect little assassin."

"Yes," I said. *No, no, no,* I was screaming, but I couldn't do anything at all to stop myself. "What should I do about Shane? And Claire?"

"Shane's of no consequence, and neither is the girl, except as a tool to be used. I've taken Myrnin out of play; without the protection of her black knight, she is no more than a pawn. But . . ." She tapped pale fingers to her lips, looking momentarily thoughtful. "You make a good point. What *of* Claire? Even a pawn may take a queen, if played properly. . . ."

She rose to her feet and paced for a moment, arms folded, head down. Hannah and I stared at each other. Her heart was hammering, and I recognized now that it wasn't fear she felt but rage. She was just as trapped as I was. If Myrnin's black knight was off the table, Hannah was Naomi's white castle, hiding secrets. And what was I?

"Ah," Naomi said, and turned back toward me, eyes shining in unholy delight. "*I* know how to play Claire. So, this is what you will do, and what you will tell her. . . ."

I listened. I hated her with every fiber of my being and every tiny bit of my soul.

But I knew I'd do what she said, even though it was going to destroy every good thing in my life.

Because I didn't have a choice.

SEVENTEEN

CLAIRE

Michael looked like the walking dead when he arrived back in the waiting room, where Claire was getting coffee for the eleven-millionth time from the machine; it ate her quarters, again, but she'd learned from one of the nurses—not the one who'd threatened Eve, thank God—how to kick the side of the dispenser in just the right spot to get the container to drop and produce about a half cup of oily, disgusting swill that kind of tasted like coffee.

It was better than nothing. But not much better.

She almost dropped the cup when she saw the boys arrive. Shane had a guarded, solemn expression, but Michael looked as though he'd been to the gates of hell and back and returned without the souvenir T-shirt.

"She's sleeping," Claire said, before either of them could speak. "Hey, are you all right? Michael?"

"Fine," he said. His blue eyes looked oddly stark and empty, and there were dark smudges under them, as if he'd been robbed of a week's sleep in just the past few hours. "I need to see her."

"Just be careful not to wake her," Claire said. "She's pretty woozy, and in some pain. The doctor said she'll probably be better in the morning. They're going to let her go then, so we can take her home. She just can't do much for a while."

"Good," he said. He hardly even glanced her way, but he took the coffee cup out of her hand and tossed back the near-boiling contents in a single gulp, crushed the paper, and dropped it on the floor as he stalked off, heading for Eve's room. Claire bent and picked up the trash.

"Wow," she said, looking after him. "What the hell, Shane?"

"Wish I knew," he said. "That was the weirdest couple of hours I've ever had. Roy—that was okay, fine, I get it. But then we went to see Cap—" By which she understood Captain Obvious, without it being spelled out. "They made me wait outside toward the end. Whatever they said in there, it was bad. He's looked like that ever since. Like somebody cut his guts out and made him swallow them."

"So you know who it is? Cap, I mean?" She kept it in a bare whisper, glancing around at the empty waiting room. Shane nodded. "Who?"

"Better you don't know," he said. "Trust me, I wish I didn't. I'm starting to wish I didn't know a lot of things."

They settled into the chairs in the waiting area, and Shane put his arm around her . . . and they were just getting comfortable when Shane turned his head and said, "Did you hear that?"

"What?" Claire felt drowsy and content nestled against his shoulder, but now that he'd woken her all the way up again, she did hear something—raised voices.

"That's Eve," Shane said, and stood up. "Something's wrong." Claire sighed and followed him on aching legs down the hall, past the empty nursing station, and arrived just as he pushed the door open.

Eve was crying. Not just crying a little, but crying in shocked, awful, painful sobs, even though she was holding her abdomen with both hands as if it were agony to even try to breathe. Michael was standing at the end of her bed, staring at her without any expression at all on his face. He'd always looked like an angel, Claire thought, but now he looked like one of those cold, remote, vengeful ones, the kind that carried swords.

It was terrifying.

"How can you say that?" Eve said, in between painful gulps for air. Crying was hurting her; Claire could hear it in the little hitching whimpers between the words. "God, Michael, don't— please—"

"What the hell is going on?" Shane demanded, and got in Michael's face. "What did you say to her?"

"The truth. Marrying her was a mistake from the beginning," he said. "And I want it over, Eve. I'll get the papers done, and you sign them, and we're finished. It's better for us both. The two of us together—Captain Obvious is right. Amelie is right. It's sick, and it shouldn't be allowed to continue. It's going to get innocent people killed."

"Dude, don't do this," Shane said, and reached out. Michael batted his hand away before it reached his shoulder. "Maybe you think this is going to keep her safe somehow, but it's not the right way, okay? And it's not the right time. I know you don't want to

hurt her. I heard you back there, with Cap. I know you're just trying to protect her—"

"Do you?" Michael turned that empty look on Shane, and
stopped him dead. "You don't know a damn thing about me,
man."

Shane actually laughed. "You're kidding, right? I know everything about you. You're my best friend."

"Think so?" Michael said, and then before Claire was ready,
before she was even aware he was moving, he had turned and
grabbed hold of her.

Michael Glass, holding her in his arms.

And bending.

And kissing her.

With tongue.

Expertly.

It took her by so much surprise that Claire could only make a
muffled sound of shock and surprise at first, and she didn't even
try to resist; her body reported in sensations in a rush—the cold
strength of him, the softness of his lips, the taste, the absolute *au-
thority* of it . . . and then her rational brain kicked in and screamed
in horror.

Michael Glass was kissing her *in front of Shane. And Eve.*

And he was doing a damn good job of groping her along with
it, with his hands slipping beneath her shirt.

Shane yelled something, and Claire felt him trying to pull her
free, but Michael held on with relentless strength. She was suddenly terrified to be between the two of them, like a rag between
two possessive pit bulls, and then Michael let go just as fast as he'd
grabbed on. That sent her crashing back into Shane, and Shane
into the wall, with his arms wrapped around her. Claire's mouth
felt bruised and wet, and her shirt was bunched up just below her

bra line; she frantically tugged it down and tried to wipe her lips at the same time, not doing a very good job of either. Michael was watching her, and the look in his eyes was awful. It wasn't love. It wasn't anything she could understand at all.

"I've been wanting to do that for years," he said. "Just so you know. Did you see *that* coming, best friend? Maybe it's been going on for a while. Maybe ever since she moved in. How do you know?"

"You son of a—" Shane pushed Claire out of the way and came at Michael, but Michael just shoved him back again against the wall and held him there, ignoring his blows. He was looking now at Eve, who was gasping and crying, curled in on herself on the bed as if he'd punched her in an open wound.

"We're done?" he asked her.

"Yes," she whispered. "Yes. Get *out*." It would have been a scream, Claire thought, except that Eve couldn't get the breath to make that happen.

Michael let go of Shane and walked away, stiff-armed the hospital door open, and disappeared in less than five seconds.

But what he left behind felt like an explosion that was still happening, the shock waves rippling on and on and on. . . .

Shane turned on Claire. "What the *hell* was that?"

"Why are you asking me?" she shot back, shocked, and scrubbed her mouth again. "I didn't ask for it!"

"He wouldn't just—" Shane was the one looking terrible now, and almost as betrayed as Eve. "Is that the first time? Is it?"

"*What?* What are you saying?" She felt sick to her stomach. One minute ago, everything had been fragile, but okay; now the whole world seemed to be splintering around her, breaking into unrecognizable fragments. "I didn't do *anything wrong!*" She remembered, with a horrible wrench, that Shane had once secretly worried about that, about her and Michael having a thing behind his back. It had never happened, but now—now it was back, all that paranoia, and the anger. Michael had chosen exactly the right spot to hit to break their trust apart. "How can you even think I would—"

"God, get out," Eve said in a small, broken voice. "Just get out. Both of you." She was crying still, but quietly now, and all her monitors were beeping and flashing red lights. "Jesus, please, go!"

The nurses came in then, crowding around Eve's bed to adjust machines and poke needles full of meds into the hanging saline bags. As Shane pushed her out into the hall, Claire heard the frantic fast beating of Eve's pulse monitor slow down. They were putting her back to sleep. Maybe, if they were lucky, Eve would think it was all a drug dream in the morning. *No. She won't be that lucky.*

Shane let go of her, and she rounded on him, still trying to pull her shirt down to a decent level. "I didn't do anything," she insisted, again. "And I never kissed him! He kissed *me*; you saw that."

"He did it like he knew exactly what you liked," Shane said. "Like he was used to doing it. And you weren't exactly struggling."

"I didn't know what to do! God, Shane—it was *fast*, and I didn't know—I didn't want that! How can you think that he and I were—"

"I don't know," Shane said, and stuck his hands in his pockets, shoulders hunched tight. "Maybe because my best friend thought it was perfectly okay to stick his tongue down your throat to make his point? Because I'm pretty sure he didn't have to do that just to break up with Eve. He didn't have to be that cruel."

"Shane—*Shane!* Wait!"

He was walking away from her, heading down the hallway with his head down. Leaving her, too.

Claire stood there, shocked and alone, feeling like the only

sane person left in the world, and when the enormity of it hit, really hit, she burst into tears and curled up in a ball on the worn
old couch in the corner of the waiting room.

How did I feel about it? She didn't want to ask herself that. She
didn't want to remember the warm rush of feelings underneath
the confusion and horror of the moment, or the way her heart had
speeded up, and her body betrayed her right down to the core. *I
didn't want it. I didn't.*

Well, hadn't she always thought Michael was a hottie? Yes, she
had. She'd always noticed, and every once in a while she'd had
the occasional little fantasy—but that was *normal*; that was what
happened when you were around someone a lot, not—not this.
Never this.

He hadn't wanted her. He'd used her, viciously and with cold
calculation, to drive Eve away, and Shane. Each of them was alone
now, in a world that didn't want or need them.

Why would you do that, Michael? It didn't make any sense. Even if
he'd decided not to stay with Eve, Michael was a good man, a nice
man; he would have done it gently and with as much kindness as
possible because he *did* love Eve; he *did*. She couldn't have been so
wrong about that. And when he'd left here before, he'd been a
knight on a mission, hell-bent on avenging her. When he'd come
back . . .

Claire gulped back the horrible, hurtful tears, and wiped her
face, and tried to think through the problem, as if it were happening to someone else. *What makes someone turn around like that, turn on his
friends?*

No. That wasn't the question. The question was, what would
make a vampire turn on his friends . . . and there was only one answer to that, really. Claire thought of Bishop, Amelie's vampire father, who could infect another vampire with his bite and command

his absolute loyalty. Amelie had a measure of that same power, but hers came in a different form. Bishop was unquestionably dead, so could it be Amelie? Would Amelie have broken Michael, as she'd once threatened to do, and made him do this?

Claire shuddered. If Amelie had done it, if this wasn't Michael's real will, then there were four victims of his cruelty, not three. . . . Michael himself was the first, and the most badly wounded of them all.

And even if it was true, even if this was no real choice of Michael's, the problem was . . .

How was she going to prove it?

In the end, Claire slept in the hospital chapel—it was quiet, calm, deserted, and she needed the spiritual support just now. She wished that Father Joe would make an appearance. . . . He was a great listener, and she desperately needed to talk to someone.

But in the end, she fell asleep reading the Bible through tear-swollen eyes, and tried to find some kind of comfort. If she did, she didn't remember.

Claire tried to call Shane six times in the morning, but her calls went to voice mail; texts went unanswered. She was surprised to see him show up around noon, but he hadn't come to talk to her, though she had a moment's pitiful hope. . . . He walked straight past her with a plastic bag, ignoring her, and into Eve's room.

When he came back outside, he sat across the waiting room and stared at the floor.

"Shane?" She took some tentative steps toward him. She wanted to burst into tears, but she knew it would only make things worse if she did. "Please, please talk to me. Please—"

"I brought her clothes," he said. "Then I'm driving you both home. Then I'm getting the hell out for a while. You take care of Eve. You do that for me."

"But—"

"Michael's stuff's already gone," he said. "He packed up last night. I don't know where he went, so don't ask me."

"Shane, please look at me." She sank down on a chair next to him. He smelled like sweat, as if he'd gone to the gym and hadn't stopped to shower. He didn't shift his gaze away from a dedicated examination of the stained tile floor. "I've never had anything going with Michael, *ever.* I don't know why he did that, but it's not what you're thinking. I've never cheated on you. I wouldn't. I've been thinking that maybe—maybe Amelie made him do this. Because I really don't think this was Michael, not the real Michael, do you?"

He didn't answer her. They sat in silence for a few dark seconds, and then a nurse rounded the corner and said, "She's ready to go."

Shane shot to his feet as if the chair had a catapult built in, and was halfway to Eve's room before Claire managed to follow, feeling slow, clumsy, and achingly lost.

Eve looked terrible—no makeup, chalky skin, bruises discoloring her swollen face. She'd let her hair fall forward to hide the worst of it, but it also hid any trace of how she felt seeing Claire come around the corner.

That was probably a blessing, Claire thought, with a horrible surge of unearned guilt. *I didn't kiss him! He kissed me!* But she couldn't insist on that, not with Eve so torn up with grief, and so badly hurt.

And I left her lying there on the sidewalk, bleeding, she thought. *I can't forget that, either.*

Shane held a wheelchair still as Eve practically fell into it; she kept her head bowed, and her hands over her stomach as if she were afraid it might break open. Claire hurried forward and took a plastic bag of clothes from the nurse, and some paperwork and pills. "Give her two of these twice a day," the nurse said. "And let her sleep. She's going to need it. No lifting anything heavier than a book for at least two weeks. She's to see the doctor again on Thursday. Someone will have to bring her to and from the appointment. No driving at all until he lifts the restriction."

Claire nodded mutely, barely able to clock in the instructions; her heart was a mess of hurt, from worry for Eve, grief over Shane, anger at Michael. *Now we have to go home and pretend everything is okay,* she thought, and the concept was pretty appalling. But what choice did she have? Leave? She couldn't. Eve needed someone, and Shane had already made it clear he'd rather run away. Michael already had.

Shane pushed the wheelchair fast, not waiting for Claire; she hurried to catch up, but the elevator doors closed in her face. Neither of her housemates looked at her directly.

She took the stairs down a floor and met them as Shane put the brakes on the wheelchair and helped Eve move shakily into the front passenger seat of the hearse.

"I can drive," Claire offered. Shane ignored her, and walked to that side of the car. He got in and started the engine, and she hardly had time to run to the back and climb into what Eve had cheerfully named Dead Man's Corner before he hit the gas for home.

It was a terrible few minutes. Claire clutched the soft bag of clothing; it smelled of Eve's latest BPAL perfume and a metallic tang she thought had to be blood. She'd wash them herself, make sure they were nice and clean before she returned them. Shane wouldn't think of that. It was something she could do, a little act of love.

Shane was careful on the drive home, avoiding the bumpy spots, and pulling up to the front curb without any jerky sudden stops. He even picked Eve up and carried her inside, waiting impatiently as Claire opened the front door.

Once Eve was settled on the sofa, with the old afghan tucked around her and a pillow beneath her head, Shane said, "You can handle nurse duties, right?" He headed for the door, again.

"Where are you going?"

"None of your business," Shane said. Claire heard the door slam behind him and felt tears clawing at her throat; honestly, it was so incredibly painful, she wanted to throw herself facedown on her bed and cry herself into oblivion. It was worse when she looked around and saw that Michael's music things were missing. He'd even taken the leather armchair with him, the one he liked to sit in while he played.

The house felt cold, hard, and empty without Shane and Michael, and without the love among all of them that had made it home.

Claire sank down beside Eve, put her head on the sofa cushions, and tried not to think about it.

"It's not your fault," Eve said, very quietly. Claire jerked her head up, hope bolting through her, but Eve wasn't smiling, and there was nothing in her swollen face that Claire could interpret as forgiveness. "He had doubts all along; I knew that. I was just— stupid enough to think he was worried about me. So maybe it's better we get it over with. It just hurts so much."

She wasn't talking about the physical pain.

"I don't know why he did . . . what he did, or why he said those things, but it isn't true, Eve. Please believe me."

Eve closed her eyes and sighed as if almost too depressed to listen. "All right," she said in a very faint, flat voice. "Doesn't matter."

Claire held her friend's loose, cool hand, and the two of them sat in silence for a long time before Claire's cell rang.

"Hello?" Her voice sounded strangled and rough; she hardly recognized it herself.

"Honey?" It was her mother. "Oh, Claire, what's wrong?"

That did it. Claire could handle the rest of it, but not that, not the compassionate warmth of her mother's voice.

She cried, and it all came out, in hitching, halting bursts—Shane, Michael, Eve, her fear, all of it. But mostly Shane, and how she was afraid it was all ruined, forever, all that bright and beautiful future she'd thought was so perfectly laid out. Somehow, she even managed to blurt that she was worried about Myrnin, too, which led to a line of questions she'd rather not have answered, but the confessional dam had well and truly busted open, and there was no going back. The call lasted at least an hour, and at the end of it, Claire lay huddled on the parlor floor, wishing the world would just suck her down into its molten core and end her misery.

She finally got her mind back in place enough to say, "I'm sorry, Mom . . . Why did you call me?"

"I just felt you needed me," her mother said. "It's a mother's instinct, sweetheart. Come home, Claire. Just come home and let us take care of you. You'll get through this; I know you will. You're a very strong girl. It'll be okay."

"I'll come," Claire whispered. "As soon as I can." She didn't have anything left to stay for, did she?

She hung up and went to give Eve her medication.

Eve was well enough by nightfall to take some food, though

not a lot. Claire made her soup in a cup, and then put her back to bed with the TV softly playing a movie she knew Eve liked well enough to sleep through.

They didn't talk much.

Miranda came back about the time that Claire was rinsing out the soup cups.

"I'm sorry," Miranda said, and hugged her. Claire threw her arms around the girl and squeezed tightly; for the first time, she felt like someone had truly forgiven her and understood how she felt. "I couldn't do anything today. Michael left; he wouldn't say *anything* to me, and then Shane—he drank too much, you know. It scared me. I thought he was going to do something—something bad. But he didn't."

It would have scared Claire, if she'd known it. "But Eve's okay; that's the important thing," she said. "We'll—we'll fix this. Somehow."

"Is it true?" Miranda pulled back to hold her at arm's length. "Shane said—Shane said you were with Michael, behind his back. But you weren't, were you?"

"No. No, never!"

"I believe you." Miranda held her hands and sat her down at the kitchen table. "I did what you asked. I got out and tried to listen to what the other ghosts were saying. I didn't talk to them, exactly, because it's dangerous to get their attention; they were still following Jenna, trying to tell her things, so that's why I was able to hear so much."

For the first time, Claire felt a surge of something that might have been hope. "Did you hear anything about Myrnin?"

"No," Miranda said. "I'm sorry. But I did hear something weird; maybe it could mean something." The hope was just a pale flicker now, but Claire nodded anyway. "One of them said a spider was in a hole under the white tree. And another one said—Claire, I'm really not sure this is about him at all, you understand—that something was climbing up, but the sun would burn it away."

That didn't help at all. Claire felt a white-hot urge to break something in frustration, or punch a wall, Shane-style, but she knew it wouldn't help. Nothing would help, except figuring something out for a change.

Think, she told herself. *Breathe.* If she could find Myrnin, that would be *something,* at least. Something positive, in all this devastation. *Something climbing. Hole by the white tree.* Was he climbing up in a hole by a white tree? That didn't make any sense. There weren't any white trees in Morganville. Was he even here, in this town? If he wasn't, she couldn't help him at all.

No, he's here. Think. Think!

White tree. That had to mean something. It must be a landmark, so it had to be something she could remember. But what . . . ?

"The ghost who was talking about the white tree," Claire said. "Do you know where he came from?"

"I think he died at the Sleep Inne over near the edge of town. You know that one?" Claire did. It was bland and forgettable, and there were no trees of any kind that way. "I guess his body is buried in the cemetery."

The cemetery, Claire thought. They'd remarked on it from the first, how it all looked so photogenic. *That big dead tree,* Angel had said. *Such a striking color.*

Because it was dead, and it was . . .

Claire's eyes opened wide. "The tree. The cemetery tree, it's *white,* right?"

"I guess. It's dead and the bark is all peeled off and it looks white."

"So it's at the cemetery," Claire blurted, and opened her eyes.

"It's got to be there, whatever this—this hole is. That's where Myrnin is. He's in the hole, in water. And there's some kind of a grate on top, with a cross; Jenna said she saw that in a vision. Mir, I have to go, right now. Can you stay with Eve?"

"I—well, yes, but you can't go out there in the dark, all alone!"

"I have to. Myrnin may be the only one left who can help us get through this, and your other ghost said the sun will burn it away. If he's in a hole in the ground, and the sun comes up, he could burn in there. I can't let that happen."

"I can't go with you! If I did, the other ghosts—they'd be all over me. I have to stay in the house. And Eve's too sick."

"Then I'll call Shane," Claire shot back, and pulled out her phone. She paced as it rang, and rang, and rang, and went to voice mail. She hung up and texted him, with a 911. No details. And finally, after five long minutes, he called back.

"Don't hang up," she said. "I need your help."

"Is it Eve?"

"No," she said reluctantly.

"Then no."

"Wait! Wait, listen to me. I have to go to the cemetery. There's—someone's in trouble, Shane. If you don't go with me, I have to go alone. Please. I know you're angry at me, but—but be angry tomorrow. Tonight, just please, do this for me." He was silent on the other end, but she could hear the uneven hitch of his breathing. "Shane, please. One time."

"Who's in trouble?"

She'd been afraid he'd ask that. But she couldn't lie. Claire squeezed her eyes shut and said, "Myrnin."

Shane hung up. Claire screamed, a raw and wild sound, and threw the phone violently on the table. Miranda's eyes were round as saucers.

"Wow," she said. "So . . . you're not going?"

"No," Claire said grimly. "I *am* going. Alone."

Eve's hearse was still parked out on the curb. Miranda argued with Claire all the way out to the picket fence, but she wasn't listening anymore. She'd put on Eve's long leather coat over her jeans and plain black shirt, and brought along a heavy canvas bag full of weapons, plus her own backpack, which had all kinds of things she might need—even textbooks, if she got study time. At the very least, they were a kind of paper-based armor she could put between herself and something attacking her.

"But—what do I do if you don't come back?" Miranda asked frantically as Claire settled in the driver's seat. The Grim Reaper on the dash shivered and nodded its head, eye-lights flashing. "Claire! Who do I call?"

"Call Shane," she said. "Maybe he'll feel bad if I'm dead. But make sure Eve's okay, and give her the medication she needs just before sunrise. Do *not* let her get up and do anything, and if she starts to run a fever, call the hospital and get them to send the ambulance. Promise me."

"I will." Miranda looked on the verge of tears. "This is bad. This is a really bad idea. . . ."

"I'm open to suggestions." When the other girl didn't offer any, Claire shook her head. "Wish me luck."

"I—" Miranda sighed. "Good luck. I'll wait for you to come back, and if you're not back before sunrise, I'll call . . . *somebody*. Amelie. I'll call Amelie."

"Don't do that," Claire said. "Because it might *be* Amelie. Okay?"

"But—"

Claire didn't give her time to argue.

The hearse drove differently from any other car she'd tried in her very limited driving experience. . . . It was heavy, hard to manage, and had terrible stopping distance, as she found when she rolled through a stop light while pumping the brakes. Luckily, no Morganville police cruisers caught sight of her. She passed some custom-tinted vampire cars. No one tried to stop her.

Claire drove the mile, give or take, out to the cemetery, which brushed the limits of the Morganville township. The place was surrounded by a thick stone wall and had heavy wrought-iron gates; the lightning-struck dead white tree loomed high, all spiky branches and intimidating angles. The gates were locked, of course. Claire considered ramming them, but she knew Eve would never forgive her for it, so she strapped the canvas bag over her shoulders, on top of her backpack, and climbed. The iron was cold and slick under her fingers, but there were plenty of crossbars, and she managed to make it to the top, then slipped down the other side.

Morganville Cemetery was an old one, back to pioneer days, full of time-sanded headstones that were hardly readable anymore, thanks to the constant wind. What grass there was grew fitfully. Nobody visited here with any reliability; the newer cemetery, Redeemer, was closer to the center of town, and that was where present-day burials were done. This was mostly just here for historical value.

It wasn't a very likely spot for vampires to hang out, at least; there hadn't been anyone with a pulse visiting the place in years. But it was still plenty creepy, all right—shadows like black knives across the ground, harsh and sharp in the moonlight. Tree branches rattled like dry bones.

Claire was headed for the tree when she saw the vampires appear on top of the wall and drop easily down, landing without breaking their stride. There were two of them, moving together. One had pale hair; the other had graying locks.

Amelie and Oliver?

She dropped to the ground behind a large carved angel and hoped that it would be enough to hide her. She also hoped she hadn't landed on one of the huge fire ant mounds that dotted the grounds; if she had, this was going to be a very short and unpleasant adventure. If the fire ants didn't bite her into a coma, the vampires would.

They passed fairly close to where she was hiding, and luck was with her; the wind had shifted, carrying her human scent away from them. And it was *not* Amelie with the pale hair shifting in the breeze, Claire realized, as she caught sight of the girl's face, her smile, her dimples.

That was Naomi. Walking with Oliver. But Naomi was supposed to be dead. *Of course,* Claire thought in horror. *Bishop's other daughter. She might have the same powers, too.* If Naomi and Oliver were in it together, Naomi could have turned Michael against them.

And Amelie didn't know.

The two of them strolled through the weeds, through tombstones and tumbleweeds, and came to a halt under the white tree. Oliver dragged a fallen piece of marble away, and Claire heard it grate on metal.

She was also close enough to hear the voices, and she heard Oliver say, "No need to go down after him. Between this and the morning sun, he's finished." He reached into his pocket and came out with a bottle Claire recognized—one of the weapons that Shane had first developed. Then he shared it with Captain Obvious and his crew. And then with the vampires, to use against the draug ... It was silver nitrate. Oliver had on gloves, but he still handled the bottle carefully as he opened the top, then poured it into the ground—no, not into the ground.

Through the metal grate on the ground.

Claire heard Myrnin's scream of raw pain and fury, and she had to press both hands to her mouth to keep quiet. There was a splashing sound, and scraping, as if he were clawing his way up from a great distance below.

"He won't get far," Naomi said. "No vampire's strong enough to make it all that way to the top before sunrise, and the silver in the grate will keep him in. If he falls, the silver in the water will finish him. Well done, Oliver. Now go back to Amelie. Our little chess pawns are almost all in place. We'll play our last moves soon."

"Yes," he said, "my queen."

"Your white queen," Naomi said, and laughed. "I like the sound of that. You're a useful blunt instrument, Oliver. I shall keep you in my court when I take my rightful place."

"Amelie," he said, and it seemed it was hard for him to get the words out. "What of Amelie?"

"What about her?" Naomi asked. She was staring down through the grate, to where she'd just condemned Myrnin to death. "A wise ruler never leaves a rival at her back. Though I might consider a merciful exile, if you beg hard enough on her behalf. Would you, Oliver? Beg?"

He said nothing. He stood with his hands locked behind his back, and from what Claire could see of him, his face was hard as stone and his eyes flaring red.

"Obviously not," Naomi said. "Your personal dignity was always more important to you than mere emotion, wasn't it? Very well." She leaned over the grate. "Myrnin? I leave you to your gods." She put her fingers to her mouth and blew him a delicate little kiss, and then she and Oliver turned away, drifting sound-lessly through the deserted graveyard, then up and onto the wall.

Then Naomi turned and looked right at Claire's hiding place, and smiled. "Did you really think I wouldn't see that ridiculous car, or sense your presence? Since your friend Eve is indisposed, I assumed it would be you rushing to the rescue," she said. "I think our little friend has outlived her usefulness after all, though it would have been a nice finishing move to use her to plant a dagger in Amelie's back. Michael. Take her off the board."

Claire gasped, because Michael jumped up on the wall next to Naomi, scanned the graveyard, and fixed his gaze right where she was.

Naomi nodded. "Adieu, Claire. It's too bad there will be no place for you in the Morganville we are to create."

She left.

And then Michael jumped down and came at her.

Claire ran.

Michael wasn't even trying hard, Claire thought; there was no real reason he couldn't catch her within ten feet. He was very, very fast, and she wasn't; the heavy leather coat she'd decided to wear was weighing her down, and so was the weapons bag. She wanted to leave it, but she didn't dare.

Are you really going to try to kill him? she asked herself, and didn't have any idea of the answer. She tripped over a fallen, tilted grave marker and went flying, rolled, and the canvas bag ripped open on a jagged piece of broken marble. The fabric was tough, but it had weakened along the zipper, and things spilled out through the gap. . . . The first one she laid hands on was a plastic Baggie full of random silver chain links, scavenged from old jewelry Eve had bought through the Internet. It made a nice, heavy handful as Claire opened it, and as she stumbled to her feet, she twisted and threw it at Michael.

The silver hit him, and where it struck skin, she saw sparks; it was more surprising than painful, but it slowed him down, giving her a moment to sort through her other available choices. She passed over the silver nitrate; she didn't want to hurt him—she really didn't.

Her hands closed on Shane's silver-tipped baseball bat, which was the biggest thing in the canvas bag, and she yanked it out.

She didn't even have time to prepare a decent swing as Michael lunged forward, but she did manage to get the coated end of the wood into place so that his momentum took him chest-first into it; the silver scorched him hard, and he veered off with a cry of pain.

Then it was a temporary standoff as Claire set her feet and took up a batter's stance, ready and watching as he paced beyond her reach.

"Michael?"

He didn't answer. His face looked as immobile and frozen as that of the marble angel behind him.

"Michael, please don't do this. I know this isn't your fault; Naomi's using you. I don't want to hurt you. I swear. . . ."

"Good," he said. "That makes it easy."

"But I will!" she finished, and took a swing at his knees as he came into reach. He jumped over the bat, landed lightly, and sprang for her with hands outstretched.

Something hit him in the neck with a soft, coughing hiss, and Michael landed off-balance, staggered, and shook his head in confusion. There was something sticking out of his neck.

A dart.

He pulled it out, looked at it in confusion, and turned away from Claire, toward the wall . . . and sitting on top of it, with a heavy rifle in his hands, was Shane Collins.

"Sorry, man," Shane said. He kicked free and dropped off the wall, flexing his knees and loading another dart into the tranquilizer gun. He aimed as he walked toward them. "You're going to feel real damn bad for a while. Don't make me hit you again. I'm not sure it won't kill you."

Michael growled something, but he was already losing his ability to function; he went down to one knee, then pitched forward to his hands, and then slowly sank down on his side. His back arched in a silent scream.

Claire dropped the bat and tried to go to him, but Shane caught her by the waist and lifted her up to stop her. She kicked and twisted, but he held her. "You get close to him, he could finish the job," he said. He slung her around and sent her stumbling well away from Michael, and from himself. "You came to get Myrnin. Go get him. I'll cover you."

There was still no hint of forgiveness in him, either for Claire or—as he looked at his fallen, suffering friend—for Michael. He was here to fulfill a duty as he saw it, and that was all.

But it was more than she'd ever expected. It was *something*.

"Thank you," she whispered.

Shane nodded, not meeting her eyes, and racked the second tranquilizer dart into place as he watched Michael writhe painfully on the ground.

Claire raced over the uneven graves toward the white tree; even uncovered, the silver grate, circular with bars that formed a simple cross, was almost invisible until she nearly stepped onto it. That would have probably broken her ankle. The grate was locked in place with an old, rusted lock, and Claire whaled at it frantically with the silver-tipped bat until it broke in two.

She threw back the cold, tarnished metal and tried to see into the dark. Nothing. Not even a hint of life.

"Myrnin?" She shouted it down. She had to cover her nose from the smell that rose up from the narrow little hole—rot, sewage, mold, a toxic brew of the worst things she could imagine. "Myrnin! Can you hear me?"

Something thumped down on the ground next to her, and Claire looked up to see that Shane had tossed over a coil of nylon rope he'd retrieved from the weapons bag. She nodded and unwrapped it, tied off one end around the dead tree, and dropped the other down into the hole. "If you can hear me, grab the rope, Myrnin! Climb!"

She wasn't sure for long moments whether he was there, or even whether he *could* get out. Maybe it was too late. Maybe he was already gone.

But then she felt the rope suddenly pull taut, and in seconds, she saw something pale appear in the dark below, gradually becoming clearer as it moved up toward her.

Myrnin climbed as if he'd learned how from his pet spider, swarming up with frantic speed. He had burns on his face and hands and lower legs, silver burns, but that didn't slow him down, and when he reached the top of the hole, Claire grabbed his forearms and dragged him out on the side that wasn't blocked by the raised silver grate.

He collapsed on his back, foul water bleeding out of his soaked and ruined clothes, out of his matted black hair, and after a second of silence he whispered, "I knew you'd come, Claire. I knew you would. Dear God, you took your time."

She took his hand, and sat down next to him.

Shane was standing fifty feet away, beside Michael, but he

looked up and jerked his chin in a silent question. *Is he okay?* She nodded.

It wasn't much, she thought. It wasn't anything to build any kind of hope upon, just that he was willing to show up here, willing to fire a rifle, throw her a rope.

But she'd take it. It was horrifying to her how pitifully grateful she was just for that smallest hint of a smile he gave her, before he turned his back.

"You're very sad," Myrnin said. He sounded faint and distant, as if he'd been a long way off in more ways than one. "You smell like tears. Did he break your heart?"

"No," Claire said, in a very soft whisper that she hoped Shane couldn't hear from where he stood. "I broke his."

"Ah," Myrnin said. "Good for you." He sat up, and suddenly leaned over to throw up a horrifying amount of black water. "Pardon. Well, that was distressing. . . . Oh no . . ."

He collapsed back on the ground, as if too weak to rise, and shut his eyes tight. His whole body was shaking and twitching, and it went on for a horribly long time. She didn't know what to do for him, except put her hand on his shoulder. Beneath the slimy clothes, she could feel his muscles locked and straining as if he were having an epileptic seizure.

He finally relaxed and took in a deep, slow breath before he opened his eyes and said, "We have to go, Claire. Quickly."

"Where?" she asked, because she was cold and scared and couldn't think of any place, any place at all, that might be safe now.

"To safety," he said. "Before it's too late."

"But you—you're not well enough to—"

Before she could finish, he was off stalking barefoot through the weeds toward the exit. He tore the chain off the fence with one hard pull and shoved the gates open with a rusted shriek.

Then he looked back with a red glow in his eyes and said, "Bring Michael. None of this is his fault. I won't allow him to suffer for it."

Shane hadn't moved during all of this, but now he bent down and pulled the tranquilizer dart out of Michael's neck. "It's going to be a few minutes before he's well enough to stand up."

"Then drag him," Myrnin said. "Unless you'd like to enjoy the comfort of my little oubliette. I'm sure Naomi will be sending Pennyfeather in a moment to be certain all of us are dead, and I'd rather not be here to oblige her. *Now,* children."

He clapped his hands and disappeared beyond the gates, and in a moment, Claire heard Eve's car start up with a roar.

She went back to Shane and took one of Michael's arms as he grabbed the other. Their eyes met, briefly.

"I'm so sorry," she whispered.

"Yeah," he said. "Me, too."

But she wasn't sure if they were talking about the same things at all.

EIGHTEEN

CLAIRE

🌙

It took them a while to drag Michael's heavy, unresponsive body over the uneven ground and out to the hearse. Myrnin stuck his head out of the passenger window of the hearse to helpfully suggest that Michael could be dumped down the same hole he'd just crawled out of. Shane suggested that Myrnin bite him, hard. Myrnin declined.

And Claire drove, leaving Shane with Michael, by his own request. She was a little anxious about that; Shane held grudges, and it was going to be hard for him to see past what Michael had done to them, but it was at least a truce for now. Mortal danger trumped emotional pain. Temporarily.

Myrnin said, "Michael seems to be under Naomi's spell, just as Oliver and Pennyfeather must be. I have no idea how many she's suborned, but it's too bad she didn't try it on me." He smiled, and his expression was bleak and dark, and it wasn't only the streaks of black water staining his face. "Greater vampires have tried, including her black-hearted father. I believe my blood made Bishop sick for a month."

"Where should we go?" she asked. He sighed.

"I suppose we really have no choice," he said. "Retreating to the Glass House will simply give them an easy point to attack, and we cannot defend the place, not from a concerted attack. So we will have to take the fight to them."

"Where?"

He shrugged wearily. "To Amelie herself. Ultimately, she is Naomi's target. Oliver's seduction of her—or at least, part of it—was Naomi's effort to weaken her, to stir up trouble against her. She must be warned of what's to come or she'll be taken unawares, by those she trusts."

"How the hell are we supposed to get into Founder's Square?" Claire asked. "Do you have some secret passage or something?"

"They're all shut up, I'm afraid," Myrnin said. "Oh, and I'm ruining your friend's lovely upholstery. Sorry about the mess. Imagine if they'd left me down there for months. That did happen, once. I was dumped into a cell no larger than a doghouse for half a year. All they did was throw down the occasional chicken or hog . . . disgusting. I seem to have lost my slippers."

"I'll buy you new ones."

"I expect we're going to have to rely on Michael," Myrnin said, switching suddenly back to the original question. "The boy has an automatic entrance to Amelie's presence, as her offspring. The difficulty is that he's hardly in a position to voluntarily assist us, and by the way, Shame, why did you shoot him?"

"It's Shane, and if you call me that again, you'll be getting the next dart."

"The question still stands."

"Because he was going after Claire. Again." Shane didn't look at her, not even a glance in the rearview mirror; Claire knew, because she was waiting for it—for some sign that his anger was starting to wear off.

"Again?" Myrnin asked, and his eyebrows rose. "My. Things change so quickly with you young people. Claire, are you enemies now with Michael?"

"Not exactly," she said. Shane cut her off.

"Last time he just tongue-kissed her," Shane said. "This time it looked a little more extreme than that. So I didn't take the chance of being wrong."

That earned her a sharp, interested look from Myrnin. "Well. We'll have to have the full story, then."

"We really don't," she said. "Something's wrong with Michael, all right. And I saw Naomi, with Oliver. They're working together."

"That—is very, very unpleasant," Myrnin said. He frowned and pulled at a stray thread on his shirt, threatening to unravel an entire piece of it. "Naomi was killed in the attack on the draug, or so it was said. I had my doubts. It seemed too convenient, considering that Naomi had begun working to undermine Amelie. I imagine she wanted to take her place even then, but Amelie's not someone who fails to respond to a challenge."

"You mean Amelie had Naomi killed?"

"Possibly. Or possibly Oliver did, to protect her. But if so, he must have had a change of heart, since, or Naomi secured control of him. I've never trusted the Roundhead, myself. A man of low character and high ambition. Naomi wouldn't be above using him to achieve her dreams of ruling."

"Then we have to tell Amelie he's stabbing her in the back."

Claire took a deep breath. "*You* have to tell her. She won't believe me, or Shane, and Michael's not able to tell her anything, even if he wanted to."

"I can't," he said. "Look at me. I'm in no fit state to—"

"You're the official bearer of bad news," Shane said, and pointed the rifle at Myrnin. "End of discussion."

"Yes," Myrnin said instantly. "Of course. No problem at all."

There was quite a lot of animated debate about how to make it into the guarded area around Founder's Square. In the end, they propped Michael up in the passenger seat, next to Myrnin, who held him upright with a friendly arm around his shoulders; when Claire rolled down the passenger window, the Founder's Square vampire guard took one look inside, saw Michael and Myrnin, and nodded them through without any questions. "Amazing," Myrnin said, squeezing rank water out of his hair. "You'd think someone might notice my general appearance."

"Funny, I'd think you'd notice that it's not that different from how you usually look," Shane said. He hadn't lowered the rifle; he sat braced in the back, aiming it generally in Myrnin's direction.

"Really? I'll have to work on that, clearly. Tell me, are you really so angry at Claire that you're willing to fire that weapon in an enclosed vehicle, with a distinct chance of hitting her?"

"I'm not angry," Shane said. "I'm careful." That, Claire noticed, didn't really answer the question at all.

It did shut Myrnin up for a while, at least until they'd parked the hearse in the underground lot of Founder's Square. Shane was forced to leave the gun, but he grabbed Claire's backpack and filled it with a selection of the handiest possible weapons.

"We're not going to be able to fight our way in, or out again," Myrnin said. "You might keep that in mind during your packing frenzy."

"Shut up." Shane put the backpack over his shoulder, and for the first time, looked at Claire directly. "He's your responsibility. Keep him from doing anything too crazy."

"I'll try," she said. It was the first real conversation—brief and businesslike as it was—that they'd had in hours, and it made her feel just a tiny bit less awful . . . until he turned his back on her in the elevator, in preference to watching the numbers flicker until they'd arrived at the right floor. Myrnin led the way, which was a good thing, because the first intersection brought them face-to-face with two of Amelie's black-uniformed guards.

"We were told you left," one of them said to Myrnin.

"You were ill-informed, then," Myrnin said loftily, and drips of filthy water ran down his feet to leave stains on the carpet. "I'm here to see the Founder."

"Like that?" The guard gave him an up-and-down look, eyebrows raised.

"Would you like me to shower and change before warning her of potential disaster? Because of course one wouldn't like to deliver that news in a less-than-pristine state."

The guard accepted that, but then he turned the analysis on Claire and Shane. "And them?"

"With me," he said. "Entourage. You know."

"Backpack," the second guard said to Shane, and gestured. He hesitated. "Now."

"Oh, give it up. I told you we couldn't use those anyway," Myrnin said. "Do it. Quickly. We have little time left, for heaven's sake."

The guards were ignoring him now, focused on Shane and the potentially lethal contents of his bag, and as soon as they'd turned away from him, Myrnin reached out, grabbed each of the guards by the side of the head, and knocked them together, hard. Claire shuddered at the sound of bone crunching. Both men dropped to the carpet, twitching.

"Come on," Myrnin said. "They won't be down for long. But don't worry, their brains aren't complicated enough to be damaged."

"But—"

"Claire, we *do not have time.*" He grabbed her by the arm and dragged her along at a run, past closed doorways, painted portraits, flickering lights . . .

And into an open doorway.

Amelie's assistant rose to her feet in alarm at the sight of them and bared her teeth, and Myrnin bared his in turn. "Announce me," he said, and then shook his head. "Never mind; I'll do it myself."

He lowered his shoulder and ran at the inner door. The lock broke, and the door swung open . . .

On Amelie, held in Oliver's arms. Not as a hostage, as Claire originally thought, but in a position that could only be called, ah, intimate. That was one hell of a kiss in progress, and there were fewer clothes than might be strictly formal.

The kiss broke off as Myrnin came to a sliding halt in the remains of the door, with Shane and Claire close behind, and said, "Well, this is awkward. Beg pardon, but I believe Claire has something to tell you."

Then he shoved her forward as Oliver stepped away from the embrace and began buttoning up his shirt. Amelie glared at Claire, then at Myrnin, then at Shane, as if deciding which of them to kill first.

Myrnin seriously wasn't going to do anything, Claire realized. He was standing back, watching. She wasn't sure what he was watching *for,* but he'd left her deliberately hanging there, wriggling like a worm on a hook.

"Well?" Amelie's voice was a crack of sound, like a sheet of ice snapping. "What could possibly be so vital that you intrude here on my privacy, like some assassin?" She grabbed Shane by the collar and dragged him close, ripped the backpack from his hands, and shredded it open, spilling weapons across the floor. "You come to use these, then? Are you in league with your father again? I warn you, this time, the cage won't go unused. You'll burn for this, you little fool."

"Shane's just trying to protect us! Oliver's betraying you," Claire blurted. "He's working with—"

She didn't have time for more. Oliver was right on her, hand gripping her throat as he lifted her effortlessly off the carpet until her feet dangled and kicked uselessly. She clawed at his hand, but he wasn't going to let her breathe. Panic blinded her, smothered her, and all she knew for a few seconds was that she was going to die before she could make things right again with Shane.

Myrnin reached down, grabbed the silver-tipped bat, and hit Oliver right between the shoulder blades, hard enough to knock him off-balance. Claire was dropped to the carpet, where she whooped in a breath.

"Enough!" Amelie said. There was pale color high in her cheeks, and a furious red glitter in her eyes. "I've had *enough* of your foolish chatter and your betrayals. You come here unasked; you threaten my consort. I am *done* with you all. I've coddled you too long. I'll start with you, Collins."

She grabbed Shane by the shirt when he tried to dart out of her way, and pulled back her other hand, claws sharp and extended. In one more second, she'd do it. She'd kill him.

"No!" Claire shouted through her agonizingly sore throat. "He's working with Naomi; Oliver's going to kill you!"

The Founder froze, and for a second her eyes went entirely

back to gray as she stared into Claire's face, reading what Claire hoped was utterly the truth as she knew it.

And then Amelie let go of Shane and started to turn toward Oliver.

Oliver grabbed the bat out of Myrnin's hands and swung it at the Founder's head with deadly, blurring speed; even for a vampire, that blow would have been fatal if it had connected . . . but Amelie moved like water, flowing out of the way and taking Oliver's arm as it passed, then twisting until the bat flew out of his grip. It shattered the windows beyond in an earsplitting crash, sending glass flying out into the night. The baseball bat whipped end over end to land almost a hundred feet away on the grass of the park below.

Amelie shoved Oliver face-first into the wall, pinned his arm behind him, and said, "Tell me why. *Why?*" She didn't doubt it; Claire saw that. Oliver's attempt to kill her had been clear enough. He cried out, and she twisted harder, though it was obvious from the expression on her face that she was hurting herself by hurting him. "Oliver, *why do you betray me?*"

He laughed. It was an awful, empty sound. "I don't," he said. "I was never loyal to you, you foolish woman. I've made a lifetime of toppling rulers. You're only the latest, and the most rewarding."

Amelie turned her head toward Claire and Myrnin. "He cannot be working with Naomi," she said. "She's dead."

"Sadly, and convincingly, not," Myrnin said. "I saw her with my own eyes. I am fairly certain Claire has her facts straight."

"And where in God's name have you been, then?"

"At the bottom of a pit," he said. "Which accounts for my current state of dress. Although Shane assures me it is not so odd."

Shane hadn't made a sound, and he hadn't moved; he'd probably judged, very rightly, that it was time to make himself a smaller target. From the way his lips tightened, he wished Myrnin hadn't mentioned him at all.

But Amelie didn't seem to care. She bent, picked up a silver-coated stake, and pressed it against the skin of Oliver's neck, just above the spine—just enough to tint the skin and start it burning. "So go traitors," she said. "In the old days, your head would have ended up as a decoration for a spike. I suppose I will have to settle for something less . . . satisfying." There were tears in her eyes, then tears coursing down her pale, still face. "I trusted you, you traitor. I suppose I should have known better. I've never been lucky in love."

"I never loved you," he said. "Kill me. It changes nothing."

"It changes *everything*," she hissed. "You'll not die yet. Not until you help me find my wayward sister. *Then* I will allow you to die. But not yet. Not yet."

"Why wait?" said a low, sweet voice from the doorway, and they all turned—even Oliver—to see Naomi standing there, with Michael behind her. And Hannah Moses, carrying a crossbow with a heavy wooden bolt already in place. And more, behind her—humans and vampires alike. "Thank you, Claire. Sometimes a pawn is the very thing to use as a sacrifice to lure the queen from hiding."

At Naomi's regal nod, Hannah raised the crossbow and fired the bolt straight at Amelie.

It was impossible that it would miss, and it didn't, but . . . something happened, a blur of movement Claire couldn't understand until it was over, and Oliver was standing in Amelie's place, swaying. The wooden bolt was in his heart.

He dropped to his knees, then collapsed.

Amelie was a blur, heading for the broken windows. Hannah had a second bolt in the bow, and Naomi grabbed the crossbow, aimed, and fired just as Amelie leaped out into the night air.

It hit her cleanly in the chest. Claire gasped and watched her tumble gracelessly down to crumple on the grass below.

"Satisfactory," Naomi said. "Though I have no notion why Oliver chose to put himself in the way. Take them all to the cage. Now."

Not even Shane tried to fight, this time.

"Great," Shane said. Claire sensed he would have been pacing, if there had been room, but the steel cage in Founder's Square was just big enough to hold her, Myrnin, and the limp bodies of Oliver and Amelie without any room left over. "Just great. I'm still going to die in this cage, after everything that's happened. That's just perfect."

"Well," Myrnin said, and shoved Oliver's limp body over to stretch out his long, dirty legs, "at least we're dying in royal company. That's something." He reached out to pull the stake out of Amelie's chest, but as he did, a thin silver blade poked through the bars and cut his hand. He yelped and pulled back.

Hannah was standing outside the bars, watching them with calm concentration. "Don't try it," she said. "No use. You leave the stakes where they are."

"Worried?" Myrnin sucked at the cut on his hand, and spat flecks of silver that burned on the floor. "You should be, Hannah. If you think supporting Naomi will win your people freedom, you're a fool. She's worse than Oliver ever thought of being, because I think she honestly believes that what she is doing is for the best—well, for *her* best, in any case." He cocked his head, staring at her, and then suddenly lunged at the bags, wrapping his hands around them. She didn't flinch, though she took a tighter grip on the knife she held. "She's Bishop's daughter. His *spiritual* child as well as his bloodline, with all his gifts. She believes humans are her property, and the world is her larder. Don't be a fool. You can't believe that Claire and Shane should be in here with us, even if you hate vampires so desperately. What has either of them done to deserve it?"

She didn't answer. Myrnin waited, then nodded, as if she'd done exactly what he expected. "I see," he said, and his voice was unexpectedly gentle. "I am well aware how being under such control feels, my dear. All will be well."

"How?" Hannah asked. She sounded indifferent, but Claire thought she heard something new in her voice: pain.

He shrugged. "No idea," he said. "But I'm quite certain that it's unfolding *even now.*"

It was the emphasis he put on the last two words that made Claire realize that by lunging forward, and drawing Hannah's full attention, he'd left Amelie partially obscured. Shane was the closest to the fallen vampire. Claire frantically gestured to the wooden stake in her heart, and Shane didn't hesitate. He pulled it out—but not all the way out. Just enough, Claire thought, to clear her heart.

Amelie didn't move. At this point, she probably couldn't.

If he'd done it right, though, maybe she *would,* when she was ready.

Founder's Square was as busy as a mall at Christmas. The big braziers surrounding the center of the square were being lit, bringing a barbaric splendor to the deep night; vampires were gathering, some looking sleepy and confused, some excited, some outright worried. There were humans, too—a group of them, herded together nearby. Claire recognized several of them, including the new mayor, Flora Ramos, and—incredibly—Gramma Day. One of them was complaining loudly. It was Monica Morrell. She certainly hadn't been rousted out of bed like the others; she was dressed to party. . . . Well, that might not be true. Claire wasn't sure she *didn't* wear tube dresses to bed.

Myrnin sank back from the bars and crossed his arms, glancing at Shane. "Well done," he said in an undertone. "Clever boy, taking it out only part of the way. I take back at least one bad thing I've ever said about you."

"What's happening?" Claire asked.

"Naomi prepares to declare her primacy," he said. "She'll have herself crowned, and then she'll spill blood—"

"Ours," Shane said.

"Oh no, not at all. It's a very old custom, one even Bishop respected. She'll kill the most influential residents of Morganville . . . Founder families, important business leaders, politicians. . . . I suppose Monica's there to represent her family; more's the pity for their memories."

"It's about more than ceremony," Shane said. "Most of those guys are on Captain Obvious's war council. I saw them. And Gramma Day is related to Hannah."

"Really?" Myrnin raised his eyebrows. "Interesting indeed. She's honoring the old customs *and* ensuring her own long-term survival. Masterful. Worthy of her father, in his better days."

"Could you maybe not admire the evil enemy quite so much, and focus more on how we're going to get out of this?" Claire asked. "Because I'm pretty sure we're going to die, too."

"Oh yes. But you and I are merely collateral damage; this is a pyre for Amelie. And I see they've made improvements. See the grates underneath us? Natural gas. It's all very fuel efficient, not like the old days with all the logs. . . ."

"Myrnin!"

He went suddenly very cool and sensible. "Bite marks," he said.

"Michael's got one on his neck. So does Hannah Moses. So, in fact, does Oliver. All a very distinctive bite distance. It takes a delicate mouth to make such marks, such as, say—" He pointed a finger, and Claire followed the line of it to Naomi, who was standing draped in silver and white a few feet away. "She's got the gift, you see. Not every vampire can compel like that. Amelie can, though she never does, and Naomi can—both of them inherited that trait from their vampire father, Bishop. So whatever's been done, you can rightly assume she's the one pulling the strings, and that no one had any choice in what's been done."

"Oh," Shane said, in a very different sort of tone. "Oh, *crap.* Michael—I left him alone with Naomi and Hannah. Hannah's Captain Obvious. I thought Naomi was just working with her, trying to get at Amelie. But its more than that. She was controlling the whole thing. And Michael."

Which, Claire realized with a sweet surge of relief, was why Michael had turned on them—and why he'd been so cruel to Eve, and to her, and to Shane. He'd had no choice. *Thank you.* She felt like kissing Shane in pure gratitude for having confirmed her suspicions, but Shane didn't look especially relieved himself; he looked disturbed. Maybe he'd just realized that he'd spent a whole day hating the guts of a friend who'd been innocent after all.

"She was controlling Oliver, too, though likely that wasn't quite so difficult," Myrnin said. "Oliver's influence on Amelie was a dark thing even without Naomi bending it to her uses. Once she had, though, she used Oliver to corrupt Amelie, agitate the town against her, create chaos and dissension . . . and then used you, Claire, to unmask him, giving her the chance to act directly while Amelie was distracted. My, if I didn't loathe her so much, I'd admire her."

"So how are we going to stop her?" Claire asked.

"We can't. Perhaps I failed to mention that we're locked in a cage and about to be burned alive . . . ?"

"Does this cage have a *lock*?"

"A very good one," Myrnin said. "Right there, on the other side of the bars. I'm reasonably certain that neither of us is a certified locksmith, however."

"Well, we can *try*."

"It's silver," Myrnin said. "I won't be able to break it."

"If the lock's pure silver instead of just plated, it's soft," Shane said. "We could use one of these stakes as a lever, maybe."

"And that will sacrifice our element of surprise," Myrnin pointed out. "You always seem to have something secreted about your person of a dangerous nature. . . . Have you nothing to contribute?"

"They took it," Shane said, "including everything out of my pockets and my belt. Just like jail."

"Not like jail," Claire said thoughtfully. "They left you your shoes."

"And? I'm pretty sure a battered-up pair of kicks isn't going to get us anywhere. . . ." Shane's voice faded at the look on her face. "What?"

"Laces," she said, and bent forward to untie her own shoes and began to pull the cords out. "Give them to me."

"I hardly think we should consider hanging ourselves, Claire," Myrnin said, looking a little worried. "And it wouldn't kill me, you know."

Claire grabbed the laces from Shane as he held them out, tied them end to end, and began quickly braiding them together with those from her own shoes in a rough twisted rope, which she wrapped around the center of the bars at the back. "Cover me," she said to Myrnin. He watched her for a few long seconds, then nodded and moved toward the front of the cage, shoving the limp body of Oliver out of the way, and began to loudly sing something in French. It sounded rude.

Claire began twisting the rope as fast as she could, rapidly getting it to the tension point. "I need something to use as a fulcrum," she said to Shane. "Something that won't break easily."

"Only thing in here is one of the stakes," he said. "Once we pull those, I'm guessing Hannah's got orders not to wait around for the official barbecue."

God, all she needed was a *stick*. . . . Claire cast her eyes about, frantic to find something, anything she could adapt to the purpose, and her gaze fell on, of all things, the headband that Amelie was wearing to keep her long, loose hair back from her face. It was a nice, wide one, not made of plastic but covered in fabric.

Maybe.

Claire edged over, leaving the rope in Shane's hand, and pulled the headband from the vampire's head. She thought Amelie's eyes flickered, just a little, but the Founder didn't move. She looked . . . dead.

Claire flexed the headband in her grip. It had a metal core that bent side to side, but not back to front. And best of all, it didn't break.

She scooted back, slipped it into the rope, and began using it to twist the strands tighter and tighter around the bars. By the fifth round, she felt the tension; by the tenth, she saw the bars actually starting to bend in the middle, yielding to the slow but inevitable force.

I love you, physics.

"Hey," Shane said as she muscled another turn out of the makeshift device. "I probably should tell you that after thinking it over, I'm an ass. And I'm—sorry."

"That must have been hard," Claire said. It was getting really difficult to turn the thing. The edges of the headband were digging into her hand deeply. She gritted her teeth and turned it again.

"Let me," he said, and took hold of the headband. For him, the next three turns were pretty effortless, and the bars bent slowly, steadily inward around the rope. "Damn, this really works. No wonder they don't let you have shoelaces in jail."

"This isn't why."

"I hurt you," he said, in the same tone of voice, without looking at her. "I swore I'd never do that again, and I did. I fell right for Naomi's easiest trick, turning us against each other. I should have trusted you, trusted him, and I didn't. So I'm sorry. And you have every right not to—" He was still turning the headband as he talked, but just then he broke off with a hissing gasp, and Claire saw the flash of red in his hand. Blood soaked quickly through the white fabric of Amelie's headband, but after a second's pause, he turned it again. "Not to trust me, or forgive me. But I hope you do."

"Let me see."

"It's just a cut, and if I let go, we're dead," he said. "It's fine." He kept turning the ever-tighter knot of cloth, and now Claire could hear the creaking of the bars. They were bowing strongly in the middle, and the gap was widening fast. Not only that, but she thought the welds at the top of one of the bars had weakened. *This can work,* she thought. *It's going to work.*

Then, with a sharp, snapping sound, the headband came apart in Shane's hands as he tried to crank it again. "Damn," he whispered, and looked at her. "Is it enough?"

"Let me see your hand."

He held it out, and there was a deep cut across the palm, one that made her ache to see it. Claire grabbed the tail of her shirt and pressed it against the cut, then fished around for the broken edge of the headband. The sheared metal in it was sharp, and she frayed enough of the cloth to rip a piece free to wrap around his hand. As she tied it in place, she looked up into his face.

"Do you forgive me?" he asked her. His eyes were warm and steady, and he had a little, tentative hint of a smile.

"No," she said. It made her sick to have to hurt him like this . . . but it was also right. It was *necessary*. "I want to, I really do, but you didn't trust me, Shane. You didn't believe me when I needed it. And that hurt me, Shane. It really did. It's going to take a little time and a lot of work for me to forgive you for that."

The breath went out of him as if she'd punched him, and his eyes widened. He'd just assumed she'd forgive him, she realized; she'd done that so many times before without any thought or hesitation that she'd made him think it was automatic.

But it wasn't. Not this time. Much as she wanted things to go back to normal, she needed him to understand that he'd hurt her.

From the look on his face, he did.

In the next second, he dropped his gaze and took a deep breath. "I know," he said. "I deserve it. If we get out of here, I promise, I'll make it up to you."

"Take the rope off the bars," she said, and reached forward to tip his chin up and kiss him, very lightly. She wanted to fall into his arms, but it wasn't the time, and it wasn't the message she wanted to send him. "And be ready for anything."

"Always." The cocky grin he flashed her was *almost* right. Almost. But there was a scared, tentative look in his eyes, and she wondered if he was thinking, as she was, *We could die here, right now, and not be right with each other.*

But she couldn't help that. She needed him to understand what he'd done to her, and to himself.

It was the toughest thing in the world, but she turned away from him. Myrnin was still belting out an endless chorus of whatever obnoxious song he was performing; no one was paying attention, but it was annoying enough that they were likely not paying much attention to her and Shane. When she tapped him on the shoulder, he coughed and broke off to say, "Are the two of you quite done with your sweet nothings? Because I might vomit."

"That would be perfect," Claire said. "It's been just a great day so far." She reached up, grabbed his pointed chin, and turned it to show him the bent bars at the rear of the cage. His eyebrows went sharply up. "Maybe you should rest a minute."

"Perhaps I should," he agreed. "Your shirt is torn. And you're wearing a lovely perfume, by the way."

"It's blood," she said. "Thanks. That's ever so comforting."

Myrnin crawled to the back of the cage, coming close to Shane as he did so. The two of them exchanged a look that made the hair rise on the back of Claire's neck; they were like two tigers sizing each other up, with Myrnin then leaning past her boyfriend to inspect the state of the bars. He made a soft *hmmm* sound and nodded, then—to Claire's surprise—pulled Shane close and gave him an utterly unexpected kiss on the cheek.

"Hey!" Shane said, and tried to wriggle free, but then he paused, because Myrnin was whispering to him. Shane's gaze darted for Claire's, then quickly away, and when Myrnin finished, Shane nodded. When Myrnin let him go, Shane moved back—way back.

Claire mouthed, *What the hell?* But Shane just shook his head and looked away. Whatever Myrnin had just said to him, it was . . . disturbing.

Myrnin didn't pause for questions. He crawled over to where Amelie was still lying very still, and pulled her into his lap as he kneeled. "My poor, lovely lady," he said, and gently eased her fallen white-gold hair back from her ivory face. "Would you rather die in fire, or in glory? Dead is dead, of course. But I feel you should choose, *now.*"

Amelie hadn't moved at all. It was possible that something had gone wrong; maybe a splinter had broken off in her heart, freezing her in place, or something else had happened. A wooden stake wouldn't kill her, but it would paralyze her. And they needed her, Claire thought. Too many vampires. Even if the trick worked to loosen the bars, even if they could break them free . . .

"Something's happening out there," Shane said. "Heads up."

Naomi was moving forward at last, stilling the confused babble of the assembled vampires in the square. She was every bit a queen in her silver and black, and her voice was warm, sweet, and compelling; she didn't need to bite people to convince them, Claire thought. She was persuasive enough without it. She'd only bothered to control the key players, and only for as long as she needed them. She was cold, but smart.

And now, she said, "My friends, I come before you in sorrow and pain to tell you that Amelie, our Founder, has lost the right to rule."

No one doubted what was going on, Claire thought, but a number of vampires out in the crowd began to voice their objections. It wasn't a lot of them, but it was enough to make it clear Naomi wasn't a popular choice.

She held up a hand in a sharp, angry gesture. "Our laws are clear: the strongest rules. My sister was strong; the past is littered with those who stood against her, and lost. Her strength carried us here, to this town, to a place where we can finally begin to regain our rightful glory. But don't be mistaken: she hesitated. She corrupted herself by compromising with humans, with their laws and morals, until she forgot what it was to be a proper vampire."

There were more shouts of protest, louder now. That might not have been what Naomi expected, Claire thought; there was a growing tension in her shoulders, and the hand she still held raised seemed to shiver, just a little. "There will be no debate on this! My sister became weak and foolish, and she was brought down by treachery. Not mine, but the treachery of a lover she trusted. She is not fit any longer to rule. Fear not; I will burn the traitor with her, and we will start newborn."

This time, no one shouted. There was an eerie silence. Claire honestly couldn't tell whether Naomi had won them over, or whether something else was happening—something that didn't bode well for the would-be queen. Vampires weren't that easy to read, especially not in large groups.

The humans in their pen had gone very quiet and still—even Monica. Frail little Gramma Day was standing very tall, hardly leaning on her cane at all. But there was someone new standing near them, almost invisible behind Monica's tall, long-legged form . . . another human, not a vampire.

Jenna? What the hell was the ghost hunter doing *here*? Trying to get a story? Was she insane?

No. She was holding hands with someone else; a small, slight form that Claire spotted as Flora Ramos shifted to one side.

Jenna had hold of Miranda's hand.

Miranda shouldn't be solid. But she was, very solid, though clinging to Jenna's hand as if to a lifeline in a stormy ocean. Maybe Jenna's psychic ability was feeding Miranda's own power and holding her steady in her nighttime form outside the Glass House, but from the strained, scared looks on their faces, it wasn't easy.

What the hell were they *doing*?

Naomi hadn't seen them, or if she had, she didn't care. She was busy trying to charm her new subjects.

"Tomorrow marks our new age, and I will lead you into it," she continued. "You have been robbed of your rights for so long, my friends—subjected to indignities, to the constant complaints and restrictions of those who are rightfully our property. And that is *over*. As a token of this, I give you the first blood of Morganville. It is yours to take, as is your right as the rulers of not only this place, but all the world." She extended her white hand to point at the people held off to the side—twenty people, including Monica.

The vampires looked in that direction. None of them moved, and then Jason sauntered out of the crowd, and said, "About damn time somebody did the right thing."

He grabbed Monica and dragged her out of the fenced-in area.

She shrieked and hit him, hard enough to make him stagger back a bit, and Claire lunged forward and yanked the wooden crossbow bolt all the way out of Oliver's chest. She threw it hard through the bars of the cage and yelled, "Monica, catch!"

Monica leaned over backward as Jason tried to drag her closer, and saw the bolt tumbling end over end through the air. In a move that was shockingly graceful—and probably couldn't have been repeated if she'd really thought about it—Monica grabbed it and jammed it not into Jason's heart, but between his teeth. "Bite that!" she yelled, and kicked her way free. Her shoes, Claire realized, had silver caps on the stiletto tips. She yanked them off and held them ready. "Anybody else want some?"

Jason spit the bolt out, looking furious and embarrassed, and when he tried to grab her, she planted the heel of her shoe into his hand. It burned.

"We have to move, right now," Myrnin said. "She creates a nice distraction, but it won't last."

"It doesn't need to," Amelie said. She pulled the last inch of wood free from her chest and smiled up at him. "I find that I choose glory, my dear Myrnin."

"Most excellent," he said. "Claire has loosened the bars, and—"

Shane held up his bleeding hand.

"And Shane helped," Myrnin amended grudgingly. "But I believe we should go *now*. Naomi is losing the respect of her peers. It will not go well for her. She will burn us out of sheer desperation."

Amelie nodded and rolled to a crouch. She studied the bars at the back of the cage, made a fist, and hit with surgical precision at the point at the top of one of the bars where the weld was weakest.

It snapped.

Her hand was burned in a bright red stripe, but she ignored it, grabbed the loose metal, and bent it in toward them with shocking strength. It, too, snapped cleanly off at the base.

"Hannah!" Shane was yelling behind them. *"Hannah, no!"*

Claire glanced back and saw that Hannah—probably still following Naomi's implanted instructions—was reaching for a button that almost certainly would turn the cage into a fry basket. Underneath them, the gas jets sputtered into pale blue flame.

"Out!" Claire screamed. "Get out *now!*"

Amelie had hit the second bar twice without breaking it, and Myrnin joined her, kicking it with his bare foot between her blows. About three seconds later, the whole thing bent and then snapped completely free.

It wasn't a huge opening, but it was enough.

Amelie lunged out, and Myrnin after her. Shane went next and held out his hand for Claire.

But Oliver wasn't moving.

"Leave him!" Shane yelled. Hannah's hand was hovering over

the button, shaking, as if she were trying desperately to fight for their lives, and losing. "Claire, come on, *now!*"

She couldn't, because Oliver opened his eyes and began to move.

Claire broke loose from Shane's grasp and lunged for the vampire.

Oliver opened his eyes as she started dragging him, and he reached out to grab the bars and hold himself in place. "No," he said. "I have to—I have to pay for what I did."

"Not like this," Claire said. "Come on!"

But he wouldn't let go. The idiot wouldn't *let go.* . . .

She saw Naomi's head turn; she saw her take in the fact that her prisoners were getting loose, and she glared sharply at Hannah—

Who lost the internal battle, and hit the button that turned on the gas burners.

"Let go!" Claire shrieked as the flames shot up. She rolled for the hole in the cage bars and felt Shane yank her free into his arms. Her shirt was burning. He slapped the flames out.

Amelie reached past them, grabbed Oliver's burning form, and yanked him out with all her strength. The bar he'd been holding snapped in half, but he slid free.

Still on fire.

Amelie stared down at him for a bare second with true horror written on her face, then threw herself down on him, smothering the fire with her body and her hands. He was scorched and smoldering, but alive.

Oliver's burned hands moved, caressing her shoulders, and he whispered, "Forgive me."

"Yes," she whispered. "Yes. Hush."

"Stop me before I hurt you again."

"I will." She sat up as he closed his hands around her neck, and she drove the wooden arrow that she'd pulled from her own chest into his heart. Oliver went limp.

But Michael and Hannah had just rounded the corner, armed and ready to kill, and there was nothing but Naomi's will in their expressions now.

They were puppets—deadly puppets.

Amelie didn't seem to know, or care. Myrnin grabbed Hannah, avoiding the silver-edged knife as she expertly sliced it at him, and tried to throw her off-balance. "Don't hurt her!" Claire cried. "It's not her fault!"

Michael was still coming. Shane let go of her and faced off with him. "Not gonna happen, bro," he said. Michael bared fangs at him, and Shane held up the stake in his hand. "Not in this lifetime. I already had a vamp kiss me today. Not going all the way—"

But the banter wasn't slowing Michael down, and before Claire could take a breath, Michael had rushed forward, grabbed Shane's arm, and was relentlessly bending it back until the stake rattled on the granite slab. It rolled toward the cage and caught on fire from the inferno raging inside.

At that moment, Claire saw Miranda and Jenna step into view behind them, and Jenna let go of Miranda . . . and the air turned darkly electric with the rush of whispers.

Even Michael paused. There was something terrifying in that sound, something *wrong*.

Claire blinked, because she could see shadows now in the glare of the fire—shadows that moved on their own. Human-formed, they rushed forward past Miranda. Some piled onto Hannah, and although Claire could hardly see them, they must have had an effect, because Hannah staggered and stopped trying to stab the hell out of Myrnin. He let go and backed away, and she swatted at the whirl of shadows around her, movements growing more and more frantic and erratic.

And weak.

And then she went to her knees, and fell.

The same was happening to Michael, a storm of ghost-fury around him, and as Shane backed away, Claire saw one of the shadows break loose from the angry swarm and come toward her boyfriend.

The small figure took on shape and a glassy kind of reality as it approached him.

"Lyss," Shane whispered, "thank you."

She held out her hand; just for a moment, Shane took it. Claire saw the power that ran between them, a burst that exploded like a star in Alyssa's shadow-body and gave her, just for a few seconds, reality.

"I love you," Alyssa said, still holding on. "I just had to tell you it wasn't your fault."

Then she let go and faded into starlight.

Gone.

Shane staggered backward, and Claire caught him. His heart was beating fast, and he felt cold despite the inferno-like temperature of the gas jets nearby.

Michael was down now, and the ghost-swarm buzzed on for a few seconds before Miranda—called them back? That was what it looked like, Claire thought. The ghosts gathered like a cloak around her, crowding and whispering, and Miranda shuddered and turned very, very pale, almost translucent.

Jenna grabbed her hand, and she stabilized again.

"Bring them," Amelie said, pointing to Hannah and Michael. She stared at Jenna and Miranda for a moment, as if trying to decide what to do with them, then inclined her head just a tiny bit. It was a bow of recognition, if not approval.

"What are we going to do?" Shane asked as he bent to grab Michael under the arms. Michael moaned, but he didn't move much on his own.

"Now," Amelie said with all of hell in her eyes, "we'll find out who plays this game better."

She was a mess, Claire thought—dress torn, smudged now with soot and blood from Oliver's scorched body, hair in a tangle around her face. But she'd never looked more savage, or more like a queen, than when she walked out from behind the cage and faced Naomi.

The whole crowd froze, a mass of a hundred or more vampires, all deciding what to do; the humans panicking in their sacrificial corral; Jason and Monica, locked in a fashionista battle stance. *Nobody* moved.

Not even Naomi, who looked utterly cool and perfect. But her smile looked stark and—just for a moment—false.

"It's fitting," she said then, "that you die at the hands of your successor. Try to do it with dignity, Amelie."

"I always loved you," Amelie said. "It's a pity you were never worthy of it." Her eyes flared bright silver white, and she nodded toward Claire, who was standing nearest. "Bring them."

Claire guessed she meant Michael and Hannah, and she gestured. Myrnin carried Hannah over, and Shane dragged Michael.

Naomi laughed. "This is your army, dear sister? Pathetic."

"Is it?" Amelie extended her hand toward Michael Glass. "I'll have my fledgling back now."

Whatever hold Naomi was keeping over him, it broke with an almost audible twist; Michael grabbed his head, and for a few seconds he looked as if he might collapse—but he pulled himself upright, wiped blood from his nose, and walked past Naomi to stand next to Amelie. Next to Shane, too. His eyes flashed over Claire, as well, and she read the horror and sorrow in them. *Oh, Michael.*

"And you, too, Hannah." Amelie moved her pointing finger to Hannah Moses. "I free you. Join your people."

Myrnin let her down, and Hannah blinked, staggered, and whipped her head around to glare at Naomi. The blind fury in her eyes was terrifying . . . but then she backed off from the vampires, and she went to where Monica was holding Jason at bay with her silver-capped shoe.

Hannah said, "Put those back on. This works better." And she handed Monica the silver knife.

"What about you?" Monica asked as Jason took a big step away.

Hannah shrugged. "If he wants to come at me, he'll find I don't need anything else. Not for the likes of him."

Jason backed all the way to the first rank of vampires behind him.

They shoved him *forward*, into no-man's-land.

"Now," Amelie said to Naomi, in the hiss of the burning torches and the roar of fire in the empty cage, "tell me again how you plan to rule in *my* town, Sister. Tell me how you will command the obedience of all these gathered here. *Show me.*"

Naomi didn't lack for guts, Claire thought. She turned to the assembled vampires of Morganville, raised her hands, and said, "You know what Amelie offers. I will give you freedom. I will give you glory. I will give you back the world that you deserve. All you need to do is take one step forward, just one, and you will be free!"

Amelie said nothing. Not one thing.

No one moved. Not even Jason, who, Claire guessed, was starting to realize just how badly he'd screwed up his newfound immortality.

Naomi's face went from impassioned to blank as the reality hit her that she had lost. Decisively.

"You missed the strong hint you were given before," Amelie said. "Many of these were present when you fell among the draug. No one bent to save you then. And none will follow you now." Her eyes blazed silver, an awful and beautiful color, and she didn't even have to raise her voice at all. "Kneel to me, Sister."

"No," Naomi said. She was shaking now, as if about to collapse, but she was grimly clinging to whatever it was that had driven her this far. "No. I was made to *rule*."

"Kneel," Amelie whispered. "I won't forgive you, but I can spare you. And I will. But you must kneel."

"Never!"

But she did. It happened slowly as if she were being crushed under a huge, impossible weight, and Claire actually felt sorry for her as she finally collapsed to her knees, bent her head, and wept.

Amelie lifted Naomi's chin, placed a soft kiss on her forehead, and said, "We share the darkest of fathers, you and I. And I don't blame you. It's a bitter thing, this blood of ours. You'll have time to think on it. So much time, alone in the dark. A hundred years of it before your penance to me is done."

Naomi said nothing. Claire wasn't sure she actually *could* say anything. She covered her face with her hands, and Amelie turned away from her to look at the vampires.

"Naomi was not wrong," she said. "I have been weak. I've allowed you to be weak as well, to indulge your passions as I indulged mine, as if there were no consequences to come. But my sister's way is the old way, and it will destroy us. . . . You know the fever that hunting brings on us, and the destruction it will cause.

Morganville was built to allow us to live *without* such risk, and with the human world encroaching on us at every turn, we cannot be weak. We cannot be indulgent." She drew in a long, slow breath. "Tomorrow, you will learn to be stronger than you ever thought you could be. There will be *no* hunting. *No* killing. You will share my sister's penance, for as long as it pleases me. And I will share it, too." She turned to Hannah, and to the humans who stood there. "You're free to go. And you may carry my pledge to the rest of Morganville: we will not kill. And if we do, the penalty for us is death, just as it would be for you to kill us. Only as equals can we keep the peace. It is not in our nature, but it is the only way to survive."

Hannah nodded. So did Mayor Ramos. Monica finally slipped her high heels back on, flipped her hair back over her bare shoulders, and said, "You ruined a great party at my place, you know." And she walked off without another word.

Claire almost laughed. Almost . . . and then Amelie turned toward her and said, "Explain to me about these ghosts."

It was a very long conversation.

Claire, Myrnin, Shane, and Michael were taken out of Founder's Square and back to Amelie's office, where workers were already sweeping up the broken glass and boarding up the windows in preparation for morning. After a glance at the work in progress, Amelie moved them into the outer office, where her assistant cleared her desk for the Founder to sit down. A couple of Amelie's guards carried Oliver in and stretched him out on the floor. He was silent, eyes shut tightly. His burns were healing, but there were still red patches all over his face, and his clothes were more char than fabric.

"I'll give the edicts now. Bizzie, be sure they are filed tonight,"

Amelie said. She looked tired, and desperately pale, but there was nothing but surety in her voice. "Myrnin, I wish you to return to your work. There's much to be done to repair Morganville. We can't do it without you, and your chances of survival outside are . . . slender, at best."

Myrnin hesitated, then said, "I'll consider it."

"I could order you."

"Well," he said, and smiled a little. "You could certainly *try*, dear lady, but—"

Amelie shook her head and cast a look at her assistant. "Just put down that he agreed," she said. "Michael, although what you did was not of your free will, you raised arms against your ruling queen and your sire. How do you intend to repay me? Think carefully about your answer. There's only one that will satisfy the debt."

He shook his head. "You always get what you want." Michael sounded exhausted and kind of . . . well, broken. He hadn't really looked Claire in the eyes, or Shane. "Eve's not going to forgive me. Not for any of it."

"True," Amelie said. "Yet there is no betrayal so bitter as that of a child. But I am prepared to allow you to go unpunished, under one condition."

"Which is?"

She gave him a very cold look. "I warned you," she said. "Again and again. I withheld my permission for your marriage not out of spite, but to protect you, and to protect Eve. She has suffered much, Michael, and some of it at your own hands; this is what I warned you against. Humans are fragile things, and we cannot resist the urge to exploit weakness. Already, you have felt this. So for your own good, I will allow you to go unpunished if you will leave your wife. Let her go, Michael. Do the kind thing."

He looked stunned—and then there was a slow-burning anger inside him that caught fire in his eyes. "You can't," he said. "You can't order me to do that."

"I am not ordering you. I am offering you the chance to avoid a heavy and very public punishment."

"Hasn't she been hurt enough? Breaking us up was what *Naomi* wanted!"

"For reasons that have nothing to do with mine," Amelie said. "I share a view with Hannah Moses, and many others. I believe that humans and vampires are best kept separate, for the safety of both. You have taken it too far. I am not angry at the girl, Michael; I am *terrified* for her. Do you understand how much danger you put her in, daily?"

He had to be thinking about seeing Eve in the hospital, Claire thought, and for a second she was sure he was going to agree, to just . . . walk away. And that was appalling.

But instead, Michael met the Founder's eyes and said, "I love her." Just that, simple and sure. "So whatever punishment you have to give me, go ahead. I'm not hurting her again."

Across from him, Shane nodded and tapped his fist against his chest. Respect. Michael gave him a small, weary smile.

"Very well," Amelie said. She didn't look pleased. "Bizzie, please note that Michael Glass has accepted punishment as decreed by his sire."

Bizzie's pen scratched dryly on the paper. "And what is it?"

"I haven't decided," Amelie said. "But it will be very public."

And then it was her turn, as Amelie's cool eyes fixed on her. "Claire," she said. "Always in the middle. What shall I do with you?" Claire stayed silent. She really didn't know what Amelie was thinking, or feeling; there was a lot of anger inside her, a lot of sadness, and it was always easy to target weakness, as Amelie had pointed out to Michael. When she didn't move and didn't blink, Amelie turned to Myrnin. "Well?"

"I need her help," he said. "Frank's off-line." Meaning dead, Claire suspected. "Without her, I'll be ages getting all of the necessary protections back online. Oh, and I'll need a brain. Something relatively undamaged. Not Naomi; I shouldn't like to have her run Morganville's systems, would you?"

"I thought you were planning to use Claire's brain," Amelie said casually, and flicked a glance back at her to see if she would flinch. She didn't. "Very well. One will be located for you. Claire, you will—"

"No," Claire said. Just that. A very simple word, but it meant throwing herself off a very high cliff. "You said I could leave Morganville once. Did you mean it?"

"Claire?" Shane blinked and took a step toward her. "What are you doing?"

She ignored him, watching Amelie, who was just as intently watching her. "Did you?"

"Yes," Amelie said. "If you wish. I can arrange for you to enter the university you wished—MIT, yes?—and have advanced study with someone who is friendly to Morganville, though no longer a resident. Is that what you require of me, as payment for saving my life?"

"No," Claire said. "That's what you *owe* me for saving all your lives, a bunch of times. What I *require* now is that you let Shane go, too. If he wants."

"Claire, this is unwise," Myrnin said. "You should not—"

"I want," Shane said, interrupting him. "I definitely want."

Claire nodded. She and Amelie hadn't yet broken their stare. It was really hard to keep doing it; there was some kind of power in Amelie that affected people even when she wasn't really trying, and it was giving Claire the shakes, and the faint outline of a head-ache. "I want you to get me into MIT. And for Shane to be able to go anywhere he wants. And for you to keep your word about Morganville. No killing. Not even to get Myrnin his brain."

"No need," Myrnin said earnestly. "There are several in the morgue who will—"

Amelie raised her hand and cut him off instantly. "Agreed," she said. "Note it down, Bizzie." Bizzie did, without lifting her head as she wrote in quick, dry scratches on the paper. "Now. As to Oliver," she said. Her voice had taken on a softer note, with something almost tentative about it. "As to Oliver, I will be seen as weak if I forgive him as well as Naomi. He was my most visible adversary, and the most visible knife at my back. So he must go. He is exiled from Morganville, until such time as I decide he may return."

Oliver opened his eyes and turned his head. Amelie's gaze fell on him, and for a moment, there was something so painful be-tween them, it made Claire want to look away. It was a kind of desperate, angry longing she knew all too well.

And then Oliver said, "Yes, my liege." And he closed his eyes. "As you wish. I accept your punishment."

"You're all dismissed," Amelie said. "Oliver, you may gather your things. You'll leave tomorrow."

She went back into her office.

And . . . that was it. It felt oddly empty to Claire, where there should have been some sense of . . . of triumph. Of *something*. But she wasn't sure of anything anymore. She just knew that she had to take control of her life, *now*, or it would never happen.

Michael stopped next to Claire and said, "So this is where I tell you how sorry I am. So, so sorry. Believe me, I—I can't explain."

"You don't need to," she said. "I was controlled by Bishop; I know how it felt."

Michael sighed and shook his head. "Dammit. It's not—I know you've got some issues with Shane, and that's on me, not on you. I'm sorry. Let me fix things, if I can."

She wasn't sure that was remotely possible, but she smiled at him. "Thanks," she said. It was the best she could manage. "But it's my life, Michael."

"I know," he said. "I—I just don't know what we are going to do without you."

"You and Eve? You'll be fine. You love her; everybody can see that now. I think you'd even give her up, if she asked you to, but not if *they* ask it. That's real love, I guess." On impulse, she stretched up and kissed him on the cheek. He flinched. So did she, a little. "I'll be back. But I need—I need to have my own life for a while. Out there. Away. You know?"

He did; she saw it in his smile. "That's what Eve and I were trying to explain to you guys," he said. "Sometimes you just . . . need that. To be sure who you really are." His smile faded. "You didn't ask for Shane to go with you."

"I didn't," she agreed, and walked away.

Shane was waiting at the hearse. He still wasn't looking directly at her, or for that matter at Michael, as the two of them approached. He leaned against the side, arms folded, and said, "Shotgun."

"Sure," Michael said. "I'll drive. Shane—"

Shane held out a palm to stop him. "Not now," he said. "I'm not ready for any apologies. You fix it with Eve, then talk to me."

Michael nodded. That wasn't what he wanted to hear, obviously, but it was the best he could have hoped for, really. *We won,* she thought. Why didn't it feel any better?

"Sorry," Shane said. He seemed flushed and awkward, suddenly, as she headed for the back of the hearse. "I—look, you should take the front and—"

"You called shotgun," she said. "It's okay."

He stared after her, clearly trying to think what to say, and failing. For that matter, she wasn't sure, either.

The drive home was weirdly silent.

Miranda met them at the door, face alight. Jenna was standing behind her, looking almost as proud. "You're okay," she said. "I knew you were going to need our help."

"Actually," Jenna said, "that was me. I had a vision of you locked in that cage, and I didn't know what to do."

"I did," Miranda said. "Once I stopped being afraid of the others and really tried to talk to them, it was easier. I still have to be careful around them, but with Jenna holding on, they can't feed on me as they could before. She can help me get out of the house. It's perfect."

Jenna didn't seem to think so, but for the moment, at least she nodded.

"How's Eve?" Michael asked. Miranda's smile faded.

"She's awake," she said. "She's waiting on the couch. We told her what happened."

"Thanks. You saved our lives." Claire hugged Miranda, then followed her into the living room. Eve was sitting up on the couch, and already her bruises were loads better; the ice packs on the floor were probably part of that.

She was watching Michael with a fragile kind of hope in her eyes.

He was a few steps away, as if he didn't dare make a move. Shane came to a halt behind him and leaned against the wall, arms crossed. Claire knew that pose; it was his bodyguard look. He was, at the moment, guarding Eve, from Michael.

But Michael didn't try to come closer.

"I hurt you," he said. "I never wanted it, but that happened. I could tell you I didn't mean it, and that it wasn't me, and that's true, but it *was* me, and I know you can't forget it. I—" He spread his hands wide. "I hate myself, Eve. That's all I can say. I hate myself. And if you want me to go, I'll go. I'll do anything. *Anything.*"

There were tears glittering in her eyes. "Miranda told me," she said. "About Naomi. About her biting you. That you didn't have a choice in what you did. But it *felt* real. You know?"

"I know," he said. "It felt real to me, too. And it scared the hell out of me."

"Don't ever do it again."

He smiled. "I won't," he said. "I love you, Mrs. Glass."

She opened her arms, and he hugged her, as carefully as if she were a fragile piece of crystal.

Shane cleared his throat. "Um, you should know that Amelie tried to make him give you up," he said. "Because Michael's probably not going to tell you that. And he refused. So now he's on her bad side, again."

"Oh, baby," Eve said, and drew back to look at Michael's face. "How bad?"

He shrugged. "Doesn't matter."

And Eve's smile was full of delight as she laid her head on his shoulder. Claire met Eve's eyes and got a very small smile. It was a little thing, but it was a start.

"I love you, too, Eve," Claire said. "I'm sorry."

"Hush up," Eve said. "Who *wouldn't* want to kiss him? Forgiven and forgotten."

That was more charity than Claire thought she could ever earn. Then Michael whispered something to Eve that clearly wasn't meant to be overheard, and the sense of intruding on something so precious and private was more than she could take.

Shane must have felt it, too; he pushed off the wall and went up the stairs toward his room. Claire hesitated, then headed that way.

"Hey." It was Michael's voice, soft and a little rough, and she glanced over at him as he untangled just a bit from Eve. "That thing, the one you were working on for Myrnin. There's something to it. I felt it. I thought you should know."

She was—surprised, she guessed, and a little elated. "Thanks," she said. The thing was sitting like a particularly large engine part on the dining room table, and she went back, retrieved it, and wondered, again, what exactly it would be able to do if she could really, truly make it work.

Something wonderful, maybe.

Or something awful.

She carted it upstairs, and at the hallway, she hesitated. All the doors were shut, including Shane's. She took a deep breath, steadied herself, and began walking in that direction.

It felt a bit like going to her own funeral.

Shane's door was shut. She knocked and got silence for an answer. *He doesn't want to talk about it,* she thought, and even though she'd wanted to keep him at a distance for now, to let him understand how badly he'd hurt her when he'd failed to trust her . . . it ached.

So she went to her room, feeling lost and alone. She left the lights off. The exhaustion, the chill, the despair, were suddenly . . . too much. She just wanted to crawl into bed and cry until she died. Tomorrow, she'd have to think about how to leave Morganville behind, how to go off to a new town, a new school, a whole new world . . . and somehow do it without Michael, or Eve, or even Myrnin.

And maybe even without Shane.

But she just couldn't face it now.

She dumped the machine on the dresser and didn't even bother to take her clothes off, just stripped back the covers, kicked off her shoes, and crawled beneath . . . and instantly felt the warmth of a body beside her, moving closer.

Oh.

Shane's arms went around her. It was slow, and tentative, and done in complete silence. He pulled her closer, and closer, until she was pressed against him, back to front. His lips pressed a slow, soft, burning kiss on the soft, tender skin at the back of her neck.

"I know you didn't ask me," he said. "I know you may not want me to go. But I'm going to Boston, and I'll be there when you need me. You don't have to say anything. I know I have to earn your trust back. It's okay."

She caught her breath, sighed, and felt her heart break all over again, in a whole new and beautiful way.

TRACK LIST

Music is important to my process of writing. It's the first thing I do before I start writing . . . pick at least ten songs for this track list. Then, as I go along, I search for more music to fill it out and keep the soundtrack in my head fresh. I think I got some particularly juicy songs for this one! Hope you enjoy them . . . and *please*, remember that, like writers, musicians exist on the money you pay for their work. So please pay to help them play.

"Seven Devils"	Florence + The Machine
"Haunted"	Kelly Clarkson
"Cold Morning"	Kitty Kat Stew
"Sonata Rapidus Revamp"	b.hantoot
"I Disappear"	The Faint
"Big Wheel"	The Bridge
"Black"	Danger Mouse & Daniele Luppi (feat. Norah Jones)
"Fresh Blood"	Eels

"Killing My Dreams"	Elysion
"Good Idea"	Peter Himmelman
"Immigrant Song"	Karen O, Trent Reznor & Atticus Ross
"The Recluse"	Cursive
"Oblivion"	Winter In Eden
"Haunted"	Evanescence
"Things Have Changed"	Bob Dylan
"Afraid"	Sarah Fimm
"What If I Were Talkin' to Me"	Louise Goffin
"Victoria"	Krypteria
"Snow White Queen"	Evanescence
"Somebody That I Used to Know"	Gotye (feat. Kimbra)
"Young Blood"	The Naked and Famous
"Stare into the Sun"	Graffiti6
"Second Chance"	Peter Bjorn and John
"Who Wants to Live Forever"	Queen
"Bullet in My Hand"	Redlight King
"Dark Horses"	Switchfoot
"Soldiers"	Otherwise
"Strangeness and Charm"	Florence + The Machine
"Ease My Pain"	Declan Flynn
"Gold on the Ceiling"	The Black Keys
"In My Veins"	Andrew Belle (feat. Erin McCarley)
"Natives"	blink-182